co's infamous Barbary Coast, Jaeger's debut, *The Dressmaker's Dowry*, is sure to captivate. Comprising both a historical and contemporary story, Jaeger spins **a tale of love, loss, and a city divided** by social class. Whether you read romance, mysteries, historical or contemporary fiction, there is something in the novel for everyone."

—Sally Hepworth, author of *The Secrets of Midwives* and *The Things We Keep*

"In this deliciously satisfying tale of love and resilience, Meredith Jaeger sweeps us into nineteenth-century San Francisco, painting harrowing images of poverty alongside excesses of wealth, weaving a multi-generational novel **impossible to put down**."

—Lori Nelson Spielman, *New York Times* bestselling author of *The Life List* and *Sweet Forgiveness*

"Meredith Jaeger deftly intertwines two tales of love and loyalty and the vast lengths to which some will go to protect those they hold dear. **A compelling debut novel that sent me racing to its final, revealing pages**."

—Kristina McMorris, *New York Times* bestselling author of *The Edge of Lost*

The Dressmaker's Dowry

The Dressmaker's Dowry

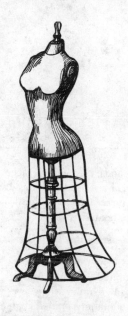

Meredith Jaeger

WM
WILLIAM MORROW
An Imprint of HarperCollins*Publishers*

P.S.™ is a trademark of HarperCollins Publishers.

THE DRESSMAKER'S DOWRY. Copyright © 2017 by Meredith Jaeger. All rights reserved. Printed in the United States of America. No part of this book may be used or reproduced in any manner whatsoever without written permission except in the case of brief quotations embodied in critical articles and reviews. For information, address HarperCollins Publishers, 195 Broadway, New York, NY 10007.

HarperCollins books may be purchased for educational, business, or sales promotional use. For information, please email the Special Markets Department at SPsales@harpercollins.com.

FIRST EDITION

Designed by Diahann Sturge
Title page illustration © a_bachelorette/Shutterstock, Inc.

Library of Congress Cataloging-in-Publication Data has been applied for.

ISBN 978-0-06-246983-0

17 18 19 20 21   LSC   10 9 8 7 6 5 4 3 2 1

For my dad, Fritz. Thank you for your adventurous spirit, which brought you to America, and for making California my home. You live forever in my heart.

Acknowledgments

Thank you to my editor, Lucia Macro. You are a privilege to work with, and I always look forward to reading your e-mails. You have shaped this novel into something wonderful with your vision of re-structuring. Thank you to my publicist, Michelle Podberezniak, and to the team at William Morrow working hard behind the scenes. Diahann Sturge, thank you for the beautiful interior design, and to my production and copy editors, thank you for making sure I don't embarrass myself!

I could not have done this without my superstar agent, Jenny Bent. Thank you, Jenny, for your keen eye, for believing in me, and for seeing this novel as a diamond in the rough. I'm also grateful to Denise Roy. I value your insights and thoughtful comments, which helped me so much when revising my manuscript.

To my critique partner, Sally Hepworth, who pushed me to dig deeper, and never to take the easy way out. I would not be writing this if not for you.

To Anna Evans, for exchanging hundreds of e-mails, keeping me sane during the submissions process, and giving me your helpful feedback on early drafts. Also thank you to Niki Robins, my most enthusiastic first reader. Your praise means the world to me. To Kat Drennan, thank you for your encouragement and suggestions.

To my mother, Carol, and my sister, Carolyn, you are my support system. Thank you to my sister, for always being a wonderful first reader—and for designing a beautiful map of the Barbary Coast for this novel. I want to be creative with you until we are a hundred years old. Mom, thank you for your unwavering belief in my writing, and for always allowing me to follow my passion.

To my girlfriends—thank you for letting me be a hermit while I worked for years on this book, and for showing me nothing but love and encouragement. You inspire me, and your laughter keeps me going. To my coworkers and former coworkers who have become my friends and confidants: you made the 9–5 worthwhile with your stories, jokes, and kindness.

To Will, my husband, for supporting me through a decade of trying make my dream of publishing a novel a reality, and never letting me give up on it. You, Bernie, and Sylvester are my whole, fur-filled universe.

And to Hazel. We haven't met you yet, but you're the most important person in the world to us. Dream big, little one. We love you more than you can imagine.

The Dressmaker's Dowry

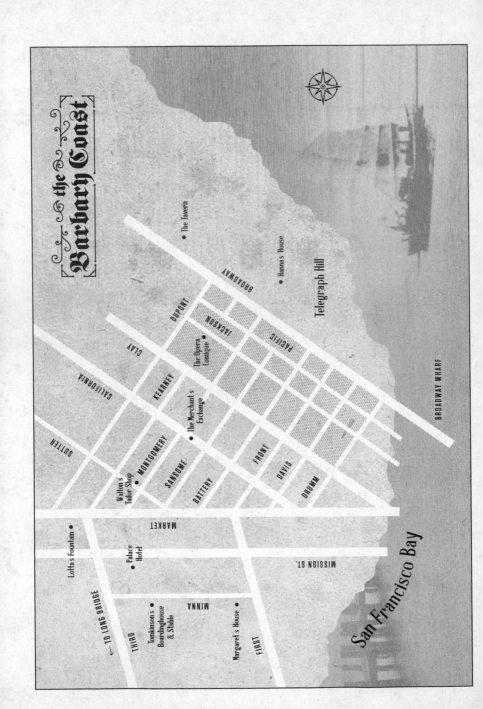

Chapter 1

Sarah Havensworth
Present Day

A doorman ushered me toward the historic garden court inside the Palace Hotel, the sequins on my gold shift dress catching the light. Men in suits mingled with women in cocktail gowns. Beneath the grand crystal chandeliers and arched glass ceiling, I felt like I'd stepped back in time to the turn of the twentieth century. Hunter stood against one of the marble columns under the elegant dome. I admired the cut of my husband's suit against his broad shoulders. His dark wavy hair was parted on the side.

"Champagne, miss?" a waiter asked.

"Yes, please."

I took a glass flute from the tray. When I sipped, the sweet bubbles tickled my tongue. With enough champagne, maybe I could relax tonight. My mother-in-law's charity events often made me feel like a fish out of water. For one, I didn't do well with crowds, and I could already feel the heat of anxiety creeping up my neck.

A gust of wind from the open door blew my bangs upward. I quickly brushed them down to hide the thin white scar on my forehead. Had anyone seen it? I took a deep breath through my nose. *I was in a safe place.* No one was paying attention to my scar. Except for me, of course. I exhaled slowly.

After walking through the sea of people, I placed my hand on Hunter's arm, giving it a squeeze. He smiled, dimples on full display, an adorable grin crafted just for me. "Hey, Kiddo. So glad you made it. How's my favorite young lady tonight?"

I chuckled. Judging from the number of blue-hairs who'd come out to the arts benefit, I *was* a young lady—a nice change from feeling ancient around Jen and Nick, my friends and former colleagues at *Pulse of the City* magazine.

On my thirtieth birthday last month, I'd realized I liked my ten P.M. bedtime, along with waking up early on weekends to go to the farmer's market sans hangover. More and more I felt estranged from hip twentysomething girls. Mostly, I didn't understand Tinder, and had trouble convincing my younger friends that it *was* possible to get a headache after only two glasses of wine.

Gwyneth appeared, gliding toward Hunter with a smile. She wore a long, pale blue dress, and a diamond tennis bracelet dangled from her wrist. I tucked my hands behind me, wishing I'd painted my nails for the event. My mother-in-law's gel manicure was perfect as usual. She kissed Hunter on the cheek and then stepped forward to hug me.

"Hello, Sarah. You look lovely tonight. I'm so pleased you could make it."

"Thank you," I said, feeling the soft warmth of her arms.

Hunter leaned down to whisper in my ear. "You do look gorgeous in that dress. I *might* be the luckiest guy in this place."

My body warmed, pleasant shivers working their way down my neck where his breath had touched me.

"Sarah, you haven't forgotten about the Canova by Moonlight gala?" Gwyneth asked. "I could use your help setting up the space before the big reveal."

Oh no. She'd told me about this. "Of course I'll help," I said, even though I had only a few weeks left to finish my MFA thesis, and I'd intended to spend them solely on writing. A hard knot formed in my stomach as I thought about my novel, languishing on my computer—a painful reminder of my writer's block.

"May thirtieth. Mark your calendar. The chair of the National Gallery of Ireland is flying in, and we'll be hosting him." She smiled proudly. "Walter is also on the board. The minister of arts appointed him for a five-year term. Walter and Colin attended the London School of Economics together many years ago. Old friends, you see."

I nodded, my father-in-law's accomplishments never ceasing to amaze me. As much as I tried to impress him, I'd never live up to his standards. But who could? He was the executive director of his own investment banking firm, Havensworth & Associates, Harvard educated, and the president of Havensworth Art Academy.

Hunter cleared his throat. "Mom, Sarah's working on her master's thesis. It's due early next month. She's pretty busy right now."

"Oh, hush," Gwyneth said, winking at me. "She can make a little time in her schedule. We're going to be serving vintage rosé, and someone has to help me sample it before the big night. You will, won't you, dear?"

I laughed. "You won't have a problem there."

"Remind me again of your thesis project?" Gwyneth asked, smoothing an imaginary flyaway into her sleek chignon. "A novel, right?"

I looked down at my hands guiltily. My square-cut emerald, set in rose gold, sparkled in the light next to my gold wedding band. Over three carats and wreathed in diamonds, the Havensworth family heirloom garnered compliments from strangers. But as much as I liked telling the story of how my engagement ring was over a hundred years old, the giant, valuable stone held an aura of mystery. No one in Hunter's family could tell me whom it had once belonged to.

I twisted the heavy ring upright. Thanks to my husband's financial support, I'd been able to focus one hundred percent on my writing. Yet somehow I'd managed to squander the opportunity. I forced a smile.

"Yes. It's historical fiction set in San Francisco's Barbary Coast, during the late nineteenth century. I'm writing about a widowed innkeeper and the quirky cast of characters who come to stay with her at the boardinghouse."

In the pause that followed, my cheeks heated. It was a

stupid idea, and I knew it. In fact, I'd been staring at my blank computer screen for weeks, utterly lacking inspiration. My characters no longer spoke to me. I was nothing more than a fraud—a former journalist, wannabe novelist, wasting my time chasing a silly dream. I couldn't believe Hunter had let me quit my day job to pursue this.

I began to babble. "I've been reading newspaper articles from the 1870s as part of my research. It's unbelievable the amount of crime that happened back then. I mean, imagine how terrifying North Beach must have been when all of the policemen and politicians were corrupt. To think I bought my beautiful Vera Wang wedding dress in the same place where people got murdered in the street!"

"Our city certainly does have a colorful past," Gwyneth said, smiling brightly as she patted my hand. "I hate to interrupt you, dear, but the chair of the De Young Museum has just arrived, and I must go over and say hello." She waved at a woman with a bouffant hairdo, and walked away.

"I think it sounds cool," Hunter said, meeting my eyes with a reassuring gaze. "I know you, Sar. Any story you write will be a good one. You've got the talent, and you work harder than anyone I know. I hope you publish your novel someday, so I can tell the world that my wife's a famous author."

"Thanks, honey," I mumbled as he kissed my forehead. I didn't have the heart to tell Hunter that I wasn't a real author, and there would be no future book tours. Anything I typed, I deleted five minutes later. I'd spent my afternoons wandering around Jackson Square, the site of my former magazine office, waiting for inspiration to strike. While looking up at the brick buildings that used to be dance halls, saloons, and bordellos in the last century, I'd never felt so lost.

I swallowed, realizing how many people had filled the garden court of the hotel. The walls seemed to close in. It was too hot in here. Why was everyone looking at me? I smoothed my bangs to make sure my scar was covered.

I could still hear the whispers that followed me down the streets of my hometown and through the halls of my high school. I felt the dark, accusatory looks, like daggers in my back. The room spun like I was drunk, even though I hadn't finished my champagne.

Don't think about it.

"Hey," I said, meeting Hunter's eyes, warm brown with specks of green. "I'm going to find the ladies' room. I'll just be a minute."

"Okay. I'll be right here."

I felt Hunter watching me as I tugged at the hem of my sequined dress, making my way quickly through the crowd. If I took deep breaths and looked at the floor, I wouldn't think about the screech of the brakes, or the jolt of the impact.

I stepped inside the ladies' lounge, appointed with plush velvet and rosewood couches. Crystal chandeliers with gold accents glinted off the shiny marble floors. Walking over to the sink, I turned on the tap to splash water on my cheeks.

My plain reflection stared back at me: a pale face with large brown eyes, dirty-blond hair, and a slightly too-big nose that sunburned easily. For Wisconsin, I was pretty enough, but I certainly didn't exude the urban glamour of San Francisco women.

I'd grown up on peanut-butter-and-jelly sandwiches and tuna casserole. On summer vacations, my parents and I camped in an old smelly tent, and "fancy" meant bringing along an air mattress. Hunter brought me into his world of yachts, summer homes, and country clubs. Sometimes Hunter asked me if I'd like to take him to Eagle River, so he could see the town where I'd spent my childhood.

My parents are dead, I told him. *There's nothing left for me there.*

Honestly, I ached to see the starry sky above the lakes, to spend the night with my husband in a rustic hunting cabin. But I could never go back. Hunter liked the person I was now, because he didn't know who I had been. I had kept myself from him.

When our two worlds had collided four years ago at the Best of San Francisco party hosted by my magazine, I'd been standing by the seafood bar, pretending I hadn't already eaten at least five raw oysters, and Hunter had come up beside me.

"Hey!" he said, grinning. "You're wearing my T-shirt."

"Excuse me?" I asked, my cheeks tingling. I cringed, bracing myself for some kind of terrible sexual joke that involved the removal of clothing.

He pointed at my gray V-neck. "That's from Have-Clothing, right?"

I rubbed the smooth fabric between my fingers. I'd bought the shirt online, knowing Have-Clothing donated the proceeds from each purchase to homeless organizations, and I'd liked the fairly traded organic cotton. Because of its softness and beautiful feather design, it had become my favorite shirt.

"Um, yeah?" I said. "How did you know?"

"I cofounded the company," Hunter said, an adorable dimple indenting his smile.

I laughed. "No way! That's awesome. I love what you guys are doing."

My body buzzed from oolong-tea-infused cocktails. Underneath the globe lights strung around the brick walls, his hazel eyes sparkled.

"So," he asked. "What do you do?"

"I'm an associate editor at *Pulse of the City* magazine." I couldn't keep the excitement out of my voice, I was so proud of my new title.

He raised his glass. "Cheers! I really like your articles. What a cool job."

I took in his fitted flannel shirt, tailored jeans, and nice leather shoes. He looked the part of the founder of an innovative start-up. But he was free of the arrogance so pervasive among rich young tech guys.

"You know, the best oysters aren't actually harvested in San Francisco," Hunter said, lowering his voice.

A wave of heat rippled through me. Of all the cute guys in the room, there was something special about Hunter. "Don't say that here," I whispered. "It's sacrilege."

He smiled again. "Ever been to Hog Island in Tomales Bay?"

I tilted another oyster down my throat, silky smooth flesh and sea brine. My mouth was full, so I shook my head.

"It's a short drive from here, up the coast through Marin. You can shuck your own and eat them right there at picnic tables overlooking the water." He paused and cleared his throat. "Want to go with me?"

"Absolutely," I said, setting down my drink. "Why not?"

After Hunter took my number and went to circulate the party, my coworker Jen came up behind me. She grabbed my arm.

"Ow! What's wrong with you?"

Jen's eyes narrowed. "Do you know who that is?"

We both turned to look at Hunter. I grinned. "Cofounder of Have-Clothing, maker of the very T-shirt I'm wearing tonight. He's cute, and cares about ending homelessness. What a seriously nice guy."

Jen brought her palm to her forehead. "Sarah. That *nice guy* is Hunter Havensworth, as in Havensworth Art Academy and Havensworth & Associates investments. Of course he has his own start-up. He's loaded! Starting to ring a bell?"

I'd passed the art academy buildings a few times on my jogs through the Financial District, but the name hadn't registered. "Like, his family owns it?"

Jen ran her fingers through her shiny black hair. "Yes, they own it! Hello? Do you know how many campus buildings that art academy has? They own this entire city. He's like San Francisco royalty."

Hunter smiled at me from across the room.

"That's not why I'm interested in him," I said, feeling a knot in my stomach.

"Well, good luck with that. Every other straight girl in this city is trying to get her claws in him. Watch out, he might be a total player."

A rich, handsome guy who didn't have to work for a living could be a red flag. But he *did* work for a living, helping those less fortunate. I didn't get the playboy vibe from him at all. Hunter seemed nice and normal.

And he was. On our first date at Hog Island in Tomales Bay, we shucked oysters and talked about everything from our childhood pets to our favorite books and sushi restaurants. Hunter was sweet, laughing when my oyster knife went flying into the water, and kissing the tip of my finger when I cut it on the rough shell. Being with him was easy and natural. For the first time in a long time, I felt like I could trust again.

Reemerging into the ballroom, I scanned the sea of suits and sequined dresses, looking for Hunter. I found him waiting right where I'd left him. He looked up and smiled, sending a warm wave of relief through me.

"Hey, Sweetie," I said, touching Hunter's hand. "Would it hurt your mom's feelings if I left early?"

Hunter's fingers curled around mine. "You okay, Kiddo? You just got here."

"I think I must've eaten something at lunch that didn't agree with me. I feel sick."

My eyes locked on his, silently pleading for him to understand. Hunter knew I had panic attacks, but he didn't know their root cause. My scar was throbbing, and my stomach churned. I had my bottle of Klonopin in my purse, just in case my anxiety started spiraling out of control. It was my fault. *My fault.*

Hunter's smile faded. "Can't you stay for an hour? I don't want to be here alone. C'mon, I'll get you some sparkling water to settle your stomach."

"No," I said, biting my lip. "I'm sorry. I really don't feel well."

Guilt surged through me, but I couldn't stand the feeling of all these eyes on me in this crowded room. I'd felt them before. There were support groups for people with alcohol and shopping addictions, groups for people strung out on heroin and cocaine. But there weren't any resources for people like me.

"Do you want me to come with you?" he asked, pulling me closer. Hunter's grip felt like a lifeline, anchoring me to solid ground.

What if I just embraced him? Or told him the truth?

"No," I said, shaking my head. "You stay."

Hunter let his hand drop, and I saw the disappointment in his eyes. I was the problem here—the reason we were drifting apart.

"Tell your mom I'm sorry," I said. "I'll see you at home."

As I walked away, I wondered what kind of person I was, leaving my husband alone when he'd reached across the divide, promising me he'd take care of me, like he always did. My panic had already begun to dissipate, and I could easily turn around. But I wasn't going back inside. I'd already made my choice.

⚜ ⚜ ⚜

Back at our apartment in the Marina, I listened to the peaceful lap of the waves and held a mug of chamomile tea in my hands. We had a chrome Italian espresso machine sitting in the middle of our granite kitchen island, but I never drank caffeine after noon, even if I needed to work late. What had *San Francisco Style* called our apartment? Modern chic? It looked nothing like my childhood home, with its Formica countertops and patchy brown carpet.

Redford crept into my lap and settled in. I stroked his orange coat. He kneaded my thigh, purring like a tiny motor. His claws snagged the fabric of my favorite skinny jeans, but he looked too content for me to set him down. Fog hung heavy and thick outside my floor-to-ceiling windows while red lights on the peaks of the Golden Gate Bridge blinked through the mist. Across the bay, the hills of the Marin Headlands cut a sharp silhouette against the purple-gray sky.

A foghorn sounded long and low. Here in the quiet comfort of my home, I was able to breathe again. I opened up a Word document on my laptop, wincing as I looked at the blinking cursor. My thesis advisor at USF had asked to meet with me next week to discuss my "progress." And all I had to show for myself were fifty lousy pages of a novel I no longer felt invested in. My main character, Mrs. McGeary, a widowed innkeeper in her forties, felt as flimsy as cardboard. Who was she, and what did she want?

I sighed as I opened my browser, preferring to lose myself in research instead. I'd always been drawn to the visual imagery of San Francisco in the nineteenth century—the beauty and harshness of the Wild West. The journalist in me couldn't stop mining the digital archives of the *Daily Alta California* and the *Sacramento Daily Union*, San Francisco's oldest newspapers, for tidbits to include in my book.

I settled into my desk chair and looked at the large framed picture of Hunter and me on our wedding day, both of us grinning like idiots. A chill passed over my body. My husband knew only the details I provided him. I was an orphan. I entered UCLA on a merit scholarship. I didn't stay in touch with my high school friends because Eagle River held too many sad memories.

When I'd changed my name on our marriage license, a weight had lifted. I was no longer Sarah Schmidt, the girl followed by rampant whispers. I was Sarah Havensworth. Hunter waited for me at the end of the aisle, promising a new life. There was a time when I thought I'd tell him the truth. The risk of losing everything kept me silent.

I let out a deep breath and Googled "Barbary Coast" because looking at images of San Francisco during the late 1800s often helped me with my writing. The screen populated with links. The red-light district of old San Francisco was nine blocks bound by Montgomery Street, Washington Street, Stockton Street, and Broadway. Today's sleek skyscrapers bore no resemblance to the cobbled streets of the past.

I clicked link after link, rejecting generic sites designed to attract tourists, and hoping for inspiration to strike. I'd been toying with the idea of developing a romance between Mrs. McGeary and a German-Jewish merchant, Herr Blumberg, who owned the jewelry shop across the street from her boardinghouse. I'd set the story against the backdrop of the Silver Rush, a time when businessmen earned fortunes from the silver found in the Comstock Lode mine in Nevada.

Much like the controversy surrounding San Francisco's current tech boom, the San Francisco of Victorian times was also a tale of two cities. The influx of wealth following the silver rush created a growing disparity between rich and poor. I intended to weave this theme throughout my narrative, focusing on the lives of the working class.

I chewed on my bottom lip, looking again at my wedding photo. I'd wanted to have a small, rustic wedding at a barn or a winery, but Gwyneth and Walter had insisted on the Flood Mansion, a magnificent Pacific Heights home once owned by James Clair Flood, one of the original "bonanza kings" and stock manipulators.

They had generously offered to pay for the wedding, and since my parents were no longer alive, I agreed. The opulent ceremony and reception with two hundred guests was beautiful, if not at all my style. My in-laws' Victorian mansion with its coveted Pacific Heights address nearly rivaled the Flood Mansion in size and opulence. Yet Gwyneth and Walter lived there alone, accompanied only by their housekeeper, Rosa.

I rubbed my temples and thought about the average people of the 1870s: the dockworkers, Chinese railroad workers, and immigrant families. Those were the people I was interested in. But somehow I had failed to bring my story to life. Perhaps I needed to introduce a new character to spark my imagination?

I clicked another link, "Events in the West, 1876," from

PBS.org. A few more clicks, and I'd found a few sourced San Francisco news stories.

> *June 8. Tom Williams drowned in the bay. A*
> *man named Jones dies suddenly in a saloon.*

> *July 3. John Miller arrested as a counterfeiter.*

> *August 7. Jim McGreevy, a tinsmith, fell*
> *from scaffolding and was killed.*

> *September 15. A child of Mrs. Wilson had*
> *his foot cut off by the streetcars.*

I sucked in my breath. How horrible.

> *October 10. The tobacco factories of Harris*
> *& Co., and Moore & Co., destroyed by fire,*
> *and a Chinese boy burned to death.*

> *November 17. Large quantity of*
> *smuggled opium seized.*

> *December 6. News received of a declaration*
> *of war by France against Prussia.*

> *January 10. Missing dressmakers*
> *believed to be murdered.*

My skin prickled. Working women in the Victorian era did not have an easy life. I clicked on the newspaper citation, January 10, 1876, *Daily Alta California*, to read more about the seamstresses. Hunter often teased me about my feminist values, but the plight of women in history would always interest me more than the countless men who'd felt it their right to rape and plunder, claiming the land of native peoples. Good. The *Daily Alta California* was part of the California Digital Newspaper Collection.

The scanned newspaper appeared on my screen as a grayed image. Zooming closer, I clicked each segment of text until I found the original article. I squinted, trying to decipher the old-fashioned font.

Missing Seamstresses Presumed Dead

It was rumored this morning that a fearful murder has been committed in the southern part of the city. The facts that can be ascertained are these: Miss Margaret O'Brien, an Irish girl, and Miss Hannelore Schaeffer, a German girl, were employed as dressmakers at Walton's Tailor Shop of 42 Montgomery Street. The young ladies introduced on this page did not turn up for their shift at eight o'clock yesterday forenoon.

Mrs. Jane Cunningham, proprietress of the shop, reports seeing from her window Miss O'Brien, accompanied by a man, walking in the direction of the saloons on Kearny Street. Several atrocious murders of young ladies with handsome countenances have been recently committed in San Francisco County.

Four months past, a prostitute was found lying dead on the Northeast corner of Hinkley Alley and Dupont Street, before a house of ill repute that sits above the Tavern. Blood was oozing from her ears as if she had received a crushing blow to the head, and there were marks on her throat and mouth, which led to the supposition that she was murdered. Could these two seamstresses have met the same fate?

Hannelore Schaeffer is about 20 years of age, dark hair and light eyes, well formed, rather bold in appearance and speaks good English with a German accent. Margaret O'Brien is about 19 years of age, red hair and blue eyes, very handsome and well formed and speaks fluent English with an Irish accent.

Though the bodies of neither Schaeffer nor O'Brien have been discovered, residents fear hearing cries of "Murder, murder, help, for God's sake, help!" once again, should the killer at large not be stopped for these dreadful crimes.

Goose bumps rose on my arms. Two young dressmakers had disappeared while a killer was on the loose? The room seemed to fade away as my screen took on a razor-sharp focus. I felt an electric energy I hadn't experienced since my days at the magazine—I knew in my gut I'd found an incredible story lead.

Closing the Word document that housed my novel, I opened a new one. Without thinking, my fingers flew across the keyboard. My novel could wait.

There was something about this story, a *true* story, that I couldn't ignore. Who were these women? What had happened to them? A shiver ran down my spine as I read the headline I'd written:

The Lost Dressmakers of the Barbary Coast

Chapter 2

Hannelore Schaeffer
San Francisco, January 1876

The sting of Father's palm spread across Hannelore's face like the burn of hot coals. He leaned in close, his sour breath reeking of whiskey. Blood trickled down Hanna's nose, the metallic taste reaching her tongue.

Raising his sinewy, soot-covered arm for another strike, Father resembled a roaring bear covered in grease. Hanna's heart pounded against her rib cage. Perhaps this time he would kill her, just as he had her mother.

Hanna shielded herself from the second blow, dropping the bowl of small boiled potatoes. It clattered to the ground, spilling its contents to the dirt floor. Hans and Katja cowered beneath the table, whimpering. Father frightened them so.

"You dumb cow!"

He spat the insult in German. Years of working as a blacksmith had hardened his muscles, and Hanna hurled herself away from his swinging arms. Martin ran from his hiding place and thrashed his fists against Father's burly chest, his twelve-year-old arms thin but strong. What a brave, stupid boy.

Father pushed Martin to the ground, where he landed with a heavy thud. Martin's chest heaved and his nostrils flared. "Stop it!" he yelled. "Don't hurt her."

Father laughed, resting his hands on his round belly. In addition to drinking too much ale, he ate his fill at the gambling houses, where men were served hot luncheon. Yet he gave nothing to his children, so that Hanna and her siblings had no means to quell their hunger. Father's laughter grew louder and louder.

"You sound like an American," he bellowed, wiping a tear from his ruddy face. The next one left a trail on his cheek before reaching his black beard.

Hanna's younger brother, Martin, had no trace of an accent, and a clouded memory of the boat that had carried them to this godforsaken place. Martin stood up, hands balled at his sides, his body shaking.

Looking at Hanna with bloodshot eyes, Father tilted his head back and cackled. She waited, holding her breath, until he stumbled backward and fell into his chair.

"Where is my money?" Father asked, pointing a thick finger at her. He was so drunk he couldn't hold it straight.

"We gave you all of our money," Martin said, stepping between them. "She doesn't have any. Tell him, Hanna. Tell him we don't have any."

"I have no money," Hanna answered, trembling as she

spoke. "I've given you every penny that I've earned, and you've spent it all!"

Father lunged for her, smacking Hanna hard across the jaw. She should have seen it coming. He would never take her accusations without a fight. Hanna held her ground. Father's eyelids drooped even as he glared. Once more, he slid into his chair. A moment later, a snore like a bear rumbled from his throat. He'd fallen asleep, drunk, his mouth open, his cruel hands hanging by his sides.

"Come now," Hanna whispered, gathering Katja and Hans into her arms. "You eat your potatoes."

She set the small spuds down on their crude wooden table, wiped the blood from her nose, and managed a smile. Katja, Hans, and Martin reached for the food with dirty fingers, and swallowed it down like wolves. Hanna's stomach growled. How she craved the fatty taste of meat. They never had bratwurst anymore.

Smoothing Katja's dark curls, Hanna kissed the toddler's damp forehead. "Eat up, little deer." Katja's soulful brown eyes darted toward their slumbering father.

"It's all right," Hanna whispered, hoping the child wasn't coming down with a fever. She'd once found her little sister curled up in the grass outside after one of Father's drunken rages, like a fawn in a meadow.

With her mother dead, and her father useless, Hanna found herself solely responsible for keeping her siblings clothed and fed. A portion of her wages from the tailor shop went to their elderly neighbor, Frau Kruger, who watched Katja and Hans during the day. The widow fed them brown bread and eggs. Thank God, for they often had nothing more than scraps. Father spent every penny at the saloons.

He beat Hanna when he thought she was withholding her coins from him. And she had been. She'd managed to stash away nearly eight dollars in a jar, which she kept hidden. Soon it would be enough money to escape.

Hanna closed her eyes and drew in a deep breath. Mountain air. Wildflowers. In her memories, she could see the green fields surrounding her cottage in Mittenwald and Mother's wise hands, rolling dough for schnecken.

But when Hanna opened them, Mother was gone. An icy wind seeped through the cracks of the ramshackle house, and Hanna shivered. While the children were eating, she pried the board in the bedroom floor loose and added more coins to her savings jar. Next to it stood the delicate plate Mother had painted. Hanna wished to live in that idyllic scene amongst the weeping willows. Trailing her finger along Mother's brushstrokes, she imagined Mother watching over her from heaven.

Hanna sniffled, pulling her shawl more tightly around her shoulders. The damp air penetrated the threadbare fabric. Setting the wooden plank back into place, she ignored her rumbling belly and hoped the children had eaten their fill. Father groaned in his sleep, causing her to flinch. Mother had been foolish to fall in love. Such vulnerability was a sign of weakness. And Hanna could not be weak if she wanted to stay alive.

Father's greed had been the reason their family had left Bavaria and come to this vile and sinful place. No man would decide her fate, not Father, not a husband, *no one*. From the doorway to their kitchen, Hanna looked at Martin, his face partially illuminated by the glow of their kerosene lamp. Her brother's lip quivered.

"Martin," she asked. "What are you feeling?"

When he turned to her, his eyes shone with tears. Hanna didn't need him to explain further. Their mother's absence ached like an open wound.

"Do you remember the ship?" Martin asked. "And the train from Hamburg, how we were loaded in like pigs?" He shook his head. "Mother was sick with pneumonia, and yet Father insisted we travel to America. We never should have come here."

Martin had been only a boy of seven when they had traveled in the belly of the steamer. It stank of feces and rot. Hanna hadn't expected him to remember Mother's rattling cough, or her ragged breaths. But perhaps it was the painful things in life that people remembered most.

"I know," Hanna said, her shoulders slumping. "Yet there is nothing we can do. San Francisco is our home now. Take the children. It is time for bed."

Father let out a grunt, and Hanna clenched her fists. She could purchase a packet of poison at one of the low groceries and slip it in his drink. But she wasn't capable of murder. Or perhaps Father could be drugged and clubbed over the head, put aboard a merchant ship to set sail for foreign lands. No one would miss him.

"Hanna, I'm still hungry," Hans said, tugging the hem of her dirndl. His blue eyes pleaded with hers. She knelt on the dirt floor and hugged him tight. Katja cowered behind Hanna's skirt, watching Father twitch in his sleep. "Ana, I scared."

"Don't be frightened," Hanna said. "I will sing you a lullaby."

The little ones nodded.

Leading Hans and Katja by the hand, Hanna entered the small room they shared and tucked them into bed. Martin stood in the kitchen, staring out the window into the darkness. What dreams did he have, kept in those stars? Hanna wouldn't relinquish hers either. Father couldn't control her forever.

"Martin," Hanna whispered. "You come to bed now?"

"In a moment," he said. "Good night."

"Sleep well."

Hanna tucked Mother's quilt under Hans's heart-shaped face and patted the thick cotton fabric. The colors had faded, but the birds and flowers formed an intricate design. Every day, Hanna silently thanked Mother for sitting by her side and teaching her how to sew. As a child, Hanna had hated sewing. But now it was her most valuable skill.

Closing her eyes, Hanna remembered the sound of Mother's voice. A song crept past her lips. She stroked Katja's cheek as she sang.

Sleep, baby, sleep.
Across the heavens move the sheep.

Hanna blew out the kerosene lamp and set it next to the bed. Her jaw ached where Father had struck her. Sucking in her breath, Hanna let her cool fingertips settle on the sore spot.

Ship bells tinkled in the distance, and she curled up against Hans's and Katja's warm bodies. In the smoky darkness, her lids grew heavy and she sank into the lumpy straw and cotton mattress.

Pushing open the door of Walton's Tailor Shop, Hanna walked past the counter into the back room. Piles of silk and taffeta dresses awaited mending, their fabrics more rich and sumptuous than anything she could ever dream of wearing.

"Be careful with those grubby hands of yours," Mrs. Cunningham said, looking down at Hanna over half-moon spectacles. "The pearls that must be reattached to the collar of Miss Jameson's gown are worth more than you could understand."

"Yes, ma'am," Hanna said, picking at her cuticles, which had become red and raw from how hard she scrubbed them with soap.

The corners of Mrs. Cunningham's mouth turned downward, her eyes resting on Hanna's jawline. "Stay in the back room."

Hanna touched her face. The bruise must have come through.

"Yes, ma'am."

When Mrs. Cunningham had gone, Hanna laid a dress flat across the table. What had this woman done to tear the pleated hem of her striped silk gown? Perhaps she'd been dancing at a private party for the fashionable set, something Hanna would never get to do. The black buttons along the bodice had become loose, as though the wearer had been careless unfastening them. Hanna threaded a needle and began to work on the large bustle, stitching a rip in the fabric.

A moment later, the bell at the shop door jingled.

"Sorry I'm late, ma'am," Margaret said, scurrying inside, her cheeks flushed from the cold. Margaret looked at Mrs. Cunningham. "My sister has got a fever. She's a wee thing, and I couldn't leave until it had broken."

"I don't care for your personal business," Mrs. Cunningham said. "There are plenty of other girls who'd be grateful to take your place."

Margaret bit her lip. She walked briskly into the back room and took a seat beside Hanna, her pretty, pale face creased with worry.

"Is it Finna?" Hanna asked, reaching out.

Margaret clasped Hanna's hand in hers. "Oh, Hanna, I'm worried sick."

Hanna nodded. "I will work late. When Mrs. Cunningham goes home, you ought to go home too."

Margaret shook her head, her deep red curls swaying against her shoulders. "You're such a dear. But there's too much work for one person." She bit her lip. "Oh, love. Does it hurt?"

Hanna shrugged. "It is not so bad."

Margaret threaded her needle. She picked up a yellow silk ball gown with short sleeves and large bows. "Drink is a curse, I tell you. And so is bloody gambling. Eight mouths to feed and me da throws money at the roulette wheel like he's Mr. Rockefeller. I need every penny for Finna's medicine."

Margaret shared Hanna's troubles, with more siblings to care for than Hanna could count. Sometimes Margaret's pale face bore purple shadows beneath her eyes. Like the other Irish immigrants, Margaret's father worked a paddy wagon, digging up the earth to carve roads from the hillside. And, like Hanna's father, whiskey was his poison.

"How much will it cost?" Hanna asked.

Margaret frowned. "Twenty cents."

Hanna reached into her coin purse. "Here," she said, handing Margaret two silver dimes. "Take it."

Margaret's eyes widened. "Oh, Hanna. Thank you, truly."

Mrs. Cunningham appeared, the lace collar of her dress tight against her neck and fastened with a large opal brooch.

"Stop chattering and get to work or you'll both be out of a job."

Hanna worked deftly, reattaching buttons and sewing knife pleats until her fingers bled. How could a woman wear so many frills? The ribbed bustle cages, corsets, coats, skirts, and hats were as elaborate as costumes in an opera. Women in the street sometimes snickered at Hanna's dirndl. The cotton dress with its floral print was respectable in Hanna's farm town, but here in America, it was nothing but a rag.

Margaret's calico day dress had been tailored closer to the day's fashions, though made of modest cotton in a simple brown. The way Margaret looked longingly at the satin ribbons, pearls, brocade, jet buttons, and lace collars of these fine gowns, Hanna knew Margaret also wished to wear something beautiful, just once.

The bell of the shop door jingled and two men stepped inside. From their top hats, gold watch chains, and fitted waistcoats, Hanna discerned they were men of importance. With silver flooding into the city from the Comstock Lode mine in Nevada, men like these became millionaires while immigrant families starved.

The elder man looked at Hanna, and ice ran through her veins. *Verdammt!* She'd forgotten to close the door to the back room. Though he had a handsome face, his green eyes sent a chill down to her bones. His long fingers, adorned with gold rings, wrapped around the head of his cane, radiated power—and the darkness beneath it.

"Hello, we've brought in a few suits for repair," the younger man said, handing the jackets and trousers to Mrs. Cunningham. His blue eyes sparkled in the light. As he removed his hat, his thick, golden curls defied the pomade he had slicked through them.

"This is women's work, Lucas," the elder said, knocking his cane against the floor. "Throw some money at the old crow, and let's be on our way."

"Have some respect, Robert," Lucas said.

In her haste to sit down, Margaret knocked the table leg with her knee, spilling a jar full of pearls onto its side. Hanna covered her mouth as they rolled to the floor. Gasping, Margaret looked at Hanna with wide eyes. "Oh, Christ! She'll can me."

Hanna darted forward, crouching to avoid the gaze of the men as she hastily picked up the pearl beads, one by one.

Mrs. Cunningham glared at Hanna, yet managed to maintain a pleasant tone. "Oh dear! I apologize, gentlemen. It appears I have quite a clumsy little fool in my shop."

"Forgive me," Hanna said. "It was my fault."

Soon Margaret appeared at Hanna's side, scouring the floor on hands and knees for the precious pearls. "Thank you," Margaret whispered.

"Here," Lucas said, bending on one knee and holding out a pearl to Hanna. "You've missed one."

Hanna looked into his eyes, blue as a summer sky. "Thank you." She opened her palm. When Lucas set the pearl inside, Hanna warmed from his touch.

The older man, Robert, who'd been standing impatiently by the door, turned and stared at Margaret as if she were a juicy piece of flank steak.

"Girl," Mrs. Cunningham snapped at Margaret. "Make yourself useful and take these suits while I write up a receipt."

Lucas smiled. "Thank you. I'm afraid I was dancing too vigorously at the Regatta Ball. The stitching on the shoulder is torn."

Margaret giggled. "You ought to see me dance a jig. It ain't easy not to rip a seam or two!"

Mrs. Cunningham shot her a look and Margaret scuttled away.

Mrs. Cunningham turned to Hanna. "What are you lollygagging for? Put those beads away before someone slips and breaks his neck."

"Yes, ma'am," Hanna said. Hurrying into the back room, Hanna turned the jar upright and opened her palm, pouring the pearls inside.

"I do apologize, gentlemen," Mrs. Cunningham said. "One of the girls will make you a cup of tea while you wait. It shall only be a moment."

Robert cleared his throat. "None for me. Thank you." He looked to Lucas. "Let's be out of here. We've a meeting at the Palace Hotel in fifteen minutes."

"Actually, I'd quite enjoy a warm cup of tea," Lucas said.

"*You*," Mrs. Cunningham hissed at Hanna, poking her head into the back room. "Make the gentleman a cup of tea at once!"

Hanna's hands trembled as she poured the steaming brew from a silver pot into a porcelain cup with a gold rim. Her stomach rumbled. How nice it would be to have hot tea on such a cold winter's day. But it was meant only for customers.

"Cream and sugar, sir?" Hanna asked.

"Yes, please," Lucas said.

Hanna felt Lucas's fingers brush hers as she handed him the saucer. Her cheeks tingled. "Here you are."

"Thank you," he said. "May I ask your name?"

Her throat felt dry. "Hannelore Schaeffer, sir."

"My, that is a mouthful," Lucas said, raising his eyebrows. He sipped his tea. "Do your friends call you Hannelore?"

She noticed the dimples that framed his smile. They gave him a pleasant, boyish appearance. "No. My friends call me Hanna. You may call me that too, if you like." Hanna's face grew hot. "Oh, sir, I am so sorry. I did not mean . . ."

Lucas laughed. "What, we can't be friends?"

Hanna smiled. "I suppose we could."

Robert snorted, and Lucas's smile began to fade. Straightening himself, Lucas seemed to remember his position as a man of society. He cocked his head, eyeing Hanna quizzically. "You're not from here, are you? You have an accent."

"I am from Bavaria," Hanna answered. "Now I have lived here five years."

"Your English is quite good," Robert said, raising his eyebrow as if in accusation. "How peculiar."

Hanna stared at the floor. "Yes, I suppose it is."

"You wear your hair differently than most women," Robert said. "Like a farm girl. Perhaps you grew up in a barn amongst sheep and cattle?"

Hanna looked up again, touching the dark plaits she'd pinned atop her head. Heat burned her cheeks. She didn't have money for false hair, curls worn long and bouncy over the shoulder, nor a fanciful little hat. Truthfully, Hanna thought the hats worn by society women to be ridiculous, adorned with ruffles and feathers, flowers, foliage, and even faux fruits. What use would she have for such a thing?

"I don't have time for curls," Hanna said.

Suddenly, Lucas's smile reappeared, indenting his dimples. "You're very practical."

Hanna looked at Lucas, his expression so inviting. Unbidden, a smile began to creep across her face. But when Robert shot Lucas a scowl, Lucas's eyes lost their sparkle. Lucas cleared his throat, straightening his ascot.

"Thank you," he said, "for mending our suits. I'm sure they shall come back good as new. And please thank your friend as well."

"What is her name?" Robert asked, his eyes cold.

"Margaret O'Brien, sir," Hanna said.

"Industrious creatures, aren't they?" Robert murmured, polishing the head of his cane with a handkerchief. "A good deal of peasant blood runs in their veins."

Hanna's stomach clenched, but she did not speak out against Robert's insult. Neither did Lucas, whose cheeks flushed pink.

Mrs. Cunningham reappeared with a paper receipt and Hanna busied herself, reaching for Lucas's dish and teacup. "May I?"

He nodded, handing them to her, so their fingers brushed again. Hanna tingled at the contact, wondering if Lucas had intended it.

"Your suits shall be ready in three days," Mrs. Cunningham said. "The total is four dollars."

Hanna's eyes widened upon hearing a sum so high. She and Margaret earned less than a dollar a day.

Robert knocked his cane against the floor. "Good. That's sorted, then. Come, Lucas."

Lucas placed his top hat upon his head. He tipped it toward Hanna. "Good-bye, Miss Schaeffer."

Hanna nodded. "Good-bye."

When Mrs. Cunningham turned away, Robert pushed open the door, letting in a gust of chilly air. Lucas followed, but paused when he reached the threshold.

"Just so you know," he said quietly, without turning around, "I like your hair the way it is."

Hanna's stomach felt like birds had taken flight inside of it.

And without another word, Lucas followed Robert out of the shop and onto the cobbled street.

When Hanna met Margaret in the back room, Margaret's face brightened. "Did you speak with him?" Margaret asked.

Hanna smoothed a pink taffeta gown against the table. "Yes."

"What a fine lad," Margaret said, a naughty look in her eye. "And so handsome! Do you fancy him?"

"He was kind," Hanna said, picking up a needle as she felt her cheeks flush. Fabric slipped between her fingers as she stitched in neat rows. "But I'm not so foolish as to have eyes for a gentleman. I know what I am."

Margaret poked Hanna in the ribs. "A fine seamstress and a good friend. He would be *lucky* to have you."

Hanna smiled at Margaret. "Not true, you silly hen."

They stifled their giggles before Mrs. Cunningham could reprimand them again. Hanna bit her lip. Would Lucas ever be interested in a girl like her? *Leave the church in the village,* as the old German saying went.

Chapter 3

Sarah, *Present Day*

"Here's where we should set the sculpture of *Amorino,*" Gwyneth said, her voice echoing throughout the marble chambers of Havensworth Art Academy's California Street campus, one of the many imposing HAA buildings planted around the heart of the city. A small army of people dressed in black buzzed around like bees with microphones, preparing the space for the Canova by Moonlight gala.

I'd taken the morning to help Gwyneth plan her event. Hopefully she wouldn't feel like I didn't make time in my schedule for her charity functions. Being unemployed, I had all the time in the world. But I looked at my phone impatiently, longing to research the missing dressmakers before the spark of this new idea burned out.

"Sarah, dear, what do you think? Is the lighting too dark?

Too *tombée de la nuit*?" Gwyneth liked to throw French words into everyday conversation.

Clueless as to what she was talking about, I nodded. "I think the sculpture will look great there. I can't believe the National Gallery of Ireland is flying it out here for the event. Isn't the marble really heavy? And fragile?"

She tucked a wisp of her blond hair behind her ear. "Oh yes! We had to pull some strings. But Walter is a close friend of Colin, the chairman of the Irish gallery board. The museum is also flying out some precious oils from their national portrait collection, very rare paintings from the early 1800s."

"Really?" I said, my eyes widening. "That's incredible."

Her cell phone jingled. Gwyneth tapped the screen with a perfectly manicured fingertip. "Hello? Yes, Gigi, darling, hello! I was just going to call you."

I walked down the hall, gazing up at oil paintings of nudes and San Francisco landscapes. This massive Italianate style building, in addition to the others, was no doubt valuable property, purchased by a Havensworth forefather who'd held an interest in the arts. Hunter came from a long line of bankers and real-estate moguls.

"Sarah," Gwyneth's voice called down the corridor. "Can you be a dear and take the stairs up two flights? At the end of the hall there's an office. You'll find an antique silver paper-weight of an Irish setter that I'd love to put on display. It was a gift to the family from a Dublin banker."

Gwyneth's heels clicked down the hallway and she handed me a brass key.

"It's pure silver, and I don't want one of these *Latinos* taking it." She lowered her voice, her eyes darting toward the workers.

"Sure," I said, trying to hide my cringe. I imagined how my friend Nick would feel if he heard Gwyneth voicing racial stereotypes. At the magazine, a rude visitor had once mistaken Nick for a janitor instead of recognizing him as our lead designer.

She patted my back. "Thank you, dear. You know how these old knees trouble me. We have to get the elevator fixed."

The key felt heavy in my hand. "Is the door on the right or left?"

"On the right."

I touched her arm. "And Gwyneth? I'm sure your workers are trustworthy."

"Yes, dear. You're probably right. But I trust you more."

I made my way up the winding spiral staircase and down the hallway. A chill came over me as my footsteps echoed in the dark. Muffled voices sounded from downstairs, yet I felt utterly alone.

I twisted the key in the lock until I heard a click. When I pushed the door open, the dark study smelled like disinfectant. Though it had been cleaned recently, the furniture hadn't been updated in years. A heavy oak desk stood in the center of the room, faded green file folders stacked on top of it. I picked up a magnifying glass with a mother-of-pearl handle and then set it down, looking for the paperweight.

An Irish setter made of solid silver sat atop a stack of yellowed papers that curled at their edges. I lifted it with one hand. Wow, it was heavy. I moved the paperweight aside so that I could peek at the papers, mostly architectural plans for the building and class rosters from the 1960s.

I picked up the canine paperweight and held it from the bottom, wondering who had used this study and chosen the artwork for the room. Above the desk hung a still life: apples, pears, and oranges in a brass bowl, sitting atop a rumpled table-cloth. I took a step closer. The painting hung vertically in a 16×20 frame, but I could make out a faint outline on the wall, the lasting image of a missing rectangle. How strange. Another painting must have hung there for quite some time. Now it was gone.

Walking slowly around the desk, I scanned the other paintings. A nude had been rendered in oils, a woman reclining against a chaise longue. I squinted to make out the signature in the corner. A student named Dan had painted it in 1981.

Purple flowers burst from a vase in another frame, a poor imitation of Van Gogh. Not that I was an art critic by any means, but the painting didn't hold any feeling in its swirling brushstrokes. It was as if the student had tried her best to copy the style of her favorite artist, but failed to bring forth emotion.

On the right wall, a large abstract piece had a series of angry red-and-black slashes, intersecting with a square drawn in a childish squiggly hand. Had Walter chosen this random sampling?

It wasn't my place to question my father-in-law's artistic sense. He was on the board of the National Gallery of Ireland, after all. But perhaps his college friendship with the chair and the amount of money he was able to donate meant more than his ability to curate a collection.

Angled into a corner of the room stood a tall, antique wooden wardrobe. I stepped closer, trailing my fingers along the elegant walnut. The keyhole was made of pewter and tarnished with age. Scanning the desk, I saw no key for the lock. I hooked my finger into the empty slot and tugged, but the door didn't budge—another gateway to the past shut tight.

It was time to return to the present. After closing the heavy door to the study behind me, I turned the key in the lock, preserving the room as it had been. Making my way down the stairs, I let out the breath I hadn't realized I'd been holding. For reasons I couldn't articulate, the study retained sadness like water inside a dam.

"Here's your paperweight," I said to Gwyneth. The cool air in the marble lobby prickled my sweaty skin.

"Thank you," she said, taking the shiny object from me and cradling it in her palm. "He's a special treasure."

"The Irish setter was out on the desk, and I wasn't sure he should be, especially if you're worried about him getting stolen. If you have the key to the wardrobe, I can put him there after the event."

Gwyneth smoothed her blond bob, avoiding eye contact. "Key? I don't know what you're talking about, dear. The setter has always been on the desk."

"I'm sure you're right," I said, unconvinced. Finding my mother-in-law's gaze, I pressed further. "Is that Walter's office?"

Her blue eyes met mine, serious and cold. "Yes, dear. Walter took over the academy presidency from his father and grandfather before him."

"I see," I said, taking a step back.

Gwyneth smiled, her eyes warm again, her hand gently touching my arm. "His study hasn't received my feminine touch, so pardon the decor. For now, I'll focus on the downstairs. This academy is a big building, you know."

I smiled back. "Yes, it is."

Checking my watch, I realized it was nearly one P.M. I'd spent more time away than I'd meant to.

"Gwyneth, I hate to leave, but I have a meeting with my graduate advisor."

The white lie brought a pinch in my stomach, but if I didn't get to work on my thesis, my mother-in-law would easily keep me here all day.

"It's all right." She squeezed my hand. "Don't work too hard now. Give Hunter a kiss for me when you get home. And Redford too."

"Of course I will."

Outside on California Street, I looked down at my phone, where Jen had pinged me with a text message.

Nick and I miss you! Meet up for beers at Zeitgeist tomorrow night around 7pm? Please? We want to tell you all the work gossip!

A smile crept to my lips. I didn't miss the politics of the magazine, one of the reasons I'd quit, but I missed my friends dearly. Not to mention, I was curious to hear about the new editor in chief, who'd been hired after I left.

I'd love to, I texted back. See you guys then!

I turned down California Street, walking toward Market, past women in black yoga pants carrying colorful leather handbags, coffee cups in hand, and countless men wearing backpacks or messenger bags over their button-down shirts. A cable car clanged its bell, and tourists hung from the handrails, awestruck as they looked up. As I passed Café Madeleine, the scent of freshly baked French bread filled the air.

On Market Street, bus brakes hissed, and notes of jazz from a street musician's trumpet carried over the din of traffic. A bearded guy on a bicycle zipped by me, his basket full of farm-fresh flowers for delivery. I caught snippets of French as I passed two men, who pointed at Google Maps on an iPhone. Nearly everyone was on a call, speaking hurriedly into the microphones of their white Apple EarPods.

My mind wandered as I walked through the bustling Financial District. There was something about that study, like a breath that had been held for too long, that needed to be expelled. With so much history, there was no telling who'd passed through the halls of Havensworth Art Academy once upon a time. Or why that wardrobe in the study remained locked. Crossing over to Kearny Street, I stopped to wait for my bus.

The 30-Stockton wasn't coming for another fifteen minutes. I sighed. Sitting down on one of the dirty benches, I pulled up the article I'd found in the archives of the *Daily Alta California* on my phone.

Though the bodies of neither Schaeffer nor O'Brien have been discovered, residents fear hearing cries

of "Murder, murder, help, for God's sake, help!"
once again, should the killer at large not be stopped
for these dreadful crimes.

Where had Margaret and Hannelore last been seen? After
an hour of searching their names last night, I hadn't found any
follow-up articles regarding their disappearance. Yet their story
tugged at me, refusing to let me go. My fingers tapped the
screen, scrolling downward.

Four months past, a prostitute was found lying
dead on the Northeast corner of Hinkley Alley and
Dupont Street, before a house of ill repute that sits
above the Tavern.

I didn't recognize those street names. Had they changed?
Pulling up Google on my phone, I did a quick search. Dupont
Street was now Grant Street. And the Tavern, San Francisco's
oldest bar, was still standing.

My eyes flickered to the digital display on the bus stop.
Shoving my phone into my back pocket, I stood up. The Tavern
was only a fifteen-minute walk away, and I could always catch
another bus.

I stopped at the corner of Fresno and Grant, looking up at a red
clapboard building with yellow trim. Tucked away on an alley

in North Beach, not far from the strip clubs of Broadway and the Italian restaurants dotting Columbus Avenue, the Tavern held its ground. Beneath the wooden street number, TAVERN, EST. 1863 had been painted on the window. I imagined seeing a mustachioed barkeep inside wearing a waistcoat. In all the years I'd lived in San Francisco, how had I never visited this place?

The bar was dimly lit and warm. A few locals sat on stools, drinking beer as a band set up their equipment on the stage. A dark wood bureau with a cracked mirror and large columns stood against the wall. My eyes moved to the layers of peeling paint and remnants of wallpaper from decades past. This place had existed when Hannelore and Margaret were alive. Had they ever come through these doors?

"What can I get you?" the bartender asked. With his weathered face, long ponytail, and leather vest, he looked like an aging Hells Angel. I checked out the two beers on tap and smiled. Pabst Blue Ribbon, my dad's favorite.

I kept a framed photo of my parents, circa 1984, next to my bed. Mom had fluffy, blond Farrah Fawcett hair and wore a tight, striped tank top while Dad had a bushy brown moustache and held a can of Pabst Blue Ribbon. His tanned arm circled Mom's waist, and she was caught mid-laugh. In that picture, they were my current age, thirty, beaming with health and happiness. It was how I liked to remember them.

My mom had smelled like lemons and had an unmistakable midwestern accent. To her, "Up Nort" wasn't a specific location, but anywhere near Lake Superior, the places we went camping and fishing in the summer. I felt my throat close up, wishing I could hear Mom's voice again, or hear my dad telling me to load up the cooler.

"PBR, please," I said to the bartender.

It was a poor man's beer, now a hipster beer. But unlike most of the bars in San Francisco, the Tavern wasn't the least bit pretentious. Not a single person tapped away on their iPhone or wore anything dressy. It was my kind of place.

Through the darkness, framed photographs on the wall came into focus. They were grainy sepia prints, images of the city 150 years ago. Horse-drawn carriages stood next to Victorian buildings. Women in black dresses held parasols along a wharf, while boys and men cast their fishing poles into the water.

"One PBR," the bartender said, setting down a frosty glass.

I gave him a five-dollar bill and pointed at the photo. "Do you know where this is?"

"That's Long Bridge."

"Long Bridge?" I said, my eyebrows pinching together. "Never heard of it."

He held his hands about a foot apart. "Long Bridge spanned the city from Fourth Street all the way to Hunters Point. It was like rapid transit for the workmen in the 1870s. But on Sundays it was where the working class would have fun."

I picked up my beer and walked around, checking out the old photographs. There were women with severe middle parts in their hair and stern expressions. Their pale eyes stared off into space, though serious faces were the norm for that era.

There were pictures of landmarks long gone, like the Cliff House on Ocean Beach, a restaurant resembling a haunted castle, perched on a headland above the water's edge.

I returned to the bar and sat down on a stool, the cracked leather crinkling underneath me. "So is this really San Francisco's oldest bar?"

The bartender coughed into his hand. "The bar was always here on the first floor, but the second and third floors operated as a whorehouse. The firemen were customers."

He pointed to a black-and-white photograph of the bar, dated 1870. Four men stood in the doorway, each with a dark moustache and a cap.

"You see," he said, his gravelly voice growing louder. "The building was burning in the aftermath of the 1906 quake, but the firemen had their priorities straight. They came to save the whorehouse."

"Good thing they did," I said. "Not many buildings left from before the quake."

He jerked his head toward the stage. "Now we host live blues almost every night of the week. You should stay awhile to really hear the bands shred. The best acts go on after midnight."

"Thanks. I can't tonight, but maybe next time."

I sipped my beer and tried to picture what this place had once been like. The piano in the corner probably had a musician playing on its worn keys, while men danced or got into fistfights. The bartender might have been here for a few years, but there had to be someone else who could verify if this saloon was once a whorehouse, someone who really knew its history.

Notes pierced the air as the blues band started to jam, first the wail of the trumpet and then the thrumming of the bass. A few bar patrons tapped their feet in time to the music. More people began to trickle through the door.

"Excuse me," I called over the din to the bartender. "Could you tell me who owns this bar?"

"Mr. Kim. It's been in his family for a long time."

"What's his first name?"

"Edward," he said, pouring a shot of whiskey.

"Thank you," I said.

I drained the dregs of my beer. How would I explain myself if Hunter found out I'd left the Art Academy this afternoon to go to a *bar*? He understood my anxiety well enough to let me quietly slip away from social functions—especially kids' birthday parties. But he didn't know about the dark memories that kept me awake at night. I wanted to let him in, but the opportunity to be truthful had already passed.

I stepped out onto the street to walk toward the nearest bus stop. Or if I was in a hurry, I could always hail a cab or get an Uber. There was a reason I'd chosen to live in a city where I didn't need a car. So far, it had suited me perfectly.

The fog had settled heavy and thick around the rooftops of North Beach's Victorian apartment buildings, the peak of the Transamerica Pyramid lost in the swirling mist. I zipped my sweatshirt up to my chin, breathing in the fog's faint ocean scent. But the shiver that ran down my spine was from more than the spring chill.

I had to find out what had happened to Hannelore and

Margaret, or the wondering would haunt me forever. My mind buzzed with ideas. I could search the library and the California Historical Society archives. What if I abandoned my novel altogether and focused on a piece of literary journalism instead? Svetlana Alexievich had won the Nobel Prize in literature for her emotional books, her histories of women, men, and children affected by war, whose stories we wouldn't otherwise know.

I admired her ability to tell a story through human truths, to portray a vanished way of life. What if I could present the story of Hannelore and Margaret not only with facts but also with human emotions? I chewed my bottom lip, thinking about how I would ask my graduate advisor if I could switch my focus.

Turning around, I looked back in the direction I'd come from. The street hummed with forgotten history. But was this truly a good idea? The walls of that old saloon held secrets. I'd held on to my own long enough to know what it felt like, and that dredging up the past could often reveal something ugly.

Chapter 4

Hanna, *1876*

Ducking beneath the clotheslines strung between the wooden houses of Napier Lane on Telegraph Hill, Hanna dodged the articles of clothing that flapped in the breeze. She pulled her shawl more tightly around her shoulders, to ward off the winter chill.

Rocks pushed through the soles of her boots as she made her way down the slope. A goat bleated while the bells of Old Saint Mary's chimed in the distance. Beyond the church steeples and streetcar tracks, the mansions of Nob Hill stood watch.

By the time Hanna reached Montgomery Street downtown, the dirt road had given way to a cobblestone thoroughfare lined with stately hotels and colorful shop fronts. Flower carts and newspaper vendors served patrons of the Palace Hotel, whose entrance beckoned with gas lamps that cast an inviting glow.

Walking arm in arm, women in towering hats and large-bustled dresses flounced about like geese.

Hanna had vowed to sew herself a dress with a bustle if she ever had the money for that much fabric. But then she'd have the trouble of finding a whalebone corset, and a hoopskirt undercarriage to give the dress its fullness. Her cotton chemise and bloomers were likely far more comfortable than the under-garments of the fine ladies who'd passed her in the street, not giving her a second glance.

Waving from a few yards away, Margaret smiled. Dressed in a green day frock, she looked as pretty as wildflowers in springtime. When Margaret came closer, she tore off a piece of white bread from the loaf in her hand. Hanna's stomach growled as she accepted the fluffy morsel. White bread was so rare it tasted like cake. Hanna couldn't remember what it felt like not to be hungry.

"Margaret, how have you got bread?"

"Don't you worry. Here." Margaret reached into her coin purse, returning the money Hanna had lent her. "Finna's right as rain now. I can't thank you enough."

Hanna smiled. "If my Kati fell sick, you would do the same."

Hanna stuck out her elbow, and Margaret looped her arm through it. For a few precious hours on this Sunday afternoon, they would be free. No chores, no piles of dresses, no furious fathers. Martin was watching the children, and in return for good behavior Hanna had promised each a piece of hard candy. How Hanna wished to catch a glimpse inside the melodeons on Pacific Avenue, where Lotta Crabtree performed inside the music halls. But even the finest of those establishments wouldn't be safe for young women.

On Long Bridge, families strolled alongside sailors and fishermen.

Crowds of men and boys leaned against the bridge's wooden railing, elbow to elbow, fishing for smelt with bamboo poles. Horse-drawn carriages rattled down the wooden causeway, passing through the marshlands on their way to the Bay View racetrack. Circling overhead, the gulls cried. Men tumbled out of Gallant and Purdy's halfway house, drunk on ale and shouting.

Margaret tugged Hanna's arm. "Let's get away from here, quick."

They took refuge at the stall of a street vendor, where Hanna bought penny candies, one for each sibling. Unfolding the waxed wrapper, she held the treat in her palm, then popped it in her mouth. The mint was sweet against her tongue. Hanna counted the seconds as she sucked, willing it not to end.

"He's a good-looking fellow." Margaret giggled, smiling at a boy in a brown bowler hat and suspenders. Factory workers walked by and whistled.

"Would you kiss him?" Margaret asked, nodding at a different young man, wearing dirty coveralls.

"Have you got birds in the head?" Hanna wrinkled her nose, her cheeks burning at Margaret's bold suggestion. The boy's skin was as pale as the underbelly of a fish and dotted in freckles.

Margaret laughed. "You speak English like no one else. He wasn't that bad looking."

"Not for me," Hanna said. "Will you marry an Irishman?"

Margaret tucked a strand of her hair behind her ear, a far-away look in her eye. "I would . . . if I could."

Margaret appeared so troubled, Hanna reached out to touch her friend, hoping Margaret would reveal the cause of her sadness. But before Hanna's fingers could brush Margaret's sleeve, Margaret's mischievous smile had returned. "He doesn't have to be Irish. I'd marry any boy if I loved him."

Perhaps Hanna had only imagined Margaret's distress. "If I knew a good German," she said, "I'd introduce you. But they are stupid as cows."

Margaret threw her head back and laughed.

"*Excusez-moi.*" A man holding a wooden box in the shape of an accordion had spoken, his English accented by his native French. "May I take your photograph?"

Hanna looked at the contraption. "Is that a camera?"

He nodded.

"Why'd you want to photograph us?" Margaret eyed him sideways. She was right to be wary of the man. Only vain women in fancy hats with little dogs had their photographs taken.

The man shrugged. "I am an artist. I capture what I see."

"Let us do it," Hanna said to Margaret. "We will act like fine ladies now."

The man crouched down and adjusted the brass lens on his mahogany box. Hanna looped her arm through Margaret's and they leaned against the wooden railing.

"Stand very still. Yes, like that. *Un, deux, trois.*" The photographer pulled a cord.

Hanna blinked. Had he finished? Margaret stood rigid as a tree, appearing unsure of whether she should change position. "Can we see it?" Margaret asked.

The photographer shook his head. "It does not work that way, I'm afraid. I must develop the plate first. What are your names?"

"Hannelore," Hanna said, her shoulders slumping. "And my friend's name is Margaret."

Perhaps some strange person would see her likeness, his curiosity piqued by the girl in the photograph. But Hanna would never know how she appeared—sullen, friendly, or frightened.

"Merci." The man scribbled on a scrap of paper. "I am François. Good day."

Margaret pressed her lips together in a frown.

"Good day," Hanna said as François packed up his things.

A ferryboat let out a loud, low rumble as it pulled away from the pier. Sleek yachts cut across the bay like herons. Hanna turned around to see the two-tiered yacht club, narrowing her eyes against the late afternoon sun. Had they walked so far already? Clinking crystal and women's laughter wafted on the breeze from the upper balcony. Craning her neck to see inside, Hanna took a step backward.

She collided with a man in a suit, causing his shiny top hat to fall to the ground. Bending down to pick it up, Hanna's cheeks burned. "Oh! My apologies."

When the man's eyes met hers, his sky-blue gaze froze Hanna in place. Lucas. Her stomach lurched, like the first time she had ridden a horse, back on a neighbor's farm in Bavaria.

Dusting off his hat, Lucas placed it back on his head. "Miss Schaeffer. Lovely to see you again."

"Oh, sir, I am very sorry. Please forgive me my clumsy feet."

His features softened. "Please, don't be sorry. It's quite all right."

Next to Lucas's wool suit and shiny black shoes, Hanna felt like a beggar, hatless and in her plain dress. Unlike Margaret, whose complexion was as pale and delicate as a lace tablecloth, that Hanna's face had known the sun branded her as working-class.

"You're from the dress shop, aren't you?" Lucas asked, turning to Margaret.

"Yes, sir." Margaret blushed, even prettier than usual, and a pang of jealousy hit Hanna like a dart.

Lucas frowned. "Remind me of your name?"

"Margaret O'Brien," Margaret said.

"Have you enjoyed your afternoon?" Lucas asked, sweeping his arm toward the pier. "It is a fine day today."

Two women holding lace parasols walked past on their way to the yacht club. They glanced at Lucas, then at Hanna's feet, their words whispered like the swish of their taffeta gowns until they could contain their laughter no longer. Hanna looked down at her boots, sticky with horse dung. Her cheeks stung with pinpricks of heat. Flicking their tails, chestnut mares munched on hay while waiting for their carriage driver.

"Yes," Hanna said. "The weather is fine. But I'm afraid we must be on our way."

The door to the yacht club swung open and Robert emerged, a scowl on his face.

"Cousin," Lucas said, clapping his hand on Robert's shoulder. "These are the girls from Walton's Tailor Shop in town, Miss Hannelore Schaeffer and Miss Margaret O'Brien. It appears we've all come out for a Sunday stroll."

The way Lucas said their names made Hanna think of grand ladies promenading gloved and veiled, not lowly shopgirls. It brought the tug of a smile to her lips.

Robert turned to Hanna. "Good day."

She bowed her head. "Good day, sir."

"Forgive my cousin," Lucas said. "Among the fairer sex, conversation does not come naturally to him. I fear he's lost his tongue."

Robert's smile didn't reach his eyes. "Apologies," he said, to Margaret this time, ignoring Hanna completely. "It is not my intention to be boorish. However, I must meet a colleague in town. Lucas and I have important business to attend to."

A heavyset man approached, a dark birthmark smudged on his cheek like a thumbprint. He gave one of the chestnut-colored horses a pat on her shiny flank. He then hoisted himself aboard the carriage with a grunt.

"Clive," Robert said. "Bring us back to town. California Street."

"Yes, sir," Clive answered, taking the reins.

"Are you heading that way?" Lucas asked Hanna.

"Yes," she said. "We will walk back."

"But that shall take nearly an hour's time, will it not?" Lucas asked, scrunching his brow. "Is it healthful to walk such a distance?"

Robert coughed into his hand. Hanna couldn't quite make out his words, but they sounded very much like *peasant blood*.

"I believe so," Hanna answered. "Nothing is better for the soul than fresh air."

Lucas nodded. "Good day, then. Enjoy the remainder of your afternoon."

Climbing aboard his carriage, Lucas tipped his hat to Hanna. "Miss Schaeffer. Miss O'Brien."

Margaret's cheeks colored even pinker, not so pretty this time, for she looked truly frightened, being addressed so directly.

"Good day," Hanna said.

"He called me Miss!" Margaret grinned as she turned to walk with Hanna. "Do you think he's gone mad?"

"Not mad, but a bit unusual perhaps."

"And quite handsome," Margaret said.

As Hanna strolled with Margaret along the bridge, a carriage full of ladies dressed in white rambled past, their faces obscured by large hats with black bows.

Margaret sighed. "Ach, they're off to the races, the lucky cows. How I would love to see the horse races."

"It would be splendid fun," Hanna said. "A shame we cannot go."

A ruddy-faced man tumbled out of a saloon perched at the edge of the pier. His wild eyes fixed on Hanna.

"You up for a ride, lass?" He bucked his hips in a vulgar gesture.

She flinched, her features contorting into a scowl. "Get away, you mongrel!"

The man grabbed ahold of her arm, bringing his face so close she could smell the whiskey on his breath. An angry red scar slashed across his cheek. "Yes, you are."

Hanna pulled against his strong grip. "No! Leave me be!"

"Let go of her!" Margaret screamed.

He grinned, like a snake. "Aren't you a pretty little trollop? You can have a ride when I'm done with her."

Hanna spit in his face. Eyes narrowing, the man raised his hand to strike her. Bracing for the sting of his palm, Hanna cowered.

"Enough!"

Lucas drew his carriage to a stop beside Hanna. His nostrils flared as he looked down at the drunk. Robert stared at Margaret, wetting his lips as if to speak out, but his eyes widened when they alighted on the scar-faced man, as if he recognized the fellow. Before Hanna could blink, Lucas had leaped down into the street, landing on two feet spry as a cat.

"Release her at once!" Lucas cried, shoving the man, hard.

The drunk fell, freeing Hanna from his dirty fingers. She watched as the vagrant sprawled in a heap across the wooden slats of the bridge.

Unsteadily, the man rose to his feet, spitting at Lucas. "You lookin' for a fight, you fancy piece of shite? I know a scrubber when I see one."

Hanna's gut told her to run. Yet her feet rooted themselves to the ground. The man pointed at her and then at Margaret.

His glassy eyes hardened. "Harlots, the both of them. Every girl in this city is a whore."

"Please, Lucas," Hanna whispered. "Do not listen to this dangerous drunkard. Get back in your carriage."

"Yes," Robert said, looking down at the commotion. "Let us keep our graces."

Lucas ignored them both, hoisting the miscreant by the collar of his soiled jacket and shaking him. "Apologize to these women. They are not trollops, you vile, disgusting creature. Apologize!"

The man struggled, wild-eyed like a captured animal. "Sorry," he shouted, spittle flying from his mouth. "I'm sorry, ladies. Please, let me down. Don't 'urt me."

Lucas relaxed his grip, and the man fell to the ground. As Lucas dusted himself off, the glint of a knife in the inebriate's pocket caught Hanna's eye.

"Weapon!" she yelled. Unthinking, she darted forward. Slick with sweat, her palm slid against the knife handle. She managed to wrench the blade from the lowlife. Hanna pointed it at him. "Stay away!"

"Give me back my knife, you little cunt!" He lunged for Hanna, but in his drunkenness, fell against Margaret instead.

Margaret shrieked, slapping him hard. "Get off me, you shit-stack!"

Before the drunkard could retaliate, Lucas pulled back his fist and punched the man hard in the jaw.

A crowd began to gather.

"Fight!" a man yelled, gesturing to his friends. "Fight, fight!"

"No," Hanna said, pulling Lucas by his suit jacket. "Leave him. We must run."

Lucas appraised the crew of ruffians that had gathered. These were hardened men eager for a fight, their arms strong from a lifetime of labor. Lucas clenched his hands into fists.

Robert cracked his whip, startling the crowd. "I suggest you disperse immediately, or I'll send for the police. I have no qualms throwing each and every one of you in prison. I'm quite well acquainted with the police chief."

"That's right," Lucas said, addressing the men. "Now leave at once!"

"Wait until your fancy boy ain't 'ere to protect you," the drunkard yelled, his eyes darting from Margaret to Hanna. "I'll find you girls and kill you."

The scar-faced man spat at Hanna's feet and then turned to dart into the thinning crowd. Hanna flung the man's knife over the bridge railing, where it landed with a splash in the water below.

"Bloody hell, that was frightening," Margaret whispered.

Hanna nodded, her body shaking.

"Are you all right?" Lucas asked, turning to Hanna. "When I saw that man accost you, I had to intervene."

"Thank you, sir," Hanna said. "You saved my life."

He held up a hand. "Please. Call me Lucas. And you were brave enough to grab that man's knife. So perhaps it is you who saved mine."

"Ahem," Robert said, looking down at them. "Now that the ruffian has left us, we must be on our way."

"How are you getting home?" Lucas asked, turning to Hanna.

"We are walking," Hanna replied.

"Please," Lucas said. "Let me accompany you." He patted the horse's flank, looking up at Robert. "Ride on without me."

Robert wrinkled his nose. "Suit yourself."

As the carriage clattered away, Hanna rubbed her arms, as if to erase the gooseflesh. Margaret placed a soothing hand on Hanna's back. "There, there. He's gone now. And we've got Mr. Lucas to walk with us."

Hanna smiled at Lucas. "Thank you."

Lucas frowned. "We must notify the police and report this criminal. I should hate to think of him plaguing others as he endangered you today."

Margaret scoffed. "I don't mean to offend, sir, but the police won't do nothing. There's enough sin in this city to burn the place to the ground."

Lucas turned to Margaret. "Is that what you believe?"

"Aye," she said, her face darkening. "The men are all drunkards, including me da. My wee brothers and sisters haven't a crumb to eat. The police don't give a damn about us Irish. They'd let us starve. That's why I work at the shop."

Lucas turned to Hanna. "Must you provide for your family as well?"

"Yes," Hanna said. "My mother died of pneumonia, so I keep house and I work. My brother Martin is a boy of twelve, and he also works from dawn until dusk."

Lucas hung his head. "I'm terribly sorry to hear about your mother. My little cousin Clara was also taken by disease as a child . . . consumption. She was Robert's sister. He's never quite been the same since she died."

"Oh," Hanna said, softening. "How sad." And here she'd been about thinking about how life was not kind to those on the fringes of society. Lucas had likely grown up in a grand home with servants, cooks, governesses, and tutors attending to his every need. He would never know the pain of a hungry belly or the danger of the back alleys of the Barbary Coast. Yet death didn't discriminate.

"It may not be of popular opinion," Lucas said, "but I don't agree with child labor. Should children not be allowed to play, at least for an hour or two?"

Hanna's nails dug into her palm.

"I'd rather my little brothers and sister learn to read," Hanna said. "For them to have more opportunities than I have had. I try my best to teach them words in English and German, but I fear they will end up working long hours in a factory."

"Aye," Margaret said, hanging her head. "I should like to read as well. I've often wondered what's inside all those books."

Lucas slowed to a halt. He stood on the wooden bridge next to the horse-car tracks, as ships bobbed in the ocean and gulls cawed. His eyes widened as he looked at Margaret. "You can't read?"

Margaret winced and then shook her head. "No. Not a word."

"Can you?" Lucas asked Hanna.

Hanna nodded. "My mother, she taught me. She was an educated woman. But I'm not so good at reading English. I haven't time to practice."

Lucas frowned. "How often must you work?"

"Until the mending is finished," Hanna said.

"But it's *never* finished," Margaret cut in. "And then when I get home, bone tired, there's the washing, the cooking, and the minding of the children."

Hanna nodded. "Sunday is the only day we do not work in the shop. Although I'm sure Mrs. Cunningham would have us stay there if she could."

Lucas shook his head. "And I've brought you my suits, creating more work for you." He smiled. "Perhaps I should learn how to mend. What a sight that would be!"

Margaret laughed at Lucas's joke. "Good thing you can't, or we'd be out of a job. We're lucky. Other girls have nothing."

"Lucky," Lucas murmured, his eyes wandering to Hanna. "Do you agree? Surely you must wish to have some leisure time. Can you play piano?"

Hanna chuckled. "What is the purpose? To play next to a dancing bear in one of the melodeons?"

Lucas eyed her quizzically, but Hanna could tell he was suppressing a smile. "Most ladies play piano in the parlor to entertain guests, although I must say, Hanna, you paint a rather amusing picture."

Hanna slowed to a stop at Market Street, where they needed

to part ways. She shivered, tugging her woolen shawl more tightly around her shoulders. "Thank you," she said, "for escorting us back to town. It comforts me to know you will try to have that man arrested."

"I must be off now," Margaret said, watching the sun dip behind the tall brick boardinghouse buildings. "I fret the wee ones have been left alone too long."

"Will you be safe?" Lucas asked. "I can accompany you the rest of the way."

"Thank you." Margaret smiled. "But I know my home streets well, and they are no place for a gentleman."

Hanna hugged Margaret tightly. "Good night, dear friend. Get home quickly."

"I'll see you in the morn."

Margaret's red hair shone beneath her straw hat, her silhouette growing smaller as she retreated.

Hanna stood in silence with Lucas, noting how handsome yet somber he appeared in profile. *He must be a kind man to forgo the comfort of Robert's carriage to walk with Margaret and me.*

"It's time I'm on my way," Hanna said. "The light has fallen."

Lucas frowned. Removing his hat, he smoothed his tousled hair, his right hand reddened and swollen at the knuckles.

Hanna sucked in her breath. "Oh, Lucas. Your hand."

His eyes met hers, sparkling under the streetlamps. "Never fear, there's an icebox at the Merchants Exchange. It is not far from here. Though my workplace is closed at present, I have a key to my office."

Placing his hat atop his head, he grew serious. "My concern is for you, a remarkable woman. The women I know don't care for anything more than the newest fashions from Paris."

Suddenly, Hanna's arms longed to embrace him. She stemmed the urge toward improper emotion with the image of Robert sending a servant to pick up the suits after Margaret and she had mended them. Lucas was from a different world—one in which Hanna had no place. It would be best not to see him again.

The cold wind penetrated Hanna's shawl, and she blew on stiff fingers. Gas lamps spread soft light onto the cobblestones, and horse hooves clattered past. Were Hans's and Katja's bellies growling? Hanna reached into her pocket, fearing she'd lost the candies she had promised them. When her hand clasped the mints, holding them tightly, she heaved a sigh of relief.

"Good-bye, Lucas," Hanna said, her chest tightening as she turned on her heel.

"Hanna, wait!" Lucas said, looking at her differently now, as if she were someone familiar to him—dear, even. "I can call you a carriage."

Hanna ran down Market Street without giving Lucas an answer. She and Margaret were stuck with their stations in life, like molasses to the bottom of a pan. Margaret's father would be drunk tonight, waiting for Margaret with heavy hands and sour breath. And Hanna's father would be drunk again as well.

But Father would not return until after the children had gone to bed. Tonight would be the same as every other night, with boiled potatoes for dinner and songs for the children. Tomorrow was another day. And Hanna would see Margaret in the morning.

Chapter 5

Sarah, *Present Day*

How's your novel coming along?" Hunter asked, placing a hand on my shoulder.

I closed my Word document quickly. "Good."

I hadn't told him yet about my decision to stop writing it. First, my graduate advisor needed to approve my new topic, and now didn't feel like the right time to bring up how unproductive I'd been. Hunter had given me the gift of pursuing my dream without the stress of working. And then I'd realized that writing a novel wasn't my dream after all. It was too embarrassing to admit.

"Hey," I said, looking over at the young, scruffy shippers Hunter had recently hired. "Are you sure you don't need help with anything? I'll happily pack boxes for the new orders if you want. It looks like you have a lot of them."

Hunter shook his head. "I asked you to come hang out at my

office so I could spend time with you, and so you could work on your book. You've already paid your dues with the masking tape, I'd say."

I chuckled, remembering the early days of Hunter's start-up, when he ran the business out of his apartment garage. We'd been dating for two years then, and I'd helped by taking orders, packing boxes, answering customer complaints, and writing the website copy. Nick had been kind enough to design the Have-Clothing website for free, even though Hunter offered to pay him generously.

"Hey, man," Nick had said to Hunter. "Anyone who cares as much as you do about treating homeless people like *people* can have my graphic design expertise gratis. I think it's cool what you're doing."

Now I smiled, looking around at the bustling Have-Clothing office. Young guys in flannels sat at MacBooks, while girls in leggings and boots kicked a soccer ball back and forth across the hardwood floors. A blonde in a beanie swung in a hammock strung between two wooden beams, taking orders over the phone. An assortment of fixed-gear bicycles lay stacked against the exposed brick wall.

All ten of Hunter's employees shared the same passion he did for helping the Bay Area's homeless. Whether they were designing T-shirts, answering emails, or volunteering at local shelters, they'd come to work for my husband because they believed in making a difference. Have-Clothing was more than just a hot new start-up featured in TechCrunch—it was social entrepreneurship in the name of doing good.

Using his own money, Hunter had rented a huge space in an old brick warehouse in the Design District, one of my favorite parts of the city. Today, South of Market was headquarters to Salesforce, Square, Airbnb, Yelp, and Pinterest, but during the mid-nineteenth century, SoMa had been a burgeoning pioneer community of recent European immigrants, who worked the factories near the docks.

"Duck!" a girl shrieked as the soccer ball went flying past my head. I dodged it, moving quickly to the side. "Sorry," she said, pushing her light hair out of her eyes. "You're Hunter's wife, right? I'm Niki. Hunter is, like, the coolest boss ever."

"Yep," I said, feeling a surge of pride. "I'm Sarah, nice to meet you."

She smiled, shaking my hand. "Sorry for taking the 'work hard, play hard' motto a little too seriously. I almost hit you there."

"Yeah," said a bearded guy, picking up the ball and throwing it at Niki. "Let Sarah work on her book in peace or she'll never bring us pizza again."

"Sorry," Niki mouthed, tucking the ball under her arm.

I shook my head. "Really, it's no trouble. And don't worry, my deliveries from Little Star won't be stopping anytime soon."

Hunter kissed my cheek. "You're the best, you know that?"

I rubbed his fingers between mine. "They're good people, and I like surprising them with lunch."

"So, I'm meeting a shop owner in Hayes Valley today," Hunter said, pulling on his jacket. "We're going to talk about possibly stocking our shirts in his store." He smiled, his hazel eyes crinkling at the corners. "This could be big, Sar. You know how badly I want to expand to brick and mortar."

I squeezed his hand. "I know. Good luck."

Hunter tilted his head. "Stay here and write as long as you like." He winked at Niki. "And make sure this one stays out of trouble."

Niki rolled her eyes. "Okay, boss man."

After Hunter left the office, I settled into my chair at the spare desk and Googled "Havensworth Art Academy." Maybe the more I knew about its history, the more Gwyneth would feel I supported her. I had the nagging sensation she expected me to be doing more outreach for her charity galas, especially now that I was no longer at the magazine. But my heart didn't lie in event planning or fund-raising.

The school's website popped up in my browser, and I opened it.

A backdrop appeared of the city's skyline, faintly visible through the fog. I read the accompanying quote.

Like the city it has called home since 1880, Havensworth Art Academy has always been a source of creativity and innovation. Take a look back at notable moments in the Academy's San Francisco history.

I clicked the first slide in the timeline. A sepia-toned photograph showed the columned building on California Street I'd visited earlier. I read the caption.

*Lucas W. Havensworth founds the Havensworth Art Academy
in the year 1880, in a purchased commercial space at 315
California Street, with 40 students. A real-estate mogul with a
silver fortune from the Comstock Lode, Havensworth establishes
the academy as a nonprofit, its doors open to any student with a
passion for the arts.*

I smiled to myself. The entrepreneurial spirit must run in
the family. How funny that Hunter was so like his forefather,
Lucas Havensworth.

Clicking through the remaining slides, I looked at pictures
of Hunter's great-grandfather and then his grandfather, a 1927
Stanford graduate, reading how the academy grew in size to
eighteen thousand students and more than ten urban campuses.

In a color photograph from the seventies, Walter sat unsmil-
ing in his study, barely recognizable with thick sideburns and
full head of hair. My mouth fell open as I read the caption.

*In 1973, Walter S. Havensworth succeeds his predecessors,
becoming president of the school and turning it into a for-profit
institution.*

So Hunter's father had turned the university into a money-
making operation when it had originally been established as
a nonprofit? *How typical of Walter.* What irked me more was
that Walter Havensworth was at no loss for lucrative streams
of income. His investment firm, Havensworth & Associates,
amassed more wealth than I cared to know about. Part of why I

loved Hunter was because of the bravery he'd shown in leaving the banking world to start his own clothing business.

"Hey," Niki said, calling over to Brian, whom I recognized as one of Hunter's original employees. "Do we have any back stock on our Mother's Day orders? It looks like our special-edition flower T-shirt has sold out already."

"Crap," Brian said, his fingers flying across the keyboard. "You're right. See if we can get more in production today."

I tried to hide the tightness in my voice as I looked up from my computer. "I'll tell Hunter. He might be able to run by the screen printer after his meeting."

"Awesome," Brian said. "Thanks, Sarah."

I nodded, swallowing hard. Mother's Day never went by without me feeling a sharp pain in my chest and heaviness in my heart. My mom had died from lung cancer five years ago, and Dad from an unexpected heart attack six months later. When I'd realized how sick my mother was, I'd flown home to spend time with her, even though I'd had a panic attack on the plane. I couldn't face the whispers in the street or the gossiping neighbors at the grocery store.

Nothing could bring *him* back.

But Mom had been diagnosed late, and I was only home for three weeks before she passed, most of which I'd spent holed up inside. I'd been grateful she'd asked to be cremated. My father and I spread her ashes to rest in Lake Winnebago, Mom's favorite camping spot. In that private moment, I'd wondered if she understood how I couldn't have read a eulogy to a room full of people, feeling the crowd's judgmental eyes.

A jackhammer struck the pavement outside, jarring me from my memories.

"God, that's annoying," Niki whined.

"Seriously," another girl said. "How are we supposed to concentrate with that awful noise?"

I peered out the open window. On the street below, workmen in vests and yellow construction hats crowded around a hole in the pavement. But the moment of silence was short-lived. The foreman placed his gloved hands around the jackhammer's handle, and resumed his pounding.

"What are they doing?" someone moaned.

Brian shook his head. "Tearing up the street to build more overpriced condos, probably. Rents are skyrocketing. I bet you could charge someone, like, two thousand dollars a month to live in one of those creepy camper vans parked under the freeway."

A lightbulb clicked on in my head. *Of course.*

I was no stranger to the sleek glass skyscrapers that had popped up around Folsom and First Street, forty-story luxury condos with names like Infinity Towers and Millennium Tower, and the endless construction around the site of the new Transbay Transit Center. A Salesforce tower was being built there, but I'd remembered reading an article about the discovery of gold rush artifacts during construction—an exhibit that was now being housed on Mission Street, over near Beale.

"Thanks for letting me hang out, guys," I said, powering off my laptop and sliding it into its leather carrying case. "You're all doing a great job."

"You're leaving?" Niki asked.

I slung my bag strap over my shoulder. "I'll be back next week."

"Thanks for the pizza!" a few employees cried in unison. I smiled, giving them a thumbs-up. "My pleasure. I'll bring burritos next time."

Outside on the street, I tugged my zipper up to my neck. If I planned to add a human element to my story about Hannelore and Margaret, I would need to know how the working class in the 1870s really lived. Maybe seeing the items they used every day would help me to feel more connected to these two women.

Twenty minutes later, the doors to the lobby of 201 Mission Street opened, welcoming me with a rush of warm air. I felt invigorated from my walk. The building was empty, and refreshingly quiet compared to the construction noise at Hunter's office.

I walked toward the glass display case along the back wall, housing remnants of the past. My eyes lingered on the plaque above the display:

WHILE CONSTRUCTION OF THE TRANSBAY TRANSIT CENTER MOVES AHEAD, WE ARE EXCITED TO SHARE AN ASSORTMENT OF ITEMS DISCOVERED WITHIN THE FOOTPRINT OF THE PROJECT SITE WITH OUR NEIGHBORS AND BAY AREA RESIDENTS. THESE OBJECTS PORTRAY THE RICH HISTORY OF SAN FRANCISCO'S GOLD

RUSH ERA. RECOVERED ARTIFACTS SHOW THE WAY NINETEENTH-
CENTURY RESIDENTS OF THE SOUTH OF MARKET NEIGHBOR-
HOOD PLAYED, WORKED, AND LIVED, INCLUDING INDUSTRIAL
TOOLS, HOUSEHOLD ITEMS, AND VESTIGES OF NEIGHBORHOOD
BUSINESSES.

I peered into a case filled with colored vials of assorted sizes. A pale blue bottle thick like sea glass read "Schenck's." That company made a syrup to cure consumption, but like most nineteenth-century medicines, it was flavored alcohol.

My eyes passed over plate fragments, ceramic doll parts, iron pulleys, bone toothbrushes, pipes, and rusted spoons. A thrill of excitement worked its way down my spine seeing the objects people had used in their daily lives over a hundred years ago.

I looked up at an enlarged sepia photograph of a clapboard building with a balcony jutting over the street. On the ground below stood horse-drawn carriages and men wearing overcoats and top hats.

1876: 57–61 MINNA STREET. THE TOMKINSON LIVERY AND
STABLE OPERATED OUT OF THE GROUND FLOOR, WITH A BOARD-
INGHOUSE ABOVE.

Fleetingly, I remembered my novel, and the boardinghouse owner, the widowed Mrs. McGeary. But my heart was already invested in finding out what happened to Hannelore and Margaret. My graduate advisor would understand. Without a spark, there would be no story—and I *knew* I had a story here.

I read the description of the South of Market neighborhood in the 1870s. It had been densely populated with Irish immigrants, many of whom worked in the nearby tar flat industries. My eyes moved to an 1876 map that showed small houses crowded together on narrow lots along Natoma and Minna Street. Had Margaret lived in one of these houses with her family?

An article from the *Sacramento Daily Union*, September 2, 1872, had been printed on the wall. I'd seen clippings from that newspaper in the digital archives online. Until it closed its doors in 1994, the *Sacramento Union* was the oldest daily newspaper west of the Mississippi. The article gruesomely depicted the murder of Mrs. Annie Brown, the wife of a sea captain. With murders so commonplace in the 1870s, the prospects did not look good for Hannelore and Margaret.

I pored over the artifacts. Victorian children's toys, red and blue marbles, had been found in the backyards of 40 Natoma and 41 Minna. A copper-plated spoon, now green and corroded with age, was recovered from 45 Minna Street.

My eyes lingered on a fragment of a blue and white plate, painted with women in traditional Bavarian dress, sitting beneath a weeping willow tree. In careful cursive, the signature read *E. Schaeffer*.

My breath hitched.

HAND-PAINTED PLATE. THE REGISTRY MARK ON THE BACK OF THE PLATE TELLS US THIS PIECE WAS MADE IN JULY 1868, BY DUHRER & CO. BAVARIA, GERMANY. ARTIST NAME: E. SCHAEFFER. PLATE RECOVERED AT 43 MINNA STREET.

I swallowed, taking a notebook out of my laptop bag and writing down the name and address. Census results online or an 1876 directory in the library archives would show me if E. Schaeffer was a member of Hannelore's family. African-American and immigrant households were accounted for after the Civil War. Though they were working-class people, the Schaeffers would have had an address.

As I stepped back out onto the street, the wind assaulted me. I shoved my hands into my jacket pockets as I walked up Market Street. At the Flatiron building, I turned onto Sutter Street, pushing open the doors to Caffé Bianco. It was one of my favorite cafés, thanks to the European feel of the decor and the delicious pastries. I ordered a raisin swirl and a chai latte, and sat down at a round table by the window. Assorted flowers arranged in glass vases filled the room with a sweet fragrance.

Scooting my chair closer to my computer screen, I typed into Google "San Francisco census, 1876, Schaeffer." Nothing. I sipped my chai latte, then tried again, typing "E. Schaeffer." Still nothing.

I sighed. My phone buzzed in my bag, and I took it out to look at the screen.

Hey chica! Can't wait to see you for beers tonight!!! Xo

My heart warmed, looking at Nick's text. We'd become close when we worked together at the magazine. Nick had taught me everything I needed to know about gay subculture (apparently he was a wolf, like celebrity wolf Joe Manganiello from *Magic Mike*), and we'd gone out for happy hour together every Thursday.

We'd bonded over how both of us had been too afraid to go to our high school proms, Nick because he'd have to "dance like a straight man" and me because . . . well, I didn't tell him the truth, but I'd chalked it up to teenage awkwardness.

I brought my fingers to my lips, remembering the laughing fit we'd had when Nick's *Men's Health* magazine arrived at the office, addressed to Nico Rogers.

"Who am I? Mr. Rogers's gay cousin?" Nick had asked, wiping a tear from his cheek. "How hard is it to spell Rodriguez?"

My eyes zipped back to the computer screen. The plate fragment from 1868 was first-rate source data. But a census would be a second source. And perhaps the census takers at the time didn't know how to spell a German name, especially if no one in the household spoke English. I thought about Schaeffer phonetically.

This time I typed: "Shaffer. San Francisco census 1870," knowing the census was taken every ten years, on the years ending in zero. Nothing came up. I tried again with one "f," Shafer.

A transcribed document appeared of the San Francisco County census taken in March 1870. I read the names.

Name	Race	Gender	Age	Birth Date	Birth Place
Shafer, Johannes	W	M	40	1830	Bavaria
Shafer, Eva	W	F	32	1838	Bavaria
Shafer, Hannelore	W	F	14	1856	Bavaria
Shafer, Martin	W	M	6	1864	Bavaria

My missing girl stared at me from the screen. The census had been taken six years before she disappeared. I thought of Hannelore's physical description: a dark-haired girl with light eyes and strong features. She was starting to take shape in my mind.

A search of the family's address on Greenwich Street revealed the early immigrant settlements of Telegraph Hill had been demolished, except for a few historic homes belonging to wealthy sea captains. What a shame. Hannelore's house was no longer standing. Likely, it hadn't been much more than a shack.

I spent another hour searching for follow-up articles using the newspaper archives online, but I hadn't learned anything other than Johannes Schaeffer's trade—a blacksmith. No information existed on him or the family after 1870. It was as if they had all vanished like ghosts into the San Francisco fog.

Great, back to square one.

Then I remembered the name of the bar owner from yesterday, when I'd visited the Tavern. Putting on my journalist hat, I looked up his phone number online, and then called, an air of authority to my voice.

"Hi, Edward," I said, reaching his voice mail. "My name is Sarah Havensworth, and I'm a freelance journalist, currently working on my master of fine arts thesis in creative writing. I was hoping you could help me with a story."

Leaving the café, I threw on my coat and picked up my laptop bag, feeling I had made some progress. With a bit more research, I'd feel confident presenting my new thesis proposal to my advisor and asking for the last-minute switch.

There was no guarantee she'd approve it, but with enough evidence to support my story, I hoped she would. After all, guidelines stated that my master's thesis had to be a *publishable* piece of work. Even after incorporating the critique from my peer workshops, my novel felt far from publishable. Plain and simple, it was crap.

But this story, finding out what had happened to these missing dressmakers, was where I felt at home. As a journalist, I had motivation, reverence for the truth, and a hunger to discover and inform. Why create a fictional account of what life had been like for working women in the late nineteenth century when I had the chance to truly show it?

As I walked up Market Street, I passed homeless men and women bundled into sleeping bags and huddled in doorways. I thought of Hunter and his open heart, his endless capacity to give. His favorite thing to say to me was, "I've got my health, I've got Redford, and I've got you. Even if I had no money, I'd still feel like the richest guy in the world. The least I can do is help those who have no one."

Suddenly, a thought dawned on me. Had Hannelore given the plate to Margaret as a gift? If Hannelore had lived on Telegraph Hill, then why had the plate fragment been found on Minna Street, an address nowhere near her family residence? I remembered a line from the artifacts exhibit.

BY THE 1870S, THE SOUTH OF MARKET NEIGHBORHOOD WAS DENSELY SETTLED, MOSTLY BY IRISH IMMIGRANTS.

Margaret and her family most likely lived in one of the row houses on Minna Street or Natoma Street. Being gifted the plate was one possible explanation. A chill ran through me as another idea hovered on the edge of my mind.

Maybe Margaret and Hannelore hadn't gone missing at the same time. I looked down Montgomery Street, staring off in the direction of the old Barbary Coast. The twinge in my gut made me wonder . . . What if Margaret had disappeared first, and then Hannelore had gone looking for her?

Chapter 6

Hanna, *1876*

Schooners bobbed in the choppy waters below Telegraph Hill, their grand masts pointed skyward and their sails billowing like wings. Wouldn't that make a pretty picture?

In Mittenwald, Hanna had once seen the artwork of a man named Renoir. There had been a girl painted in oils, with flowing red hair like Margaret's, and a scene of people dancing beneath the Paris streetlamps. They were the most beautiful compositions Hanna had ever seen, breathing life into her like a flame.

Today she had stolen moments in the early dawn, the sky streaked poppy orange. No one could claim her here: not her mind or the product of her hands. With her mother's brushes and paints, Hanna lent beauty to the gritty landscape, the factory smoke fading away. Mother's soul did not reside in a dark church, where the pastor's eyes bored into Hanna's. Mother was here in the wind rushing through Hanna's hair and in the ocean spray.

I love you, Mother.

Hanna's silent words caught in her throat. Steadying her hand, she signed her name and the date with her smallest brush, forming the letters how Mother had taught her to. Mother had given her everything she needed to make her own way in the world. Hanna stared up at the sky, wishing she could see her mother's face.

Frau Kruger's chickens clucked as Hanna set the painting down to dry. No one would discover it behind the chicken coop. She crouched low to open the gate, then reached for the eggs. Frau Kruger could not bend as easily as she once had, and allowed Hanna to keep two eggs in exchange for bringing her the rest.

With the warm eggs cradled in her hand, Hanna looked down at the steamboat chugging its way across the bay. She nearly had enough money saved for her passage, along with Martin, Hans, and Katja, to Sacramento. From there they would take the train to the Sierra Nevada Mountains, where she could mend and wash clothing for men in the mining towns. Would Margaret run too? Hanna would ask, but not until it was time.

Plumes of gray smoke rose into the air from the cluster of small houses on the hillside, fires burning in their hearths. It was a hopeful day. In another month's time, Hanna would be gone like the smoke, vanished in the wind.

⚜ ⚜ ⚜

"Girls, I'm stepping out for luncheon. I expect you'll keep everything orderly until I return at two o'clock. Is that understood?"

"Yes'm." Margaret bowed her head.

Mrs. Cunningham looked at Hanna, her cold eyes appraising Hanna's face. "If I hear of any trouble, you'll both be out of a job."

"Yes, ma'am," Hanna answered.

With a curt nod, Mrs. Cunningham picked up her full skirt and walked in that clipped way she had, as if astride a trotting horse.

Margaret smiled. "She looks like a big-bottomed buffoon with that bustle."

Hanna giggled. "It isn't kind to say such things."

"She isn't a kind person," Margaret said, smirking.

Hanna eyed the clock on the wall. It was noon.

"Shall we have tea?" Margaret asked, a glint in her eye.

Hanna looked at the gold-rimmed teacup and felt her mind return once again to Lucas's summer-blue eyes. Margaret clinked a spoon against the saucer, puncturing Hanna's daydream.

Hanna bit her lip. "Perhaps we can take a little tea, but not the cream and sugar. Mrs. Cunningham will notice if there is less than before."

Margaret shook her head. "Oh, but Hanna, that's the whole fun of it! Can you even remember the taste of sugar? Real white sugar?"

Hanna's mouth watered. It had been so long since she'd had any.

Before Margaret could pick up the teapot, the shop door

jingled. Hanna straightened her posture. In strolled two society women, gowns tiered like layer cake trailing behind them. One had an upturned nose, like a pug dog, and tight blond curls. Her dark-eyed brunette friend appeared more handsome, with a face of sharp angles.

The pug-nosed woman sniffed. "My name is Miss Delia Heathcoate. I'm here to pick up my evening gown."

"Yes, ma'am," Margaret said.

The brunette laughed. "Ma'am? Delia, you're not yet married."

Miss Delia glared at Margaret. "It's Miss Heathcoate, as I stated."

Margaret reddened. "Apologies, miss."

"And I'm Miss Juliet Livingston," the brunette said, cooling herself with a beautiful floral fan in the overheated shop. "Please find my gown as well."

Margaret paused. "What colors are they?"

Miss Delia frowned. "We gave you our names."

Margaret froze, wide-eyed.

The thought seemed to dawn on Miss Delia as she laughed derisively. "You can't read, can you?"

Margaret's face fell.

"Go on," Hanna whispered to Margaret. "I'll come in a minute."

With a nod, Margaret darted to the back room to search for the dresses, while Hanna walked to Mrs. Cunningham's office to locate the receipt book.

The brunette giggled. "Even though you aren't *quite* a ma'am yet, you shan't be single for long. You've got your eye on Robert, haven't you?"

Miss Delia smiled as if she had a secret. "Perhaps."

"Yet there are other fine men in that family. Lucas is quite the gentleman."

Hanna stopped and held her breath.

Both women erupted into laughter.

"Oh, Jules, stop. It's not polite to suggest I should fancy both cousins. I can't help having multiple suitors."

"I saw the dark, mysterious way he was looking at you at the Governor's Ball. Robert would be my choice."

Hanna fiddled with a loose thread on the pocket of her dirndl. Surely Lucas hadn't taken a liking to the awful blonde. She'd been unkind to Margaret.

As Hanna picked up the receipt book, she heard Miss Delia giggle.

"Lucas has asked to meet me tonight at seven in front of Lotta's Fountain. He's purchased tickets for us to see Lotta Crabtree perform. But Viscount Theodore Wharton is in town, and I intend to make *quite* an impression on him."

"Delia!" Juliet cried. "Will you not send a calling card to let Lucas know you've canceled?"

Hanna covered her mouth, her ears attuned to every word.

"Indeed not," Delia said. "Mother and I are seeking the best possible husband. I ought to be a baroness, not the wife of a lowly real-estate man. We're attending a private party tonight at Fanny Reynolds's mansion, and I shall look irresistible."

"But Lucas shall be waiting for you," Juliet said.

"He's so dull." Delia cackled. "Waiting will suit him."

With the receipt book in hand, Hanna met Margaret in the back room. Margaret's cheeks had flushed from the encounter. "Cows, the both of them."

"Yes," Hanna said, slamming the book on the table. How could such a horrible woman leave Lucas waiting, after he'd gone to the trouble of purchasing tickets to the theater? And to see the most famous actress in America, no less!

"Are you all right?" Margaret asked.

Hanna shook her head. "I will explain later. Have you found the dresses?"

"I couldn't. I'm sorry."

Hanna sorted through the frocks on the clothing rack, pushing them aside until she lifted a pink silk brocade gown with Miss Juliet's name written on the tag and a green velvet evening gown that belonged to Miss Delia. Margaret helped her carry the dresses, holding the folds of fabric aloft so they wouldn't touch the ground.

"Here you are," Hanna said, laying the gowns flat on the countertop.

"Is that the dress you wore to the Regatta Ball?" Juliet asked, wrinkling her nose. "What a darling cap sleeve."

Delia's expression darkened. "What?"

Juliet shook her head. "Nothing at all, only it's not the newest from Paris. The three-quarter-length sleeve is a la mode again."

Flaring her nostrils, Delia glared at Hanna. "Take it away."

Hanna froze. "But, miss, it's been mended and . . ."

"You heard me," Delia said. "It's a rag and I don't want it."

Margaret gaped at Hanna. To give away such a fine dress? It was unthinkable.

"Miss," Hanna said, steadying her voice. "Mr. Heathcoate has paid in advance."

"Are you deaf?" Delia said, speaking more loudly than necessary. "I don't care if Father paid for it. Dispose of it now."

Juliet raised her eyebrows and picked up her pink dress. "Come, Delia, don't work yourself into a tizzy."

"It doesn't matter," Delia said, opening a pearl-handled fan with a flick of her wrist. "You see, Jules, I'm buying a new dress this very instant. Come along. We shall see what's just arrived from Paris. We're going to Lord & Taylor."

Miss Delia tossed her blond curls and walked with purpose. Miss Juliet followed behind her, carrying the garment bag. The bell tinkled and a burst of cold air charged through the door before it closed. Hanna stared at the green dress in front of her, touching the soft velvet. The jet-black buttons on the bodice were as smooth and round as stones.

"It's gorgeous," Margaret said.

"But what are we to do with it?" Hanna asked.

"We'll decide later. Let's have our tea."

After helping herself to the cream and sugar, Margaret carried over a tray laden with two steaming mugs.

A shiver of pleasure ran through Hanna as she placed her lips on the rim of Mrs. Cunningham's porcelain teacup. How scandalous! Warming her from the inside, the first sip of Hanna's tea held hints of cloves and spices mixed with a creamy sweetness. A woman with Mrs. Cunningham's erect posture walked past the shop, and Hanna nearly dropped her saucer. Once the woman's face became visible, Hanna's shoulders relaxed. The lady on the street bore no resemblance to their supervisor.

Margaret set down her teacup and twisted her ring. Glinting in the light, the silver band encircled two hands holding a heart, topped with a crown.

Margaret caught Hanna looking. "It's me gran's wedding ring."

"Do you miss her?" Hanna asked.

Margaret's eyes glistened with tears. "Aye. She's the kindest person you'll ever meet."

Hanna reached for Margaret's hand, knowing nothing she could say would bring comfort. Margaret would never see her grandmother again. Nor would Hanna see her Oma, who had wept when Hanna boarded the ship for America, waving goodbye for the last time. Only the elderly and frail were left behind. No one returned from America. And letters from home were not the same as a warm laugh or a cup of tea shared on a cold day.

"She's got no one to care for her," Margaret said, wiping away a tear. "She's all by herself, in a drafty old cottage in County Cork. She'll die alone."

Hanna remembered disembarking the ship, her legs shaky. There were those unfortunate people who didn't pass inspection. Families separated in America and asked to reboard the very ship that had taken them here. She'd seen women in babushkas crying out as they clutched at their grandchildren. It was her first sign that America was no glittering land of promise.

"Your gran loves you," Hanna said, squeezing Margaret's hand. "You did what you had to. She is better in Ireland. It is the only home she knows."

Margaret looked at the ring on her finger. "Gran gave me this before we boarded the ship. It's the most special thing in the world to me. I'll never take it off, Hanna. No matter how hungry I am."

"These hands here," Hanna asked, touching the silver. "What does it mean?"

Margaret smiled, allowing Hanna to inspect the design. "The hands represent friendship, the heart love, and the crown loyalty. It's called a claddagh ring."

"That is lovely," Hanna said, smiling at her friend.

Margaret stared at her finger, a look of sadness passing over her face. Hanna swallowed. Was Margaret thinking again of her grandmother, or of a boy she wished to marry? If Margaret had a sweetheart, surely she would say something. Margaret loved to gossip, chattering like a little sparrow in the spring time.

The shop door jingled and Hanna set down her teacup. She and Margaret both stood to attention, their skirts obscuring the tea set behind them. Hanna's breathing eased when she realized their visitor was only a small boy. Soot covered his face, and he wore a tattered cap.

"Shoo!" Margaret said, bending down. "You best be out of here before I tell your mother. We haven't got money. This is not a shop for grubby boys."

In his outstretched hand he held a folded piece of paper.

Hanna took the note from him. "Who gave you this?"

He grinned, revealing two missing teeth. "A man in a big hat gave me a silver dime. He said I ought'a find the two pretty shopgirls."

Margaret's eyes widened. Unfolding the piece of paper, Hanna's hands trembled. The penmanship was neat, written in black ink.

Dear Hanna and Margaret,

I'm terribly sorry I haven't been able to stop by the shop for a visit. I hope that you both arrived home safely. Please know that while I may not seem to understand your struggles, your conversation has remained with me. I will do what I can to reform the current labor laws, by advocating against them, so that your siblings shall not work too hard, and that you may spend more time with your families. Wishing you all the best.

Lucas

"What does it say?" Margaret asked, tugging the paper from Hanna's hands. Margaret's brow wrinkled. "Oh, bloody hell. Why would I even try to make sense of it?" She turned to the boy. "You said the man had a hat? What kind of hat? Was he a handsome man?"

The boy shrugged. "It was a rich man's hat, shiny and black. How am I to know if he's handsome?"

Margaret giggled. "Well, I suppose you're right. Be off now."

He pushed open the shop door and scurried down the cobblestone street.

Margaret fixed her eyes on Hanna's. "Who is it from?"

"From Lucas. I do not understand all of the words, but he says he hopes our siblings shall not work as hard as we do, and that he remembers our conversation. He wishes us well. It is very kind."

Margaret sighed. "What a man, I tell you."

Tightening her hand around the paper until it crinkled, Hanna's brow furrowed. "Lucas invited Miss Delia to the theater with him tonight, to see Lotta Crabtree."

"Lotta Crabtree?" Margaret said. "He invited that awful blonde? The lucky wench! How I would love to see Lotta sing and dance."

Hanna sighed, placing Lucas's letter on the countertop. "But Miss Delia is not going. And worse yet, she is not sending a messenger to tell Lucas of her cancellation. He shall be waiting for her at Lotta's Fountain at seven, only to feel the fool."

Margaret clasped Hanna's hands in hers. "Hanna, listen to me. You *must* go tell him. Lucas ought to know. No woman should treat him like that."

"Yes," Hanna said. "You're right."

Margaret's eyes twinkled, looking at Miss Delia's green velvet gown, lying in a crumpled heap beside her. "I've got an idea."

"Oh no," Hanna said, recognizing Margaret's mischievous look. "You're not suggesting that I pretend to *be* Miss Delia. Are you?"

"Not quite," Margaret said. "But when Lucas sees you so pretty like, and hears what a cow that woman is, he'll see the true kindness of your nature. And it would be an awful shame to waste those tickets, would it not?"

Hanna pictured Hans's and Katja's rosy little faces, the way their eyes lit up when she returned home. "It's a completely foolish thing to do, as it could go terribly awry. And who would mind the children for me?"

Margaret put her hands on her hips. "I can mind the children. I'll pick the wee ones up from Frau Kruger's if you tell me where she lives. I'll mind them until you come back, which, if you're successful, won't be 'til late."

Hanna shook her head. "I can't."

"Yes you *can*," Margaret pleaded. "Show him you're a kind, decent, respectable person." She smiled. "And wearing that dress, he'd be blind not to see it."

Walking down Market Street toward Lotta's Fountain, Hanna could scarcely breathe, for her corset had been pulled so tight. Somehow she'd allowed Margaret to talk her into not only taking Miss Delia's dress, but also into borrowing the necessary undergarments from another customer. Hanna's cheeks burned, as if the mark of a charlatan were stamped upon her.

Hanna and Margaret had hidden the clothing in a laundry bag, which they took out back and set down next to the rubbish bin. At the end of her shift, Hanna picked up the bag and walked with Margaret to the back entrance of the Palace Hotel. In the maids' quarters, Margaret helped her into the hoopskirt and whalebone corset and buttoned all fifty tiny black buttons of the sumptuous green velvet dress.

"I'll never be able to lace so tight," Margaret said as she unraveled Hanna's plaits and pinned the mass of dark hair atop Hanna's head, letting a few curls hang loose.

Only Hanna's boots, hidden beneath the heavy folds of velvet, were the very same she wore each day. Hopefully no one would notice the scuffed toes and holes in the soles. How very strange to feel men in fine hats looking at her, not as a poor immigrant, but as a woman of society. Ladies, too, regarded her as if she were one of them. Hanna pressed her hand against her chest. Her bosom swelled from the low-cut bodice, drawing many sets of eyes toward her. This lovely dress was quite different from the high-necked day frocks many women wore to do their daily shopping.

When she reached Lotta's Fountain, Hanna looked about for Lucas. Women talked in hushed tones behind their gloved hands as they waited to greet friends or lovers. Trailing her fingers along the bronze monument, Hanna spotted him standing to the side. Lucas held his pocket watch in his hand, frowning.

Hanna flattened herself against the lion's head, immediately regretting her decision to intervene. Perhaps Lucas would believe Miss Delia took ill, and he would soon be on his way. But when Hanna snuck another glimpse, the nervous look on his face tugged at her heartstrings. Taking a deep breath, she strode toward Lucas.

He looked up, his eyes widening as he recognized her. "Hanna. I did not expect to see you here. Have you come to meet someone?" His gaze passed over her body. "You're a vision. That dress . . . Green truly becomes you."

"Thank you," Hanna said, bowing her head. "I received your note today. It was very kind. Margaret thanks you as well."

"Good," Lucas said. "With Father's influence in the Senate, I hope to pass new legislation. Though it isn't an easy thing to do."

Looking again at his watch, Lucas smiled. "I fear my date for the evening is fashionably late." He sighed. "This is my mother's doing. She's trying to thrust me upon every eligible socialite in San Francisco. To be honest, they bore me to tears."

Hanna swallowed. "Your date is not coming."

"Excuse me?" Lucas asked, wrapping his gloved hand around the silver head of his cane. "And how have you come to know this information?"

"Miss Delia stopped by the shop today. I overheard her conversation." Hanna paused, looking into Lucas's eyes. "She is attending a private party tonight, to catch the eye of a viscount. Forgive me. I realize it is not my place to tell you this. But I thought you should know her true nature."

Lucas's brows drew together, and Hanna feared she had upset him. But then he broke into a dimpled grin, and a laugh escaped his mouth. "You're joking."

Hanna shook her head. "I'm afraid not. I came to tell you, because I believe you deserve someone far better."

The blue of Lucas's eyes seemed to burn with intensity. "So

you haven't come here tonight to meet someone? You've only come here to tell me this so that I would not be left waiting?"

Hanna's cheeks tingled. "Yes. Again, please forgive me if it was too forward. I will be on my way now."

As Hanna turned to leave, she could feel Lucas watching her. Perhaps it had been wrong to surprise him. Had she embarrassed him?

"Hanna, wait!"

Turning around, Hanna looked at Lucas, who strode toward her in his black suit. He rubbed his jaw, as if troubled by an inner conflict.

"I want to thank you. Your honesty is admirable. And Delia Heathcoate is nothing more than an obnoxious social climber, spoiled by her father's money."

Hanna smiled with relief. "You are welcome."

They stood together beneath the gas streetlamps, listening to the rhythmic clopping of horses' hooves. With a gust of wind, Hanna caught a whiff of pine needles and cigar smoke, the scent of Lucas's skin.

"Now that Miss Heathcoate has abandoned me," Lucas said, "I don't suppose you would wish to go in her place to see Lotta Crabtree perform?"

"Thank you," Hanna said, ignoring the flutter in her stomach. "But I would not wish to trouble you. Surely there is someone else you wish to invite?"

Lucas smirked. "I'm afraid all the women I'm acquainted with are attending the party for Viscount Theodore Wharton. And I am but a lowly real-estate investor."

"That is not true," Hanna said, shaking her head. "You are a good man. And I would love to go."

"Come then," Lucas said, taking a step toward Montgomery Street. "If we meet any of Mother's gossiping friends, we shall say you're the Baroness of Bayern, visiting from Europe. Having never seen you before, they shall be none the wiser."

Hanna giggled, covering her mouth. "If you say so."

It was ridiculous to think she could pass for nobility, considering she wore no diamond jewelry, nor had the manners of a lady. But Hanna quite enjoyed Lucas's silly sense of humor, so different from his brooding cousin.

Strolling on her way to the theater in a beautiful dress, Hanna glided past shop windows as if she weighed no more than a feather. Catching her reflection in the glass, she saw a handsome, proud woman staring back at her.

As Hanna walked with Lucas down Kearny Street past the dance halls and saloons, he held his cane with purpose, as if ready to use it as a weapon. Hanna dared not go near the Opera Comique on Jackson and Kearny, better known as Murderer's Corner. The pretty waiter girls there were known to put on the bawdiest and most obscene shows of any melodeon or concert saloon on the Barbary Coast. Hanna had heard of those girls selecting their victims, usually a sailor or miner, and giving the man a drugged drink. Once he'd lost his faculties, the poor fellow would be knocked unconscious and robbed blind—then rolled into a back alley and left for dead.

But that was how it was here, kill or be killed. Horrible crimes beyond comprehension befell women of these saloons.

Hanna shivered as a man's dark eyes passed over her. San Francisco was not a safe place for anyone.

Lucas and Hanna turned onto Bush Street, where other couples had formed a queue, men in tailcoats and top hats and women bedecked in jewels and feathers. The California Theatre loomed before Hanna, an impressive marble structure.

An usher led them upstairs to a private booth overlooking the stage below. Inside the theater, the gilded ceiling, red velvet curtains, and frescoes adorning the walls brought a silent intake of Hanna's breath. The array of colorful silks and plumed hats and the glint of diamond bracelets dazzled her. She had mended fine dresses many times, but to see the fabric shimmer under the stage lights brought the garments to life.

"Please, sit." Lucas gestured toward a plush bench.

When Hanna did so, she nearly cried out. The whalebone corset constricted her lungs. Surely women couldn't tolerate such torturous devices every day?

"Champagne?" the waiter asked, holding a silver tray with two crystal glasses.

"Yes, please." Lucas took one and handed the other to Hanna.

"*Prost,*" she said, touching her glass against Lucas's while looking him in the eye. "It means 'to your health.'"

"I like that," Lucas answered. "And to your health as well."

The champagne bubbles tickled Hanna's throat, lovely and sweet, unlike anything she had ever tasted before. The crowd cheered as the velvet curtain rose, and Hanna looked down to see Lotta Crabtree onstage. There she was, the actress's

lively, diminutive figure immediately captivating the audience. Hanna clapped her hands as Lotta began to sing and
dance.

Lucas bought Hanna a second glass of champagne. Through
a pleasant haze, Hanna watched Lotta perform *Little Nell and
the Marchioness*. Portraying little Nell, a virtuous girl of fourteen, Lotta told the story of how the character was orphaned.
Nell's grandfather cared for her, attempting to earn her a good
inheritance through gambling. Both Nell and her grandfather
came into misfortune due to her grandfather's gambling debt,
and they were forced to run away.

"Have you tried oysters?" Lucas asked, handing Hanna a
silver fork so small it could have been used by a porcelain doll.

Hanna shook her head.

"Here," Lucas said, giving Hanna a scalloped shell with a
fleshy gray lump inside. "Squeeze a bit of lemon on it. You can
eat it with the utensil or simply let it slide down your throat."

Hanna stabbed the oyster with her fork, prying it loose.
When it reached her tongue, the briny, soft, and almost creamy
flavor pleased Hanna, despite the strange consistency.

"Do you like it?" Lucas asked.

"Yes," Hanna said, though her stomach grumbled. What she
would give for a hot loaf of brown bread with butter.

Hanna gasped as Nell's evil brother searched for the young
girl with the malicious, deformed dwarf, Daniel Quilp.

"Oh no," Hanna whispered. "Please tell me he doesn't find
them."

Lucas smiled with kindness in his eyes. "You're quite enraptured by the story. Have you read Dickens's *The Old Curiosity Shop*? The novel inspired this play."

"No, I haven't. I would like to."

Even if Hanna had the time to read for pleasure, it would have to be done by candlelight, away from Father's unforgiving gaze. The Dickens book probably contained words far too difficult for her to comprehend. Hanna swallowed, anxiety creeping through her heady buzz. If she was to run away, would Father look for her, just as these evil men never relented in their search for Nell and Nell's grandfather?

Hanna thought of the children. Were they all right? Surely Margaret had kept them entertained. Margaret was always full of stories and games. Hanna bit her lip. What if Father came home whilst Margaret was still there? *Unlikely.* He preferred to drink until the small hours of the morn. But if he did . . .

Hanna exhaled to dispel her anxiety, except the corset was too tight, her breath catching in her throat. Sweat glistened on her upper lip.

"What's wrong?" Lucas asked.

"It's late," Hanna said. "And the children. I fret for them. I ought to leave."

Lucas stood up and took her arm. "Of course. I shall take you home."

"Thank you," Hanna said.

As they descended the stairs, Lucas looked about with darting eyes, as if he feared encountering someone he knew. He had been all too eager to leave, perhaps because he was embarrassed to be seen with her.

Outside of the theater, Lucas helped Hanna into his carriage. The wind cooled her skin as they rode toward Telegraph Hill. Her stomach sank, knowing she had cut a wonderful evening short, but she had already asked such a great favor of Margaret. Hanna would feel better seeing the children safe in their beds.

As they passed the foulest of dives on Pacific Street, the carriage lurched forward, causing Hanna to fall, her bare hand landing atop Lucas's. Her body warmed with pleasure at the contact, but she cringed in embarrassment. "Forgive me!"

Lucas slowly pulled his hand away. "It is quite all right. These streets are terrible and badly in need of repair."

As they rode through Devil's Acre, men hollered at one another and smashed bottles as women with bare feet and hair askew stumbled out of saloons.

"Have you ever been inside one of those melodeons?" Hanna asked.

Lucas shook his head. "No. Though many of my contemporaries enjoy the bawdy shows at the Bella Union. You'll see men of respectable family connections, their parents dozing away in their residences on Rincon Hill, under the impression that their worthy scions are attending the Young Men's Christian Association."

Hanna laughed at the vision. "They haven't any idea that their sons are watching waiter girls do the cancan?"

Lucas smiled. "Not a clue. What the rich don't want to

believe, they ignore, even if it's taking place right under their noses."

Hanna breathed in the faint scent of Lucas's coat, cigar smoke and pine, as they rode together in silence. Closing her eyes, she savored the warmth of his body next to hers. When Hanna opened her eyes again, the carriage had turned onto the dirt road leading toward the clapboard houses of Telegraph Hill.

"Stop here," Hanna said to the driver, who brought the carriage to a halt in front of Frau Kruger's house.

Lucas stepped out and helped Hanna down from the carriage. The chickens clucked inside their coop and the smell of goat dung filled the air.

"Is this your house?" Lucas asked, turning to Frau Kruger's wooden cabin.

The home, though modest, was nicer than Hanna's. "Yes. That is the one."

Hanna took a step back and knocked something over with her foot. Looking down, she saw leaves and sticks, mottled brown against the damp earth. And then her eyes alighted on a painted canvas, lying facedown in the dirt. "Oh *drat!*"

Hanna bent down and picked up the painting. Seeing that no leaves had stuck to the oils, Hanna smiled in relief. It had dried in the sun. "Thank heavens."

"What is it?" Lucas asked. "May I see?"

Hanna handed him her rendering of the landscape.

Lucas stared at it for a long time. When he looked at Hanna, his eyes were serious. "Did you paint this?"

Hanna's cheeks tingled. "Yes. I know it is a foolish hobby. But my mother was an artist and I . . ."

Lucas smiled. "Hanna, it's lovely, finer than the paintings done by my sister Georgina, and believe me, she's had only the best instructors. Did your mother learn from a master of the arts, or was she self-taught? You have inherited quite a skill."

"Thank you," Hanna answered. "My mother learned from a tutor. She was an educated woman who came from a good home. Though my father was the town blacksmith, she married him in spite of their differences."

"Ah," Lucas said, gazing at the painting. "For love."

Hanna nodded. "Yes."

Lucas would never know the truth of how that love had turned rotten, like a peach riddled with mold and worms, or how Mother had been cut off. Father's sour breath and tobacco spittle flashed in Hanna's mind. Father would slice the canvas with his knife, just as he had broken Mother's porcelain plates beneath his heavy boots.

"Please." Hanna looked into Lucas's eyes. "You should take this."

"Do you mean it?" he asked. "Surely it would look fine on your mantel."

"Yes," Hanna said, lowering her voice to a whisper. The last thing she needed was Frau Kruger pulling back her curtain to eavesdrop. "I want you to have it."

Lucas stepped closer, his face a hairsbreadth from Hanna's. "Then I will cherish this beautiful work of art."

Gently, he took Hanna's chin and tilted it upward. "How you intrigue me, Miss Schaeffer. You are not at all what you seem."

The air charged with an electrical current, like the sky before a thunderstorm. Hanna trembled, hardly daring to breathe. His lips were so close.

"Good night," Hanna whispered, turning her face away.

The intensity in Lucas's eyes faded. Sliding his thumb ever so softly over her bottom lip, he let his hand fall by his side. "Good night."

Hanna lifted the hem of her velvet dress, turning to leave. Lucas tipped his hat toward her. "Tonight was a pleasant surprise. Thank you for accompanying me to the theater. I've never seen someone enjoy it as much as you did."

"It is you I should thank," Hanna said. "For an experience I will never forget."

As Hanna walked toward her father's house, her insides felt warm. Had Lucas meant to kiss her, or had she imagined that moment between them? Hanna pulled open the door, willing it not to creak. Margaret had likely tucked the children in their beds, and Father would be at some debased saloon or grog shop. Hanna couldn't wait to tell Margaret how their plan had *actually* worked.

With a loud crack, pain flooded Hanna's skull. She fell and shielded her head as fists pummeled her ribs. She gasped for breath as her stomach clenched from the impact. Piercing needles of pain penetrated her insides.

Rolling over, Hanna looked into her father's dark eyes,

bloodshot and fiery. She wiped a tear to clear her vision. Her German words hardly came fast enough, tumbling out of her mouth. "Where are the children?"

From her position on the floor, Hanna could not see Katja, Hans, or Martin. Where had they gone? Dear God, were they safe?

Father unfastened his belt from his trousers so his massive belly hung low over his dirt-stained pants. With a firm grip on the leather, he held the belt aloft. The metal end of the buckle glinted in the moonlight.

"They are with me, you whore."

Hanna's blood ran cold. What had he done? She couldn't breathe. Her corset and the heavy folds of the velvet dress restricted her movement. Sweat pooled under her arms and trickled down her back.

Katja cried out from the other room. Hanna recognized Hans's whimpering as well. They were safe behind the bedroom door. For now. The belt came down across Hanna's back, the corset doing little to lessen its bite. Hanna screamed. Father tore open the dress, buttons popping off one by one as the velvet ripped apart.

"Margaret!" Hanna yelled. "You must take the children away from here."

No one answered. Hanna's gut writhed like maggots eating away at her flesh. Something had gone very wrong.

With the dress and corset torn open, Hanna inhaled deeply. Pain stabbed her ribs, but she needed to move. If Margaret wasn't behind that door, where had she gone? Hanna rolled onto her back and pushed herself to her feet. The room spun, like she'd drunk too much champagne. But a surge of energy prompted her to act.

Father stood before her, belt in hand. Hanna lunged for the iron frying pan and grabbed its handle. Steadying her grip, she held it aloft. "Move now. Or I swear to God I will kill you."

Chapter 7

Sarah, *Present Day*

At a long wooden table in Zeitgeist's beer garden, I sat wedged between Jen and Nick. The sound of laughter carried on the breeze and marijuana smoke lingered in the air. Pink painted elephants danced along the brick wall. My eyes roamed the graffiti art as my mind wandered to Hannelore and Margaret.

"Hey, Sarah, you want another beer?" Nick lifted a pitcher of pilsner.

I looked down at the glass in my hands, still half full. "No thanks, I'm good. Tell me everything. I *miss* you guys. How've you been?"

"Ugh," Jen said, rolling her eyes. "Not great. Our new editor in chief, James, is totally tech-obsessed. He doesn't like any of my pitches."

"Not even the one about the mass exodus of working-class

people to the East Bay?" I asked. "What about the families who've had to move as far as Sacramento?"

She took a swig of beer, then set the glass down. "It's like he's oblivious to the fact that my rent has been raised an unholy amount, forcing me to move to Oakland . . . and it's all the fault of these assholes with 300K salaries, who came into the city like they own it." Her eyes grew sad. "No one cares about the original residents."

I nodded sympathetically. "Were you able to write your piece about the teachers who can't afford to live in the district on their teaching salaries?"

"Nope," Nick said, cutting in. "I think the last meaningful piece we published was the one that you wrote six months ago about sex trafficking."

My eyes moved from Jen to Nick. "*My* piece?"

It had been a heartbreaking feature on the sex-slave industry right here in Chinatown, the underbelly of San Francisco's massage parlors. Hundreds of readers had written in, to express outrage at what had been going on right in our own backyard. I'd had a tough time writing that one, but the article had prompted the mayor to pass new legislation to protect victims, and to increase funding to advocacy groups.

I shook my head. "Have things really gotten that bad since I left?"

Jen rubbed her face. "Yes, they have. Every time I pitch a story idea, it gets shot down. James doesn't want to hear about the Mexicans and Filipinos who've lived in the Mission for generations, and who are being pushed out because of gentrification." She looked at me. *"Pulse of the City* has totally lost its soul."

Nick threw an arm around Jen's shoulder. "I promise I'll come visit you in Oakland. And you can crash at my place in the Castro anytime."

She looked at him meaningfully. "Will you still be living there in three months?"

"Rent control. My building is old as hell."

"Yeah, well just wait until they knock it down to build condos for the tech scum. Did you hear the tiny studios in Civic Center are renting for three thousand a month?"

My stomach tightened with guilt. I also disliked the wave of change taking over the city, but unlike my friends, Hunter's money protected me from eviction. I didn't have to worry about finding another job, because I could afford not to.

"You're so lucky," Jen said, as if reading my mind. "You get to do exactly what you want, and Hunter supports you one hundred percent."

"I know," I said, looking down into my beer glass.

"Hey now," Nick said, giving me a bright smile. "Jen's just jealous. We love you, Sar. You hang on to that hot, dreamy husband of yours."

I swallowed, my chest constricting. "I'll do my best."

Three years ago, before Hunter had proposed, I'd sensed things becoming serious between us and made up my mind to tell him the truth about my past. My stomach had knotted as I'd waited for seven o'clock—and Hunter—to arrive. I'd decided to tell him over burgers at this very beer garden, hoping it would ease the blow. My chest had tightened when I'd glimpsed Hunter walking onto the patio.

"Hey, Kiddo!" Hunter had said, giving me a kiss on the cheek. I'd managed to find us a private table in the back, out of earshot from the other bar patrons. Then noticing my obvious discomfort, Hunter had asked, "What's wrong?"

Like ripping off a bandage, I'd let my words loose in one swoop. "I need to talk to you about something."

"What is it?" he'd asked.

I'd taken a deep breath, readying myself, but then Hunter's phone had jingled its ringtone. He'd reached for it. "It's my dad. I'll call him back."

"No," I'd said, eager for an extra moment before I changed everything between us. "Take it. Honestly."

He'd glanced at the screen. "Okay. I'll be quick." He'd pressed the phone to his ear. "Hey, Dad, I'm out to dinner with Sarah . . . Okay, go ahead." Hunter's smile had faded slowly. "Fired him? But why?" He'd listened solemnly for several seconds, and then exhaled. "Wow. Yeah, I understand. No, Dad— it's fine, you did the right thing." Holding up his finger to let me know he'd be another moment, Hunter had frowned. "I agree. We'll look for someone else. Bye, Dad."

"Everything all right?" I'd asked when he'd hung up the phone.

Hunter's thick brows had drawn together. "Yeah. It's just, remember my friend Andy, the guy I used to work with at my father's firm?"

"Vaguely."

"HR had been doing a routine background check, and my dad found out he has a criminal record. Andy was arrested twice for DUI and twice for reckless driving." Hunter shook his head. "He could have killed somebody!"

I'd felt cemented to my chair. "So your dad . . . fired him?"

Hunter had nodded. "Tough decision, of course. Andy was one of our best analysts. But it was the right one. We can't have people like that associated with our business. It looks bad for our family, and we have a reputation to uphold."

The open-air patio had felt too crowded. I'd felt like all eyes in the beer garden had suddenly focused on me, on my scar.

"Sarah?" Hunter had asked, placing his hand over mine. "You okay? What was it you wanted to talk with me about?"

"Oh. I—" My mind had raced. Before I could stop myself, I'd blurted out the three little words we hadn't yet spoken. "I love you."

The silence had seemed to stretch for an eternity. My cheeks had burned like they were on fire. Of all the things I could have said!

But Hunter had smiled. "I love you too, Sarah. I didn't think the first time we'd say it to each other would be sitting here at Zeitgeist." He'd leaned forward and whispered, "That scary biker guy in the corner might have heard us."

I'd laughed. And then Hunter had reached across the table and kissed me. Selfishly, I'd given in—too blissfully happy to ruin the moment.

Hearing a loud clack, I jumped, the memory of Hunter popping like a bubble. Someone had knocked over a pitcher of beer.

"Oh, sorry!" the girl shrieked as it sloshed across the communal table, seeping through the cracks in the wood and soaking my jeans.

"Party foul!" a tattooed guy yelled.

She hiccupped and started laughing. "I'm so sorry, guys! I'm wasted."

I stood up and wiped my hands on a napkin, the cold wind harsh against the damp fabric of my jeans. I should have told Hunter that night, and now it was too late.

"Let's get some paper towels," Jen said, standing up. I followed her to the bathroom. We pulled a wad of paper from the dispenser, and I dabbed at my jeans.

"Poor girl," I said. "She looks like she's about to throw up."

Jen raised an eyebrow. "You're too nice. I wanted to smack her."

I smiled. "But weren't we all like that when we were twenty-one?"

Jen's phone buzzed with a text. She squealed. "Oh my God! It's Mark!"

I looked at her blankly.

"You *know*," she said, scoffing. "The guy who works at Twitter."

"Twitter?" I asked, shaking my head. "Last time we talked, you wanted me to meet someone from *Tinder*. Besides, I thought you hated Twitter!"

Jen shoved me playfully. "Tinder guy is old news. I really like Mark. I know you're thinking I'm a giant hypocrite. But he's not your average tech scum. He works there because he has to pay off his student loans, but he's also a musician."

"So are you guys going on a date tonight?" I asked.

She shrugged. "He wants me to hang out with his friends over at Maggie McGarry's. I don't think that counts as a date."

"In North Beach?"

Jen grabbed my hand. "Please come with me? I'll look pathetic if I show up alone."

"So now it's a pub crawl?" I asked, wondering when the hell I was going to get my research done. "It's a Wednesday."

Jen rolled her eyes. "Thirty is not dead. Don't you dare pull the old-lady card. I won't let you."

"Just wait until it's your turn," I said, giving her a knowing smile. "Suddenly all you'll want to do is wake up at dawn to drink a latte without a headache."

"Whatever. I'm getting an Uber right now to come pick us up."

"Jen, I really think I should—"

She brought her finger to her lips. "Uber will be here in five minutes. I already typed in the request."

Inside a rowdy, dark pub, overgrown frat boys threw back pitchers like they were filled with water. Jen's date, Mark, cocked his head toward the guys at the end of the bar.

"I don't know about you ladies," he said, pushing his black-rimmed glasses up his nose. "But this isn't really my scene. I heard they have a great live blues band tonight down the street at the Tavern. You want to go?"

"I love blues," Jen said. Mark had no idea that Jen's music

library had more Britney Spears than B. B. King. She shot Nick and me a warning look. "Let's go."

I followed Jen, Nick, and Mark into the street. Girls in vintage coats took drags from their cigarettes, the tips burning bright in the dark alley. Looking up at the Tavern, I felt a shiver work its way down my spine. Maybe the apartment building above the bar really had been a brothel back in the Victorian era.

"I'll stay out with you guys for a bit longer," I said. "But then I'm taking the bus home. I'm getting tired."

Nick raised his eyebrows. "The bus? Girl, you can afford to Uber."

Jen shook her head. "I don't get why you don't just buy a car."

I drew in a sharp breath. When I finally got behind the wheel again after reinstating my suspended license, I'd hallucinate images on the roadway and pull over shaking with fear. I hadn't driven in over ten years. "Too much of a hassle."

"Sarah," Jen said, looping her arm through mine, "Nick wants me to invite Mark to see Peaches Christ, because he thinks Mark will say no to a drag show."

"And this proves?" I asked.

Nick dropped his voice to a whisper, nodding at Mark, who was ten paces ahead of us. "That this Twitter guy Jen's dating is probably another tech asshole, the scum taking over our beloved city. Why not show him some *real* San Francisco culture?"

"Oh, shut up," Jen said, shoving Nick. "Mark is nice. He's not like that."

"Whatever," Nick said. "Maybe if he made more of an effort

to *talk* to me I would like him, but I think you can do better."
His phone beeped with a text and he grinned. "Sorry, ladies,"
he said, turning to us, "but there's this guy I'm seeing and he
wants me to come meet him at a party in the Mission."

"You're leaving us?" Jen said.

Nick nodded. "I really like him. Text me later if you want
to come too."

"Okay," I said, waving good-bye to Nick. "Be safe."

I showed my ID to the bouncer, making my way into the
dark room. A band jammed onstage, sweating through their
shirts as the trumpet wailed and bass thrummed. People
bumped against me, jostling for space at the bar.

"I'll grab us a beer," Jen said.

"Let me pay for it," Mark answered. "PBR okay with you
guys?"

I nodded. "That's great, thanks."

At the end of the bar, a middle-aged man, who was tall and
thin with short, dark hair, drummed his hands on the wood
to the beat. A chubby guy wearing a beret smiled and clapped
him on the back. "Ed, my man! How's it hanging?"

"Good," Ed said, shaking his hand.

"Hey, Jen," I said, moving closer. "I think this guy might be
the owner. I'm going to go talk to him."

"What?" she yelled, over the music.

"Never mind!" Pushing through the sweaty bodies, I tapped
Ed on the shoulder. "Excuse me. Are you Edward Kim, owner
of this bar?"

He gave me a hearty handshake. "Yep. Call me Ed."

I smiled. "Ed. I've been trying to get in touch with you. My name's Sarah Havensworth. I left you a message about a story I'm working on."

"Oh yeah," he said, nodding as if he remembered. "Sorry I haven't gotten back to you. Things around here get a little crazy."

I struggled to make my voice heard over the music. "Listen. How about coffee tomorrow? Do you have time?"

"Maybe." He paused. "You know Caffé Sapore?"

"The one on Lombard? I sure do."

"I'll make you a deal. You buy me breakfast, I'll meet you there at eleven."

I smiled. "Consider it done."

More of Ed's friends crowded around, seeking his attention. I slipped back to my table against the wall, where Jen handed me a cold glass of PBR.

"Who's the old guy?" she asked.

"The owner." I took a swig of beer, then set the glass down. "I'm glad we ran into him. I'm working on a story about two missing seamstresses who disappeared in 1876."

"Cool!" Jen said. "But I'm confused. Aren't you working on a novel for your thesis project?"

"I was," I said. "But I'm changing my focus to narrative non-fiction."

"Ha!" she said, smiling at me. "You're still a journalist after all."

As I tapped my feet in time to the music, I thought about how right Jen was. For some reason, I'd always dreamed of writing a novel. But maybe it wasn't what I was meant to do, especially if it didn't come naturally to me. I would never be the next great American author. But that didn't mean I couldn't write a great story.

Sitting at my writing desk with a mild headache, I frowned at my wedding picture. I hadn't slept well last night. When I'd gotten in at eleven-thirty, Hunter had slung his arms around me, nuzzling my neck in the darkness. I'd closed my eyes, feeling his hardness pressed against me, then I'd guided his hand between my legs.

"*You know,*" he'd whispered. "*Maybe you could go off birth control.*"

And just like that, my body had seized, my muscles turning rock solid. When he'd tried to comfort me, I'd pushed him away.

"*Hey,*" Hunter had said, stroking my hair. "*I'm sorry. I shouldn't have brought it up. I know you're not ready yet. But you will be, right? Never mind. We don't even have to talk about it right now. Let's get back to kissing.*"

But the mood had been lost. Feeling the muscles of his strong back and smelling the familiar piney scent of his skin and aftershave, I couldn't. He'd sighed as I'd rolled off him, mumbling an apology. And then I'd curled up in the fetal position feigning sleep, tears pricking my eyes. I would have to tell him what happened. My secret was going to catch up with me eventually. And then everything would fall apart.

My phone buzzed with a text, jarring me from my memories.

Feel like shit. You were smart to go home early.

I smiled, my fingers tapping the phone keyboard.

Told you so! Thirty is coming for you, Jen. ☺ Drink lots of water. Coffee will only make you feel worse. Trust me on this one.

My phone buzzed again. Thank you for coming out. It was great to see you. PS. Mark is a really good kisser!

I chuckled, turning back to my computer screen. In spite of feeling slightly groggy, I was glad I'd gone out with my friends. So much of what Jen had spoken to me about really resonated with me. I'd left the magazine because I'd sensed the new editor in chief would be the type to care more about Jack Dorsey and start-ups with Series C funding than artists, laborers, and educators.

And now I had the freedom to write my own story, about two working-class women who vanished from San Francisco's gritty streets a hundred and forty years ago.

I glanced at the clock. It was ten-thirty, and the walk to Caffé Sapore in North Beach would be a welcome escape from my apartment, where the rumpled bedsheets served as a painful reminder of the gift I could never give Hunter.

Inside Caffé Sapore, the smell of coffee beans filled the air. Speaking to one another in French, tourists sipped their espressos. I looked up as Ed entered the café, beckoning him over to my table with a wave.

"Thank you so much for coming," I said, gesturing to the menu above the espresso bar. "Anything you want. It's on me."

Ed settled into his chair. "That ham-and-egg bagel looks good, and I'll take a black coffee."

"Great," I said, standing up. "I'll place your order."

Back at our table, I leaned forward on my elbows, notebook at the ready. "So tell me, Ed, how did you come into ownership of the Tavern?"

"My father bought the place back in the 1980s. It had fallen into disrepair, but I think he saw its potential." He paused to sip his coffee, and then set the mug down. "It's part of our neighborhood. I grew up in Chinatown on Grant Avenue. My father still calls the street 'Du Pon Gai.' He wanted to preserve a piece of San Francisco history."

I scribbled as much as I could on my notepad. "That's really cool. Who did your father buy the bar from?"

Ed rubbed his chin. "The Heinrichs. The great-great-great-grandfather, George Heinrich, opened it in 1860 and got one of the city's first liquor permits. It stayed in the family for generations, but eventually they didn't want the burden of it anymore."

I wrote down the name George Heinrich. "And do you stay in touch with any of them?"

"Oh yes." He smiled. "Anna Heinrich. She lives up in Sacramento, but sometimes she comes into the city to hear the bands jam."

"Are the blues bands your addition?" I asked, holding my latte.

He laughed. "No, that was my wife's idea. She convinced me to turn the bar into a live music venue, because she's a big fan of blues. I decided to do just that, while maintaining the integrity of the old Tavern."

I nodded, tapping my pen. "The photographs on the wall, some of them date back to the 1870s. How did you end up with that collection?"

Ed took a bite of his bagel. I waited for him to swallow. "Funny you mention them," Ed said. "They don't really fit the vibe of the bar, but they were always a part of it. When I was a kid they kinda freaked me out. It was like looking at pictures of ghosts."

"So your father put them up?" I asked.

"He found them in a box in the back room when he was fixing up the old place. I don't know why he decided to hang them. For the history, I guess."

"Would you mind if I got Anna Heinrich's email address or phone number from you? I'd like to ask her a few questions."

He shrugged. "Sure."

With any luck, Anna might have kept old newspaper clippings related the murder of the prostitute that took place outside. "Do you own the whole building, including the apartments?" I asked, taking another sip of my latte.

Ed set down his bagel. "I sure do. Why, are you looking for a place to live?"

I laughed. "No, thank God. I've heard people compare apartment hunting in San Francisco to *The Hunger Games*. But I'd love to see one of your units if that's possible."

Ed's face lit up. "I've got a corner unit for rent that the painters are working on now. You're welcome to take a look before the open house on Thursday morning. Probably best to avoid the crowds and the fight to the death."

I smiled, putting the cap back on my pen. "Perfect. When can I stop by?"

"Tomorrow night at seven, if you're free." Ed wiped his mouth. "Give me a ring and I'll have one of the tenants buzz you in. It's unit number thirteen. The door will be unlocked."

"Sounds lucky," I said, picking up my latte. "Thanks so much, I appreciate it."

Learning about San Francisco's wild past was what I loved most about living here. This city had so much more to offer than start-ups, gourmet food, and overpriced coffee. Digging beneath its shiny veneer, I never knew what I'd uncover next.

I twisted my heavy ring upright on my finger, looking into the mysterious depths of the emerald. In 1876, a prostitute had been murdered in the alley next to the bar. And perhaps the person behind the door to unit number thirteen had seen what had happened.

Looking down at my notes from my interview with Ed, I felt confident in the research I'd done so far. Taking a deep breath, I pulled my phone from my purse and dialed my graduate advisor's number.

All of the faculty members at the University of San Francisco were fantastic, but my advisor intimidated me. She had a *New York Times* bestselling novel, a PhD in English lit from Princeton, and an MFA in fiction from Columbia. Part of why I'd chosen to focus on a novel in the first place was because she'd wanted me to leave my comfort zone. And now here I was, right back in the world of nonfiction.

"Mariko Sanders," she said.

"It's Sarah," I answered, my heart beating faster.

"Sarah," she said, her voice lightening. "How's it going? Are we still scheduled to meet tonight after the fiction seminar?"

"Yes," I said. "Absolutely. But about that . . . I've decided to change the focus of my thesis project. And I can't wait to tell you about it."

Chapter 8

Hanna, *1876*

Hanna gripped the iron frying pan and steadied her shaking arms.

"Did you hear me? I'll kill you if you've hurt the children!" She repeated herself, this time in German. Hanna's heart beat like a trapped bird flapping its wings. Despite the pain radiating from her head and sides, she prepared to fight.

Father lunged for her, belt in hand. Hanna swung the pan as hard as she could. It cracked against his skull, the impact sending vibrations through her body.

He toppled from the blow, blood trickling from his hairline. Hanna gasped.

"Dumb slut," he muttered, falling to his knees. Father slumped against the wall, appearing completely lifeless.

God in heaven, had she done it? Sweat chilled Hanna's goose-pimpled flesh. Holding her breath, she took a step toward him. Father's chest rose and fell while dark blood congealed in the wound.

Thank the lucky stars. He was not dead, merely unconscious. But he would be mad as the devil when he awoke. Hanna and her siblings could no longer stay in their home. Hanna ran to the bedroom and pounded her fist against the door.

"Martin! Let me in."

A chair dragged across the floor and Katja cried out. Martin must have propped it under the doorknob to keep Father out. Martin pulled the door open, his right eye purple as an eggplant, the lid swollen. Hanna threw her arms around him, feeling his tear-stained cheeks pressed against hers.

Martin sniffled. "Hanna, I thought he would kill you. Why didn't you come home?"

"Forgive me," Hanna whispered.

What had she been thinking, going with Lucas to the theater? Little Hans and Katja stared up at Hanna with frightened eyes. Bending down, she pulled them into her arms, her bare shoulders protruding from the torn corset.

"What happen the pretty dress?" Katja asked, touching the fabric.

Hanna kissed her sister's cheek, the cogs of her mind spinning faster than carriage wheels with a horse at full gallop. They had to depart now, before Father came to. There was no time to collect another month's wages for their train passage north.

"Martin," Hanna asked. "Did Margaret come to mind the children?"

Martin shook his head. "No. Frau Kruger brought them here and asked for extra money because she had to watch them longer than usual. Father got too drunk today to keep working, and so Mr. Thomas at the livery sent him home early."

Hanna winced. Martin did not have to tell her how Father had reacted to that request. But why hadn't Margaret kept her word? Hanna pulled open wooden drawers, taking out the few extra dresses and trousers for the children.

"Turn around," Hanna said, beginning to undress.

Martin did as he was told. Hanna's body ached as she struggled out of the corset and torn gown. The clothes did not hold beauty anymore, reminding her only of the consequences she had suffered for pretending to be someone she was not.

Hanna stepped into a pair of bloomers and pulled a chemise over her head. The pain in her ribs stabbed her like a blade. Hanna took her blue Sunday dirndl from the closet and fastened the hooks, hastily putting it on. With her shawl slung around her shoulders, she laced her boots tightly. Father could awaken at any moment.

"Get the children's coats," Hanna said to Martin. "We leave tonight."

Martin nodded. Hanna pried the board loose from the floor and removed her savings, along with her mother's painted porcelain plate.

Martin's eyes widened when he looked at the glass jar, nearly full. "You *were* stealing from Father?"

Hanna tied both items inside Mother's quilt. "Saving for our future is not stealing. I earned that money. We must go now."

Martin nodded, wordlessly following her like someone in a trance.

"Close your eyes," Hanna said, marching the children past Father's bulky form. "And no peeking." Katja and Hans obediently covered their faces with their little hands. Martin helped the toddlers as Hanna grabbed a hard loaf of bread from the kitchen cupboard. She pressed her lips together, not knowing where their next meal would come from. Then, pulling open a drawer, her fingers wrapped around a spool of thread with a needle tucked inside. Martin stared at Father's bloodied head, his mouth gaping.

Hanna put a hand on his shoulder. "I had to do it. Go now."

Putting the loaf of bread and the thread into the satchel with her belongings, Hanna led her siblings out of the house. One by one, they snuck away quietly, until their footsteps pattered along the dirt road. Under the cover of darkness they walked in silence. Chickens clucked as Hanna hurried past their coop.

"Where are you taking us?" Hans asked.

"Shhh," Hanna whispered. "We will go on an adventure."

She swallowed the lump in her throat. They required a place to stay the night. The boardinghouses on Kearny or Jackson where prostitutes turned their tricks were far too dangerous. Perhaps Margaret's neighborhood would be better.

"Ana, I'm tired," Katja whined.

"I'm sorry, my love." Giving the blanket bundle to Martin, Hanna scooped Katja up in her arms. The little girl was heavier than she used to be, and Hanna's side throbbed. "We're nearly there," Hanna said, blinking back tears. In truth, they had two miles to walk, and Hanna's legs felt as though they would give out.

But three quarters of an hour later, Hanna and her siblings had reached the Tomkinson livery and stable on Minna Street. The horses whinnied, swishing their tails. Hanna looked up at the boardinghouse above, hoping it would be safe.

The inn was not far from where Margaret lived. Hanna struggled to remember which of the row houses belonged to her friend. It had been a wooden house, crowded against two others on a narrow lot on Minna. Yes, she would find Margaret in the morning. First she needed to get the children inside and put them to bed.

"Martin," Hanna said. "Go in that building and tell the man we require a room. State our name as Mueller and say I am a widow. Do you understand?"

Martin nodded and ran across the wooden planks of the sidewalk, toward the entrance. Mueller had been their mother's maiden name. As they waited in the darkness, Hanna's breath formed a white cloud in the evening chill.

Hans started to cry and stomped his feet. "Hanna, I want go home. It's cold."

She patted his head. "Tonight we will play pretend. Dry your tears now."

Katja looked up at her. "Ana, I'm frightened."

Hanna squeezed her sister's hand. "Do not be frightened, little one."

Two men emerged from the stable beneath the boardinghouse, staggering onto the street. Hanna's stomach lurched. Praying they would not see her, she crouched down next to Hans and Katja, hugging them close. "We must get past a big dragon to hide in our cave. But to do that we must be very brave. Can you be brave?"

Hans looked up at Hanna beneath his long lashes and nodded.

"A dragon?" Katja whispered, her eyes wide.

Martin returned, out of breath. His cheeks had flushed from the chill, and he held a key in his right hand. "We have a room for the night."

The knot in Hanna's stomach loosened, only slightly. "And you told him our name is Mueller?"

"Yes. Hanna Mueller. The man wrote it in a book."

"All right," Hanna said, standing. She led Hans and Katja by the hand, while Martin picked up Mother's blanket. They trudged toward the boardinghouse. Inside, the rickety stairs creaked beneath their feet as they climbed to the upper level. Piano music and women's laughter filtered through the cracks in the walls.

Hanna turned the key, opening the door to their room, then shut and locked it behind them. Lighting the kerosene lamp on the bedside table, Hanna watched as one large bed came into view, a threadbare quilt thrown over it. A window looked over the street below. Hanna shivered from the chill seeping through a crack, but the vantage point assuaged her fears. Should Father come for them, they would have time to flee.

Hanna unfolded her mother's quilt and laid it atop the bed. Looking around the room, she searched for the best place to hide Mother's plate. Her body ached with exhaustion, making it difficult to think. Knowing the money to be her most important resource, she tipped the bills and coins out of the jar. Carefully tearing apart the seam at the hem of her dirndl, Hanna folded the bills and slipped them inside.

After threading the needle, her fingers stitched from muscle memory, sealing her hard-earned savings away from pickpockets.

The plate was less likely to be stolen, but Hanna would not take chances. Kneeling on the dusty floor, she gently slid the porcelain dish behind the bed's wooden headboard, where it rested snugly against the wall. No one would ever find it there, unless the innkeeper decided to rearrange the furniture.

"Come now, into bed," Hanna said to Hans and Katja, lifting them onto the mattress. Hanna tucked both children under the blankets. Through the thin walls, a man's voice grew louder, yelling about gambling debts.

"Who's that?" Hans asked, his eyes widening.

"That's the dragon," Hanna said. "We must stay very quiet so he doesn't find us."

Hanna looked at Martin, leaning against the wall. His eye had swollen shut, but he managed a smile. "Don't worry, I'll keep us safe," he said, drawing an imaginary sword from its sheath. "I can slay the dragon with this."

Katja pointed at his face. "Ouch!"

Hanna stroked her sister's cheeks. Lying down next to Hans and Katja, Hanna's body sank into the mattress.

Martin stretched out on the floor. He was a boy of twelve, too old to share a bed with his sister. Hanna took the shawl from her shoulders and gave it to him. She tried to hand him her goose-down pillow as well, but he waved her away.

"You keep it," Martin said.

Hanna nodded, setting the pillow back in place. Soon Katja's eyes closed, and a snore escaped Hans's mouth. He looked like a sleeping cherub with his blond curls, while Katja curled up like a little fawn. Reaching over to the bedside table, Hanna extinguished the kerosene lamp, embracing the darkness.

Sunlight crept under the gap in the curtains. The fabric reeked of cigar smoke, yet Hanna feared opening the window, lest someone see her.

"Martin," she said. "Repeat what I have told you."

"Keep the drapes closed and the door locked. Do not open it for anyone, until I hear three quick knocks and two slow ones. Then I will know it is you."

Hanna smoothed Katja's dark curls and gave Hans a kiss on the cheek. "There is bread for when you have hunger. I will be home by forenoon."

Katja clung to Hanna's skirts. "Don't leave, Ana. Stay here."

Hanna swallowed. "I will come back soon. I promise."

A crease divided Martin's brow.

Hanna placed her hands on his shoulders. "I must find Margaret. When I have spoken to her of our plans, we can depart. Remember, the door must stay locked."

Martin's fingers curled around the brass key. With a nod, he shut the door behind Hanna, and she heard the lock click into place.

Horses whinnied as Hanna walked away from the livery toward the row of small, narrow houses on Minna Street. Her gut told her to turn around, and she stopped where she stood, breathing in dust from the road. Hanna shook her head. The children were safe inside, and she would travel more quickly to Margaret's house alone.

Perhaps Margaret had fallen ill or had a fainting spell. Hanna's boots crunched along the gravel, every pebble like a knife through the thin soles. She kept her head down, each dark-haired man with a beard causing her heart to seize. Father was likely awake now, head throbbing and temper raging.

Children shrieked and scampered across Minna Street. Women emptied chamber pots into the road. Covering her nose and mouth, Hanna attempted to block the stench of urine and feces. Some of the street children eyed her with caution, her face unfamiliar in the Irish neighborhood. Laughing as they walked, men in overalls speckled with yellow clay made their way toward the nearby tar flats.

A hunchbacked woman with a silver plait hung laundry on the line.

"Excuse me?" Hanna asked. "Do you know the house of Margaret O'Brien?"

"Aye," the woman said, pointing toward the east. "Walk down the road a wee bit that way. It's the fourth house on the left."

"Thank you," Hanna replied.

She picked up her skirt to prevent the hem from dragging through a puddle of mud, and scattered a flock of geese. The fourth house on the left had a sloped roof and flaking white paint, with a porch that sagged in the middle. Four children sat outside on the ramshackle stoop, their pale skin smeared with dirt. A girl of about ten held a crying baby in her lap.

"Does Margaret live here?" Hanna asked.

The girl's eyes narrowed. "That's me sister. Have you seen her?"

"Did she not come home last night?"

The baby shrieked and Margaret's sister bounced it on her knee. She stuck a grimy finger in the child's mouth for it to suck on. The girl's eyes were the same brilliant shade of blue as Margaret's, like snowmelt in the mountains. She talked fast, making it difficult for Hanna to keep up.

"I waited and waited, caring for the wee ones. Pa was madder than I've ever seen 'im. When Margaret didn't come home, he said he'd kill her. Murder her dead."

The girl's brow furrowed and Hanna saw the restraint it took to hold back her emotions. But then her features formed a hard mask. Like Hanna's brother Martin, Margaret's sister had grown up too fast. In these dark times, tears were wasted effort.

"What's your name?" Hanna asked, looking down at her soiled clothing.

"Cathleen." Margaret's sister stared at Hanna with hardness in her eyes, like she would take a swing at her if she had to.

"I'm Hanna Schaeffer," Hanna said. "A friend of your sister."

A group of scrawny children fought over a chicken bone in the street. Wishing she'd brought something to give Cathleen, Hanna offered a smile instead. Perhaps this small kindness would be enough.

Cathleen chewed her bottom lip. "Is it true what they say in the papers? That there's a madman on the loose, murdering pretty girls? I can't read, but my friend Moira told me it was true."

Hanna thought of the newspaper headline she'd seen a few months back. *Murder! Murder!* it had read, describing a prostitute found dead in front of a brothel somewhere in Devil's Acre. A shiver worked its way down to Hanna's bones.

Cathleen's lip trembled. "What if Margaret has been killed?"

Hanna shook her head. "We must not think that way. Ask every person you know if they have seen Margaret. We will find her."

Cathleen shook the squealing baby as it wriggled to break free from her grasp. A woman hollered from inside the house.

"Cathleen, you daft git! Come 'ere right now."

Cathleen's eyes widened. "I'm here, Ma," she said.

A heavyset woman with ruddy cheeks stumbled onto the porch, eyes flashing like a rabid dog's. Instinctively, Hanna took a step back, but not before she smelled the whiskey. This woman reeked like Father after a night out at the saloons. Every fiber of Hanna's body told her to run, but she forced herself to hold her ground.

Mrs. O'Brien placed her plump hands on her hips. Her bloodshot eyes locked on Hanna's. "And who the hell are you, comin' round my house?" Mrs. O'Brien's wild reddish-gray hair gave her the appearance of a madwoman.

"I'm Hanna, a friend of Margaret's." Hanna stood taller. Was Margaret's mother to push her, she wasn't afraid to push back. "I haven't seen Margaret since yesterday, and I have come to see if she's all right."

One of the younger children ran forward, grabbing Mrs. O'Brien's leg. "Mama! I'm hungry."

With a deft movement, Margaret's mother slapped the child. He began to cry. "What is it you want, then?" Mrs. O'Brien spat. "My daughter has run off."

"Why do you think that?"

Mrs. O'Brien hacked and coughed, spitting greenish mucus at Hanna's feet. She wiped her mouth and glared. "Margaret has been foolin' around with that McClaren boy. Don't you know nothin'? If you's such good friends, you'd have seen the lad always comin' round here."

The acrid odor of burned eggs and urine clogged Hanna's nostrils. Margaret had never mentioned a sweetheart.

"McClaren?" Hanna asked. "Has he a given name?"

Margaret's mother spat again. "Kieran. Works the dock over by Clark's Point. I told her he wasn't no good. But she don't listen to me."

"I will find her," Hanna said, glaring.

Mrs. O'Brien laughed without mirth. "Don't fret your pretty little head. That daft trollop is good as dead, she is."

And with that, Mrs. O'Brien turned and waddled into the house. Hanna fought the panic rising in her chest, fast as the incoming tide. Margaret's own mother didn't care what happened to her daughter. Hanna took a deep breath, knowing who could help. Picking up the hem of her dirndl, she ran down the narrow road.

The dirt gave way to cobblestones, and laborers thronged the wooden sidewalks whilst newsboys chanted the morning papers. Men in top hats with stiff brims walked past. Hanna reached out and touched a coat sleeve. "Excuse me, sir?"

The man stepped back, his eyes wide.

"Please," Hanna asked. "Which way to the Merchants Exchange?"

He pointed to the north. "Straight ahead, five blocks or so."

"Does an employee named Lucas work there?"

The man stroked his moustache, likely wondering what business Hanna might have in a building where powerful men traded money and secrets.

"There's a Lucas Havensworth. You will find his office on the ground floor." The man tipped his hat. "Tell him Mr. Collier sends his regards."

"Thank you, sir," Hanna said, bowing her head. "I will do that."

Picking up her skirts once again, she ran past women strolling idly from one shop window to the next, giggling as they pointed at garments. Her chest heaved. Lucas Havensworth was Hanna's only hope to find Margaret before it was too late.

Chapter 9

Sarah, *Present Day*

I looped my arm more tightly through Hunter's as I walked up the staircase to his parents' Queen Anne style mansion. The white paint made the Pacific Heights stunner appear like a haunted castle looming above the city. The proud bay windows reflected the May sunshine but, I was certain, the curved glass of the round turret harbored stories long untold. The ocean shimmered in the distance, and the peaks of the Golden Gate Bridge stretched proudly toward the blue sky.

"Hey," Hunter said, interrupting my reverie. "I got tickets for tomorrow night's Giants game. The seats are great. The vendor I met with earlier gave them to me. He's going to stock our T-shirts in his shop. Want to come?"

I gasped. "He's stocking your shirts? You got a brick-and-mortar shop! Of course I'll come. We have to celebrate!"

Hunter picked me up and swung me around in a circle.

I pressed my nose against his. "You're the best, you know that?"

Slowly he lowered me so that my toes skimmed the ground. "You're pretty special yourself." He grinned at me. "Game starts at seven. Meet me at work? We can head over there together."

"Shoot," I said, remembering my appointment to see Ed's apartment. I hadn't told Hunter yet about my decision to write the story of Hannelore and Margaret. "I might be a little bit late."

The heavy door swung open and Gwyneth smiled, ushering us inside. "Hello, dears! I'm so glad you're here. Come in! Come in!"

Our conversation had been cut off before I'd had a chance to explain my article and how important it was to me. But I'd make my announcement soon enough. Tucking the bottle of merlot under my arm, I followed my husband into the foyer.

Gwyneth pulled Hunter into a tight hug. "I miss you, son. It's been too long since your last visit."

"I know, Mom," he said, patting her back. "I'm sorry."

The parquet floors and grand entryway dating back to the nineteenth century were part of what I loved about my in-laws' house. Of course "house" wasn't really the right word. With eleven bedrooms, one staff bedroom, and seven bathrooms, Gwyneth and Walter had over sixteen thousand square feet of living space spread over four levels.

They'd renovated over the years to impeccably restore the original Victorian details, while adding twenty-first-century comforts like a home theater and a spa.

"Hello, Sarah!" Gwyneth said, enveloping me in a hug and her signature Chanel perfume. "Good to see you!"

"Gwyneth, it smells amazing in here," I said, drinking in the scent of rosemary, butter, lemon, and garlic.

She chuckled, holding me at arm's length. "Well, I wish I could take credit for it, but Rosa does all the cooking. We're having roasted chicken with garlic mashed potatoes and Brussels sprouts with caramelized onions and bacon."

My stomach rumbled at the description. "That sounds delicious."

"Oh!" she said, looking down. "You brought wine. Fabulous! I have a bottle of Domaine de la Romanée-Conti open, but we can open this too."

"Rosa," Gwyneth called toward the kitchen. "Take this bottle of wine, please."

"Sorry for the wait!" Rosa said, walking in from the kitchen wearing a black dress and white apron, her hair pulled back in a bun. It was a costume fit for *Downton Abbey*.

"Thanks so much," I said to Rosa as she took the wine bottle. Hopefully Gwyneth never made her use the second staircase, which I wasn't allowed to use. *Oh, that old servants' passageway needs to be fixed!* Gwyneth would trill, every time I tried to take the narrow spiral stairs. But I couldn't imagine anything in this magnificent mansion not being up to code.

Classical music played softly from the sound system as we passed the reception parlor, beneath heavy crystal chandeliers.

"Would you like a cocktail?" Gwyneth asked. "Come take a seat in the family room. Relax."

"Sure," I said, removing my jacket. "If you have any grape-fruit juice, a greyhound, please."

"And I'll have a bourbon," Hunter said. "But just one, be-cause I'm driving."

The grand family room had soft, plush couches and peach-toned wallpaper. After sinking into the sofa cushions, I nestled against Hunter. His shoulders relaxed beneath the weight of my head. He stroked my hair, and I let out a deep breath.

"I'm not going to be able to meet you at work before the game. I'm working on some research for my thesis, and I have to see an apartment first."

"An apartment?" He asked, turning to face me. "Your novel is set in the 1800s, right?" He smiled. "You're not trying to divorce me and get your own place, are you? Because I'd be heartbroken if that was your secret plan . . . I don't like secrets."

"Never," I said, feeling the familiar heat of anxiety creeping up my neck.

Gwyneth returned with our cocktails, and we clinked glasses.

"To my favorite dinner guests," she said. "Cheers."

"Cheers," I replied, warming. Though Gwyneth's formal dinner rituals were nothing like the microwaved meals in front of the television I'd grown up with, I appreciated the comforts provided by Gwyneth and Walter. Their home was a beautiful place where I was always welcome, and they'd given me so much.

When we finished our cocktails, Rosa took our glasses and we made our way into the formal dining room.

As I sat down at the impeccably set dining table, I clung to the futile wish that we were at my parents' home for dinner. I would have loved for Hunter to meet my mom. All I could think about was her smile, her laugh, and the way she liked to sing along with the radio when she cooked her tuna casserole. I would have given anything to hug her, to talk to her about everything going on in my life.

"Hello, son," Walter said, startling me as he walked into the room. Hunter immediately set down his glass and stood up.

"Dad," Hunter said, clapping him on the back as they embraced. "I see life has been treating you well."

I half stood up, hoping Walter would also offer me a hug, but he simply nodded, before taking a seat at the head of the table. "Hello, Sarah."

My cheeks flushed. "Hello, Walter."

I sat back down, like I hadn't just made an effort to greet him. I looked at Walter, who, like Hunter, stood six-foot-three, his skin tanned from hours on the golf course. The way his eyes narrowed, I couldn't help but feel like I'd done something wrong. Walter wasn't exactly chummy with me, but tonight he seemed openly unfriendly.

"Son," Walter said, leaning toward Hunter. "How's business?"

"Good," Hunter answered. "Busy."

Walter shook his head. "You let me know when you drop this little side hobby of yours and come back to finance. The firm's waiting."

Hunter laughed nervously, but I stiffened.

"I'm proud of what Hunter is doing," I said, staring Walter in the eye.

Hunter looked at me, slightly alarmed at my daring to confront his father, but gave me a sheepish smile. I smiled back at him.

"Oh good," Gwyneth said, clapping her hands to break the tension. "We're all here. Rosa! Please bring the first course."

I placed my napkin in my lap, eyeing the assortment of forks and spoons. When my parents were alive, my mom would talk about her workday, imitating each coworker until my dad and I couldn't stop laughing. My talent for writing came from my mother, a natural-born storyteller. As I thought about how she always supported me in following my dreams, my eyes started to sting. Both she and my dad encouraged me from a young age to embrace my creativity, watching every silly play I put on for them and clapping like they'd been to see a Broadway performance.

Rosa set a steaming plate in front of me, the roasted garlic wafting into the air.

"Thank you," I said. "This looks delicious."

She smiled, warmly. "You're welcome."

Setting dinner plates in front of Hunter, Gwyneth, and Walter, Rosa asked if we all had enough wine, and then disappeared into the kitchen. I wished Rosa could sit with us at the table, mostly because she'd be more fun to talk to than Walter.

Gwyneth raised her glass. "*Bon appétit.* To health, life, and a growing family."

My glass felt shaky in my hand.

"Mother," Hunter said. "It's not growing yet."

Gwyneth winked. "Perhaps not yet, but I want to see grand-children before I'm old. I'm sure Sarah understands that."

I stabbed a Brussels sprout with my fork. My stomach churned. I thought of the woman I'd seen last week at the park. I'd watched as she snuggled her baby close, kissing the little one's chubby cheeks. In that moment, my desire for a child was so strong I had to turn away, fighting back tears.

Gwyneth wagged her finger at me. "Well, don't wait too long. You know what they say about women over thirty."

I braced myself for the familiar lecture, literally, by placing my other hand on the table. Now that Hunter had hinted about having kids, it made me feel claustrophobic.

Taking a long sip of her wine, Gwyneth got ready to regurgitate whatever article she'd read recently in one of her women's magazines.

"Sarah," she said, clicking her tongue. "The risk of something going wrong increases. Those children have terrible defects." Her voice dropped to a whisper. "Down syndrome. Autism. *Retardation*. Can you imagine?"

No, I couldn't imagine. I'd already made something far, far worse happen. My palms began to sweat. Gwyneth looked at me for an answer, but I took a bite of mashed potatoes and chewed. So long as my mouth was full, I wouldn't say something rude that I'd regret later. Couldn't my mother-in-law see how red my cheeks were? This dinner was making me feel like a caged animal at the zoo—a freak species, an impostor. I felt the panic rising like a wave in my chest.

"We're going to wait a few more years," Hunter said, setting down his fork with a clack, as if to end the conversation with an exclamation mark.

Gwyneth pursed her lips. "I know, I know. You're both young, focused on your careers. But why risk a dangerous pregnancy? Too many women get caught up in their work and forget the importance of family."

"Mom," Hunter said. "*Stop*. Please?"

Gwyneth held up her hands. "Okay, I relent!"

"So." I set down my wineglass, my cheeks burning. "I'm looking forward to your event with the pieces from the National Gallery of Ireland. It's wonderful what your family has done for the arts."

Gwyneth perked up. "Mayor Ed Lee is going to give a speech. And I've found a fantastic designer to transform the space for our fete. It's going to look even more beautiful than the exhibit at the National Gallery in Dublin, a bit Edwardian Baroque."

Walter cleared his throat. "My wife has quite a penchant for the arts. I'm glad she has something to keep her occupied while she spends my money."

I pressed my lips together. Gwyneth had probably set aside her own dreams so that Walter could focus on his business. Surely she'd made sacrifices.

"Your great-grandfather founded the academy," I said, staring at Walter Havensworth. "He must've valued the arts."

When Walter's eyes met mine, they were as cold as ice. He spoke without smiling. "I didn't know you'd taken an interest in our family history."

I sliced into my chicken. "I understand Lucas Havensworth originally started Havensworth Art Academy as a nonprofit, open to any student with an interest in fine arts. Does it still operate that way?"

Walter studied my face, his mouth a stern line. Though his hair had gone completely white and he'd grown a potbelly, he looked formidably strong.

"No," he said. "It's a for-profit institution."

"Do you offer any scholarships of academic merit?"

Walter stabbed a Brussels sprout, popped it in his mouth, and chewed. He often liked to make me wait for his responses, as if my questions were inane, the chatter of an obnoxious little bird.

He turned to his wife. "Gwyn, pour me another glass of red, will you?"

She nodded. "I'll just pop into the kitchen."

We sat in uncomfortable silence.

"Hunter," Walter said, looking at my husband. "We have an IPO bake-off on Friday. I was hoping you could help me with the pitch."

"Um, sure," Hunter said. "Do you have the market overviews and bank introductions sorted out?"

"We've lined up a few tombstone slides to show recent M&A deals, IPOs, and debt offerings that I've advised on. Plus the league table slides that show how we rank in equity issuances."

Heat boiled under my skin. Not only had Walter not answered my question, but also he was sucking Hunter back into the banking world, when Hunter had fought so hard to leave the profession.

What the hell? *Just leave him alone!* I wanted to scream. Have-Clothing wasn't profitable yet, but they were breaking even. Hunter loved his work—believed in it.

"Sarah," Gwyneth said, locking her eyes on mine as she returned with Walter's wineglass. She appeared as eager as I was to cut the banking talk short. "Tell me how your novel is coming along?"

Suddenly the room fell silent and everyone turned to stare at me.

"Well," I said, my heart pounding in my ears. "Actually, I've stopped writing it."

Hunter's eyes grew to the size of our dinner plates. *"What?"*

I rubbed my chin nervously. "It wasn't coming naturally— the characters felt stiff and wooden. Nothing about the plot felt right. But something amazing happened when I was researching the 1870s." I looked into my husband's hazel eyes, terrified he'd see me as a fraud. "I discovered an article on two dressmakers who disappeared in 1876, a German girl and an Irish girl. I was so captivated by their story, I asked my graduate advisor if I could change the topic of my thesis."

Gwyneth coughed, her face reddening. "Oh dear! Please excuse me." She patted her chest. "That sip of wine went down the wrong way."

"So if you're not writing your novel," Hunter asked, his eyes narrowing, "what's the focus of this story? Is it fiction, nonfiction?"

"Narrative nonfiction," I said, looking quickly from Hunter to Gwyneth, then Walter. "I felt inspired by Svetlana Alexievich, who won the Nobel Prize in literature. This is going to be a long piece on what happened to these two women, illuminating the struggles of working-class immigrants during the late nineteenth century."

"Do you know what happened to them?" Hunter asked.

I bit my lip. "Not yet. But my research is leading me there." I smiled at him. "You know I won't stop until I find out."

He chuckled. "That much is true. But you've given yourself quite a challenge, trying to solve a 140-year-old mystery."

"And your graduate advisor," Gwyneth asked, her eyebrows drawing together. "She approved this topic? Do you intend to publish it?"

I nodded. "She did, and yes, I do. I have connections from my old job at the magazine, not to mention my wonderful advisors at USF. I'm going to submit to *Slate*, *The Atlantic*, maybe even *Vanity Fair* and *The New Yorker*."

"That's rather ambitious, don't you think?" Walter said, his dark eyes studying me with hawklike intensity.

Heat rose under my skin. "Perhaps. But I want to reach a national audience. If I'm rejected, I'll publish in one of our local magazines instead. I have contacts at the *San Francisco Chronicle*. They'd love a piece like this."

For a moment, everyone sat there in silence while my words hung in the air. My heart began to pound, a burst of adrenaline threatening to send me spiraling into a panic attack. Why was everyone so interested in my thesis all of a sudden?

I slid my chair back and stood up, sweat beading on my upper lip. "Excuse me."

Hunter's eyes locked on mine, and I squeezed his shoulder before I turned to walk down the hall. I let out a deep breath as I heard conversation resume without me.

Reaching into my purse, my fingers clasped the hard plastic tube of my Klonopin bottle. I'd pop a pill, head back to dinner, and in about ten minutes I wouldn't give a damn what Walter and Gwyneth were talking about.

I had a sharp pang of longing for my parents. If Mom and Dad were alive, I would have done housework after dinner, cleaning up like a normal person, instead of letting a maid do it. I'd have told them how I was really feeling—my self-loathing, not this polite management of emotion that Hunter practiced with his parents. Why couldn't he stand up to his dad? Sometimes Mom and I yelled like banshees at each other. We weren't always nice, but at least we were honest.

As I traveled down the hallway toward the bathroom, I glanced in at Walter's study. The cherry-paneled room was dark and smelled faintly of cigar smoke. I knew he kept the Cubans in a humidor, and expensive forty-year-old Scotches in the glass cabinets lining the wall. Hunter liked to stay late, sipping Glenfarclas with his dad.

Something on Walter's desk caught my eye. I blinked. There atop a file folder on Walter's mahogany desk sat a pewter skeleton key. Its coloring looked nearly identical to the antique lock on the wardrobe in Havensworth Art Academy, which Gwyneth had pretended to know nothing about. Could it be the key?

Glancing over my shoulder to make sure nobody was watching, I stepped inside the study. I picked up the key, which felt cool and solid in my hand. Before I had time to think, I stuffed it into my pocket. Footsteps sounded down the hallway, heavy and slow. I froze. "Where are you going?" Gwyneth's voice called.

"To get a cigar," Walter muttered.

No! I darted into the hallway and then ran toward the bathroom. I stopped in front of the bathroom door, breathing heavily. Placing my hand on the handle, I turned it, ready to slip inside, as if I'd been there all along.

"Ahem."

Turning around, I gasped. Walter stood before me in the dim light, his broad shoulders filling the space between us.

"So," he said. "Are you sure it's a good idea, writing about these missing women?"

"Excuse me?"

Walter's eyes studied my face, calculating and cold. "Maybe it's best if you find another topic."

I kept my expression neutral. "I think the lives of working-class women are often overlooked in history books. I'd like to shed a little light on them. Also, it's an interesting mystery. My graduate advisor is enthusiastic about it too."

Walter stared off into space, as if lost in thought. "Exposing secrets can be dangerous." But then his eyes met mine. "And everyone has secrets, don't they?"

The air in the hallway felt uncomfortably close. I blinked, a strange, unsettling feeling coming over me.

"Dad?" Hunter appeared around the bend, my knight in shining armor. He looked at his father with a raised eyebrow. "Everything okay?"

Walter's face relaxed. "Fine, son. Everything's just fine."

"Good," Hunter said. "Because it's a little early for cigars and Scotch, don't you think?" He threw his arm around his father's shoulder. "And Mom needs help with something. Why don't you come with me back to the kitchen."

As Hunter steered Walter back down the corridor, I struggled to regain my breath. Had my father-in-law just threatened me? Reaching into my pocket, I wrapped my fingers around the key. This was my moment to put it back right where I'd found it—to do the right thing. But against my better judgment, I didn't.

Chapter 10

Hanna, *1876*

Hanna ran down Montgomery Street as if her father himself chased after her. Stabbing her insides like needles, a sharp pain caused Hanna to gasp for breath. She stopped short, holding her ribs. In that moment, Mrs. Cunningham's bustled form emerged from Walton's Tailor Shop.

God in heaven!

Quickly, Hanna stepped into a nearby doorway, hiding beneath its striped awning. She lowered her head so Mrs. Cunningham would not see her. Between the events of last night and her haste to find Lucas, Hanna had forgotten neither she nor Margaret had turned up for work this morning. Leaning forward, Hanna glanced around the corner. Mrs. Cunningham stood in the street, speaking with an elderly gentleman.

Fragments of their conversation carried on the breeze, Mrs. Cunningham's voice barely audible. ". . . I always knew the O'Brien girl was trouble. No doubt she has gone the way of the devil. It's the other one who has surprised me. She didn't strike me as the type to run off. But you know how these shop-girls are, easily swayed by vice."

The man stood before her with brows as thick as caterpil-lars, which drew together as he frowned. He shook his fist, jingling his gold pocket watch.

"No matter how grave the situation, I demand workers forthwith. I'll not shut the doors of my business due to the antics of two fickle girls. Can you not find them? Where were they last seen?"

Mrs. Cunningham appeared shrunken before him, like an apple that had withered in the sun. Perhaps she would be out of a job. From his fine suit and shiny top hat, Hanna presumed this man to be the shop owner.

Mrs. Cunningham dropped her voice. "I last saw the O'Brien girl at supper hour. Unbeknownst to her, I watched her from my apartment above the shop. She stepped out with a rough-looking man, walking toward those debased saloons on Kearny Street."

Straining to hear every word, Hanna covered her mouth. Mrs. Cunningham had seen Margaret! And what on earth had been troubling Margaret, causing her to walk toward the dan-gers of Old Sydney Town? Murderers and crooks swarmed the dives that stood along Kearny Street. It was hardly a safe place for a woman.

"Does the girl have any family you can contact?" the man asked.

Mrs. Cunningham lifted her nose. "I do not associate with the likes of Irish immigrants such as Mrs. O'Brien. The girl couldn't even write her address."

"And what of the other girl?" he asked, throwing up his hands. "Call on her family and bring her into the shop immediately. I care not if she is on her deathbed."

Mrs. Cunningham pursed her lips. "The German girl wrote her address as Napier Lane. I suppose I could send a messenger to the home."

The gentleman paced back and forth in front of the shop. "Please do so. In the meantime, call on whomever you must. I want seamstresses here within the hour. I shan't leave my customers waiting."

Mrs. Cunningham bowed her head. "Understood."

"If the girls cannot be found . . ." The man removed his top hat and rubbed his silver hair. "Terrible misfortune may befall them. You must call the police."

Mrs. Cunningham frowned. "Yes, sir, Mr. Walton."

Hanna stood still as a statue. Pray that unfortunate messenger would not encounter Father in a drunken rage. Her palms began to sweat. If the police were to search for her, would she be arrested for stealing the beautiful velvet dress?

Bowing her head, Hanna left the doorway and walked quickly in the opposite direction. Turning right, she ran the remainder of the way to California Street. Her boots stopped before the imposing marble structure that housed the Merchants Exchange.

Hanna looked at the dirty hem of her dirndl, which had

dragged through the mud. Tugging her shawl more tightly around her shoulders to shield herself from the cold, she blew hot breath on her reddened fingers.

You shall do this for Margaret. You must.

Walking with purpose, Hanna entered the building. She held herself erect, as though it were perfectly natural for a girl of her position to enter a place such as this.

A man with a waxed moustache sat at a desk in the lobby. "Excuse me," he asked. "May I help you?"

Hanna's mouth went dry as cotton, but she managed to form words. "Yes, sir. I am here to see Mr. Lucas Havensworth."

His eyes narrowed. "And Mr. Havensworth is expecting you?"

Hanna crossed her hands to hide the trembling. "Yes, sir."

The man's moustache twitched as he spoke. "Mr. Havensworth is quite busy. He may well be in a meeting this very moment."

"Please," Hanna said. "Mr. Havensworth expects me."

The man's expression softened. "This way."

Her footsteps echoed in the marble halls as she followed him down the corridor. Hanna's eyes darted to the gilded columns, the glass windows, and the oil paintings. How much wealth could be contained in a single embellishment, while children outside starved in the street? She stopped before a frosted glass door, painted with a gold number 17. The man rapped his knuckles against it.

Lucas pulled the door open, his blue eyes meeting Hanna's. Even under such terrible circumstances, seeing him again pleased her.

"Sir," the mustachioed man said. "This woman states she has an appointment with you." He looked at Hanna as if she were a mouse that had scurried inside. "But I am happy to escort her out if that is not the case."

"Please do no such thing," Lucas said. "I am expecting Miss Schaeffer. Hanna, do come in. Bernard, you may leave us now."

"Thank you," Hanna whispered to Lucas, watching Bernard turn away. Lucas shut the door behind them. Looking at Hanna, he reached up to touch her face where the bruise had come through. His cool fingertips settled against Hanna's sore skin.

"Good God, Hanna. Who is the brute who did this to you?"

His touch was so tender she managed not to flinch. "My father."

The cobalt ring around Lucas's eyes deepened. "How dare he raise his hand to you! Are you all right?"

Hanna shook her head. A hot tear trickled down her cheek. "Lucas, I am sorry to trouble you, but Margaret . . . she is gone."

"Gone?" He patted the chair next to him. "Here, sit down. I'll bring you tea."

Hanna sat on the soft chair upholstered in velvet. A silver dog rested atop Lucas's desk, holding a stack of papers in place. That trinket could buy a family enough food to last a year. And here it sat, helping no one.

"What happened?" Lucas asked, pouring tea from a silver pot into a porcelain cup. Few men possessed his kindness, a special quality indeed.

Hanna reached into her dirndl pocket for a cloth handkerchief. Dabbing at her eyes, she recounted last night's events. "I asked Margaret to mind the children while you and I were at the theater, and she agreed. But when I returned home, she was gone. The children told me she never arrived. My father was drunk, and he struck me."

Lucas curled his hand into a fist. "What kind of man raises his hand to his own daughter?"

"Drink is a curse. Margaret's father also beats her."

Handing her a teacup and saucer, Lucas sat down next to Hanna. "How do you know Margaret didn't return home?"

Hanna lifted the cup with both hands, allowing its warmth to comfort her. "I visited Margaret's family early this morn."

Margaret's dreadful mother with her wild eyes and spittle was not a woman Hanna wished to encounter again. "Margaret was not there. Her mother told me she had been seeing a boy named Kieran McClaren."

"Margaret had a sweetheart?" Lucas asked.

"I do not know," Hanna said, hanging her head. "And I thought I knew everything about Margaret."

"Do you think she's with him now?"

Hanna sipped her tea, taking time to think. "She may well be. I heard Mrs. Cunningham speak to the owner of Walton's Tailor Shop. She had seen Margaret on the arm of a man last night, walking to the saloons on Kearny Street."

Lucas furrowed his brow. "And Margaret was not known to frequent saloons?"

"Of course not! She is a virtuous girl."

"Forgive me," Lucas said. "It was not my intention to offend.

I am only trying to piece together the events of the evening. When did you last see Margaret?"

"At six o'clock. We were together when she helped me dress . . ."

Hanna's throat tightened, remembering the smile on Margaret's face as she fastened each jet button of the borrowed velvet dress. Margaret had brushed Hanna's hair out for her, and pinned it atop Hanna's head, copying the hairstyles of fashionable women she had seen in the street.

"Can you recall what she was wearing?" Lucas asked.

Hanna closed her eyes, trying to picture her friend. "Her brown day frock. She wore no ribbons in her hair, nor did she have any jewelry save for her grandmother's silver claddagh ring. She never takes it off."

"And according to Mrs. Cunningham, she was last seen with a man, walking in the direction of the saloons on Kearny Street?"

"Yes," Hanna said, her shoulders slumping. "That is all we know."

"Well then," Lucas said. "We must make a statement to the police."

"Mrs. Cunningham has done so already," Hanna replied. "And I fear they will not act quickly enough. We must find Margaret before it is too late."

Lucas placed his hand on Hanna's. "Pray tell me then what you wish to do."

Hanna sucked in her breath at the unexpected contact. But she felt reassurance in the warmth of Lucas's touch. "May I ask you to accompany me to Devil's Acre?" she asked softly. "And to prepare for the worst."

Lucas clenched his teeth, setting his jaw in a hard line. "Have you no one else who can travel with you? Your brother, perhaps?"

"No. He's too young. I do not wish to expose him to such vice." She swallowed. Perhaps Lucas would refuse, leaving her with no one.

But Lucas nodded. "Then my decision is made. I would not wish any harm to befall you, especially when your father has already done enough."

"Thank you," Hanna said. "Now we must hurry."

Even with Lucas by her side, Hanna felt her skin prickle with nerves as she walked down Kearny Street. Working girls stumbled onto the wooden sidewalk, their eyes glassed over from smoking opium. They wore lipstick, rouge, and little else. Even the pretty waiter girls employed at the melodeons donned gaudy costumes such as see-through shirts and frilly knickers to display their charms for the taking.

Lucas held Hanna's arm tightly as the neighborhood grew rougher. She looked up at the signs above the grog shops, saloons, and dance halls: THE COCK O' THE WALL, THE DEWDROP AND THE ROSEBUD, BROOK'S MELODEON, THE MONTANA. Which of these horrid cellars could Margaret have entered, and why?

When Hanna and Lucas reached the corner of Pacific

Street, they stood in front of a dank saloon. Some called it a deadfall, for not many a man emerged from it with his life. It was known as the Billy Goat. A middle-aged woman stood outside smoking a cigarette. Her deep-set eyes shone black beneath frizzed hair, and skin hung from her face like dough.

"Aye, come inside," she said, turning toward them. "Drink spirits and I'll 'ave a right show for ye."

Spitting tobacco on the dirt road, the barkeep stopped to wipe her mouth. The street smelled of urine and rotting vegetables. Hanna took a step forward, her muscles tensing as she prepared to follow.

"Are you mad?" Lucas whispered.

"Please," Hanna said, navigating her way past a broken bottle. "The barkeep might have seen Margaret and known the man who accompanied her."

The hag smiled, revealing blackened stumps of teeth. "What 'ave we here, a fine man and his slapper."

Lucas's eyes hardened, but Hanna squeezed his arm.

"Yes, we would like a drink," she said. "May we enter?"

The barkeep laughed. "No need to be polite round 'ere, girl. This is Old Sydney Town, where the next fool you meet could stab you in the back."

Lucas looked nervously over his shoulder. The woman beckoned them toward a stairwell leading down to a cellar. "Come in. Me name's Pigeon-Toed Sal."

Walking down, Hanna covered her mouth and nose. The repulsive combination of odors included sweat, urine, goat dung, and stale beer. Her heart pounded as she forced one foot in front of the other. When her eyes adjusted to the darkness, Hanna saw men in soiled coveralls sitting on stools around the bar.

From their sun-browned skin and wiry muscles, they looked like sea captains, dockworkers, and miners. They stared at Hanna, wetting their lips and stroking their beards. Turning to the crack of light seeping under the door from the street above, Hanna wondered how quickly she could run up the stairs.

"Fine lass you got there," said a ruddy-faced man with chipped teeth, his fingernails embedded with dirt. "How much?"

Lucas made a noise like a growl. "She's not for sale."

Pigeon-Toed Sal waddled behind the bar and poured beer into a sullied mug, taking her time. Passing it across the bar to Lucas, Sal didn't seem to mind when the drink sloshed everywhere. Nor did she make an effort to clean it up.

"Ten cents," she said, her whiskery mouth sneering.

Hanna cleared her throat. "Excuse me, ma'am. Have you seen a girl by the name of Margaret O'Brien?"

Sal studied Hanna with her birdlike eyes. "It don't ring a bell."

Hanna lifted her skirt as she climbed onto the barstool. Bits of wet sawdust clung to the hem of her dirndl. "She's a girl of nineteen. She has long red hair and a comely face. She wears a brown dress. Please?"

A rail-thin man leaned forward on his elbows. The whites of his eyes shone a sickly yellow. "I seen the lass. Real pretty like. Seen her yesterday."

"You did? Pray, tell me where."

He stroked his chin. "What're you gonna give me if I tell you?"

"He's lying," Lucas whispered. "He wants money."

"Please," Hanna said. "I'm frightened for her."

The miscreants around the bar chuckled. A fat sailor leered at Hanna. "Your grovelin' won't get you far, sweet cheeks. But I like the look of those cat's heads."

He stared at her breasts like they were juicy peaches.

Hanna's face burned.

Jumping to his feet, Lucas knocked over his barstool. "Enough!"

Every man in the room stood up. One pulled a knife from his pocket, while another held a wooden club, ready to bludgeon someone to death. Hanna sucked in her breath, her muscles tensing in readiness for a fight.

"Oy! Settle down," Pigeon-Toed Sal bellowed. "It's not yet noon. Put yer weapons away or I'll throw ye out on the street. And shut your bone boxes. Have more drink, you idiots."

The men grumbled at one another, then appeared to relax.

Sal poured a round of beers and vile-smelling whiskey, passing the oily glasses to her patrons. "On the house. Drink up, you cheap bastards."

Hanna's body shook as if with fever—such was her desire to run.

Pigeon-Toed Sal looked long and hard at Lucas. "You 'aven't touched your ale, and you don't want to hurt me feelings. Bottoms up."

Lucas met Hanna's eyes. Despite the fear etched on his

face, he picked up the mug and raised it slowly to his lips. The faint smell of something chemical wafted toward Hanna. The free drinks for the others . . .

Sal hoped to catch a much bigger fish. With a quick swipe of her arm, Hanna knocked the mug from Lucas's hands. It clattered against the wooden bar, beer spilling everywhere as it toppled toward the sawdust-covered ground.

Hanna wiped her hands on her dress and smiled at Sal. "Forgive me. I am so clumsy—"

Sal's eyes narrowed. "Well, ain't you a smart little trollop." She reached across the bar and wrapped her thick fingers around Hanna's wrist like a shackle.

"Let go!" Hanna yelled, tugging to break free.

"When he's knocked senseless," Sal spat, her eyes glinting darkly. "I'll see how much I can get for you. After each man here has had a ride, I'll take you upstairs for even more silver."

Lucas grabbed the fallen beer mug and swung it at Sal's head, knocking her sideways. Sal clutched her face. "I'll kill you, you swine!"

Pushing Hanna in front of him, Lucas sprinted toward the staircase leading to street level. Hanna stumbled, but caught herself, using the handrail to steady her grip. Shouts erupted behind them. Hanna glanced over her shoulder, seeing a roughened man had Lucas by the collar.

"I'll put you in your eternity box," the vagrant yelled, pulling Lucas downward.

"No!" Hanna screamed, raking her nails across the man's face.

Letting go of Lucas, he swiped for Hanna. "You cunt!"

"Give her an anointing!" cried the skinny man.

"Go," Lucas said, hoisting Hanna upward. "Go now."

Hanna reached the top step and pushed open the door. Lucas followed behind her, tumbling into the sunlight. Hanna's breath came in ragged gasps as she turned to see two men from the pub, quick on her heels. "Run faster!"

She and Lucas ran the length of Pacific Street, dodging vendors hawking their wares, newsboys, and street children. Even when the shouts faded into the distance, Hanna didn't dare turn around. She narrowly missed the wheels of a carriage, which could have crushed her foot. At the corner of Montgomery Avenue, Hanna doubled over, gulping in air. Her lungs burned.

"Are they gone?" Hanna asked, looking to Lucas.

Lucas held his sides. "I believe we lost them."

"Good," Hanna said. "I have bellows to mend."

Lucas smiled, his breathing equally labored. "I do as well." With a shaking hand, he smoothed his hair into place. "Are you all right? Blazes! That was terrifying."

"Yes, thank you. I am sorry we went inside."

Lucas waved a hand toward the saloons lining the street. "These pestholes of debauchery and corruption should all be shut down."

Hanna wiped her sweaty palms on her dress. "Now you see why I fear for Margaret."

"We will find her." Lucas reached for Hanna's hand and held it in his own. "We'll bring Margaret home."

Hanna held her breath, stunned by the warmth of Lucas's large hand keeping hers safe. She should not have brought Lucas to this befouled place. But what choice did she have? It would have been more dangerous to travel these streets alone. And Margaret needed her. She had no one else.

"This man in the bar," Hanna whispered. "Do you truly think he has seen Margaret?"

"I cannot say. It could be a mendacious report. If he has seen her, then others have too. We must keep looking."

Hanna's boots crunched along the gravel- and straw-covered road. Passing the melodeons frequented at night by criminals and society men alike, popular for their cancan shows, she saw gamblers, pimps, sailors, and miners, degenerates of every description. These hardened men looked as though they had not washed in months, and stank of sweat, whiskey, and tobacco.

In the doorway to a melodeon stood a man with a snow-white ruffled shirt, in the bosom of which sparkled an enormous cluster of diamonds. He also possessed a very large silky brown moustache, and wore the tightest lavender trousers Hanna had ever seen. His hair curled out in two poufs beneath his plug hat.

"Good day," he said, smiling. "My name is Happy Jack Harrington."

"Good day," Hanna answered, unable to hide the tremor in her voice. Glancing behind her, she checked to see if they were still being followed.

"Do you care to see a show?" Happy Jack asked, his blue

eyes sparkling. "We've singing and dancing, the most fun performance in town. Come inside!"

Hanna looked up at the building's marquee. It read "The Opera Comique."

"Are you the owner of this establishment?" Lucas asked.

Happy Jack smiled. "Why yes, I am! And trust me, we have far better shows than you'll find at the Bella Union. You'll have the grandest time."

"Please sir," Hanna said. "Have you seen a pretty red-haired girl? Her name is Margaret. She may have passed by here yesterday night."

Happy Jack chuckled. "My dear, I cannot keep note of every comely redhead that has walked through these doors."

Lucas reached into his pocket and removed a silver fifty-cent piece. "Perhaps this will jog your memory?"

"Well then," Happy Jack said, stroking his moustache. "There was a ginger girl who passed by last night. She appeared quite drunk. A man with a nasty scar across his cheek practically dragged her down the road."

Hanna gasped. "A scar?"

Happy Jack nodded, his face grave. "Long and raised, from his eye to the jaw. Quite the brute, I'm afraid."

Icy terror coursed through Hanna's veins. She turned to Lucas. "Recall the man from the pier with the knife? He said that . . ."

Lucas touched Hanna's arm, his eyes soft. "I know what he said."

Neither of them spoke the awful words aloud.

"Where have they gone?" Hanna asked.

Happy Jack pointed toward Montgomery Avenue. "Up that way. They turned onto Dupont Street, then I lost sight of them."

"And the girl appeared to be drugged?" Hanna asked, feeling sick to her stomach.

Happy Jack nodded, his gaze sympathetic. "Or very drunk. She did not have her wits about her, I'm afraid."

"Thank you," Lucas said. "If you see this girl again, please send word to the police commissioner immediately. Her name is Margaret O'Brien. I will make sure that you are compensated for your trouble."

Happy Jack tipped his plug hat. "Good luck to you both."

As Hanna walked with Lucas in the direction of Dupont Street, women ambled toward them, their fleshy curves barely contained by their corsets. Hanna gazed up at the three-story building next to Sullivan Alley. Men inside the dance hall guffawed and hollered. The sound of shattering glass pierced the air, causing her to jump.

"*Scheisse!*" she muttered, feeling like a skittish horse.

A girl Hanna's age with heavily rouged cheeks and kohl around her eyes darted at Lucas, tugging at the waist of his trousers. "Hello, handsome. Fancy a taste?"

"Miss," Lucas said, stepping backward. "Let go of me immediately."

She giggled, jiggling her breasts. "Oh, don't be shy now."

"Leave him be," Hanna said, stepping in front of Lucas.

"Don't act so fancy," the girl slurred, struggling to stand

straight. "You're no better than I am. You may well find yourself working at the Bull Run soon enough."

A small circle of waiter girls gathered around, their breath smelling of whiskey. What kind of establishment allowed the women to drink spirits? Looking upon their vacant eyes, Hanna did not wish to know what horrors they had been subjected to.

"This place is mad," Lucas whispered. He turned to the women, throwing up his hands. "Have you no shame? Where is your decency?"

A voluptuous brunette with a dead tooth shook her finger at him. "Don't tell me I ain't got no decency. I'm not a common whore."

"Right," a freckled girl piped up. "We're performers. Waitresses. Not slappers the likes you'll find in Madame Susan's house above the tavern on Dupont Street."

"Up there." The brunette waved her hand, pointing to a red clapboard building. "Seventy-five cents will get you a ride."

The freckled girl smiled at Lucas. "I'll give you one for a dollar."

"No, thank you," Lucas said, his cheeks reddening.

The girl puffed out her bottom lip. "I can do better'n you anyway."

"Wait!" Hanna said. "What type of girls work for Madame Susan?"

The freckled girl glared at Hanna, her collarbone jutting sharply beneath her bare shoulders. "The kind who ain't got nowhere else to go. Opium addicts, the lot." She shuddered. "God help 'em."

"Thank you," Hanna said.

"Do you think Margaret was taken there?" Lucas asked, pausing at the corner of Dupont Street and Sullivan Alley.

Hanna looked up at the building before her, painted red. Black curtains covered its windows, lending it an ominous feel. Only the tavern below had a clear view of the interior, where a barkeep polished glasses with a rag.

"Let us go inside," Hanna said to Lucas, leading him by the hand into the welcoming warmth of the bar. A tune carried from the piano, and cigar smoke hung in the air like a thick blue mist. Coughing, Hanna made her way toward the barkeep, her boots crunching the orange peels and peanut shells that littered the floor.

"Sir," she said. "I must speak with you."

When the man's eyes met hers, they were green as the sea and sunken deep, his appearance skeletal. Hanna shivered.

"Yes," he said, his voice soft. "How can I help you?"

"There's a man," Hanna started, her hands trembling. "With a long scar down the right side of his face. Was he here last night, with a red-haired woman?"

The bartender frowned. "I know of no such man."

Hanna looked past the bartender, for a crack in the wall that might lead to a door. How would one get upstairs from here? Men such as those in the Billy Goat watched her like dogs salivating for a scrap of meat. Every hair on Hanna's body stood at attention. But this green-eyed man was not telling the truth. She could feel it.

"Where you from, girl?" asked a vagrant smoking a porcelain pipe. His boil marks gave him the appearance of having been homeless.

"From Bavaria," Hanna answered, moving closer to Lucas.

He laughed. "Another immigrant, just what this city needs. Perhaps we should put you to work." He nodded at the bartender. "Jim, think you could use a barmaid? Look at the form of this one."

Hanna crossed her arms over her chest, shaking with anger. The scent of flat beer and cheap perfume had caused her head to spin. Already she had spent too much time here. The children were waiting for her at the inn.

"Let us go," Hanna said to Lucas.

"Are you sure?" he asked.

"Yes," Hanna said. "We can resume our search tomorrow."

As she turned to leave, Hanna heard a chair screech against the floorboards, while the man with the pipe stood up. As he made his way across the room, his breath sounded wet and ragged. He slapped a heavy hand on Lucas's shoulder.

Hanna spun around, glaring at the man's red, lumpy face. "I will not work for you. Lay your hands off him!"

The pustule-covered man grinned at Lucas, his gums and teeth blackened by tobacco. "She is a feisty one. You'll have to tame her."

Lucas swatted the man's hand away. "State your business!"

The man wet his lips and stared at Hanna. "I overheard you, girl. And I know who you're looking for. The man with the scar."

Hanna held her breath, praying for a crumb of information.

The vagrant turned his palm upward, his fingers fat like sausages. "Give me a dollar."

Hanna's skin crawled as if cockroaches burrowed beneath her dress. Everyone wanted money, and yet no one could be trusted.

Lucas reached into his waistcoat for his coin purse, his eyes on Hanna.

"Don't," Hanna said, shaking her head. "It's far too much."

The boil-faced man leaned in close, his breath sour on her cheek. "I ain't lying. I know him."

"His name," Lucas said, retrieving a dollar. "And step away from her, you brute."

The man snatched the money from Lucas's hand with his thick fingers. "Sam O'Grady. Folks here in Devil's Acre know him well."

"Thank you," Lucas said, placing a hand on Hanna's shoulder.

"I wouldn't cross him if I was you," the man replied. "Best to keep away."

Hanna's stomach growled. She'd hardly eaten and walked quite far. Martin, Hans, and Katja sat in the boardinghouse, awaiting her return. It was now past noon, and she had promised not to take long. Her search for Margaret would have to wait.

"Hanna, are you all right?" Lucas asked, slipping his arm around her waist to support her. "You look pale."

"Perhaps I should take a drink," she said, warming at his closeness.

"One soda water with bitters," Lucas said to the bartender. Turning to Hanna, Lucas frowned, his face creased with worry. "I'll call us a carriage. We've walked quite a ways. And this dreadful place has taken its toll on you, I fear. It is no place for a lady."

Though the soda water soothed her parched throat, Hanna felt overcome with dizziness. Snapping his fingers, Lucas hailed a carriage driver.

On the bumpy ride, the rhythmic clopping of the horse's hooves lulled Hanna to sleep. She slumped against Lucas's shoulder, floating in and out of consciousness. Visions of Margaret appeared before her, and then the brutish face of her father, his features contorted with rage. Perhaps he walked the streets now, looking for her.

"Hanna," Lucas whispered. "Are you awake?"

She opened her eyes. The stately hotels and gas lamps of Montgomery Street allowed her to get her bearings.

"Where shall I take you?" Lucas asked.

Hanna pointed to the right. "I'm lodging at a boardinghouse on Minna Street."

Lucas frowned at the waste thrown into the street and the scraggly dogs running about, looking for scraps of meat. "All right then."

Arriving in front of Tomkinson's livery and stable, the carriage slowed to a halt. A man sprawled out in the dirt in front of the boardinghouse, a whiskey bottle in hand. Hanna shuddered, smelling his stench even from yards away.

"Thank you," she said, smiling at Lucas. "For everything."

"You're welcome," Lucas said, tipping his hat.

Climbing down from the carriage, Hanna crossed the dirt road, making her way toward the entrance of the inn. But as she got closer, the drunk awoke, sitting up and rubbing his matted hair. With his eyes fixed on Hanna, he licked his lips.

"Oy!" he called out. "Aren't you a bushel bubby? With those cupid's kettledrums, you could let me into cock alley, I'd say."

Hanna recoiled, sucking in her breath. Before she could turn around, she felt Lucas's hand on her arm, guiding her away from the lecherous prick.

"Forgive me," Lucas said, looking over his shoulder. "I should not have brought you here. Surely you cannot stay there? Such places are not safe."

Hanna sighed. "I am aware of that, but I have nowhere else to go."

"Have you no other family?" Lucas asked. "Aunts, uncles?"

"They are in the old country," Hanna said. "I am on my own."

Lucas held her gaze. "It is a difficult life you lead. More and more, I see that now."

The blue of his eyes seemed to intensify. It was not pity, but determination that Hanna saw in his expression.

"Come with me," Lucas said. "My home is quite large. I shall invite you and your siblings as my guests. You may stay the night."

Hanna let out a deep breath. What would Lucas's family think if he took in four immigrants? She could not fathom such hospitality. And yet, to remove Martin, Hans, and Katja from the dangers of the inn . . .

Hanna shook her head. "It is not proper."

Lucas took her hand. "Please, accept my offer."

His eyes, blue as a cloudless sky, told Hanna he meant his words. Wherever Lucas lived, it would be far removed from Father, drunken vigilantes, and the corruption of Devil's Acre. Hanna thought of her young siblings, alone in the horrid inn.

"All right," she said. "We will come with you. But only for tonight."

Lucas smiled. "I am glad you will accompany me. I shall introduce you to my parents. Please, do not take offense at how they might react. I don't often invite Prussian families for tea. You understand."

Hanna could not bring herself to laugh at the joke. Deep in her belly, she had a horrible feeling about how poorly she and her family would be received. Turning to look behind her, Hanna imagined she saw Margaret standing in the shadows.

Chapter 11

Sarah, *Present Day*

I buried my nose in the crook of my elbow, light-headed from the paint fumes trapped in the small apartment. Pushing open a window, I breathed in a gulp of fresh air. My thesis deadline loomed before me like a dead end.

I stared out at the twilit streets. Past Grant Avenue, the Zoetrope Building stood before the Transamerica Pyramid. I liked the juxtaposition of San Francisco's most famous skyscraper with the Zoetrope's aged green copper spires, two centuries standing side by side. Even Columbus Avenue was visible from here.

In the narrow alley below, two guys leaned against the wall, smoking cigarettes. I got the amused feeling I had as a child when I used to spy on my neighbors. Whoever snagged this North Beach apartment wouldn't be at a loss for people watching.

Taking one last look, I tried to picture a turn-of-the-century brothel with undergarments flung haphazardly across cots and perfume bottles sitting on the vanity. But the room looked like an ordinary city apartment. Soon it would be filled with Ikea furniture and twentysomethings drinking bottles of cheap wine.

I sighed, wondering what, exactly, I had hoped to find here. It had been nice of Ed to let me inside, but I hadn't found any information to use for my article. Perhaps the descendant of the original owner, Anna Heinrich, would have more insight into the murder of the prostitute that had occurred in 1876.

Pulling my phone from my purse, I composed a quick email, explaining my research and asking Anna Heinrich if she'd be willing to meet with me. The original photographs and newspaper clippings that Ed had mentioned sounded fascinating, and I hoped that she had kept them.

I checked my watch. The game had just started. If I caught an Uber now, I could be at AT&T Park in twenty minutes.

As the Uber wove through traffic, I looked out at the houseboats and high-rise condos lining the waterfront at Mission Bay. This used to be where Long Bridge began; a pedestrian walkway that Hannelore and Margaret might have used.

Beneath the dominating glass skyscrapers, a working-class neighborhood had once thrived. Strangely enough, a lone blacksmith shop still stood on Folsom Street near First Street, a squat building from 1906, tucked in between the apartment towers. I admired the owner's stubborn loyalty to tradition.

"Thanks," I called to the Uber driver, hopping out in front

of the baseball park. As I went through the Public House entrance, my mouth watered at the scent of bratwurst and garlic fries. I pulled my ticket from my pocket, looking at my seat number. From my knowledge of the park, it was somewhere behind home plate.

I made my way through the crowded restaurant and toward the entrance to section 115 of the stadium. An usher directed me to the Field Club, a fenced-off area with a private bar. I felt the chilly ocean breeze on my face, carrying with it the scent of wet fog and sea brine.

Zipping my down jacket up to my chin, I welcomed its warmth. It was black, and I'd worn an orange scarf to show my team colors, along with my Giants baseball cap. My heart went out to the tourists who didn't know how to layer, huddled together shivering and wishing they hadn't worn shorts in May.

Pardoning myself as I squeezed past a row of people, I beamed, recognizing Hunter with his ball cap slung low over his eyes. Completely transfixed by the game, he mouthed instructions to Buster Posey, as if the catcher could hear him. Who knows, maybe he could? We were right behind the batting cage.

I put my hand on Hunter's shoulder. His head snapped around, then his eyes crinkled at the corners as he smiled. "Babe! You made it!" He was on his feet, enveloping me in a bear hug that made me feel like I was his favorite person in the world.

Throwing my arms around his waist, I breathed in the piney scent of his cologne. "Did I miss much? Are we winning?"

Hunter hugged me tighter. "Fourth inning. We're up by two. Man, you missed an epic home run by Pence! But don't worry, he'll score another."

"How do you know that?"

"Because," Hunter said, kissing my forehead, "now I've got my lucky charm by my side."

"You're so cheesy," I teased, gazing up at him. But secretly I loved how affectionate Hunter was with me in public. His kindness and his honesty made me want to open myself up more, even though it hurt.

As we sipped bottles of Anchor Steam, munched on sandwiches from Crazy Crab'z, and snuggled against each other, I relaxed. My emerald ring sparkled under the stadium lights, and I gazed into the stone as if into a crystal ball. Meeting Hunter had changed the course of my life for the better. Who would I have been without him?

"Whoo!" the crowd roared, the sound puncturing my thoughts. "It's another homer!" Hunter yelled, tugging me to my feet. My beer sloshed onto my sneakers, but I didn't care. I whooped and hollered along with my husband and the other bundled-up fans, our cheeks flushed from the wind, watching as Posey rounded the bases.

Honestly, I didn't even care if the Giants won or lost. What mattered was being here, in this moment, with the man I'd chosen to spend my life with. It had been silly of me to worry that Hunter would be angry with me for no longer working on my novel. He trusted me and understood my heart was with this new story—the story of Hannelore and Margaret. In spite of his parents' strange reaction, at least I had my husband's support.

"Did you see that?" Hunter said, his hazel eyes sparkling like a kid's on Christmas. "We're up another run!"

"I love you," I said, throwing my arms around him.

Hunter pressed his nose against mine. "And I love you more each day."

For once, the crowd didn't cause my panic to rise. Right there in the midst of thousands, I kissed Hunter as if we were the only two people in the world.

"Learn anything helpful from visiting that apartment yesterday?" Jen asked, slipping into her leather jacket. Red blotches bloomed on her cheeks, and she seemed distracted, like something wasn't quite right.

"Nope," I said, looking around my former magazine office with a pang of nostalgia. A few employees typed away at their MacBooks while the familiar hum of the copy machine buzzed in the distance. The building was nearly empty now, past six P.M.. Normally Jen would be chatting my ear off, complaining about work or gushing about Mark, the guy she was dating, but tonight she was surprisingly quiet.

My eyes settled on my former desk, now occupied by someone else.

"You miss being a reporter, don't you?" Jen said. Her smile didn't reach her eyes.

"I do," I said, looking around the room. "I told Hunter I'm not working on my novel anymore. Narrative nonfiction is where my heart is. I emailed a woman whose family owned the Tavern back in the 1800s. Hopefully she'll have a lead."

A deep voice boomed down the corridor, causing Jen to flinch.

"I'm done with this whole East Bay versus San Francisco debate," the voice said, footsteps coming closer. "Oakland has no culture. I mean, come *on*."

I whipped my head around. A blond man, over six feet tall, ran a hand through his tousled hair as he strode into the room on long legs. He wore expensive-looking dark jeans, leather shoes, and a checkered button-down shirt.

My skin prickled with an instant dislike. His blue eyes met mine and he raised an eyebrow, as if in recognition, though we'd never met before. Then a smile spread across his face, showing off his huge white teeth. He exuded confidence, like someone who'd often been told he was handsome. Luckily, I wasn't into overgrown frat boys.

"Well, hello," he said, extending a giant hand. "You must be the infamous Sarah Havensworth. You're just as pretty as your photo."

My cheeks prickled. "Thanks. And you are?"

He squeezed my hand a little too tightly. "James Bradley. Editor in chief. I've read a few of your pieces. Very . . . how do I put this? Sensational."

"Excuse me?"

James dropped his hand and then placed it heavily on Jen's shoulder. She recoiled, as if a tarantula had touched her.

"We don't focus on the poor prostitutes of Chinatown or the elderly Mexican residents being pushed out of their homes anymore." James grinned at Jen. "I'm afraid Ms. Chang here has tried taking a page out of your book. She's always pitching me some crazy feminist story idea. But she'll be covering Disrupt SF in September."

"The tech conference?" I asked, my eyes narrowing. "But that's not Jen's area of interest."

"It is now," James said, locking his gaze on mine. "Our content needs to be pushing the needle. We live in a cutting-edge city. I want articles on tech and on hot start-ups. We're done with San Francisco history fluff pieces."

I clenched my hands into fists, my nails biting into my palm. Jen looked like she was about to cry. Who the hell did this guy think he was?

"It's not fluff," I said, wrestling down my anger. "I think our city's past is as important as its future."

"A nice notion," James said, releasing his grip from Jen's shoulder. "But now that I'm in charge, *Pulse of the City* is moving forward, not backward." He sneered at me. "Jen tells me you're working on a novel. You know, less than one percent of books get traditionally published. Do you have an agent?"

"Not yet," I said, glowering at him.

"Good luck," he replied, with a taunting look in his eye. "I've got to run, but you girls have fun tonight. It was a pleasure meeting you, Sarah."

I clenched my jaw as he walked away. Jen had warned me

James was difficult to work with, but I hadn't been prepared for *this*.

"What a prick," I muttered under my breath.

Jen's lip began to tremble.

"What's wrong?" I asked, taking Jen's hand. The office was empty now, quiet except for the sob that escaped Jen's mouth. Her shoulders shook, and tears streamed down her cheeks. I pulled her into a hug, but her eyes darted to the door where James had exited, and she quickly wiped her cheeks with her jacket sleeve.

"It's bad, Sarah."

"What is it?" I asked, my voice dropping to a whisper. "Is it James?"

She nodded. "Today he told me that all his ex-girlfriends are Asian, and how I look like the one he never got over. Except that I'm *hotter* than she was."

I wrinkled my nose. "*What?* That's totally inappropriate."

"I know. It made me so angry. I'm not some submissive China doll he can boss around, here to cater to his yellow fever. I feel really uncomfortable around him."

I swallowed. "Did he say anything else?"

Jen was silent. Then she exhaled. Freeing herself from my hug, she looked at me with hurt in her eyes.

"He told me that he only dates Asians because we fuck better than other women."

"That's disgusting," I said, heat rushing to my head. "Jen, this isn't okay. You have to report him to HR. Have you told anyone?"

She shook her head. "Only you. Besides, we were alone in the office when he said it, so no one else heard him."

"It's harassment," I said, my voice rising. In the five minutes I'd spent with James, he'd commented on my looks, belittled my writing, and treated me in an incredibly demeaning way. I could only imagine how bad things would get for Jen . . . perhaps even dangerous, if she didn't do anything. My stomach curdled.

"I don't want to be alone with him," Jen said, pulling her jacket more tightly around her. "I know I should quit and interview at another magazine, but I'm in the middle of moving, and I can't risk losing my job right now."

"You won't lose it," I said. "You're telling the truth. I can go with you when you report him. I was here to witness his behavior."

Another tear trickled down Jen's cheek. "It hurts, you know? Asian women are practically invisible in the media and in pop culture, and yet there's this ridiculous stereotype that we're better in bed than other women."

"Report him," I said loudly, just as James appeared around the corner.

Jen sucked in her breath and quickly wiped her tear-stained cheeks. My heart started to beat faster. Had he heard us?

"Hey, ladies," James said, his cold eyes meeting mine. "I hope I'm not interrupting anything. I forgot the keys to my Lexus."

We sat in silence while James walked over to his desk. His fingers curled around his key fob, a menacing fist.

He looked at me, breaking into a charming smile. "Gosh, I'm so forgetful. Anyways, I didn't mean to make the outlook appear grim when I talked about the slim chances of getting an agent. I'm sure you'll get one soon."

His eyes twinkled, and he gave a friendly wave. "See you."

My heart sunk into the pit of my stomach. James had turned on his nice-guy charm with the flip of a switch. There was no doubt he would contest any charges Jen brought against him. But underneath his handsome exterior, I could sense something dark lurking there. And I wouldn't rest until I knew that Jen was safe.

Chapter 12

Hanna, *1876*

The white mansion loomed before Hanna like something out of a storybook. As she suspected, it perched high on a hill overlooking the city. The spire reminded Hanna of castles she had seen in Bavaria. Nearly four stories tall, it appeared to belong to nobility. How would it feel to have so much land, like a king looking down on his kingdom?

"Is it a castle?" Katja asked.

"Are you a prince?" Hans turned to Lucas and bounced on the carriage seat, barely able to contain his excitement.

Lucas chuckled. "No, children. It's not a castle and I am not a prince."

Katja's bottom lip protruded.

"Or maybe he only pretends he is not a prince," Hanna said with a wink.

Katja smiled at Lucas. "You a prince."

Even Martin's lips tugged into a smile, though Hanna could tell from his furrowed brow that he was as nervous as she. The carriage came to a halt and the horses whinnied, swishing their long black tails.

"Here," Lucas said to Katja. "Let me help you down."

Katja squealed in delight as Lucas lifted her from the carriage before setting her gently on the ground. At first the children had been hesitant when the strange man in a top hat arrived at the boardinghouse. But now they had warmed to Lucas, especially after he'd produced coins from behind Hans's and Katja's ears—coins he let them keep.

Martin stepped down from the carriage and dusted off his dirty trousers. Hanna had done her best to mend the holes. But they were poor and it showed.

"Let's go, shall we?" Lucas asked.

Following Lucas up the long staircase leading to the grand entrance, Hanna's stomach tightened. Lucas rapped his knuckles on the wood. Hanna stood behind him, admiring the beautiful bay windows, very fashionable for a modern home.

A girl about Hanna's age opened the door. She wore a maid's uniform and tucked her dark hair beneath a white cap. When her eyes met Hanna's, the maid frowned.

"Hello, Frances," Lucas said, stepping inside the foyer. He gestured to Hanna. "This is Miss Hannelore Schaeffer. And these are her siblings, Martin, Hans, and Katja."

"Good day," Frances said, dropping into a curtsy.

"Good day," Hanna replied, bowing her head. Perhaps she should have curtsied as well. Martin removed his tattered cap and stared at the interior of the house. Light spilled in from the windows onto the floor of the parlor. The wood had such rich and varied colors that it reminded Hanna of a rainbow trout Martin had caught while fishing.

Frances shut the door, eyeing Hanna suspiciously.

Removing his hat, Lucas spoke. "Frances, could you please fetch Mother and Father? Inform them we have guests. Also, kindly ask Gertrude to run a hot bath and to ready two of the rooms. Our guests shall be staying the night."

Frances's dark eyes grew to the size of saucers. Hanna half expected her to protest, but Frances composed herself. "Yes, sir."

Hans ran into the sitting room and trailed his fingers along the velvet cushion of an upholstered gentleman's chair.

"Feel it, Hanna!" he cried. "It's soft like a kitty cat."

"Hans, no!" Hanna admonished, darting over and holding his tiny, dirt-caked hands in hers. "It's not our home. We cannot touch the nice things."

Lucas looked at Hanna with a smile. "Nonsense. I wish for you to feel welcome here. You may touch whatever you like." He bent down to eye level with Hans. "I broke a very nice vase once. I was playing stickball in the sitting room."

Hans giggled, covering his mouth.

Lucas whispered, "I was a boy too. And sometimes I behaved poorly. If you do something naughty, I won't tell." He ruffled Hans's hair, and a surge of warmth shot through Hanna, as if she stood in a pool of sunlight.

Footsteps echoed off the walls in the foyer. Hanna turned

just in time to see figures emerge on the level above. A tall man with graying hair descended the grand staircase, his woolen waistcoat and trousers snug against his portly frame. Behind him trailed a woman with a large sapphire brooch fastened at her neck, bedecked in a floor-length royal blue gown. Even at her age, she remained quite beautiful.

Hanna looked down at the floor, too petrified to speak. When she looked up again, she saw a lovely blonde, who wore an exquisite pink gown with a low bodice and three-quarter-length sleeves. The blond woman appeared to be slightly younger than Lucas. Behind her came Frances, wearing an expression as glum as ever.

Standing straight as a pole, Hanna hoped to do a proper curtsy. The man, whom she presumed to be Lucas's father, peered at her over his spectacles. Under the light of the gas lamps, his gray eyes glinted. Bushy sideburns covered most of his face, but Hanna discerned a frown. He looked at her as if she were a specimen in the zoo.

The patriarch cleared his throat. "Son, what have we here?"

When his stern gaze passed over Martin, Hans, and Katja, they cowered in the corner like frightened mice.

Mr. Havensworth shook his head. "Lucas, you know my policy that our staff shall not bring their children to our home. They detract from one's work ethic." He rubbed his head, turning to his wife. "Elizabeth, have you acquired a new maid?"

Lucas's mother pursed her lips. "No, indeed I have not."

Hanna's cheeks burned. When she looked at Lucas, his face had also reddened, but he held his jaw firm.

Before Lucas could speak, Mrs. Havensworth glared at Frances, as if the maid had conspired to bring Hanna inside. "Did you know about this?"

Frances shook her head. "No, ma'am. First I heard of it."

Lucas let out a deep breath. "Mother. The woman before you is not a servant. She is a friend of mine, Miss Hannelore Schaeffer. I ask that you please allow her to stay the night in one of our guest bedrooms."

Mr. Havensworth's mouth fell open, and Mrs. Havensworth's face went completely white. Hanna wished to slip out the door, as if she had never been seen.

Taking advantage of the silence, Lucas nodded at Hanna. "These are my parents, Mr. William Havensworth and Mrs. Elizabeth Havensworth."

Hanna curtsied as she had seen Frances do. "Pleased to meet you."

Mrs. Elizabeth gasped, as if she might faint. Mr. Havensworth made a noise like he had choked on a piece of mutton. He glared at Hanna. "This woman brings her children into our home? Is she unmarried? Son, I forbid it. This is unacceptable!"

"They are not my children, sir," Hanna stammered. "They are my younger siblings. And no, I am not yet married, sir."

A little bit of color returned to Mrs. Havensworth's cheeks. The young blonde, who had been standing behind her parents, stepped forward. She smiled at Hanna and dropped into a curtsy. "Hello," she said, standing again. "I am Mrs. Georgina Havensworth Chapman. It is very nice to meet you, Hannelore."

Georgina's small act of kindness felt like a welcome ray of sunshine. "Pleased to meet you," Hanna said, finding her voice. She lifted the hem of her skirt and leaned forward, while bending her knees, a poor imitation of what Georgina had done.

Lucas grinned. "Georgina is my younger sister. She lives here with her husband, Charles, and their small children, Annabelle and Marcus."

Georgina kneeled down, smiling at Katja and Hans. "Why hello, dears! My own son and daughter are about your age. What are your names?"

Hans stared dumbly at Georgina. Katja, however, smiled at her. "My name's Katja. I am two. You very pretty."

Georgina laughed, patting Katja on the head. "What a darling girl."

Hanna placed a hand on Hans's shoulder to help him feel more at ease. "This is my brother Hans," Hanna said. "He is four." She nodded to the corner. "And that is my brother Martin. He is twelve."

Martin held his cap so tightly his knuckles had gone white. Hanna ached to reach for his hand. Like her, Martin knew they had no place in this home.

Lucas cleared his throat. "These children have lost their parents. I beg of you to let them spend the night. They have nowhere else to go."

"Poor dears!" Georgina cooed, rising to her feet.

Mr. Havensworth turned to Lucas. "Son, that is unfortunate. However, we're not running an almshouse. I fear this family will have to find elsewhere to stay."

Hanna felt as numb as if she had been standing barefoot in the snow. Bending down to eye level with Hans and Katja, she whispered, "Go play outside." Without missing a beat, Frances opened the door. Hans took Katja's hand, and they ran into the garden. Martin shrunk into the shadows, like a boy hoping to vanish.

"Father," Lucas said, his voice steady. "As I stated before, Miss Hannelore Schaeffer is a friend. She has nowhere else to go. I have welcomed her here as my guest, and I would appreciate your cooperation."

While Hanna admired Lucas's belief that the world was an inherently good place—a place where she would be welcome—she did not share it. There would be more nights in the boardinghouse above the livery, and perhaps nights on the streets. She shuddered, thinking of the perils of homelessness.

Georgina placed her delicate white hands on her father's coat sleeve. "Papa," Georgina said, her deep blue eyes filled with determination. "Have you no compassion? These children require a place to stay. It is our duty as Christian people to help those less fortunate than we are. Is that not what we are taught in church?"

Mr. Havensworth studied his daughter's face. The deep frown lines around his mouth drew downward. "My dear, we cannot . . ."

Hans and Katja pushed open the front door. Breathing so heavily he could barely speak, Hans ran to Hanna, grabbing the hem of her skirt. "There's a robin outside! And a squirrel too! Hanna, you must come see him. He has a big tail!"

Mr. Havensworth's expression softened. He turned to Georgina and sighed. "When will I ever learn to say no to you?"

"Thank you, Papa!" Georgina cried, grabbing hold of his hand.

Mr. Havensworth looked at Hanna. "Although my daughter has quite silly notions at times, I suppose it would not be Christian of us if we were to turn you away."

Hanna let out the breath she didn't realize she'd been holding. "Thank you. You are too kind."

Perhaps Lucas's family was Catholic like Margaret, or some other type of Christian faith. That was of no importance to Hanna. All that mattered was she and her family had a place to stay the night—a true blessing indeed.

"All right. That's settled then," Georgina said with a smile. "I'll have Gertrude run Hans and Katja a hot bath. When they're ready I shall introduce them to my little Annabelle and Marcus. How it shall delight my children to have friends to play with."

Georgina turned to Katja. "Would you like to get cleaned up?"

Katja shook her head. "When I take a bath I stand in the cooking pot and Hanna washes me with the dishcloth. It's cold and scratchy."

Hanna stroked her sister's hair, though her cheeks stung at the child's admission of their poverty. "It's all right, little deer. Go with the nice lady. Hans, you go too."

A man in dirty coveralls appeared in the foyer, removing his hat as he knocked once on the open door. Hanna recognized him as the Havensworths' carriage driver from the dark mark on his cheek. He had taken Robert into town on the Sunday Lucas and Hanna had walked the length of Long Bridge with Margaret.

"Pardon me, sir," he said. "But the carriage wheel is broke. It came right off. I been hammerin' at it tryin' to set it right, but it don't want to go back."

"Well, that won't do, Clive," Mr. Havensworth replied. "I've a meeting at the Merchants Exchange that I am to attend after supper."

Clive rubbed his head. "I'd call on Zeke over at the livery and stable, but his lady took sick, so he ain't working today."

Martin looked up, his eyes brightening. "I can fix it."

Mr. Havensworth turned to Martin. "But you're not more than thirteen."

"I am twelve, sir," Martin said. "And I've worked the past four years with my father as a blacksmith."

Though Hanna wished Martin were in school, she felt a small swell of pride. For his age, her brother was strong. He could handle a hot iron with care and precision.

"Well then." Mr. Havensworth lifted one bushy eyebrow. "I suppose you can make a go at mending the carriage wheel. But please don't damage it further."

"Yes, sir. Thank you, sir."

"Clive here will show you to the stable."

Clive beckoned Martin. "Come wiv me, lad."

Martin followed Clive out the door into the garden, his shoulders relaxing as he made his way toward more familiar surroundings.

"Hanna," Lucas said, "Frances here will show you to your room upstairs. There will be a hot bath waiting. I shall see you for supper."

"Thank you," Hanna said, meeting his eyes, which sparkled like deep blue pools. She yearned to hold his hands in hers, which she knew to be soft and not calloused, so different from the hands she'd seen of longshoremen, bricklayers, and miners.

Following Frances up the wooden staircase and down a long hallway, Hanna passed several doors leading to different rooms. Gas lamps illuminated the dim corridor, and crystal chandeliers twinkled overhead. She could not help herself from staring.

"You look surprised," Frances said.

"I've never seen lights like this before," Hanna murmured.

Frances smiled wryly. "Then I suppose you don't have running water in your home neither."

"No," Hanna said.

"Well then," Frances answered. "Enjoy it while you can."

The cryptic comment sent a shiver down Hanna's spine. True, she could not stay here forever, and believing in such fantasies would be foolish.

Frances turned down the hall, pointing to a room on the left. "In here," she said. "Gertrude will help you."

"Thank you," Hanna replied, stepping inside. Rich peach drapes matched the light pink wallpaper. A few framed watercolors of lilies hung on the walls. Perhaps Georgina had painted them, for Lucas had mentioned his sister's art lessons.

A pleasantly round woman appeared from the washroom.

"Hello, dear," she said, her rosy cheeks lending her a kind appearance. "I'm Gertrude."

"Hello," Hanna answered, her eyes skimming the low dressing bureau, washstand, easy chair, and chaise longue. This chamber held more furniture than Father's entire home. "I am Hannelore, but you may call me Hanna."

Gertrude looked Hanna over. "Let's get you out of those clothes."

Slowly, Hanna unbuttoned her dirndl, hunching her shoulders and turning away so Gertrude would not see her naked flesh. Hanna's sides ached when she lifted her arms above her head, slipping out of her chemise.

When Gertrude noticed the purplish bruises that bloomed on Hanna's rib cage, she covered her mouth. "Oh, my word. You poor dear."

The lashes on Hanna's back from Father's belt buckle hurt, especially with the rush of cold air. Hanna shivered, wishing to cover herself.

Gertrude clucked her tongue like a protective mother hen. "Come with me," she said, leading Hanna into an adjacent room. A large basin sat in the center, filled to the brim with steaming water. Odd metal pipes connected the bath to the wall. "Go on, step in," Gertrude said. "It's only a tub. Don't be afraid."

Hanna slowly lowered herself into the soapy water, sucking air in through her teeth. The lacerations on her back stung. But within a few moments the pain subsided and the hot water wrapped Hanna up like a blanket. She moaned in pleasure.

"We're going to give you a proper clean," Gertrude said, taking a sponge from a hook on the wall. "Go on. Scrub yourself with this."

Hanna did as she was told, scrubbing her arms, her chest, and her legs. The filth of Old Sydney Town sloughed off Hanna's body, dirt from years of living amongst the evils and sin of the Barbary Coast. Soon after, the water took on a muddy hue.

A lump rose in Hanna's throat when her thoughts turned to Margaret. Was she trapped in a dark brothel, surrounded by low women and vile men? Nearly a whole day had passed since Margaret had disappeared. Was she . . . Hanna couldn't even think it.

Gertrude turned a silver knob, and water poured from the tap into the bath. "Ha!" Hanna exclaimed, sticking her hands beneath the stream. "How is it possible?"

"Modern plumbing," Gertrude said, rubbing soap into Hanna's scalp. Her strong fingers sent shivers of pleasure down Hanna's spine. "Magic, ain't it?"

Gertrude drained the dirty water, filled the basin again, and let Hanna soak in the tub for what felt like a very long time. When Hanna's fingertips had wrinkled like prunes, Gertrude helped her out and toweled her off, the rough cloth invigorating Hanna's skin. Careful to avoid the bruises and cuts, Gertrude managed to be gentle.

"Turkish towels," Gertrude said. "Good for the health. I'm going to shine you up like a copper teakettle."

Hanna's eyes welled with tears. Gertrude's cool hands reminded Hanna of her mother's, and the way Mother used to braid her hair while she hummed.

"It's all right, dear," Gertrude said, hanging the towel back on the hook. "Follow me, let's get you dressed." She smiled, opening a wooden bureau. "You see here? Miss Georgina has generously lent you a few gowns."

"Oh!" Hanna put her hand to her chest. "She needn't have. I will wear my dirndl."

Gertrude shook her head. "I've already put that in the washbasin for a good scrubbing. When you have it back it will be good as new."

Once again, Hanna's cheeks prickled with heat as she stood stark naked, feeling useless while Gertrude puttered about. Tugging open a drawer, Gertrude coughed as a puff of lilac powder filled the room. She reached inside, removing a handful of frilly undergarments. "Here," she said, handing Hanna a pair of lace-trimmed bloomers. "You can put these on yourself. I'll help you into the crinolines and the corset."

As Hanna tugged the chemise over her breasts, she noted how the lace sleeves matched the trim of the drawers. Gertrude wrapped the corset around Hanna's middle and tugged the ties tight, expelling Hanna's breath from her lungs. Next Gertrude lifted a crinoline around her, encircling her waist like a birdcage.

Made from the same whalebone as her corset, it felt surprisingly heavy. While Hanna struggled to get used to the weight, Gertrude pulled an evening gown from the bureau. It was the shade of the ocean at midnight, the silk shimmering under the lights. Hanna covered her mouth, taking in the exquisite knife pleating along the bodice. She knew the difficulty of those stitches, her fingers thick and calloused from sewing them.

"What a beautiful dress," Hanna murmured, touching the collar trimmed with black lace. She drew back her hand, admiring the tiers of pleats like a wedding cake and a bustle big as a hot air balloon. Hanna had seen lovely dresses in the tailor shop before, but none quite as magnificent as this one. She simply stared, unable to move.

Gertrude chuckled. "The dress won't bite you, child. Now, raise your arms."

Tugging the dress over Hanna's head, Gertrude clucked happily. "Fits like it was made for you, don't it?" Then Gertrude bent down to pull the yards of fabric over the hoopskirt. Hanna stood there like a doll. It was necessary to keep a maid just to coax oneself into the contraption.

"Thank you," Hanna said, smiling. "I do not think I could have put it on myself."

"Oh no, dear," Gertrude said, tugging a brush through Hanna's tangled wet curls. "That's what I'm here for. Now, let's make you up pretty."

Hanna's scalp prickled as Gertrude yanked, and Hanna pressed her lips together.

"My, that's quite a lot of hair you've got," Gertrude said, twisting pieces into place at the crown of Hanna's head.

"Yes," Hanna replied. "I don't pay it much attention."

Gertrude pinned a large plait across Hanna's part and pulled at sections of hair, muttering to herself. The hairstyle felt heavy at the front, but long pieces hung free in the back. Hanna had seen women toss their follow-me-lads flirtatiously, curls hanging low over their shoulders. Never did she expect to do the same.

Smiling at her creation, Gertrude tucked a tortoiseshell comb into the braid. "Go on," she said to Hanna, pointing at the mirror on the vanity. "Take a look."

Hanna gazed into the looking glass, unable to believe the woman staring back at her. With this shimmering dress and lovely hair, she appeared far comelier than usual, her strong features softened. But Hanna was no lady, even if tonight she resembled one. She gently touched her hair, to see if it would hold in place.

Turning to Gertrude, Hanna shook her head. "I—I am not this person. I do not belong in such finery."

Gertrude took Hanna's hands in hers. "Love, I don't know what you've been through, but I know it ain't pretty. You deserve some happiness, and I think this dress suits you." Gertrude's eyes shone bright as her rosy cheeks.

Hanna squeezed her fingers. "You have shown me much kindness. Thank you, truly."

"It's an unkind world we live in," Gertrude said, frowning. "We have to help each other when we can. Now, go on, get yourself to supper."

Taking a few steps forward, Hanna practiced walking in a pair of Georgina's satin high-heeled shoes. They fit a little snugly, for Georgina's feet were smaller than Hanna's. But unlike Hanna's boots, the heels felt comfortably soft and had sturdy soles.

"One more thing," Gertrude said as Hanna turned to leave. "Wear these." She handed Hanna a pair of black silk gloves.

"Thank you," Hanna said, slipping the first one onto her hand. She bit her lip. "Do I wear them when I eat?"

"No, dear," Gertrude said. "You take them off when you reach the table."

Hanna exhaled, fearing she would make a fool of herself, unfamiliar with the customs of the wealthy. "I cannot go downstairs," she whispered, looking to Gertrude's kind face for guidance. "I do not belong here."

"Hush," Gertrude said. "You will do just fine. Go on now."

After leaving the bedroom, Hanna descended the grand staircase, steadying herself on the banister. Beneath the glow of the gas lamps, the dark wood creaked like it was whispering to her. Hanna stopped, wondering if she had heard a cry. Perhaps one of the children called out? No, it was merely the wind.

Shaking her head to clear the uneasy feeling, Hanna walked down the remaining stairs and slowly made her way to the dining room. When she entered, Hanna found a long table laden with porcelain plates rimmed in gold. White tapered candles flickered next to a bowl of white flowers, and the silver shone to such a high gleam, Frances must have polished the utensils for hours.

Laughter emanated from the other room. Hanna hesitated, wondering if she ought to follow the sound or stay in place. The door behind her creaked, and she spun around. Lucas stood there, holding a crystal glass. His eyes swept over Hanna's dress and then her face. He covered his mouth with his hand.

Hanna held her breath, waiting for him to speak.

"Hanna," Lucas said, his hand falling at his side. "You are a vision. I am thunderstruck."

"Thank you," she whispered.

The air crackled with static, like the rumble of the new cable cars. When her eyes met his, the room seemed to slip away. Lucas took Hanna's gloved hand, raising it to his lips. How she wished she could feel his mouth against her skin instead of the fabric. Did he feel the charge in the air, or was his kiss only customary?

"Ahem."

Hanna dropped her hand, gasping. When her eyes met the pale eyes of the man in the doorway, a jolt of nerves shot all the way from the crown of her head down to her feet.

"Robert," Lucas said. "You've given poor Miss Schaeffer quite a fright. Hanna, you do remember my cousin, don't you?"

Robert placed a hand on his stomach and bowed. "Good evening. Forgive my shock. I did not expect to see you here."

"Good evening, sir. It is I who apologize." Hanna stared at the floor, feeling more out of sorts than a fish in a stable. She should have helped Frances polish the silverware.

Lucas pulled a chair out and gestured to Hanna. "Please, sit."

"Thank you," Hanna said, trying to keep the full skirt from becoming trapped beneath the wooden leg. Her corset pulled in her stomach, hindering her breathing.

"Care for a glass of sherry?" Lucas asked.

Judging from the scent of his drink, it had to be some kind of *Schnaps*. Did ladies drink alcohol around the dinner table? Lucas had offered, so perhaps it was safe to assume that they did. Hanna smiled. "Yes, please."

While Lucas and Robert disappeared into the adjacent room, Hanna looked at the arrangement of engraved cutlery. On the right side of her plate lay two large knives and a small knife, next to a very small fork. On the left side three large forks lined up next to a tablespoon. *Heavens!* In her home, they'd had only one silver spoon, which had belonged to her Oma on her mother's side. But then Father had pawned it. Most often, Hanna and her siblings tore bread with their hands, sharing what little they had.

Hanna stood to attention when Mr. William and Mrs. Elizabeth Havensworth entered the dining room, smoothing the fabric of her dress. Georgina followed, resplendent in a green gown with pearl buttons. She had changed from the pink gown she had been wearing when Hanna arrived. Did ladies always change clothing before supper?

Mrs. Havensworth regarded Hanna with a thin raised eyebrow. Hanna had scarcely heard Lucas's mother speak a word. Perhaps this was customary, as every proper woman believed herself to be merely an extension of her husband, silent and passive. Mr. Havensworth sat down in a chair at the head of the table.

"Miss Schaeffer, you look lovely in my blue dress," Georgina said, taking a seat adjacent to Hanna. "I thought it would suit you. Please, sit down."

"Thank you," Hanna said, wondering how she could ever repay Georgina's kindness. "Please, if you require any help, I can mend your dresses."

Mrs. Havensworth sniffed like something stank.

Georgina smiled. "Why, thank you. I do have a few dresses in need of mending. I should have learned to do it myself."

No lady would ever do her own washing or mending, and they both knew as much. Georgina's hands would only ever touch the ivory keys of a piano.

With a burst of laughter, Lucas, Robert, and a third man entered the room.

Georgina waved the newcomer over to her side. "Hello, dear husband. Charles, this is our guest, Miss Hannelore Schaeffer."

Charles turned to Hanna, his face pleasant. "Good evening, Miss Schaeffer."

"Good evening," Hanna said, lowering her head.

Taking a seat next to Georgina, Charles turned to Hanna, twisting the end of his waxed moustache. "I hope conversation has been harmonious thus far. My wife, whenever she entertains, chooses guests for their beauty, wit, talent, or money."

Mr. Havensworth coughed. Hanna stiffened, but Charles hardly seemed to notice. He smiled at Hanna. "With these four necessities, the hostess may eat her dinner in comfort, secure in the knowledge that the verdict of her guests will be in her favor. I see she's brought you into the fray."

Georgina giggled. "Oh, Charles, stop."

"Tell me, Miss Schaeffer," Charles said. "Which category do you fall into?"

Georgina touched her husband's arm. "Charles, Miss Schaeffer and her siblings have lost their parents. We have extended our Christian kindness to them by offering respite at our home. They are immigrants from Prussia."

Charles stared at Hanna. "Veritably so? I'm quite sorry. And have you no other family?"

"My grandparents are in Bavaria," Hanna said. She swallowed, looking about for Hans, Katja, and Martin. Hanna turned to Georgina. "Will the children eat with us?"

Georgina's eyes softened. "No, dear, with Claudia, our governess."

Hanna nodded, as if she understood.

Georgina sipped her sherry and then blotted her lips with a napkin. "Your brother Martin asked to take supper with Clive in the carriage house. We extended the invitation to him to dine with us, but he insisted."

"Perhaps he is more comfortable there," Hanna said.

Mr. Havensworth coughed again, his face growing red. Mrs. Havensworth fanned herself vigorously. Suddenly, the room felt far too warm, and Hanna's corset too tight. She had not meant to offend, simply to state the truth.

"Miss Schaeffer," Charles said. "Tell me, what is your father's line of work?"

Hanna sucked in her breath, picturing Father wild-eyed, wandering the streets in search of her. Sipping her sherry, Hanna tasted the sweet burn of alcohol. After she set the glass down, her nerves abated slightly.

"He worked as a blacksmith," Hanna said, looking at Charles. "But he has died."

Lucas turned to face his parents. "Hanna speaks quite well. You can see she has learned much from her mother, who was an educated woman."

Hanna shook her head. "Your son misleads you."

As Frances refilled their glasses and conversation flowed along with bottles of champagne, Hanna could not join in the spirit of felicitation. The men laughed through courses of various soups and sliced into their juicy steaks. The appeal of the rich foods diminished when Hanna thought of Margaret.

Where had Margaret gone?

Hanna looked out the window into the darkness. Tree branches scratched against the windowpane. Moaning like a phantom train, the wind seemed to carry the hint of a scream. Hanna shivered. When she found Margaret, she prayed she would find her alive.

Chapter 13

Sarah, *Present Day*

My footsteps echoed in the marble lobby of Havensworth Art Academy, where a security guard manned the front desk. It was late now, and quiet. On an impulse, I'd decided to stop by, emboldened by the glass of wine I'd had at dinner.

I'd tried to cheer Jen up at our favorite Italian restaurant, but she hadn't laughed at my jokes and had managed only a few forkfuls of pasta. I'd urged her to tell Nick what James had said to her, but she didn't trust Nick not to spread the news.

I had half a mind to report James to HR myself. Could I do that? I hadn't liked the way he'd looked at me after he'd reentered the office, his eyes beady and cold. He seemed like the type of man to be threatened by a strong woman.

I cleared my throat. The security guard looked up, his dark eyes meeting mine.

"Hi," I said warmly. "My name is Sarah Havensworth. I'm

here to help my mother-in-law set up for her event, the Canova by Moonlight gala."

The guy sat up straighter, his shiny badge catching the light. My mouth felt dry. "And um, well, there's some paperwork in the upstairs office that she asked me to get for her tonight. I was wondering if you might have the key?"

His bushy brows drew together. "You got ID?"

"Yes," I said as I dug around in my purse. Pushing my ID across the desk toward him, I pasted a smile on my face.

He picked it up with both hands and studied it. "Sarah Havensworth, huh? Okay, looks like you're part of the family."

My shoulders relaxed. "Thank you," I said, adrenaline pumping through me. The security guard removed a large key ring from a hook. He sorted through the jumble of metal before handing me a square brass key that I recognized.

The security guard smiled, almost making me feel guilty. "Bring it back when you're finished. I'm here all night."

"Great," I said, turning on my heel. "I won't be long. Thank you again."

Taking the stairs two at a time, then traversing the dark corridor, I reached Lucas Havensworth's office as if propelled there by an unseen force. Shutting the door behind me, I approached the wooden wardrobe in the back corner of the room. My hands shook as I stuck the skeleton key into the lock. It was a perfect fit. My breath shuddered as I grappled with my conscience. Was I doing the right thing?

What if there was something horrible behind that door—something I didn't want to find? But it was too late; I twisted my wrist to the right and pulled on the key with both hands, tugging the stubborn door open. At first I thought the wardrobe was empty.

But then I blinked, noticing a canvas lying on its side. Stuffing the key into my pocket, I reached into the wardrobe with both hands and pulled out a painting in a gilded frame. Sneezing once, I buried my nose in the crook of my elbow.

I brushed off the dust, my eyes drawn to the beautiful color of the oils. Curving coastline faintly resembled Telegraph Hill, long before it had been developed. The hillside rippled vibrant green, and the sky swirled pink and orange, like the hues of early dawn. A schooner with billowing white sails bobbed in the water.

The thick brushstrokes transported me into the scene. I yearned to sit on that grassy knoll with the breeze in my hair and to experience the quiet of the city as it once had been— over a hundred years ago.

The German word *sehnsucht* popped into my mind. I'd once written an article on thirty untranslatable words. Yes, the Germans managed to capture this feeling perfectly: nostalgia for a place or experience I'd never had.

I looked at the dimensions of the frame. My eyes darted above the desk, meeting the faint outline of a rectangle. Could this have been the painting that had once hung above Lucas Havensworth's desk? It was the right size and shape. If so, why had it been taken down? And by whom?

Tapping my chin, I stared at the swirl of oils, once again transported into the ethereal beauty of that place. Just below the frame, the looping letters of a signature poked out. Carefully pressing back the canvas with two fingers, I could make out the black letters of the artist's name and the date.

HANNELORE SCHAEFFER, 1876.

Blood rushed in my ears. It couldn't be. I sneezed, waving the dust particles away. Reading the cursive again, the signature was unmistakable. My pulse started to race as if I had downed too many cups of coffee.

My missing girl had known my husband's great-great-great-grandfather? She'd been a poor German immigrant and he'd been—what, a real-estate mogul, with a fortune in silver from the Comstock Lode? It didn't make any sense. The art university hadn't been founded until 1880 and Hannelore had gone missing in 1876.

Nothing added up, and yet here was Hannelore's name. I wiped the sweat from my forehead, my mind racing. If Hannelore and Margaret had been such good friends, was it possible Lucas Havensworth had been acquainted with both of them? I shivered, running my hands along the goose bumps prickling my arms.

By unlocking this wardrobe, I'd unleashed the skeletons in the Havensworth family closet. Slipping my phone from my pocket, I steadied my shaking hands and snapped a photo of the painting. Deep in my gut, I felt a twinge. If Lucas had known what had happened to Hannelore and Margaret on the night of their disappearance, did that mean Gwyneth and Walter also knew something they weren't letting on?

My phone pinged in my hand. I pulled it out, swiping the screen. A Gmail notification popped up, the sender's address: anonymous0982561@gmail.com. I gasped, my eyes racing across the two lines of text.

I know what you're doing. And I strongly advise you to stop.

Chapter 14

Hanna, *1876*

Hans and Katja sat at a small round table, their fingers fumbling with silver spoons. The walls of the room had been painted in gay bright colors, and all around them were blocks and storybooks. A bit of porridge stuck to Hans's cheek. Wiping it away with a cloth napkin, Hanna smiled at her brother's new clothes. Hans looked such the little gentleman in his brown trousers, while Katja wore a frilly pink frock.

"Did you enjoy your breakfast?" Hanna asked.

Katja nodded, a bow holding her dark curls in place.

Hans spoke with his mouth full. "This is the best food I ever had."

Georgina's son, Marcus, let his spoon drop into the bowl, then set his chin on his tiny fists. "It is only boring old porridge and I've had it a thousand times before. I want eggs Benedict. Mother, tell the cook to make me some."

Georgina smoothed her son's hair. "Now, Marcus, eat your breakfast like Hans and Katja. It is not polite to complain."

He stuck out his lip. "They are poor. They can't even speak properly. They probably think porridge is something grand because they eat slop for pigs."

Georgina reddened. "Marcus William Havensworth Chapman, I will not tolerate such language. Go to your room!"

He threw down his napkin and stomped away. For a boy of six, he was quite a little terror.

Annabelle continued to eat her porridge quietly. She had Georgina's blond curls and rosy cheeks. Hanna hoped Georgina's daughter and Katja would become playmates, but in the time they had spent together, the child hadn't uttered a word.

"I'm sorry about Marcus," Georgina said, her eyes apologetic. "He has a temper."

"It must be difficult for him," Hanna said. "He has many strangers in his home."

"Oh, please do not feel like a stranger." Georgina clasped Hanna's hand. "It is my hope that we shall become friends."

"I would like that," Hanna replied, touched by Georgina's kindness.

Georgina let go of Hanna's hand, motioning toward the stable. "Your brother Martin fixed the broken wagon wheel that Clive could not. Father was very impressed."

Hanna smiled. "Good. I am glad to hear that."

Georgina smoothed her dress. "I've spoken with Father, and he has agreed to allow you to stay until you've made other arrangements. Your brother has proven himself useful in the stables, and I will take you up on your generous offer to mend my clothing."

Hanna exhaled, her fear of walking the streets amongst stray dogs fading from her mind. "Thank you," she said. "Truly."

"Annabelle," Georgina said, stroking her daughter's cheek. "Katja shall join you in your lessons today. Would you like that?"

Annabelle looked up at her mother. She gave a tiny nod.

Georgina straightened the hem of her daughter's dress. "The children are reading Hans Christian Andersen's fairy stories. They are also practicing arithmetic and French."

Hanna swallowed. What if Marcus was to poke fun at Hans for being unable to read? If Hans felt ridiculed, he might strike the boy.

"My siblings are not schooled," Hanna said. "They cannot yet read, write, or do arithmetic. And they do not know French, I am afraid."

Georgina's face fell. "Oh. I'm terribly sorry. Our governess has been with us for so long, I fear I've taken her services for granted. But I understand that not all families are so fortunate." She appeared to sense Hanna's unease. "Annabelle is still learning her letters. Hans may join the girls in their lessons. It will allow him to catch up."

Hanna kissed the top of Hans's and Katja's heads. "Did you hear that? Today you have lessons. Listen to your governess, and be polite."

"Yes, Hanna," Hans said.

Hanna patted his arm. "You will thank Mrs. Chapman for her hospitality."

Hans turned to Georgina. "Thank you, ma'am."

"Should Martin join the lessons as well?" Hanna asked, hoping her eldest brother would take an interest in learning.

Georgina frowned. "He's with Clive, at the stable. Unfortunately I don't believe we have a tutor available for a child his age."

It was Father's life Martin wanted, even though he was capable of becoming so much more. But he enjoyed stoking the fire and putting shoes on the horses.

"Go now," Georgina said to the children. "Mrs. Blackford is waiting."

Katja, Annabelle, and Hans scampered down the hallway hand in hand toward yet another room, where they would have their lessons.

Rising to her feet, Georgina turned to Hanna. "Will you join us in the drawing room today? Mother and I shall practice our needlepoint, and perhaps later, piano."

Though Hanna could not play piano, she had confidence in her needlepoint ability. However, a day spent on such leisurely pursuits would be time wasted. It was imperative to find Margaret.

Hanna raised a hand to her forehead. "Forgive me. I feel a bit faint."

"Oh dear," Georgina said. "Are you all right?"

With a slight roll of her eyes, Hanna allowed her knees to buckle. Falling to the floor, she lay motionless.

Georgina gasped. "Frances! Come quickly. Miss Schaeffer has swooned. Please see her to her room, immediately."

Hanna blinked. "Heavens. What has happened?"

Touching Hanna's forehead, Georgina clucked her tongue. "You've had a fainting spell. Please, you must retire to your chamber. I insist."

"Thank you," Hanna murmured. Frances narrowed her eyes, helping Hanna to her feet. Did she see through the charade?

"I am all right," Hanna said, brushing off her dress. She felt awful for deceiving Georgina, after Lucas's sister had shown such kindness. But Margaret needed help. "I can see myself upstairs. Thank you."

"Are you sure?" Georgina asked.

Hanna nodded. "Yes, thank you. A bit of rest will do me good."

She made a show of leaning heavily against the banister as she climbed the stairs. But once she reached her bedchamber, Hanna shut the door quickly, struggling to unbutton the cumbersome taffeta gown Georgina had lent her.

Hanna removed the whalebone corset from around her waist, and the heavy hoopskirt, stepping out of both. She smiled, able to breathe once more. To think she and Margaret had once dreamed of wearing such finery.

Gertrude had washed and dried Hanna's dirndl, which Hanna slipped over her head. Quickly, she fastened it, and then stuffed two pillows under the duvet, to make it appear as though she lay in bed sleeping.

Slipping off Georgina's satin shoes, Hanna laced up her dirtied boots, which she'd begged Gertrude not to take from her.

Sneaking down the servants' staircase, she held her breath. The labyrinthine nature of the mansion would befuddle anyone. But these stairs would take her to the kitchen, Hanna knew that much. Tiptoeing the remainder of the way, she succeeded in slipping by the staff unnoticed.

The side door creaked as she opened it. Looking to her right and left, she darted across the wet grass, past hedges trimmed into circles and cubes. Where were the potatoes, tomato plants, and chickens? With so much land to grow food, it was a wonder the rich did not use it. Checking behind her, she saw no one.

As Hanna passed the stables, chestnut mares whinnied and stomped their hooves. The sweet smell of hay bales reminded her of home in Bavaria. Beneath her boots, a twig snapped. She winced. Before she could run, a figure appeared in the doorway.

Hanna gasped. "Martin! You frightened me."

Her brother wore a leather apron and a dirty shirt. A crease divided his brow. "Where are you going?"

Hanna's voice dropped to a whisper. "I must find Margaret."

Martin nodded toward the house. "Do they know what you're doing?"

"They think I took ill. I put pillows under the blanket in my room to make it appear I am in bed."

Martin grinned like a boy, instead of a serious young man. "Don't get caught, then."

Hanna squeezed his hand. "Have you eaten enough? You missed supper. The Havensworths are wealthy, but they are kind. You ought to come inside."

Martin shook his head. "They don't like us, Hanna. And they don't see us as equals. I don't want to pretend to be something I'm not."

His words stung like the lash of Father's belt. Hanna gestured toward the hay and horse dung. "You like working here?"

"Yes. We work hard, and then we eat. Clive's wife made us a mutton stew with potatoes." He patted his belly. "I haven't eaten so well in a long time. I think I may finally grow some muscles, like a real man."

Hanna chuckled, ruffling Martin's hair. "I'm glad you're well, brother. I will go to Broadway Wharf now. Do not tell a soul. I will return before noon."

"Please be safe."

"I will," she whispered. "Do not fret."

But as Hanna ran from the stable toward the street, she knew she could not promise to stay out of danger. In the Barbary Coast, every day was a roll of the dice.

The gulls cawed and circled overhead. A steamer ship sounded its foghorn while men hollered at one another, hauling nets bulging with cargo onto scow schooners. Hanna smelled the overpowering stench of rotten fish, while giant rats scurried about the planks of the boardwalk. She squealed as one ran across the toe of her boot.

"Move!" a boy shouted, throwing himself onto his belly, capturing the rat beneath an upturned bowl. Hanna had never seen a child covered in such filth, as though he hadn't washed in his life. He sneered, looking up at her.

"This big 'un gonna get me a dollar in the fights."

Hanna recoiled. "The fights?"

The boy coughed, his face bruised and ear bloodied. "Big rats like these can kill them little dogs. If my rat wins, I win money. That's why I catch 'em. Or maybe I'll set 'im on the belly of a Chinaman. I'd like to see it eat right through his yellow skin."

Hanna gasped. "Why do you say such hateful things?"

He spat at her, his rat clutched to his chest. "You want these Orientals running our city? Me and my crew, we'll beat him with a hickory stick till he's near dead. Then slit his ears and his tongue so he can't say nothing 'bout who did it."

Hanna knew of the hoodlums, who grew in numbers. The anti-Chinese gangs had taken over the neighborhood by the wharves, harassing the railroad workers. What had the Chinese done other than provide for their families? They were immigrants, like her.

"Horrible child!" she hissed, though she knew he would not understand her native German. As Hanna watched him scamper away, it pained her to see that this harsh environment had bred such hatred in his heart.

The water slapped the wooden pilings as Hanna walked along the wharf, past men in tweed caps wearing coveralls stained with clay. Sinewy-armed stevedores unloaded barrels and boxes onto the ships. Sitting in groups on the pier, other men mended the nets. Hanna stopped, looking about for Kieran.

"Aye, you girl!"

Hanna turned to see a fishmonger in a stall, frizzy gray hair sprouting beneath a red kerchief. "Buy a head of trout from us?"

The rotten fish heads in the woman's bucket stared up at Hanna with dead eyes.

"No, thank you," Hanna said, trying not to gag. "Do you know a boy by the name of Kieran McClaren? He works the docks here."

The fishmonger frowned, hairs poking from a mole on her mouth. "I know the McClaren boy. He's down on the wharf a wee bit farther, right that way."

"Thank you," Hanna said, picking up the hem of her dirndl so she could walk more quickly. "I'm sorry I've no money for fish. Next time."

The woman grunted, waving a dirty hand. "Be off with you, then!"

Walking toward a scow schooner with its hull jutting over the water, Hanna drew her shawl tighter. Men tugged ropes, lifting large boxes up toward the deck. The pulleys squeaked and the waves splashed in the choppy water below. Others sorted through bins of oysters, crabs, and herring. Those would bring a pretty penny at the market.

Hanna's eyes landed on a man with sun-browned skin. As he clenched his teeth, sweat trickled from his hairline down his wrinkled brow as he lifted a net of cargo. His bright eyes shone like moonstones in his weathered face. But underneath that sandy mop of hair, Hanna could tell he was no more than twenty, though working out in the elements had given him the lines of a man much older.

A foreman called out commands until the sagging contents finally reached the deck of the ship. Stevedores began to unload the boxes, barrels, and hay bales. The sandy-haired boy let go of his rope, wiping perspiration from his brow.

Hanna took a step toward him, clearing her throat. "Are you Kieran McClaren?"

He wiped his hands on his coveralls. "Who's askin'?"

"Hanna Schaeffer."

He tilted his head. "You don't look familiar."

"I'm searching for my friend, Margaret O'Brien," Hanna said, swallowing as she noticed the ropelike muscles in his arms. "Have you seen her?"

He shook his head. "I ain't got time for trouble. Can't you see I'm working?"

"Margaret is missing. Her mother told me you were her sweetheart. Now, is your name Kieran or not?"

He pulled tobacco rolled in newspaper from his pocket and struck a match, lighting the cigarette. Taking a long drag, he blew the smoke in Hanna's face. "The old bitch ain't got no right talking about my business. And yes, me name's Kieran."

Hanna coughed, waving the cloud away. "Were you courting Margaret?"

"What's it to you?"

"I fear she's been taken against her will. And if you've done anything to harm her, I will go straight to the police."

Kieran sucked his tobacco. "Margaret's a sweet girl. I wouldn't do nothin' to harm her. But she don't listen. And she ain't brought me nothing but trouble."

"What do you mean?"

Kieran stared at the sun. "Margaret knows I have a fiancée. I love me Bridie. We been together since we was fifteen. But I got a little something on the side."

Hanna's mouth fell open. "Margaret would never."

Kieran laughed, his cigarette dangling between two fingers. "Oh, she would. And she did. I'd sneak round her house after midnight, and we'd go in the empty lot behind Sutherland's pharmacy, or up against the shed at the McGregors' house."

Hanna closed her eyes. Margaret *wouldn't*. Had she truly given herself up before marriage, and to a man who had promised himself to someone else? When Hanna opened her eyes again, Kieran was smirking at her.

"Don't look so shocked, love. Margaret wasn't no virgin."

Hanna slapped him hard. Kieran reached up and touched his cheek. Hanna flinched as Kieran's eyes flashed with anger in the same way Father's did. This time she had asked for it.

"What'd you slap me for?" Kieran asked, rubbing his face.

Hanna raised her fists to her face. "For speaking that way about Margaret. She's a good girl."

Kieran's eyes grew softer. "I'll forgive you, but only because you're more innocent than I thought. You're a *maighdean*, ain't you?"

Hanna's cheeks prickled. She would not give Kieran the satisfaction of admitting he was right. "Please. Did you see Margaret the night before last?"

"Last I saw her was five days ago. She came down here and told me she was up the duff. I told her to get rid of it."

"You mean Margaret was pregnant?"

Kieran sucked his cigarette and nodded. "Told me she was havin' my child. But I don't want no wee ones. Not yet. And I told her I ain't leaving my Bridie."

Hanna clutched her head, thinking back to the morning she and Margaret had last sewed together side by side. Margaret's face had been a little fuller, and her clothing had fit a bit tighter in the bust. But other than that, there had been no signs. Margaret hadn't been sick or tired. She had been rosy and happy as the friend Hanna loved.

Hanna steadied herself against a metal pole, the wharves spinning around her. This time, perhaps she *would* faint. A lump rose in Hanna's throat. Unable to stop the tears, Hanna sobbed in front of Kieran. Margaret was pregnant and alone—in far more danger than Hanna had ever imagined.

"Hey now," Kieran said, touching Hanna's arm. "She'll be all right. I told her the name of a woman I know, to get the baby out."

"You vile man!" Hanna yelled, slapping his hand away. "You are a monster!" Heat surged through her. "Such a doctor could kill Margaret. I thought your faith taught you life is sacred."

Kieran laughed, but his smile did not reach his eyes. "Catholics say you'll go to hell for killing a baby. That's what Margaret thought too. But I don't believe in hell. It's right here." He gestured at the skinny street children by the wharf. "Just look around."

"Did anyone else know about the baby?"

Kieran stubbed out his cigarette. "If her pa found out, he'd probably kill her himself. You don't go shaming your family like that. She's ruined now."

"Because you ruined her!" Hanna yelled, her eyes welling up with tears again. "And your Bridget, she stays with you?"

"I provide for her, like a good man does. And I put a ring on her finger. Why should she leave me?"

Hanna slowed her breathing, trying to regain control of her emotions. Had Kieran hired the scar-faced man to force Margaret to get rid of the baby? *God in heaven*, perhaps that's why Margaret was drugged? In houses of prostitution, there were many women with the potions and know-how to conduct such surgeries.

"Oy, McClaren, back to work!" yelled a burly man with a thick black moustache. He ambled toward them, glaring at Hanna. "You, girl. Get out of here."

"Please," Hanna said, as the man grabbed her arm. "Did you send Sam O'Grady to come after Margaret? The man with the scar?"

Kieran frowned, taking hold of the rope. "O'Grady? He's a common criminal. A con man. I don't mess with the likes of him."

The foreman's grip tightened around Hanna's arm. "Leave now," he hissed. "You're costing me time and money. Stop talking to my workers."

He let go of Hanna with a push, and she stumbled to the ground. A few of the stevedores laughed. Hanna brushed her hands on her cotton dress and stood up. "Kieran! You must help me find Margaret."

Kieran tugged on the rope, his moonstone eyes hard. "You won't find her here."

Hanna's blood ran cold, watching the rope uncoil—rope that could be used to tie someone up or to hang them. Rope pulled by the arms of someone strong enough to strangle the life out of a girl carrying an unwanted child.

Chapter 15

Sarah, *Present Day*

"Thank you so much for meeting me." I smiled at Anna Heinrich as she sat across from me in Caffé Bianco on Sutter Street.

Anna brushed her gray-streaked auburn hair away from her face. For a fiftyish woman, she had a youthful glow radiating from her laugh lines.

She set down her coffee. "It's cool you've taken an interest in Papa's old bar. It's a shame we couldn't keep it, but it was just too much work. Ed does a great job. And we love what he's done, bringing in the blues bands."

"I heard one the other night with some friends. They had great energy."

Anna shook her head. "If it was all good vibes, I could've kept the place. But there were too many fights. People getting drunk and smashing bottles over each other's heads. One regular died from a head wound, right after I called the cops. That's when I decided I couldn't deal with it anymore."

I winced, holding my latte. "Wow, it sounds as bad as it was back in the Barbary Coast days. I don't blame you for not wanting to put up with that."

"Those days were worse than we've got it now." Anna sipped her coffee, then set it down. "Oh, which reminds me! I brought the photos." Reaching into her backpack, she pulled out a battered shoebox. "They're all in here. My grandpa kept everything his father had saved. Lots of action happened around that bar."

"Thank you so much," I said.

"Any time," Anna replied. "I hope you find something useful." She checked her phone. "I gotta run, honey, otherwise I'll hit traffic on the way back to Sacramento. But you keep those as long as you need to."

"Thanks again!" I called as Anna walked away from the table. After she left the café, I lifted the lid off the old shoebox, a musty scent filling the air. Reaching inside, I pulled out a stack of sepia prints, many hand-tinted with watercolors. Some had scalloped edges, and my fingers traced the smooth corners of the others. At the bottom of the box, daguerreotypes printed on thin pieces of metal stuck to a clump of photos. Where to start?

I held a picture toward the light, between my thumb and forefinger, examining it. A society woman stifled in her high, ruffled collar. Watercolors accentuated her sad blue eyes, blond hair, and thin pink lips.

In the accompanying photograph, an older man wore a black

suit and bow tie over a collared shirt. His big beard gapped without a moustache, in the style of Abraham Lincoln. Watercolors tinted his eyes blue.

Turning his photograph over, I read, "Captain John Worthington, taken in his San Francisco home, 1878, François Dupont." The same handwriting marked the woman's photo: "Edith Worthington, wife of Captain John Worthington."

I jotted their names in my notebook. A photographer named François Dupont had taken most of the pictures, although someone named A. J. Merckel had taken others. Some had no writing, leaving the identity of the people in the photograph a mystery. Nonetheless, the window into the past transfixed me.

Sipping my latte, I pulled another photograph from the box. Children with somber faces stared up at me, sending tingles all the way to my toes. The watercolor tint couldn't mask what was wrong in this photo. The little red-haired girl at the center of the photograph was too stiff, her pale cheeks too rouged, and her eyes vacant. Without turning the picture over, I knew she was dead.

A dark-haired boy of about twelve laid a hand on the shoulder of the redheaded girl. Pillows propped her up in bed, her head haloed by a garland of red roses. To her right stood a younger boy, his hair sandy colored, and next to him a blond girl who clung to a teddy bear. She couldn't have been more than three or four.

Postmortem photography was common in the Victorian era, but that didn't make it any less disturbing. I shuddered, looking away from the children and focusing instead on the furniture in the room. From the chandelier overhead and the velvet chairs, I could tell this family was wealthy. Even the privileged couldn't escape death. Turning over the picture, I read the small, neat handwriting.

> *Robert Havensworth with his sister Clara Havensworth*
> *[deceased] and cousins, Lucas Havensworth and Georgina*
> *Havensworth—taken in the home of Mr. William*
> *Havensworth and Mrs. Elizabeth Havensworth, San*
> *Francisco, California, 1858.*

I nearly choked. Havensworth? It wasn't a common last name. Looking again at the chandelier, the way the brass curled and the crystals hung in tiers . . . I recognized it. And the chair—I knew that chair.

Setting the photograph down, my hands trembled. There was a reason Hunter's parents' mansion had always given me the creeps. A little girl had died in that house, in one of Gwyneth and Walter's many rooms.

A car pulled away from the curb with a screech—a Lexus with darkened windows. An uneasy feeling washed over me. Was I being paranoid, or had someone been watching me?

"How's your story coming along?" Mariko asked.

"It's good," I said, noting the concern in her deep brown

eyes. "I'm making headway." Bouncing my heel beneath her desk, I hoped she believed me.

I averted my eyes, looking instead at the pretty potted plants in Mariko's office, the leaves of spiral bamboo shoots pointing toward the ceiling. My graduate advisor had trusted me when she'd given me permission to change my thesis topic, and now I feared my lack of progress had caused Mariko to regret her decision.

But hadn't I always done well when given the opportunity to use my voice? Frank, the former editor in chief of *Pulse of the City* magazine, had taught me so much about finding the right hook and reeling our readers in with a good story. I knew telling the tale of Hannelore and Margaret was the right one. I needed to figure out what had happened to them and to write my best piece of journalism yet.

"Are you sure you'll be able to finish your article within the next two weeks?" Mariko asked, her perfectly penciled eyebrows drawing together.

I swallowed. "Yes, that won't be a problem."

With the discovery of the painting at Havensworth Art Academy I had a new and unexpected lead, the connection between Hannelore and Lucas. But time was running out, and I still didn't know what had become of Hanna and Margaret.

"Remember," she said, her expression serious. "If you want to brainstorm with me, or if you need to refine the direction of your pitch, I'm here to help. I'll provide you with constructive feedback, but I expect a completed draft by May 30."

"I understand," I said, gripping the base of my chair. "I'll have it ready by then."

Mariko pressed the tips of her fingers together. "You still have your novel to fall back on." She sighed, and then shook her head. "I don't know, Sarah. I'm glad you're excited about this new idea, but my concern is that the story will feel too rushed."

In our series of meetings over the past year, we'd always had a good working relationship. Mariko had provided me with extensive feedback on the early drafts of my novel, pushing me to delve into fiction. I'd tried flying by the seat of my pants, going where inspiration pulled me, but nothing I'd written had felt right.

"I want to publish this," I said, meeting Mariko's stern gaze. "And I promise I won't turn in something half-baked."

She smiled. "I like your determination. You've shown promise in your writing, and that's why I'm allowing you this last-minute change. I want you to prove to me, *and* to the graduate committee, that this is your very best work."

"I will," I said, standing up. The fog had begun to settle like a blanket around the white spires of St. Ignatius, the Catholic Church at the heart of the USF campus.

Mariko shook my hand. "Good luck, Sarah. See you next week."

Leaving Mariko's office, I watched through the window as tendrils of mist clung to tree branches in the courtyard. Even within the warm hallway of the faculty building, I shivered, thinking of the email on my phone. *I know what you're doing. And I strongly advise you to stop.* Was it from Walter or someone else?

My chest tightened as I thought of James. I'd said aloud that Jen should report him to HR, which would threaten his job. Had he heard me?

Exiting the building, I zipped up my sweatshirt. As I walked down Fulton Street, toward the Panhandle, I smelled eucalyptus, mingled with the scent of the ocean, carrying over from the outer avenues. On weekends, Hunter and I liked to ride our bikes through Golden Gate Park, sometimes all the way to Ocean Beach. I enjoyed the sleepiness of the Sunset District and the Outer Richmond, a few of the last remaining neighborhoods where longtime San Francisco residents lived.

A pang hit me, thinking of a happy family, cozy in one of the small, stucco houses: a mom, a dad, and two little children, laughing as they played together in the living room. I swallowed, hard. That would never be my life.

Pulling my phone from my purse, I dialed Nick. I'd promised Jen I wouldn't say anything to him, but that didn't mean he couldn't help me.

"Hey," Nick said. "What's up, Sar?"

"Hey, buddy. I need to ask you something."

"Wait, don't tell me," he said. "You want help making your Instagram account better so you can get more followers. I already told Jen to download Afterlight, but even a great filter can't help a mediocre photo. The trick is in finding the right subject and the right mood. And please, no more brunch photos. Food is meant for eating."

I laughed. "What? I don't care about my Instagram. I need your help with some computer stuff. Do you know how to trace an IP address?"

The smile in Nick's voice disappeared. "What's going on, *chica*?"

"I got this creepy email from an unknown sender who calls himself Anonymous."

"Yikes. What did it say?"

"I can't tell you. But I need to find out who it's from."

Nick's voice went up an octave. "Oh, *really*? Well, don't get yourself into too much trouble, Nancy Drew. Forward me that email."

"So you think you can do it?"

"It won't be easy." He paused. "If you ever want to find the IP of an email sent to you, you can investigate the message's headers—you know, that stuff that looks like a keyboard exploded on the message. Then you do a ping on a known address, or a 'who is' check, where the information will be sent out to a database, queried, and then returned with the registration information for that IP address."

My eyes glazed over. "Nick? You know, you might as well be speaking Spanish right now, because I don't understand a word you said."

"Okay, then *Déjame en paz!*"

I laughed as I rounded the corner, spotting my bus stop. "That wasn't nice."

"Oh, so you *do* understand Spanish."

"Not really," I said. "Only the stuff you taught me. Anyways, I'm about to catch my bus, so I'll let you go. Thanks for helping me out."

"Wait," Nick said. "Before you go, I have to ask you something. Do you think Jen has been acting weird lately?"

I pressed my lips together. "Not that I've noticed. Why?"

"She seems skittish at work. She hasn't been laughing at my jokes."

"Can you blame her?" I smiled. "Your jokes are terrible."

"Hey, they're not that bad. But honestly, I'm a little worried about her. She's been really quiet at her desk, and it seems like something's on her mind."

"Why don't you ask her?"

Nick was trustworthy. I wanted Jen to tell him about James. The more friends she had on her side, the better. "Talk to her. Find out what's going on."

"Okay," Nick said. "Will do. Bye, hun. Let's chill again soon."

"Bye," I said, feeling a bit guilty as I hung up the phone. But I hadn't told Nick what had happened. I'd only encouraged him to find out for himself.

As I stood at the bus shelter, waiting for the 5R to arrive, I heard my phone ping. When I swiped the screen, my breath hitched. This time, the email had an attachment. My knees buckled underneath me, and I sank to the concrete, the world around me going dark.

Unless you want people to see this, stop what you're doing now.

Chapter 16

Hanna, *1876*

Hanna crept through the side door of Lucas's house, her pulse racing. Margaret was with child. But why hadn't she been forthcoming about her predicament? And Kieran McClaren hardly seemed trustworthy, having sent Margaret to an abortion doctor. Had Margaret been forced to go through with it?

Hanna steadied herself on the counter in the servants' pantry, breathing deeply. The potions and surgical methods used to rid women of their children could kill Margaret. Surely she would never endure such a procedure. But then again, Margaret hadn't told Hanna she'd given up her virginity, and Hanna had been none the wiser.

"What have we here?" Frances said, crossing her arms as she entered the room. "A little mouse, sneaking round the kitchen, up to no good?"

Beneath her frilly white maid's cap, Frances's eyes shone black.

"Oh, hello, Frances," Hanna said. "I've come to look for . . . potatoes."

Frances scoffed. "Potatoes? You ain't wearing your fancy clothes no more, and now you're after potatoes? What for?"

"I would like to help cook supper," Hanna answered.

Frances stuck her hands on her hips. "I know your kind. Herr Schmidt, who runs the jewelry on Market Street, he's always scheming good folk out of their hard-earned money. You lot are a bunch of dirty Jews."

Hanna frowned. "I am not Jewish. Not that it would matter to you, thinking all German people are the same."

Frances threw up her hands. "And you don't think all Irish are the same? You call us Micks and give us dirty jobs. If me ma knew I was working for a family of Protestants, she'd roll over in her grave." Making the sign of the cross over her chest, Frances sighed. "I should've stayed in Dublin, even if I would've been no more than a chambermaid."

"Frances, you were right about the potatoes," Hanna said. "I was lying. That's not why I am here."

Frances's eyes widened. "I knew it! You've come to steal the silver."

"No," Hanna said, her voice breaking. "I haven't come to steal anything. My dearest friend, she's Irish, an immigrant from Dublin, like you."

The hard line of Frances's mouth softened. "Go on."

Hanna sniffed. "Her name's Margaret. She's gone missing.

And I've learned she's with child. I'm terribly frightened for her, and I am looking to find her."

"What's her family name?" Frances asked.

"O'Brien," Hanna said. "Margaret lives on Minna Street, by the boardinghouse above Tomkinson's livery. Do you know her?"

Frances smirked. "I know the O'Briens. Not well, mind you. But the wee ones are always running amok. Her ma's a drunk, just like her da. It's not a good life down in Irish Town. That's why I've been raised up. Brought meself here." The kindness in Frances's eyes disappeared. "And if I tell Mr. Lucas you're sneaking around searching for your pregnant friend, he won't think you're such a nice girl then, considering the company you keep."

A surge of anger swept through Hanna. "Lucas knows about Margaret. He will help me find her."

Frances turned around, grabbing a knife and peeling the skin from an onion. She brought the knife down with a loud slice. "Good luck then. But don't expect to live in this house like a fine lady. I know what you are."

Hanna's eyes stung as she made her way up the servants' staircase. Lucas's kindness could be extended only so far. It was as Frances said—she didn't belong here. Pushing open the doorway at the top of the stairs, Hanna peeked down the hall. Seeing it was empty, she moved quickly and quietly across the carpet.

Rounding the corner, her body collided with a man. She slapped her hand over her mouth to stifle her scream.

"Hanna," Lucas said, taking both of her hands in his. "You look as though you've seen a ghost. Whatever is the matter?"

Hanna trembled, breathing in the piney scent of his cologne and faint cigar smoke. "Oh, Lucas. It is Margaret. Things are worse than I ever imagined."

"There now," he said, stepping closer. "I heard you had a fainting spell, and I came upstairs to see if you had recovered." He studied her face, and then the dirty hem of her dirndl. "But you appear quite well. I gather you haven't been truthful with Georgina?"

"I am sorry I lied to your dear sister. She has been lovely to me. But I had to speak with Kieran McClaren."

Lucas's eyes widened. "You went down to the wharves alone? Hanna, that was very foolish. It is too dangerous a place for a woman."

Hanna glared. "You may believe that, but I am familiar with such places. Do not think me to be a delicate flower who wilts at the sight of vice." But even as she spoke, her lip quivered. Lucas touched it with his thumb, bringing on a rush of longing.

He smiled. "You may not think yourself a flower, but to me you are a rose."

A tear trickled down Hanna's cheek. "Margaret is with child. She went to Kieran for help, but he is betrothed to another girl. He sent Margaret to an abortion doctor."

Lucas's face grew pale. "Do you believe it to be true, that Margaret is pregnant?"

"I know not. Perhaps the seams on her dress pulled more tightly than usual. She had taken on a bit of weight." Hanna's throat tightened. "We must find her. It is more important than ever that we bring her home safely."

"This abortion doctor," Lucas said. "Do you know her name?"

Hanna frowned. "I do not."

Voices carried from downstairs, and Hanna tensed. Taking her by the arm, Lucas guided her into an alcove. They stood merely inches apart, their noses almost touching. Perhaps Lucas could hear her heart beat, for Hanna heard it ringing in her ears. Lucas's mouth, full and perfect, was close enough that she felt his breath.

"Have you this morning's paper?" Hanna whispered, looking at Lucas. "Doctors such as these place advertisements."

"Yes, I can bring it at once."

For a moment, neither of them spoke. Though the voices abated, they remained hidden in the alcove, their bodies nearly pressed against each other. The air filled with a charge like lightning, the same way it had outside Frau Kruger's house on the night Lucas had taken her to the theater. This time, Hanna knew she was not imagining things. Lucas's mouth was a hairsbreadth from hers.

When his fingers cupped her chin, tilting it upward, Hanna closed her eyes. And in the exquisite moment when Lucas kissed her lips, tingles shot through Hanna as the hairs on her arms stood to attention. Warmth flooded her body, as though she were butter melting in a hot pan. Parting her mouth to feel his tongue, Hanna lost herself in the lightness of her being. She couldn't resist him any longer.

After a time, Lucas drew back, breathing heavily. "Forgive me," he said, taking her hands gently in his. "I have been too forward. I do not know what overcame me."

"Do not apologize," Hanna said. "I did not stop you."

"My dear Hanna," Lucas said, leading her back into the corridor. "Perhaps you should rest before resuming your search for Margaret."

"No. Not when it is imperative that we find her. Will you come with me to town?"

Lucas sighed. "All right. Change into one of Georgina's dresses, and meet me downstairs in the parlor. I shall tell my family we are taking the carriage into town together. They might find it improper, but Margaret's safety is of more importance than abiding by protocol."

"Thank you," Hanna said as they walked down the corridor toward her chamber. "I cannot tell you how much your help means to me."

Lucas nodded, a faraway look in his eyes. "I know how it feels to lose a friend unexpectedly. I do not wish it upon anyone."

Hanna waited for Lucas to explain further, but she did not wish to press him.

Dropping his voice to a whisper, Lucas pointed toward the bedroom door. "Gertrude shall expect to find you in bed. I'll send for her, to help you dress." He winked. "What better cure for a fainting spell than a carriage ride in the fresh air?"

❖　❖　❖

As the horses' hooves clattered against the cobblestones, Hanna pointed to an advertisement on the back page of the newspaper. "You see? There."

Lucas squinted. "This one? But it does not mention anything of note."

"It must be discreet."

Lucas read the advertisement aloud. "To the ladies, Madame Costello, female physician, still continues to treat, with astonishing success, all diseases peculiar to females. Those who wish to be treated for obstruction of their monthly visits can consult Madame C. at 34 Kearny Street, at all times."

He wrinkled his brow. "I don't understand."

Unfortunately, some of the words had eluded her. "What does it mean, 'obstruct'?"

"To block."

"There you have it. She treats female diseases and also treats when there is a blockage of a woman's . . ." Hanna's cheeks grew hot.

Lucas was a quick study. He gave the address to Clive.

"Yes, sir," Clive said, pulling the reins so that the horses trotted faster. Hanna watched as the grand homes of Nob Hill faded into the distance. The wind whipped her face, and she nestled into Georgina's elegant coat, protected from the cold.

By the time they reached the city center, it was lunch hour. Men in high hats walked with young girls in furred opera coats toward the theater. Ribbon counters, dressmakers, and milliners strolled arm in arm idly from window to window, taking in the air during their break. Hanna's throat tightened, remembering strolls with Margaret.

Ducks and geese scattered when the carriage barreled down Kearny Street. Barefoot women and children held out their cupped hands, begging for food on the planks of the sidewalk. Hanna sucked in her breath, watching girls with hollow cheeks and too much rouge collect tidbits of junk they could sell for a glass of opium.

If not for the kindness of Lucas and his family, Hanna would also be there amongst the stray dogs, searching in the rubbish for scraps of meat.

"Whoa," Clive called to the horses, pulling the carriage to a halt. Hanna stared up at the facade of a building with darkened windows. On the ground floor, a small wooden sign bore the name MADAME COSTELLO, FEMALE PHYSICIAN.

"This is the place," Hanna said.

Lucas stepped down from the carriage and held out his hand. Struggling to move beneath the weight of Georgina's dress, Hanna maneuvered the hoopskirt through the carriage doors as Lucas steadied her. Once both of Hanna's feet were planted firmly on the ground, she noticed the young girl who stood outside Madame Costello's office.

"Wait here," Lucas said to Clive. "We shan't be long."

Approaching the girl, Hanna realized she could not be much older than Martin. Green eyes peered out from her strikingly beautiful face, her plump lips lacquered cherry red.

"Are you waiting to see the doctor?" Hanna asked, placing a hand on the child's shoulder.

The girl nodded, clutching her stomach. "Aye. I've got to get rid of it or the madame won't let me back in the house."

Hanna's insides clenched like she'd drunk spoiled milk. "What house, dear?"

The girl tilted her head in the direction of Pacific Avenue. "Madame Evangeline's house. If I don't get the baby out, men won't lay with me and I won't get paid. Madame says men pay good money for girls like me."

Hanna touched the girl's cheek. "How old are you, dear?"

"Thirteen," she said.

Hanna swallowed. "And what is your name?"

"Molly."

How could a girl so young have already lost her innocence? And to grown men? Molly must have a family, someone to take care of her.

"Where are your parents, Molly?" Hanna asked.

Molly picked her cuticles. "My mother is dead. My father sent me away."

Lucas's face went as ashen as a stormy sky. Perhaps it was not often he saw the world outside his mansion's walls for the cruel and dangerous place it was.

Lucas patted Molly's bare shoulder. "Are you warm enough, child? Have you enough to eat?"

A coy smile played at her lips. "You could buy me something to eat. I can show you what I've learned from the French girls."

A crease divided Lucas's brow. "No, my dear. You mustn't speak that way." He took off his coat and put it around her shoulders. "You are but a child in need of help."

Molly's lip trembled. "Madame Costello will help me. She'll get the baby out, and then I can work again and have my old room back."

Hanna turned to Lucas. His eyes mirrored what she felt.

"There must be another way," Lucas said, rapping his knuckles on the door to the building. "A convent or a safe place. I will gladly pay for it."

A man with thick spectacles and a white moustache pulled open the door. Across his barrel chest hung a gold pocket watch. He glared at them. "State your business."

"We are here to see Madame Costello," Lucas answered.

The man looked down at Hanna's stomach. "Do you have an appointment?"

Hanna placed a hand over her belly, feigning concern. "Madame Costello's advertisement stated we could visit during any hours."

"Make haste," Lucas said. "And this matter requires some privacy."

"One moment," the man said, shutting the door behind him.

"Molly!" Hanna cried out, watching as the girl stumbled backward. Hanna steadied Molly by the elbow, but her complexion had taken on a greenish hue. Touching Molly's forehead, Hanna's fingers came away damp. "You're burning up."

"I drank some potions," Molly mumbled. "They're s'posed to get the baby out. But Madame Evangeline told me to come here, just to be sure." She bent over and retched on the wooden planks of the sidewalk.

Hanna pulled Molly's long, straggly hair away from her face

and held it back. "Lucas," Hanna said. "We must call a doctor. I will not send her in there."

Recognizing the somber expression on his face, Hanna swallowed. Frau Kruger had given her the same look when Hanna's mother had died.

"Dr. Jones is our family physician," Lucas whispered. "I'll send Clive to call on him. He can take the girl. We'll do without a carriage for now."

Molly's eyelids fluttered and her eyes rolled back to show their whites.

"Molly," Hanna said, taking her hand. "We will help you. Clive will take you to a real doctor."

"But I'm here to see Madame Costello," Molly moaned.

"A witch doctor," Lucas muttered. He lifted Molly into the carriage and pressed a few dollars into her palm. "Take this. Use it to start a new life. You must never return to Madame Evangeline's house of ill repute. There is hope for you, child."

Lucas turned to Clive. "After she has seen Dr. Jones, make sure she is taken to the convent of Saint Mary's."

"Will the nuns care for her?" Hanna asked, biting her lip. Molly did not need judgment or shame for the state she'd ended up in.

"I studied at the convent as a boy," Lucas said. "It is a safe place across the bay in Berkeley, far removed from the Barbary Coast and its vice."

"Can I keep my baby?" Molly asked, holding her stomach.

Hanna looked into the girl's sea-green eyes, still taken aback by her youth. Only God would decide what happened to that baby, and he was not always kind. Clasping Molly's clammy hands in hers, Hanna smiled. "Godspeed. Be well."

Clive shook the reins and the horses snorted.

"Please hurry!" Hanna called to him.

With a start, the carriage rattled down the cobblestone street, taking Molly away from the dark groggeries, theaters, gambling dens, and smoke-filled saloons. Hanna could only hope she would find a better life for herself and her child, if both survived.

Once again, the door to Madame Costello's office swung open, and the bespectacled man beckoned Hanna inside. "The madame will see you now."

Hanna and Lucas entered a dim parlor, the door shutting behind them with a thud. It smelled of herbs and musky perfume. As she followed the man to a desk at the back of the room, Hanna's eyes set upon a woman dressed completely in black. Her unruly dark curls were piled atop her head beneath a large feathered cap.

When she looked up, her blue eyes flashed, sending a shiver through Hanna. Madame Costello's voice came out harsh as gravel. "How may I assist you?"

Hanna hesitated. Despite the madame's handsome features, she looked the type to slit a man's throat without second thought. To her right, a leather-bound ledger sat on her desk. Hanna strained to make out the names and dates written on the page.

"I'm here for the obstruction of my monthly periods," Hanna said.

Madame Costello pursed her lips, false sympathy in her eyes.

Lucas removed his hat. "Unfortunately that is the case. May we obtain your services?"

Madame Costello flicked through her ledger with a clawlike nail. Then her unsettling gaze met Hanna's. "How long has your monthly cycle been obstructed?"

"Several fortnights," Hanna answered.

Madame Costello turned around, pulling a green glass bottle from the racks of potions on the shelf behind her desk. "Dr. Hart's medicine for feminine ailments," she said. "Removing from the system every impurity."

"I've already drunk it," Hanna lied, looking at the woman's ledger. "And it has been a week's time, and my impurities are not yet removed."

"She requires your *other* services," Lucas said, dropping his voice.

"I see." Madame Costello picked up her quill pen, raising a thin eyebrow. "My services are fifteen dollars."

"Must it be paid at once?" Lucas asked.

"You may pay half now, and the other half once the procedure is finished." Opening her palm, she held it out to him. "Eight dollars."

"That is more than half," Hanna muttered, but Lucas reached into the pocket of his waistcoat, retrieving his coin purse.

"Here," he said, handing the awful woman the bills.

Madame Costello smiled like a snake. "Then we have a deal."

Standing up from her desk, she glided toward Lucas, ledger in hand. Opening the book, she pointed to the page. "You will sign your name here. And the name and age of the patient here."

Putting a firm hand on Hanna's shoulder, the bespectacled man steered her toward the back room. "This way. Time to undress."

He pushed Hanna down the narrow hallway. Pulling back a stained curtain, the assistant revealed a coffin-like room with no windows. It smelled of turpentine. Hanna sucked in her breath, seeing the blood-spattered sheets covering a cot. On a table, hooks, needles, a spoon, and scissors shone beneath the lamplight. Hanna shuddered, recognizing the longest, sharpest needle, identical to one she'd used at the tailor shop.

In a metal pail beneath the cot, blood-soaked rags were piled in a heap. Hanna covered her mouth. There was no way out except the doorway through which she had come.

"Remove your clothing," the man instructed.

"I— Please give me a moment," Hanna said, pressing her hand against her forehead.

The assistant blocked the doorway, taking a step closer. "No time for second thoughts. Your man in there has already paid. We shall get this over and done with."

"No," Hanna said, pushing past him. "I cannot!"

She ran down the dark hallway, steadying herself against the wall. Perspiration pooled beneath her arms in Georgina's tight gown.

Reemerging in Madame Costello's office, Hanna ran straight to Lucas. He hugged her close, his eyes wide with concern.

"I fear your girl requires some convincing," the elder man said, breathless.

Lucas returned the ledger to Madame Costello. "We don't require your services."

The madame smiled like a cat toying with a mouse. "I wager you'll return. And when you do I shall be waiting. I'm keeping the eight-dollar deposit."

"You will not," Hanna said. "And we will not return."

"My money," Lucas said, extending his hand. "Or I'll notify the authorities of your unsavory business practices."

Madame Costello reached into her purse, holding the money between thin fingers. She paused a moment, then allowed Lucas to pluck the bills from her talons.

"Please," Hanna whispered. "I want to go."

"All right," he said, placing his hat upon his head. He tipped it toward Madame Costello and her male secretary. "Good day."

When Hanna opened the door onto the street, the stench of rotting garbage and horse manure had never felt so welcome. Sitting down on the rough planks of the sidewalk, she held her head in her hands. Hanna couldn't erase the image of those blood-soaked rags. Lucas sat down, slinging his arm around her shoulders.

"Pray tell me Margaret's name was not in that book," Hanna whispered.

Lucas tilted his head toward her. "It was not. I managed to discreetly thumb through the pages. Margaret never came here to see this woman."

Hanna dropped her hands, looking at him. "I am glad for that."

"As am I."

Hanna rested her head against Lucas, her stomach sinking as the terrible truth set in. "We are no closer to finding her."

Lucas pressed his lips together, his eyes shiny with determination. "What of the man with the scar? What was his name?"

"Sam O'Grady. Perhaps if we find that criminal, we can find Margaret."

"Ah," Lucas said, stroking his chin. "But for one small problem."

Hanna bit her bottom lip. "What is it?"

"We've sent Clive away with the carriage."

Hanna stood up, brushing the dirt off the full silk skirt of her gown. "Then we will go on foot. Why do you give me that look?"

Lucas smiled. "Hannelore Schaeffer, I have never met anyone like you. Will you be all right to walk in that ponderous dress?"

Hanna chuckled. "I am not one to care about ribbons and feathers. The dress is heavy, but I will manage."

Standing, Lucas brushed off his trousers. "Where shall we begin?"

"The man, Sam O'Grady, he is known in Devil's Acre. I fear we may see Pigeon-Toed Sal again if we walk that way."

Lucas wrinkled his nose. "I do wish to avoid the Billy Goat, if possible."

Hanna took Lucas by the elbow, trudging up the hill toward

Pacific Avenue. "We will go wherever we have to. And we must keep our wits about us."

"Do you really suspect the boy Margaret was courting, Kieran McClaren, might have harmed her?"

A tremor passed through Hanna as she recollected the uneasiness she'd felt this morning at the wharves. Hanna clenched her teeth. "When he said he'd sent Margaret to the abortion doctor, I saw the look in his eyes. It was beastly."

When Lucas turned toward Hanna, his face was pinched. "Do you believe Kieran might have paid Sam O'Grady to drug Margaret, and to force her into an abortion doctor's office against her will?"

Hanna's mouth went dry. Lucas might not have thought much of fifteen dollars, but Kieran McClaren would never have that sum of money. Madame Costello's services were far too expensive for a man like him.

Yet a house of prostitution, such as the one above the Tavern on Dupont Street, would likely offer women's services at cheaper prices. There would be no bespectacled man, no ledgers, no desks, and no office. These back-alley procedures bore unspeakable risks, and a much higher cost—one Margaret might have paid with her life.

Chapter 17

Sarah, *Present Day*

The Victorian homes and tree-lined streets surrounding my bus stop faded to black when I opened the email attachment. I couldn't breathe. The newspaper article appeared on my phone screen as a PDF file. I squeezed my eyes shut, and panic washed over me like a tidal wave. I knew what the clipping said without having to read it again. Those words would haunt me for the rest of my life.

November 3, 2001

Eagle River, Wisconsin—A plea agreement for the 16-year-old driver charged with hitting and killing a 3-year-old boy as he crossed a street was rejected by a Vilas County Court judge on Thursday and she was sentenced to one day in jail.

The teenage girl was charged with careless driving resulting in death and two counts of careless driving resulting in injury for the fatal collision on November 3 at East Main Street and South Wood Boulevard, outside the popular Bott's Ice Cream store.

Police did not release the driver's name, citing her age and concerns about retaliation.

Leah Nichols, 33, was walking with her toddler, 3-year-old Connor Nichols, at an intersection near Bott's Ice Cream. Authorities say the teen's vehicle collided with another car, which then hit the mother and son as they crossed the crosswalk.

A man who witnessed the crash told *Eagle River News* that Nichols was bleeding from her face and had a broken arm. Another witness said he saw a body fly through the air in the crash. Connor Nichols was taken to a hospital but died the next day.

The female teenage driver had accepted a deal with prosecutors that would have avoided jail time. But during an emotional hearing, the family of the little boy brought photos of him and placed them around the courtroom, then asked Judge Kerry Smith to reject the plea, which included 200 hours of community service and a driving class.

"You can't be that reckless," Connor's father, Jim Nichols, said in court.

Judge Smith then asked: "What do you think would be the appropriate sentence?"

"I would never want her to drive again," replied Nichols, saying the teen should receive the maximum sentence. "We have to live with this every morning and every night."

Judge Smith then sentenced the teenage girl to one day in jail, 30 days of home confinement, 200 hours of community service, and to complete a driving course.

At the crash scene, a crowd gathered after the accident, adding to the candles, stuffed bears, balloons, and flowers. One of the balloons read, "One more angel in the sky."

When I opened my eyes, I was reliving my worst nightmare. I still remembered my junior year of high school like it was yesterday.

I'd been speeding in the rain because I'd overslept, and my time card would show I hadn't clocked in for my morning shift. I'd been working as a cashier at Gino's Pizza for only a few months, but Mom really needed the extra money. She'd been so proud of me for getting this job.

I'd been thinking about the disappointed look on Mom's face—the way her mouth would turn down at the corners if I told her I'd lost my paycheck—when I saw the car stopped in front of me. Thinking quickly, I grabbed my emergency brake and pulled it up by the handle. "Come on, come on!" I pleaded. But time seemed to move in slow motion, and I slammed hard into the bumper of the silver Toyota. *Smack.*

I felt a punch to my face like the time I'd been hit with a fly ball during softball practice. Touching my forehead, my fingertips came away covered in blood. I sucked in air through my teeth, the cut stinging. *Ouch.* My windshield wipers squeegeed back and forth, but the cab of the truck had fogged up entirely, so I couldn't really see what was going on outside. The defroster in Dad's old Ford didn't work at all.

This is what you get. This is what you get when you mess with us.

I breathed in and out, like a woman in labor I'd seen on TV. I'd crashed—I'd crashed Dad's truck. I could've killed myself, and now Dad was going to kill me. The hood was all crumpled up and we didn't have the money to fix it. My Radiohead cassette continued playing in the tape deck, while panic swelled like a balloon in my chest.

For a minute there, I lost myself, I lost myself.

Thom Yorke's voice taunted me. What had I been thinking, speeding in this weather? I chewed on my bottom lip, feeling sick with worry that I'd hurt the person in the Toyota. With shaking fingers, I pulled up the lock on the door. Rubbing my sleeve against the condensation, I watched out the window as a man ran down the street toward the accident. Was it that bad? Other cars had stopped in traffic, drivers gaping at me with their mouths open. Why were they looking at me like that?

When I opened the truck door, stepping down into the rain-soaked street, a scream pierced the air. Suddenly I was hit with a pang of dread. I felt it deep down in my gut, like something rancid. The car in front of me, the silver Toyota, looked okay aside from a dent, and the girl screaming didn't seem to be hurt. She was about my age, her brown hair pulled back in a ponytail, and her pink winter parka splattered with raindrops.

"Are you okay?" I asked, slowly taking a step forward. "I'm so sorry I hit you. I don't even know what happened—I pulled up my emergency brake but my car wouldn't stop. Do you need me to call 911?"

An unearthly wail carried into the air, and I noticed the crowd of horrified people who had gathered around the crosswalk. Shivering as the rain hit my face and my shoulders, I looked around desperately for a pay phone.

With a sob, the girl pointed to the sidewalk where the wail had come from. "Look what you made me do!" she yelled, her face contorting. Turning completely white, she doubled over and vomited on the wet pavement. "Oh God."

Peeking around her, I gasped when I saw the woman lying in the road. Blood gushed from her forehead, matting her wet blond hair. The woman's left arm bent back at a sickening angle, like a chicken wing.

"My son!" the blond woman screamed. "Connor!"

The man I'd seen dashing across the road cradled her in his arms. When his dark eyes met mine, he looked at me like I belonged in hell. "Are you the driver?" he asked, the lines of his face drawn in judgment. "Did you do this?"

"I—I didn't mean to," I said, barely above a whisper.

"I found him," another man called, running from the median strip. He carried a tiny body in his arms, legs dangling limply, one shoe missing.

"My son!" the woman screamed again, struggling to sit up. "Connor! Please God, tell me my baby is all right."

The man's face crumpled as he lowered the child onto the ground, placing him at his mother's feet. Bile rose in my throat. The boy couldn't have been more than three, and he had a huge lump on his forehead and blood dripping from his mouth. His pallid face had bluish eyelids, closed like he was sleeping, framed by long lashes.

"No!" the woman in the crosswalk screamed, thrashing as the men tried to restrain her. "My baby! My baby! Connor!"

I felt the eyes of a hundred people on me. Heard a thousand whispers. The mother continued to scream, her face red and twisted as her howl came out raw with pain. She stopped fighting and collapsed. A sob escaped her mouth.

"Why?" she cried. "God, why?"

"No," I whispered, sinking to my knees on the wet pavement. "No!"

I couldn't speak. My arms lay there like two limp fish, shaking at my sides. The mother cradled her toddler in her lap, her body racked with sobs. Tears pressed against my eyelids. I needed to help, but I couldn't move. The little boy . . . What had I done?

"I think she's in shock," a woman said, placing a firm hand on my shoulder. "Are you hurt? It looks like you cut your forehead. Come on, let's walk this way."

"It's her fault!" the Toyota driver screamed at me as I marched past, her face streaked with tears. "My car was stopped at the crosswalk like it was supposed to be. I was waiting for them to cross the street. She hit me! It's *her* fault!"

"You can both give your statements to the police," said the woman guiding me by the shoulders. Her curly blond hair poked out from underneath a beanie. "I'm a nurse," she said quietly. "I saw what happened. Breathe. It was an accident."

My leaden right foot moved in front of my left. It was my fault. *My fault.*

Looking over my shoulder, I couldn't stop staring at the little boy in the crosswalk or his mother, screaming as a police officer restrained her with his arms wrapped around her waist. When had the police gotten here? I felt as though I was having an out-of-body experience. This wasn't happening.

Another officer taped off the intersection with yellow caution tape, the lights of his cruiser flashing red and blue against the gray sky. A puddle of blood had pooled around the little boy's middle, a dark crimson. I bent over and threw up on my sneakers.

"Keep moving," the nurse said, pushing me forward.

More and more people gathered around the intersection, staring at Dad's truck, at me, whispering, sirens wailing—people shouting and crying.

I had caused all of this chaos.

Only thirty minutes ago I'd been at home in my bedroom, throwing the covers off when I realized I'd slept through my alarm. I'd gotten dressed, grabbed the keys, and driven over the speed limit like an *idiot* the whole way into town, worried about clocking in late to Gino's Pizza. I'd cursed and sworn like a normal teenage girl on her way to work, thinking about prepping the pizza dough.

But nothing was normal anymore.

"Can you come with us down to the station?" An officer had a firm hand on my shoulder, leaning in so close that I could smell the coffee on his breath. His eyes were blue as icicles. *Where did the nurse who'd been helping me go?*

I couldn't tell how much time had passed, minutes or hours.

"I—I—" I looked again at the boy lying in the street, his face now covered by an oxygen mask. Two paramedics lifted a stretcher and loaded him into an ambulance. "Is he going to be okay?" I swallowed. "Do you think he's going to—"

But I couldn't finish my sentence.

I wanted to rewind time, just like I could rewind "Karma Police" on my tape. I needed to go back to this morning, so that I'd never have woken up late for work, never have driven too fast in the rain, and never have made any of this happen.

"Let's go," the officer said, guiding me toward his cruiser. "You can give us your statement at the police station."

"My parents," I said, tears streaming down my cheeks. "I want my mom."

The officer nodded, pushing me into the back of the police car like a criminal, right behind the metal partition. "We'll call them for you."

Pain stabbed me like a knife twisting in my gut. That little boy on the stretcher had a mom too. The desperate look on her face would be forever burned into my mind. I didn't need the officer's answer to know what I had done. That little boy, Connor, was dead. And I was the monster who had killed him.

Chapter 18

Hanna, *1876*

Sawdust peppered the streets, the stench of rotting garbage and human waste growing stronger. Hanna wrinkled her nose, lifting the hem of Georgina's dress. Men with picks and shovels slung over their shoulders pushed against her, knocking Hanna aside. With their workday half done, they took to the saloons in droves.

"Oy!" a man with a glass eye hollered at Lucas. "Come 'ere to old Bill's Tavern. Free drinks for the lady, and I'll give you a whiskey on the house."

Hanna's grasp tightened on Lucas's arm. Dressed so nicely, they were prime targets for robbery, even in broad daylight.

"Do you think he knows Sam O'Grady?" Lucas whispered, cocking his head toward the tavern keeper.

"No," Hanna said, picking up her pace. "All he wants is

your silver. It is best we go back to that saloon where Sam is known."

"But the last time we were there, the bartender was not forthright with us. He wouldn't even give us the man's name."

"Correct," Hanna answered. "But the working girls, they will talk. One of them might have seen Margaret."

Lucas's eyebrows shot toward his hairline. "The harlots? Heavens, Hanna, I thought you had enough of their company the last time we visited."

"Yes, they are troublesome. But it's not an easy life for them. Who can say it is a path they have willfully chosen?"

She shuddered to think Margaret had been forced to lie with a man against her will. Hanna would be torn to pieces if her friend had encountered such a fate.

Lucas pulled Hanna closer. "You show such compassion toward others, an admirable trait indeed. Now then, what is our plan?"

She warmed at the eagerness in his eyes. Lucas could have stayed home, sipping tea in his sitting room. Instead he trudged through the filth of Pacific Avenue, willing to revisit the dark haunts of Sullivan Alley.

Hanna tapped her chin. "To find Margaret, I must get upstairs to where the girls are sleeping."

Lucas paled. "Hanna, I don't think—"

"You will remain downstairs," Hanna said. "Close enough to hear me scream. Buy a drink from the bartender and converse with him. Do everything you can to learn of Sam O'Grady. I will sneak upstairs and do the same."

Lucas grimaced, dodging the splash from a puddle as a horse-drawn carriage rambled past. "What if the girls are . . . engaged?"

"It is too early. The girls are creatures of the night. And most men are still asleep, nursing their headaches."

They slowed to a stop, standing in the street as the tavern came into view up ahead, with its red-painted clapboard and yellow trim. Chickens clucked as they walked past, flapping away from the grocer who tried to grab one by the neck.

Lucas sighed. "Take no more than a quarter of an hour, or I will not be capable of waiting any longer. I fear for your safety."

"Here, this is the alley. I will look for a side entrance."

Chinese men with pails balanced on ends of broomsticks spoke in their native tongue, passing Hanna on her right. She stepped aside to make room.

Lucas squeezed Hanna's hand. "Scream as loud as you can, should you encounter any danger. I will occupy the barkeep downstairs."

Hanna looked into his eyes. "You must also be careful. There are many pickpockets about."

Lucas patted his vest and the coins jingled. "I've hidden my dollars in my back pocket this time. The small change is merely for show."

Hanna smiled. "I see you have learned."

Beyond the street vendors hawking their wares, homeless men searched for bits of junk in the shadow of the building. The wind blew, carrying the scent of urine from the alley. Before Hanna could lose her nerve, she squeezed Lucas's hand once and then let it drop. Darting away as the next group of Chinese passed, Hanna entered the alley.

Holding her breath, she crept past an old man sprawled on the ground, a bottle of whiskey clutched to his breast. Hanna walked along the side of the tavern, looking for a door. Piano notes filtered through the walls. For some, it was never too early for folly.

A crack of light caught her eye. The outline of a door. Pressing herself against the wall, Hanna peered through the gap at an empty corridor and a rickety wooden staircase. The piano music grew louder. She looked at the metal latch locking the door in place. It was no more than a hook resting inside a screw.

Aside from the drunk in his stupor, not a soul moved about. She wedged her fingers inside the crack, attempting to jiggle the lock, but Hanna could not stick them deep enough.

A knitting needle would have been the perfect tool. Hanna's skin prickled as Madame Costello's bloody chamber came to mind. Looking down, Hanna spotted a twig, thin and sturdy enough that it might work. Picking it up, she moved to the doorway.

"Clarence, this keg is done," a man bellowed. Hanna sucked in her breath, pressing her body flat against the wall. Silently cursing Georgina's hoopskirt, she wished she did not have so much fabric hindering her movements.

"Run and get another barrel of ale," a different man hollered.

Something scraped across the floorboards. Heavens! If

either man were to step outside, she would have to run in the opposite direction.

"Dammit, this is heavy," someone grumbled. Hanna waited, barely daring to breathe. But slowly his footsteps faded.

She peeked through the crack once more. With the hallway empty, she pushed the stick against the metal hook, applying steady pressure. Unhitching, the hook of the lock swung to the side. Slowly Hanna pushed open the door.

Shutting it behind her, she quietly set the latch back into place. With a deep breath, she looked up the staircase at a red door. Hiking up her skirts, Hanna took the stairs as quickly as she could. When the doorknob twisted in her hand, she let out her breath like a whisper of wind. Once again, lucky.

Creeping inside the room, Hanna blinked, trying to adjust to the darkness. Heavy curtains obscured the windows. Rows of cots lay side by side, occupied by sleeping women. Bloomers and chemises had been cast haphazardly across chairs, while others hung on twine to dry. In the corner, a wooden vanity with a cracked mirror held a washbasin and a few combs. The room smelled of smoke, perfume, and sweat.

As one of the girls turned in her cot, her hair spilled over the side, shining a brilliant red. *Margaret!* Running to Margaret, Hanna crouched at her friend's side, wiping the sweat-soaked strands of red hair from her face. Stroking Margaret's cheek Hanna whispered, "Margaret, wake up."

But when the girl blinked, a blade of panic whisked through Hanna. This girl was not Margaret. Deep purple circles shadowed her dark eyes. Her hollow cheeks gave her face a skeletal appearance. As she turned to Hanna, the girl's cracked lips parted.

"Who are you?" she croaked.

Hanna's eyes darted to the other girls, still sleeping. But for how much longer? The madam or a john could enter at any moment. A dozen or so girls snored lightly, their arms hanging over the sides of their cots.

"Please," Hanna whispered. "Do not raise your voice. I am not here to hurt you. My name is Hanna. I am looking for my friend Margaret. Have you seen another girl with red hair and fair skin? She would have arrived only a few days ago."

The girl's eyes focused momentarily and then clouded like sea glass. "The red-haired girl. Yes, I remember . . ." Her eyes fluttered closed.

Hanna squeezed the girl's hand. "What do you recall?"

A prostitute coughed and rustled the thin sheet in her cot. Hanna crouched low in the shadows. The floorboards squeaked as women moved in their beds.

"Please," Hanna hissed, shaking the girl's arm. "Wake up."

The girl's brown eyes opened again, lucid. "Her screaming, it was awful. Sam hit her. Then she was quiet."

Hanna felt the sting of Father's palm and winced for Margaret. No woman deserved to feel the slap of a man's hand. Her body shivered with cold, though the room was warm. "Sam? Do you mean the man with the scar?"

The girl rolled her head as if she couldn't control her neck. Her words came out too slowly, thick as molasses. "Yes, him. His breath smells of whiskey. He is the worst. He's so rough, he is."

A lump rose in Hanna's throat. Was lack of sleep blurring the girl's senses, or something else? Hanna bit her lip. "Did Sam take her . . . in here?"

The girl's eyes began to close again, and Hanna squeezed her hand tightly. "Please. What is your name?"

"Johanna," she murmured, staring at the wall. "But round here I'm Little Jo."

Holding tightly to Jo's hand, Hanna took a deep breath, dreading the question she did not want to ask. "Did Sam O'Grady force himself upon Margaret?"

Little Jo turned her head, looking dazedly toward the window. "He said he couldn't spoil her. He's saving her for the man who paid him."

Hanna felt as though she'd swallowed glass. "Who paid Sam?"

Little Jo stared at Hanna. "Her husband."

"Why do you say that?" Hanna asked. "Margaret was not married."

"Little hands, a little heart." Jo sighed, her lips rough as burlap. "Wish I had a silver trinket like that. So pretty."

Goose bumps prickled Hanna's arms. Jo had seen Margaret's claddagh ring. Hanna covered her face, shaking. Cots creaked and sheets rustled as the girls stirred from their slumber.

"Jo, please," Hanna whispered. "What man paid Sam O'Grady so that he would not spoil Margaret? What man?"

Little Jo's head lolled to the right. "The man at the window."

Hanna looked to the window, the black curtains obscuring the view. Who had been standing on the street down below?

"Carriage," Jo mumbled.

As she closed her eyes, Little Jo's mouth parted. Her fingers unfurled, and an object fell, landing with a clink on the floor. Rolling toward Hanna's feet, a glass vial slowed to a stop. Hanna picked it up, smelling the telltale chemical scent. *Opium.*

"All right, girls, rise and shine!" a voice bellowed.

Hanna sucked in her breath as footsteps thundered up the creaking staircase. The disembodied voice was male, perhaps one of the two men she'd heard earlier.

"Rent don't pay itself," he hollered. "Get up!"

Lucas had asked her to scream should anything happen. Ought she to do it? Cowering next to Jo's cot, Hanna contemplated hiding behind the curtains. But the bulk of her dress would give her away. There was nowhere to run. Bracing herself for the worst, Hanna watched as the doorknob twisted.

"Pardon me, is this the way to the lavatory?"

Hanna relaxed, recognizing Lucas's voice.

"Oy," the other man snapped. "You don't come up here wivout paying. It's seventy-five cents for a roll in the hay, or a dollar for a real looker. The girls ain't up yet, but I could wake one for you."

Lucas scoffed. "Are you speaking of harlots? I want no such business. I am asking if your establishment has a lavatory."

The man growled. "A what now? You can use the outhouse round the corner like the rest of us do. Or go piss in the alley."

Hanna waited in a crouched position. This man could still open the door at any moment.

"Please, let us keep our graces," Lucas said. "Show me to the bar."

In a flurry of curse words, two sets of heavy footsteps descended the stairs. Hanna let out her breath. Gathering her skirt, she looked one last time at Little Jo and the other women slumbering in their cots, aching to help them.

Pushing the door open, this time she did not step softly as she ran down the stairs. Reaching the bottom, she turned left, grasping the latch on the door and tugging it open. She stumbled into the alley, then picked up her skirts and ran.

The silhouette of a man appeared at the end of the street. Hanna sucked air through her teeth, backing away. But as his face came into focus, she smiled, running toward him while her skirt dragged. Lucas wrapped Hanna tightly in his arms.

"My dear, that took longer than expected. I was terribly concerned," Lucas whispered into her hair. "I shouldn't have permitted you to venture upstairs alone."

Looking into his eyes, Hanna spoke with a new surge of hope. "I met a girl who has seen Margaret."

Lucas's mouth fell open. "Veritably so?"

"She described Margaret's claddagh ring. That awful man, Sam O'Grady, took Margaret upstairs. For what purpose, I dare not say. But the girl—Little Jo—she told me Sam was paid to bring Margaret to another man."

"What man would pay that criminal to capture Margaret?"

Hanna turned back toward the brothel. "I haven't a clue. I thought the McClaren boy might, but I cannot make sense of it now. Perhaps Margaret's own father . . ."

"Why such keen travail to have his own daughter captured?"

Anger rippled through Hanna, thinking of her vile father.

"Men believe they own their children. We are like chattel to them."

"But why would Margaret's father ask Sam O'Grady to take Margaret to a house of ill repute against her will only to bring her back?"

Hanna shrugged. "Perhaps it was a lesson, to frighten her. If he knew Margaret had lost her virtue, then possibly he wanted to show her the life of a harlot."

Lucas frowned, appearing unconvinced. "It seems an awful lot of trouble."

Hanna thought back on how Little Jo had mentioned the word "carriage" and a man standing at the window. Or was it merely the opium speaking?

"Come," Lucas said. "We've spent quite enough time here. Clive will have returned by now. Let's walk back to Madame Costello's."

"All right," Hanna replied.

But the workings of her mind spun like the insides of a pocket watch, ticking and ticking yet finding no solution. She looked down at the hem of Georgina's dress, the fine blue silk covered with dirt.

"*Scheisse*," Hanna said. "Look what I've done to Georgina's frock. This would not have happened on an ordinary carriage ride."

"Oh," Lucas said, grimacing. "I'm afraid you're right. We can't very well tell Mother we were traipsing around Devil's Acre." His face brightened. "I've a suite at the Palace Hotel. We shall have Clive take us there instead."

The Palace Hotel was the last place she had seen Margaret, when Margaret helped her change into Miss Delia's stolen dress. Hanna's throat tightened as she pictured Margaret's ready smile.

"What troubles you, Hanna?" Lucas asked, falling in step beside her.

Hanna wiped a tear from her eye. "Margaret. I miss her so."

"Hush now," Lucas whispered. "We shall find her."

By the time they reached Madame Costello's office, Clive sat waiting with the carriage. Lucas helped Hanna aboard and Hanna sank against the seat cushions, her legs pleasantly tingling with relief after their long walk.

Shouting erupted on the street. As Clive tugged on the horse's reins, Hanna turned to see a drunkard standing before a saloon, his black hair matted and his fingers caked in dirt. *Father.*

Shoeless and shaking with rage, Father yelled at another man. But when his dark eyes met Hanna's, he fell silent. Her muscles tensed, bracing for the onslaught of insults. Would he drag her from the carriage by her hair down into the filth?

Yet Father stood there, slack jawed, staring at her. She touched Georgina's silk dress and fur-lined jacket, remembering she appeared to be a woman of society. Father stumbled forward, spittle flying from his mouth. He fell to his knees in the dirt before the carriage, nearly getting trampled by the horses.

Reaching his arms out, Father cried, "Help me, my daughter. Please!"

Hot tears pressed behind Hanna's eyelids. But how many times had she felt the lash of his belt against her flesh and his hot whiskey breath on her face? Father was the monster of Hans's and Katja's nightmares, a man who drank himself blind so that his family hadn't enough food to survive.

"Do you know that man?" Lucas asked, giving Hanna a worried glance. He hadn't understood Father's plea in German.

Hanna swallowed. Perhaps Father would die in the streets, homeless and alone. A kinder person would offer him forgiveness. But she was not that kind. And she would never suffer at his hands again. Lucas did not need to know the truth.

"No," Hanna said. "He's merely a drunkard."

Hanna peered down at the cobbled street from the fourth floor of the Palace Hotel. Horse-drawn carriages waited out front beneath the stately gas lamps. Women in silk with large bustles took evening strolls with their beaux. Laughing, shopgirls walked arm in arm at the end of their workday. Hanna pressed her eyes shut.

When she opened them, the girls were gone. A knock sounded at the door.

"Who is there?" she asked, spinning around.

"It is I," Lucas responded, his voice muffled. Hanna walked toward the door, wearing nothing but a sumptuous velvet bathrobe over her chemise and bloomers. A maid had taken Georgina's dress to clean, though Hanna had tried to insist on washing it herself. "Yes?" she said softly, leaning against the door.

Lucas cleared his throat. "Please pardon my intrusion. I wanted to see that you are well. I fear I might fret for your safety more than I ought to. Yet I cannot help myself." He paused. "I've begun to care for you a great deal."

"I am well," Hanna answered, placing her hand against the wood, imagining Lucas's fingers on the other side, mirroring hers. "Thank you."

In the silence, Hanna heard only his breathing. Closing her eyes, she slid her hand to the door handle. It would be a sin for Lucas to see her in such a state of undress. And yet her heart implored her to do so as it never had before.

"Forgive me," Lucas said. "I shall return later."

"Wait!" Hanna called, clasping the brass. She pushed open the door, looking upon Lucas. He stood in the hall, hat held in his hands, his youthful golden curls slick with pomade. When his eyes alighted on Hanna's, his mouth parted.

"Please," Hanna whispered. "Come inside. I do not wish to be alone."

Color rose in Lucas's cheeks as he stepped over the threshold. "Your hair," he said quietly. "I am utterly enchanted."

Hanna's hair hung long and loose over her shoulders. She felt freer this way, without the cumbersome weight of it piled atop her head. "Thank you. Mrs. Cunningham once told me I could not wear it long, for it looked like a mongrel dog's tail."

Lucas set down his hat. "She is a fool. It's beautiful."

Shutting the door behind her, Hanna trembled. From what she had believed until now, romantic love was merely an illusion. But in the time she had known Lucas, a yearning had built inside her, so great it was nearly painful. She gestured toward the walnut settee. "Will you take a seat?"

Without breaking Hanna's gaze, Lucas lowered himself onto the cushion. He reached out, guiding her toward the empty space beside him.

As they sat side by side, their knees almost touching, her body hummed like a lightning rod. Taking a deep breath, she prepared to ask the question that had plagued her conscience for days. Hanna wet her lips. "Why do you trouble yourself for me? You are not like the others of your station. I should be invisible to you."

Lucas nodded, sadness in his eyes. "It is unfortunate, but you speak the truth. For it was only when I got to know you that I saw the true beauty of your soul."

In spite of Lucas's kindness all this time, she had feared Lucas was no more than a gal-sneaker, a man devoted to seduction. But his blue eyes glistened, and Hanna knew then that he spoke from his heart.

Lucas stroked her cheek. "But you could never be invisible to me now. Your sparkle lights up a room."

Hanna shook her head. "I know my position, Lucas. You would not see me in this light if some person did not change you first."

Lucas gave her a sad smile. "Remember when I told you that I too had lost someone?"

She did remember. "It is the reason you help me in my search for Margaret, is it not?"

Lucas sighed. "Yes. When I was a very young boy, I had a nanny named Berta who came from the Russian Empire. I can still recall the sound of her voice. Every night she sang me a lullaby."

"She cared for you?"

"More so than my own mother. I have no memories of Mother holding me or comforting me after I had taken a fall. But Berta, she would gather me into her arms and sing to me until I was soothed. She had the most beautiful voice, like an angel."

Hanna pictured small Lucas, his chubby hands and rosy cheeks. "How long did Berta live with you?"

"Until I was a boy of six. Then one day I came home and she was gone." His voice cracked. "She loved me as if I were her son. And I loved her back."

Hanna squeezed his hand, taken aback by the show of emotion on Lucas's normally stoic face. "What happened?"

"I believe my questions unsettled my parents. Like many young children, I wanted to know why Berta did not dine with us at supper, and why she was not permitted to use my mother's parasol."

"Do you think they sent her away?" Hanna asked.

Lucas took a deep breath. "Yes, now I do. But as a child, I thought she had vanished, for she had promised never to leave me. When I asked my parents where Berta had gone, they refused to answer, pretending as though she had never existed."

"How horrible," Hanna murmured, shaking her head.

Lucas smiled. "Berta lived in a room off the kitchen no bigger than a closet. It's a pantry now. But the size of her chamber made no difference to me, for it was my favorite room in the house. Berta kept lavender in a jar by the window."

"How lovely. My mother, she always picked lavender too. Whenever I smell it, I am positively filled with happiness. It reminds me of her."

Lucas gripped Hanna's hand more tightly. "The rules of society did not matter to me then, nor should they matter now. Why can we not reclaim the purity of heart we had as children?" His eyes burned with intensity. "I do not wish to judge my fellow man by his wealth or station, but by the strength of his character."

Hanna drew in her breath, taken aback by Lucas's passion. Something stirred low in her belly, a desire to feel his skin warm beneath her fingertips.

"Lucas," she whispered as his face drew closer to hers. "If you have any regard for me at all, you will leave me in peace."

"I cannot do that," Lucas answered, his breath warming her face, "until I know whether my love for you is reciprocated."

Hanna scarcely dared to breathe, her stomach fluttering.

"Hanna," Lucas said. "I feel that I must reveal to you my feelings and my hopes. Trusting that my attentions have, in a measure, prepared you for what I'm going to ask, please do not be frightened."

Without letting go of her hand, Lucas lowered himself onto the floor, kneeling before her. Hanna's heart began to pound, faster than when she'd been frightened by the men in the Billy Goat. She had neither the manners nor the breeding to become part of Lucas's family. He knew that. Yet never before had she seen Lucas so nervous.

He cleared his throat. "If I know my own heart, it has an unalterable affection for you. And that is why I must ask for your hand in marriage."

Hanna blinked back tears. "Please, do not tease me."

"I am entirely serious, Hanna. Must I repeat the question?"

Hanna could not speak. Mr. and Mrs. Havensworth would find her nothing more than an unsuitable social climber, after their family name and their estate. "Your father," Hanna whispered. "He will never allow it."

Lucas frowned. "I am prepared for that. And I am sorry that my father is such an old stick. We must work on him together, you and I. Perhaps he will see how fond I am of you and his resistance will melt. Your character is so much purer than that of the frivolous upstarts he'd have me marry. But even if he cannot accept it, my affections for you will not change. Please, tell me yes, or my heart will be irreparably broken."

Hanna smiled through her tears. "Yes. A thousand times yes."

Lucas rose and pulled her into his arms, then pressed his lips against hers. Heat pooled in Hanna's center. For this man she would compromise her morals. Her lips parted and they kissed in a way that was reserved for a man and his wife. A longing like she had never experienced filled her, so strong was the want.

Lucas pulled back, bringing his hand to his mouth. "I am a fool! In my haste to propose, I have forgotten to give you your ring."

Reaching into the pocket of his waistcoat, Lucas removed a black velvet box. His fingers pried open the lid. A square-cut emerald, green as a lake beneath a canopy of trees, glittered in the light, wreathed by twelve diamonds.

Hanna's voice deserted her as Lucas slipped the large jewel onto her finger. Never in her life had she seen a thing of such beauty or value. The rose gold ring was fit for a queen, and no doubt cost a fortune. "Lucas, this is much too—"

"Shhh," Lucas whispered, brushing Hanna's hair aside. "You are my betrothed, and I am not ashamed of you. This is your ring now."

Hanna closed her eyes as Lucas moved his hand from her cheek to the curve of her waist. Planting tiny kisses along her neck, Lucas sent shivers down to her toes. Then he stopped. "Hanna, you're trembling. Are you cold?"

"No," Hanna said hoarsely. "Merely frightened of what I am feeling."

Lucas continued to kiss her, brushing the side of her face, her neck, and her collarbone with his lips, sending heat to Hanna's insides in a powerful wave.

"There is nothing to be frightened of," Lucas whispered. "We are to be man and wife." He lowered his hands, gently caressing her hips.

Kissing him deeply, Hanna lost herself in his scent of sweet cigar smoke and pine needles. He smelled like the forest in Bavaria—like home.

When Lucas pulled back, her body ached. She almost cried out so that he would not halt his attentions. Her breath shuddered against his cheek.

"Hanna," Lucas said throatily. "I can stop now. This is enough." The desire in his eyes was unmistakable, but he managed to regain his composure.

"Do not stop," Hanna whispered. "I want to feel you."

With a groan, Lucas removed his waistcoat. Slowly he unraveled his ascot. Hanna shivered as he undid the silver cuff links on his shirt, throwing them hastily on the floor. Her entire body flushed, acutely aware of his arousal. After Lucas had stripped away his clothes, he stood before her, a perfect statue of a man.

Gently Hanna traced Lucas's skin with her fingertips, delighting in the soft curls of his chest hair. Breathing deeply, she moved her hands lower, touching every ridge of his hardened muscles. Lucas slipped her bathrobe from her shoulders, letting it fall in a crumpled heap on the floor. Then he peeled away the thin layers of fabric from her body, leaving a trail of sensations over every area he touched.

His mouth and his fingers sloped over the curve of her bare breasts and the tautness of her belly, her toes curling at his touch. Grabbing her hips, Lucas pulled her to the edge of the settee so that her legs splayed before him.

Hanna gasped when Lucas's mouth met the mound of hair between her legs, and her eyes rolled back in her head when his tongue parted her. Never in her life had she felt such exquisite pleasure. She bucked her hips to meet him, pulling him deeper as he tasted her. Lucas came up for air, breath-less.

Undoing the buttons on his cotton drawers, Lucas paused. "Hanna, are you sure?"

She felt the wind prickle her bare skin as she stood on the edge of a precipice, about to dive into a pool as deep as the emerald on her finger.

"Yes," she said. "I am sure."

"I love you, Hanna," Lucas whispered, laying her down against the settee cushions.

"And I love you," she breathed, clutching his strong back.

Lucas straddled her and pushed his girth inside. Hanna cried out as she felt a sharp pinch. But Lucas's words were the only assurance she needed, and soon the pain faded and the building pressure flooded her with unbearable ecstasy.

As she rose to meet him, Hanna's muscles tightened around the man who was to be her husband. She groaned in pleasure, her legs quivering. Whoever had taught women to lie back and "endure" this act had been sorely misguided. The settee creaked beneath them as she pulled Lucas closer, their bodies rocking and melding into one. Giving herself to Lucas fully, with a final shudder, Hanna moaned in joyous release.

Chapter 19

Sarah, *Present Day*

Hey, are you okay?" the bus driver called to me between the open doors. My emotions felt raw. I sat shaking on the concrete sidewalk underneath the bus stop awning. That article. The accident. It had all come back to me.

"Yeah," I said, rising to my feet and brushing off my jeans. Robotically, I boarded the bus and pressed my clipper card against the plastic panel, listening to the beep.

I averted my gaze from the prying eyes of other riders. Gripping the overhead rail, I watched as houses and trees blurred together. My hands continued to shake, but I managed to keep my balance.

I thought of the email from Anonymous: *Unless you want people to see this, stop what you're doing now.* A chill worked its way down my spine. Hunter could never see that article, not before I had the chance to explain. I bit my lip, hating myself for not coming clean three years ago. Now I had to live with the lie. Who had found the article? And *how* had they found it?

My blood ran cold. Could it be James? He'd likely overheard me when I'd told Jen to report him, which would put his job on the line. What if he was holding all the cards in his hand, ready to expose my criminal record if I decided to help my friend? I thought of his manipulative smile and his calculating eyes.

I couldn't imagine what would happen if Hunter learned about my darkest secret. A fight, or worse . . .

I squeezed my eyes shut, wishing I'd paid my lawyer to remove that horrible article from the Internet. Not that it would have helped. Every local paper in the entire Vilas County metro area had covered the accident. It had taken me ten years to expunge the crime from my record. But that night I spent in jail was a memory I'd never forget.

I covered my mouth as a lightbulb went off in my head. *Of course!* Opening my eyes, I yanked on the chain to announce my bus stop. We were passing by the Civic Center library, and I wanted to pinch myself for not thinking to do this earlier.

Maybe someone had paid to remove the article that solved the mystery of what had become of Hannelore and Margaret from the online newspaper archives. But the library would possibly have records of the original newspaper.

Research was the only thing that could distract me from the pain in my chest and my racing, anxious thoughts. How dare James threaten to send an email about my car accident to people! I'd struggled for fourteen years to move past it. Half of my life spent thinking every day about Connor, his lifeless body, and his grief-stricken mother.

I'd sent her a letter of apology soon after the accident, pouring my sixteen-year-old heart out, telling her how absolutely horrible I felt, and how I knew nothing I said or did could make it any better or bring her son back. Then my lawyer had told me to take the plea deal, making it look like I didn't think I deserved jail time. Seeing photos of Connor in court, his rosy-cheeked, gleeful face—he was the reason I could never have a child of my own. Connor's father had wanted me never to drive again. Instead, I'd given myself a much harsher punishment.

My throat tightened. Would Jen ever look at me the same way if I told her the truth? Would Nick? I couldn't imagine losing both of my best friends in one fell swoop.

The bus door opened onto Market Street, the wind whipping my face. Pressing my lips together, I pushed the thought of Connor away. Hannelore and Margaret were leading me down a rabbit hole, and in the process, I was losing control of my own life. What was it that I wasn't meant to find?

"The devil sold my soul to an alien!" a homeless man covered in tattoos screamed at the sky, shaking his fist. He spat on the ground.

I stuck my hands in my coat pockets and walked faster. Despite the city's attempts to clean up Mid-Market, trash and used needles littered the street. The copper dome of City Hall gleamed in the distance, a bright spot in the gray landscape. The library stood to my right, a modern building with tall glass windows. Walking through the automatic doors, I strode over to the front desk.

My eyes pricked with tears, remembering Connor's limp body, but I pushed down the lump in my throat. I looked at the woman behind the desk. "Can I speak with a reference librarian, please?"

She nodded, clicking her pen. "Someone will assist you in a moment."

An older woman with a long braid appeared, her bracelets jingling as she moved. "Can I help you?"

"Hi," I said. "I'm looking for a newspaper article from January 1876 in the publication the *Daily Alta California*. Do you have any of the originals?"

"No, unfortunately we don't. But you can use the computers to check the archives online."

My hands hung at my sides. "Thanks. But I really need an original."

Her eyes brightened. "Try the California Historical Society over on Mission Street. Their collection is much more extensive than ours. They've got newspapers, periodicals, and photographs—you name it. Admission is five dollars, but they don't charge for the use of their research library."

"Thank you so much," I said.

"Good luck!" she called as I turned on my heel, jogging out of the building.

Flagging a cab, I climbed in and rode the short distance over to Mission and Third. Rain had started falling in fat droplets, and I didn't have an umbrella with me. Paying the driver,

I pulled my sweatshirt hood over my head and darted toward the doors of the California Historical Society.

Inside, I took off my hood and brushed the water droplets from my jacket. A girl looked up and smiled at me. She couldn't have been older than twenty, probably still a student.

"Are you here to see the exhibit?" she asked.

Artifacts from Yerba Buena in the 1700s filled the white-walled space. I craned my neck to look down the hall. "No, actually I'm here to speak with the reference librarians. Are they available?"

She tucked her hair back, showing off the crescent moon tattoo behind her ear. "Go straight to the back and you'll see a glass door. The library is through there."

"Thank you," I said, walking in the direction she'd pointed.

Pushing open a frosted glass door, I entered a small room with no windows. Lights hummed overhead and wall-to-wall bookcases filled with encyclopedias surrounded a long table. Hanging on the wall was a framed black-and-white picture of Yosemite, probably taken by Ansel Adams.

From behind the desk, a woman in a plaid skirt looked over her tortoiseshell glasses. "Hi, how can I help you today?"

I chewed my bottom lip, bracing for another rejection. "Do you have originals of the newspaper the *Daily Alta California* from 1876?"

She nodded. "Sure. What month?"

"Let's start with January. But if you have the issues through July, I'd like to see those as well. And photographs, if you have any from that time period."

"Is there something in particular you're looking for?"

"Yes. I'm looking for a Lucas Havensworth from 1876 and two girls, Hannelore Schaeffer and Margaret O'Brien."

"Your ancestors?"

I paused. "Well, one's my husband's ancestor. But the girls are of no relation."

She tapped her pen on the desk. "Would these have been working-class people?"

"The girls were," I said, taking off my jacket. "But the man would have been someone of society, I think."

The librarian smiled. "That's a great start. Just wait here a minute and I'll get you the directories from 1876, and the newspapers you asked for."

"Directories?" I asked. "Like a phone book, without phones?"

She laughed. "Exactly. They were the white pages of their day. The blue book was for members of high society, and the other directory included immigrants, laborers, and domestics, sort of like an everyman's book. I'll bring both of them over."

I settled into a chair, throwing my jacket over the back. After a few moments, the librarian returned with two books, one blue, the spine about an inch wide, and the other a black, leather-bound volume nearly half a foot thick. I opened the blue book first. In fancy old-fashioned script it read:

Of those whose position or wealth has made their names familiar; together with their city and country residences. A blue book has always been deemed an essential adjunct to the literature of every prominent family in the leading Eastern cities and European capitals.

Fanning through the pages, I reached the "H" section. I trailed my finger down the names until I found "Havensworth," and next to it, Gwyneth's Pacific Heights address. Reading the names of the residents, a chill passed over me.

Mr. William Havensworth
Mrs. Elizabeth Havensworth
Mr. Lucas Havensworth
Mrs. Georgina Havensworth Chapman
Mr. Charles Chapman
Mr. Marcus Chapman (child)
Miss Annabelle Chapman (child)
Mr. Robert Havensworth
Miss Clara Havensworth (child, deceased)

The book only confirmed what I already suspected. Lucas had lived in Hunter's parents' house, and Lucas's young cousin Clara had died there. She'd been the little girl I'd seen in the postmortem photograph taken by François Dupont.

I cracked the spine on the black leather volume, my eyes widening at the extensive list of San Francisco's other residents—those unworthy of the blue book—who had built our beautiful city. There were laborers, gas fitters, longshoremen, drivers, boot fitters, bakers, dressmakers, and sailors.

I read through seven pages of O'Briens. No wonder San Francisco still had its fair share of Irish bars. On the last page, my eyes alighted on "Margaret O'Brien, dressmaker," a resident of 23 Minna Street. She had eight siblings and a father who worked in the tar flats. I traced her name with my fingertip.

Flipping to the back of the book, I located Schaeffer. Of the six Schaeffers listed, Hannelore's name was printed next to an advertisement for Yerba Buena Bitters, which claimed to cure indigestion and dyspepsia: "Hannelore Schaeffer, dressmaker."

"Here you go," the reference librarian said, setting down a stack of newspapers in front of me. She handed me a pair of cotton gloves. "Make sure you wear these when you're going through the newspaper clippings and photographs."

"Thank you," I said, slipping them on.

"Use the index cards to write down which papers you have removed. And please be careful. Oil from your skin will damage these historic documents."

"I understand," I said.

Starting with the first issue of the *Daily Alta California* from January 1876, I read through each article that pertained to a murder or disappearance. My gloved fingers rested on the yellowed page. Using a magnifying glass to make out the tiny lettering, I turned the newspaper over. But neither Margaret nor Hannelore was mentioned.

The clock on the wall ticked loudly as I sorted through the stacks. Raising my arms above my head, I cracked my back. Nearly an hour had passed, and I hadn't found anything. When the librarian approached, she pointed at the time.

"We close in ten minutes," she said. "Just be aware of that."

"Okay," I answered. Maybe I wouldn't find anything at all. When I checked my phone, the screen was blank—no missed calls, no text messages. Hunter hadn't found out yet. Sighing with relief, I picked up another newspaper. James was bluffing. He wouldn't be so callous as to expose me. Then my breath hitched as I read the headline.

Murder of Margaret O'Brien Solved

Without warning, tears filled my eyes. I'd known this was the most likely outcome, but that didn't make it any easier to read.

At eight o'clock in the morning of January 14, 1876, the lifeless body of Margaret O'Brien was found floating in the water at California Street Wharf. Though some speculate the girl had drowned, the heavy rope around her neck indicates she was strangled to death. The coroner has also determined that she was with child at the time of her death. Stevedore Kieran McClaren is accused of the crime.

Neighbors of Margaret O'Brien lend credence to the claim that Kieran McClaren was the father of her unborn child. In a fit of rage, it is believed McClaren took Miss O'Brien's life to terminate the life of the unwanted babe.

Prostitute Johanna "Little Jo" Schroeder gives

testimony that she had seen Margaret five days ear-
lier, in Madame Susan's brothel on Dupont Street.
How the O'Brien girl came to be there is unknown.
Decidedly, she arrived in a state of distress.

Little Jo insists a man with a mark in a carriage
parked on Montgomery Avenue took Miss O'Brien
away. Yet no other witnesses can confirm seeing
such a man.

Johanna Schroeder's testimony has been dis-
missed due to the impossibility of the claim. Montgomery Avenue cannot be seen from such a distance,
a heavy dose of opium clouded her senses, and a
prostitute's fickle mind cannot be trusted.

Miss Margaret O'Brien met a terrible misfortune. Yet many believe she was not the innocent,
young country girl she portrayed. Her impropriety
sealed her fate, and now Kieran McClaren, a man
engaged to another, will hang for the crime.

The room felt very cold. Shivering, I slipped my arms into
my jacket, zipping it up to my chin. What a horrible end for
Margaret. She'd been pregnant and killed by her lover? I
dabbed my eyes, wishing she'd met a different fate. However,
there had been no mention of Hannelore at all. Maybe she'd
managed to escape.

But escape what? Or whom?

I scoured newspaper articles through January of 1877 as
quickly as I could, but found no mention of Hannelore Schaef-

fer. Pulling my laptop from my bag, I powered it on and searched Kieran McClaren's name. Instead of finding a link to the newspaper article, I got a surprising hit: McClaren's Pub. I'd gone once with Jen and Nick for happy hour. My fingers tapped on my keyboard, pulling up a recent census.

A Bill McClaren in his late sixties lived in the Dogpatch. The website for McClaren's Pub confirmed that he'd owned the bar for the past three decades. Going to the white pages online, I scribbled down Bill's phone number. If this was how Margaret's story ended, I wanted to hear it straight from Bill himself.

Pulling out my cell phone, I called Bill and left a message, asking if I could talk to him about the history of his bar. Not exactly a truthful lead-in—but I wanted to get him warmed up enough to call me back. The librarian glared at me, wagging her finger. "Sorry," I whispered, hanging up. "It was an important call."

"You'll have to finish up in here," the librarian said. "We're closed."

Taking off my gloves, I set them on the table. When her back was turned, I snapped a picture of the article detailing Margaret's murder with my phone.

"Thanks for your help," I said, shoving my phone in my back pocket. With my laptop bag slung over my shoulder, I walked through the building, and then stood outside in the rain, looking for a cab. Suddenly my cell began to vibrate in my pocket. I bit down on the inside of my cheek, thinking of James.

When I looked at the screen, I saw an unfamiliar 415 number.

"Hello?" I answered, my mouth dry. "This is Sarah."

"Sarah," a gruff voice replied. "Bill McClaren. I got your message. You said you want to write a feature on my bar?"

My shoulders slumped in relief. "About that," I said, sticking out my arm as a cab with its light on caught my eye. "I was hoping we could talk in person."

"Well, I'm down at the bar now," Bill said. "If you want to drop by."

The cab pulled over for me, and I tugged on the door handle. "Perfect. I'll be there in five minutes."

But as the cab pulled away from the curb, an uneasy feeling came over me. Behind us followed a black Lexus with darkened windows, a car I was sure I'd seen somewhere before. Yes! It had been parked outside Caffé Bianco on the day I'd met with Anna Heinrich over coffee. I slunk lower in my seat. James drove a Lexus. I remembered that now—he'd grabbed his car keys that night when Jen was crying. Was it black, though? When I peeked in the cab's rearview mirror, the Lexus was still behind me.

In the smoky interior of McClaren's Pub, Bill frowned at me, hands folded in his lap. With his silvery moustache and weathered face, he reminded me of my dad—rough around the edges, but sweet beneath the tough shell. He sighed, looking at me with baggy eyes. "You understand why I had the story removed from the Internet, don't you?"

"I do," I said, wishing I could tell him just how much I understood.

We'd been over Margaret's murder, and I'd come clean about the reason for my visit, my phone holding proof that the original article existed.

Bill stared into his whiskey glass. "Listen, honey, it's hard getting business in this town. People these days, they go to dance clubs, trendy places, not Irish bars. I don't need anybody smearing my great-grandfather's good name."

I nodded, leaning forward on my stool. "So you're sure Kieran McClaren didn't kill Margaret? I mean, if he didn't, who do you think did?"

"Who knows?" Bill said, rattling the ice cubes in his glass. "They couldn't hang the guy who committed the crime, so they got my great-gramps instead. Cops were corrupt back in those days. Nobody liked the Irish, that's for damn sure."

"Did your great-grandfather have an alibi?" I asked.

Bill met my eyes. "Sure did. He was working on the boats. But when they arrested him he'd been drinking, so he couldn't defend himself."

I jotted notes on my legal pad. "Do you have any employment records? Or know the name of the shipyard where he worked?"

Downing the rest of his whiskey, Bill eyed me sideways. "Are you going to write about this? I don't want to read some magazine piece about the crime."

I shook my head. "I'm searching for the truth. I won't write about Kieran murdering Margaret if that's not what happened. I'm not after an easy answer."

Bill rubbed his temples. "You must think I'm crazy. Who gives a damn what happened back then? But it's my family name. I ain't got much, but McClaren means something to me. Can you understand that?"

My throat felt dry. The rich and powerful cared equally about protecting their family names, and it made sense that Kieran had been a scapegoat.

"I do. And I think if we can prove that Kieran McClaren was working, we can clear him of this crime, even though we're a hundred and forty years too late."

Bill rubbed his chin. "I think he worked for the Boole and Beaton Shipyard on Channel Street on a scow schooner, the *Anna Louise*. I have some old papers at home, passed down from my father. I can take a look."

"That would be great," I said. "Anything to show that Kieran was working on the night of January 8, 1876. That's when Margaret disappeared. In fact, if you can prove he was out of town, that'd be even better."

Standing up, Bill poured two beers and slid one across the bar to me. "On the house," he said.

"Thank you," I answered, raising my glass. "Do you mind if I hang out here for a bit? I have some work to do."

The bar was completely empty, and a dry respite from the rain.

Bill waved toward the empty tables in the pub. "Not at all. Make yourself comfortable. It's nice to have a bit of company." Shuffling toward the back room, he called out, "Let me know if you need anything."

"Thanks," I said, setting my laptop on a cozy table in the corner. Even though Bill hadn't produced any papers, I wanted to believe Kieran McClaren was innocent, which left me no closer to finding Margaret's killer.

Staring down at my notes, I tried to make sense of things. Hannelore had known Lucas Havensworth in some capacity. Margaret had been killed. Kieran McClaren was named as a suspect and hanged for the crime. Lucas had lived in Gwyneth and Walter's house with his family during the time of Hannelore and Margaret's disappearance.

Though I didn't want to look at it again, I pulled out the postmortem photograph of Clara from my bag, her dead body surrounded by roses and dolls. Shuddering, I flipped the picture over, reading the photographer's name, which was written on the back.

I typed "François Dupont, San Francisco photographer" into Google. Judging from the people he photographed, François was in a unique position to mingle with members of high society, though he himself was only a tradesman. He had a foot in both worlds, something that allowed him to see what others didn't.

A newspaper advertisement from 1870 popped up in the image search.

François Dupont. Photographer. No. 103 California Street, near Montgomery Street. Makes a specialty of fine portraits of all sizes. Old pictures copied, enlarged, and finished in crayon, India ink, watercol-

ors, or oil colors. All work guaranteed satisfactory,
and done at the very lowest price possible. Views of
business houses, private residences, lawn parties,
family groups, etc. attended on short notice.

I typed another image search into Google. "François
Dupont. Havensworth residence." Holding my breath, I waited
for the screen to populate. As the pictures loaded, women in
white dresses sprawled on the grass of a grand estate with
picnic baskets. But instantly my eye was drawn to a mansion
with a Queen Anne tower. Clicking on the image to enlarge it,
I stared at a sepia photograph.

It was Hunter's parents' house. I recognized the slope of
the roof, the gables, and the sheer size of the Victorian. Two
men with moustaches stood in front of a carriage, next to their
driver. The light-haired man wore a dark suit with a gold watch
chain. He had a strong jaw, wavy hair, and his lips bore the
hint of a smile. His dark-haired friend stood beside him, taller
and thinner. His sharp and angled features formed a serious
expression. Both men were handsome, and probably in their
mid-twenties.

My eyes leaped to the caption.

*Cousins Robert and Lucas Havensworth, taken in front of the
Havensworth Estate, San Francisco, 1876.*

So this was Lucas Havensworth. Unlike most of the sub-
jects I'd seen in Victorian photographs, he seemed friendly,

like the kind of person who'd smile at you on the street. Robert appeared stiffer, perhaps more traditional. I looked at the heavyset man holding the reins to the carriage. He had a hard expression.

I gasped. The birthmark on the carriage driver's cheek! That was what the prostitute "Little Jo" had described in her testimony. Johanna Schroeder, opium addict or not, had spoken the truth. I'd seen the view from that corner unit above the Tavern, exactly where the brothel would have been. Not only was Columbus Avenue—then called Montgomery Avenue—visible from there, but a distinct mark on someone's face would be too. The carriage driver had killed Margaret.

I opened a Word document on my computer, my fingers flying across the keyboard as I began to type an outline for my article. Tires screeching, a black car zoomed past, splashing through a puddle.

It was the Lexus with the tinted windows—the same one that had been following me earlier. I reached into my purse, my fingers wrapping around my phone. Maybe I could call Hunter, ask him to come pick me up. This was starting to get creepy. But before I had the chance to dial, my cell phone pinged.

I swallowed, seeing another message in Gmail from Anonymous.

I warned you, but you didn't listen. You'll have to suffer the consequences. You left me no choice.

Chapter 20

Hanna, *1876*

"Clive," Hanna said, speaking into the darkness. "Clive, are you here?"

He emerged from the shadows of the stable, his shirtsleeves rolled up above his powerful arms. Wiping his sweaty brow, he grunted. Hanna wondered if Clive wished to wipe away his birthmark, like a smudge of dirt on his cheek.

Gripping a hot poker, Clive stared. "Are you lookin' for Martin?"

"Yes," Hanna said, the straw crunching beneath her boots as she took a step closer. "Is he here?" The barn smelled strongly of horse dung, and for a brief moment Hanna felt faint, trapped between the heat of the fire and the door.

Perhaps Clive would attribute the color in her cheeks to a long carriage ride. Had he any idea the impropriety of Hanna's transgression, Clive would think her a common whore. Hanna's betrothal to Lucas scarcely felt real, other than a slight pain, a reminder of the passionate moment they had shared. But she had already removed the large emerald ring from her finger, tucking it safely into her bodice.

"Martin!" Clive called into the stable. "Your sister's come round." And with that he set down his poker, shuffling off toward his cabin.

"Thank you," Hanna said, fanning herself. Her hips hurt beneath the weight of her hoopskirt. Perhaps her dirndl would be more suitable attire for Lucas's announcement. He wished to tell his parents of their engagement at supper. Hanna believed it braver to stand before them in plain clothes than to hide behind Georgina's finery. No amount of silk would obscure her lowborn status.

Martin appeared, leading a large chestnut mare by the reins. The horse whinnied and flicked its tail. Martin smiled. "Hanna! You're back. Are you all right?"

"Yes, you see? Right as rain."

"Did you have any luck searching for your missing friend?"

Hanna could not tell Martin of abortion doctors and whorehouses with darkened windows. But her brother saw the distress on her face.

"I'm sorry," he whispered.

"Martin," Hanna said, taking his hand. "How would you feel if we stayed here for a while longer?"

He kicked the dirt. "I like Clive well enough. The food is good. But why would we not leave to make a home of our own? I thought that was what you wanted?"

Hanna swallowed. Lucas had promised she could speak to Martin first, before they revealed their news to the rest of the family.

"If Lucas was a part of that home," Hanna asked, meeting Martin's gaze, "would that be all right with you?"

Martin laughed, gesturing across the lawn toward the mansion. "And why would he leave all of this?"

Pressing her lips together, Hanna stared at the grand home. Many women of her station had tried to marry men of society, and whispers passed between gloved hands. They were called social climbers, charlatans—women who would never possess the manners or breeding to fit into their new surroundings. What if Lucas's parents threatened to cut off his inheritance? Would he still love her then?

"Lucas and I are to be married," Hanna whispered. "Look."

She stuck two fingers in her bodice, retrieving the large emerald and diamond ring. Martin's mouth fell open. "Holy smokes! Is that real?"

Hanna nodded. "Lucas will break the news at supper. But I wished to tell you first. Please say you are happy for me?"

Martin stared at the jewel. "It must be worth a fortune. Hanna, you could sell this. We could buy a house or a stable full of horses. We could start a business."

She sighed. "Martin, I could never. Why would I sell it?"

He frowned. "You really want to stay here? Do you love him?"

"Very much," Hanna said, tucking the ring safely back inside her dress. "Lucas is a kind man. And his sister, Georgina, is lovely. Is she not?"

Martin shrugged. "I want you to be happy. But what if Georgina does not see you as her sister? She is kind now because she enjoys dressing you up, like a little pet dog. What will happen when she tires of you?"

Hanna said nothing.

"Forgive me, Hanna," Martin said. "That was rude. Please don't be sad."

"If you would give Georgina a chance, you would know her kindness," Hanna replied. "Why don't you clean up for supper so that we may eat in the house tonight?"

Martin shook his head. "I do not want to go in there."

"Please, Martin. I would feel much better to have you with me."

His face softened. "*Fine.* If you say so."

"Thank you. We eat supper at six."

"All right, then," Martin said, running his hand through his tousled hair. "I s'pose I ought to take a bath."

Hanna laughed. "The horse dung is not so welcome inside, yet I don't mind it. It smells like the fields back home in Mittenwald."

"Go on," Martin said, waving Hanna away. "Your prince is waiting for you."

Hanna rolled her eyes, picking up the hem of Georgina's dress. Then she dashed across the lawn toward the house. Martin was a smart boy, and perhaps it was true Georgina saw her as no more than a plaything. But Hanna would not know for sure until Lucas had made his announcement.

As Hanna slipped through the door and rounded the corner,

Georgina appeared in the foyer, her blond hair falling onto her shoulders in ringlets.

"There you are!" Georgina exclaimed. "I'm glad to see you're faring better. There's some color to your cheeks. The children have been asking after you."

Hanna dropped her head. "Thank you for minding them. Truly, I appreciate it."

"It is no bother," Georgina said, waving her fan. "Claudia, our governess, is quite taken with them. Katja is such a bright child. She has learned the alphabet. She will be so happy to recite it for you."

"She has?" Hanna asked. "That is wonderful."

Georgina began to walk, her long silk skirt swishing. "And Hans, he is such a darling boy. He quite fancies cats. He made me a drawing." Georgina turned, giggling behind a gloved hand. "The whiskers are a bit askew, but it is charming."

Martin was wrong. They would be lucky to have Georgina as a part of their family. Surely such kindness could not be a ruse?

Following Georgina up two flights of stairs, Hanna entered a sitting room flooded with sunlight. Hans and Katja played on the carpet with colorful marbles and building blocks. They looked up from their game, squealing when they saw her.

"You came back!" Hans cried, clinging to her skirt. Katja threw herself at Hanna's feet. "Ana! I miss you." Hanna gathered the children into her arms, holding them close with their baby-soft cheeks against hers.

Katja fluttered her lashes against Hanna's face. "I give you a butterfly kiss."

"Thank you, little deer," Hanna said, planting a kiss on her sister's forehead.

"Hanna," Hans said, pointing to the floor. "Look at my castle I made from blocks. The man that lives there, he is a prince and he has a pet dragon."

"A pet dragon?" Hanna asked, smiling at Georgina. "That sounds a bit dangerous."

Hans stuck out his bottom lip. "No, Hanna, he is a good dragon. He only breathes fire on the bad people."

"What bad people, dear?" Georgina asked.

"My papa," Hans said. "He frightens me."

Hanna sucked in her breath. "Come now," she said to Hans. "Show me your drawing of the kitty cat."

Perhaps Georgina would dismiss the remark as a child's overactive imagination. But Hanna had seen Father's wild face and left him to fend for himself in the street. She would rather he rot in prison than frighten or harm her siblings.

Lucas stepped into the room, his eyes sending a bolt of electricity through Hanna. In a flash, she saw their tangled naked bodies, and drew in a sharp breath. Her hands tingled at the memory.

"My dear Georgina," Lucas said. "It is lovely to see you."

"You too, dear brother," Georgina said, dropping to a curtsy.

Lucas removed his hat. "And Miss Schaeffer. I see that you are well."

Heat flooded Hanna's cheeks as she took in his secret smile. "Yes. Thank you."

Lucas bent down, opening his arms to Hans and Katja. "Hello, children!"

They ran to him, melting Hanna's heart like snow from the Alps. Perhaps someday she and Lucas would have children of their own. Hanna did not know if she could bear such happiness, for it felt like nothing but a dream.

"Hans made a drawing he would like to show us," Hanna said to Lucas. "And Georgina tells me Katja has learned her letters already."

"What a talented bunch," Lucas said, smiling at the children. "I fear you know more than I do. Now the alphabet, does it go A, G, K, L, V . . . Z?"

Hans and Katja giggled. In unison, they shouted, "No! It's A, B, C, D, E, F, G."

"Ah," Lucas said. "Drat. I thought I had it right." He turned to Georgina. "Dear sister, would you mind if I spoke to Miss Schaeffer alone for a moment?"

Georgina hesitated before she offered her consent. "Of course. I shall be with the children in the drawing room. I take it you won't be long?"

"Not long at all," Lucas said.

When Georgina had gone, Hanna bit her lip. "Do you think she suspects us?"

Lucas stroked Hanna's hair. "Even if she has caught wind of our engagement, we shall make it known in a few hours' time. We will brace ourselves for resistance from my family, but together we shall stand strong." He frowned, rubbing Hanna's bare finger. "You're not wearing your ring?"

"I will put it on later," Hanna answered. "Only Martin has learned of our betrothal."

Lucas nodded. "How did he take the news?"

Hanna thought of her brother's creased brow, but she formed a smile. "He is happy. How do you imagine Georgina and Robert will feel?"

Lucas took Hanna's hand in his. "Georgina will be overjoyed. She adores you and your brothers and sister. She is a pure rare soul who does not look upon social class as a hindrance. I am sure we shall have her support. Robert . . ."

"What is it?" Hanna asked. "He will not accept me as part of your family? I am not surprised."

"Perhaps," Lucas said, his eyes somber. "Robert is very traditional. He may appear cold, but he's been dealt a poor hand. You see, when we were children, he lost his younger sister, Clara, to consumption. She was only eight."

"Yes, I remember you telling me this," Hanna murmured, recalling the sick children who'd perished on the boat passage to America.

"You may never have noticed," Lucas said, "but Robert wears a pin tucked in his jacket which contains a lock of Clara's hair. It's a lovely shade of red."

Hanna had not kept a lock of her mother's hair, for she believed it a strange custom, but she understood the desire to carry a piece of a loved one. Hanna's throat tightened, remembering her mother's kind gray eyes. How Mother would have liked to see her married. "Lucas," Hanna said softly. "What if your parents disown you?"

Lucas's eyes smoldered like embers. "Nothing will deter me from marrying you. If I were to lose my inheritance, I would be monetarily poor but rich in love. I am willing to take that risk. I have an entrepreneurial spirit, and we could start anew." He smiled. "Come, I would like to show you something."

Leading Hanna into a large sitting room, Lucas stopped before a wall of oil portraits. A fire burned in the hearth, flames dancing in reflection on the surface of a marble-topped table. Hanna sat down in a red velvet gentleman's chair, with roses carved into the wood. She recognized Lucas's likeness in a portrait, his blue eyes gleaming from the canvas. The artist who had painted him truly captured his features.

"You are very handsome," Hanna said, nodding at the painting.

Lucas laughed. "You thought I have brought you here to show you a portrait of myself? I hope you would not find me so arrogant."

Dimples indented his smile. He pointed above the fireplace. "Look there."

Hanna looked up and saw her oil painting, the hillside from her father's house overlooking the ocean. Lucas had set the art in a gilded frame with ornate corners, as if the work had been painted by Renoir, and not a poor, unknown immigrant girl.

"Do you like it?"

Tears welled in Hanna's eyes. When she had given Lucas the painting, she simply hadn't wanted Father to destroy something of beauty she had created. But never in a thousand years did Hanna expect to find her artwork adorning the walls of a fine home.

"I fear I do not deserve a place on your wall," she said, shaking her head.

Lucas kneeled beside her. "Hanna, you have a place in my heart, and I want your painting here for everyone to see."

Hanna clapped a hand over her mouth. *No! Had she forgotten it?*

"Whatever is the matter?" Lucas asked.

Hanna blinked back tears. "My mother painted a beautiful plate. It is very special to me, and I have left it at the boardinghouse!"

"There now," Lucas said, rubbing Hanna's shoulder. "We'll travel with the carriage to retrieve it. Never fear."

"I cannot believe in my haste to remove my siblings from that place, I forgot my most precious belongings. I've left Mother's quilt as well."

Lucas took Hanna's hands in his, pulling her to her feet. "The sentimental value of those items cannot be seen by a common crook. We shall get both back."

"Thank you," Hanna said. "I dearly hope so."

Lucas smiled. "When you are my wife, I shall buy you all the paints in the world. You can make enough art to fill this entire house."

"With a house so large, it would take many years."

Lucas kissed her hand. "And that is what we shall have, many, many years together, until we are old and gray and befuddled."

Hanna looked into Lucas's eyes, as though she could see straight into his soul. "I would love nothing more."

"Martin?" Hanna called out in the dim light of the barn, her boots crunching across the straw-strewn floor. If her brother hadn't bathed yet, he wouldn't be ready in time for supper. Hanna wiped her brow, the heat from the fire causing her to sweat. Tools and pokers hung from hooks along the wall.

The mares whinnied, but the barn stood empty. She sneezed, walking toward the door that led to Clive's quarters. Made of clapboard and similar in size to Father's home, the carriage house emanated light from the windows. White smoke puffed from the brick chimney into the darkening sky. No wonder Martin felt more at ease here—such coziness could not be found in the mansion.

Hanna rapped on the door with her knuckles. "Clive? Are you at home?"

No one answered, yet the floorboards creaked inside. Perhaps he had not heard her. "Clive?" Hanna called, more loudly this time. The door swung open, Clive's bulky shape filling the frame. Looking down at her, he curled his lip.

"Forgive me," Hanna said, suddenly overcome by a sense of unease. "I do not mean to interrupt your supper. Have you seen Martin?"

Peering into the room, she saw a fire crackling in the hearth and a stout wooden table standing against the wall. Laundry hung from a line pulled taut between two beams, and a narrow bed with rumpled sheets sat beneath the window. A few plates and jars decorated the mantel, reminding her much of her own living room.

"He's out back," Clive said. "I boiled some water and gave him a brush for scrubbin' and a basin to stand in. He ought to be finished soon."

In the flickering firelight, the gleam of something silver caught Hanna's eye. There, resting on the edge of the fireplace, sat a silver ring. Gasping, Hanna ducked under Clive's arm and pushed past him, running to the back of the room.

"Oy! What the hell do you think you're doin'?" Clive bellowed, stumbling after her. Grabbing a hot poker lying next to the fireplace, Clive picked it up and pointed it at Hanna's face. "Don't move."

But all she could hear was the sound of her heart pounding. A wail escaped her lips. *My God!* Reaching into the soot, Hanna grasped Margaret's silver claddagh ring, the cherished gift from her grandmother.

"Why have you got this?" Hanna yelled, turning to Clive.

His hair stood out wildly at the sides, like a man caught in a windstorm. Pointing the glowing amber tip of the sharp poker at her, Clive glowered, his dark eyes gleaming like mud puddles, watery and brown. "You best be leavin' now."

Hanna rose to her feet, shaking with rage, Margaret's ring held out in her palm. "Where is she? Did you hurt her? Tell me!"

Clive shook his head, his eyes frantic like a startled animal.

"I didn't want to 'urt nobody. I did what I had to." Spittle shot from his mouth as he looked at the ring. "*He* told me to destroy it. I—I put it near the fire, but I couldn't drop it in."

Hanna's voice trembled. "*Who* told you to destroy it?"

"Please," Clive said, taking a step forward. "I don't want to harm you. Leave this place. Take your brother Martin, and your young 'uns, and leave right now." He nodded at the mansion through the window. "That house is evil."

Hanna's fingers wrapped tightly around Margaret's ring. "Clive, put that poker down. Tell me now. Where is Margaret?"

Clive lowered the poker, letting it fall to the floor with a clang. He shook his head, his voice breaking. "I gave her to him. I took the ring because he didn't want proof of what he'd done. I can't lose my job. But I didn't harm the lass, I swear!"

"Whom did you give her to?" Hanna asked. "Tell me!"

When Clive's eyes met Hanna's, they shone with tears, the answer already in them. "Robert. But I fear she's already dead. God rest her soul."

Icy claws gripped her flesh. "No!" Hanna screamed, looking out Clive's window at the mansion, its lights burning like a jack-o'-lantern in the darkness. "Margaret is *not* dead. I will find her! Dear God, is she in *there*?"

"Aye," Clive answered, his face ashen.

Hanna's body began to convulse as if she had a fever. She could not stop the fit, sinking to her knees and rocking back and forth. She had taken baths in that house, been dressed by servants in Georgina's satins. And all the while her dear Margaret had been held captive, locked in one of the many rooms.

She and Lucas had searched every saloon and back alley of the Barbary Coast, while Margaret lived beneath their roof.

Hanna stood up, though her legs felt weak. Her sweaty grasp tightened around Margaret's ring. *Robert.* Hanna dared not let herself imagine what he had done to Margaret. Why could she not see what a horrible creature Robert was, hidden beneath his fine suits? A monster! The crime he'd committed was unforgivable. Beautiful Margaret, who would never harm a soul! Why had he taken her?

Stumbling, Hanna ran toward the door. She would find Margaret and save her. And then she would kill Robert with her bare hands if she had to.

"No!" Clive yelled. "Don't set foot in that house. Get away from this place while you still can!"

Hanna knocked a chair sideways in her haste to leave Clive's cottage. He hollered behind her as she dashed across the lawn, but Hanna didn't turn around. Her eyes stung with tears, focused only on the side door leading to the servants' pantry. As she sprinted across the grass, Hanna's lungs burned.

Throwing herself against the knob, Hanna burst into the kitchen. Frances gasped, dropping a plate of beans. "You stupid cow! Look what you've made me do. What trouble are you up to now? Hey! Clean this up."

Ignoring Frances, Hanna pounded up the steps of the servants' staircase, taking two at a time. Bracing her arm against the wall, she climbed higher and higher, toward the fourth floor. The sound at night she'd thought was the wind. Had that been Margaret's screams? Hanna shuddered.

Blinking back tears, Hanna steadied herself at the top of the dizzying spiral. When the stairs reached an end, she pushed open the door, emerging into a wing of the house she had never seen before. Through an oval window, she glimpsed Clive's carriage house far below. Her breath came hard and fast, looking at the many doors.

Running down the corridor, Hanna pushed open each one. "Margaret!" she screamed. "Are you here? Where are you?" But each time, dusty furniture covered in white cloth greeted her like ghosts, every room empty and silent as a grave. The wind howled in the trees and rattled the window glass. At the end of the hall, she spotted a narrow wooden staircase. As she dashed toward it, her lungs burned.

In this rabbit warren of corridors, stairways, and hidden rooms, what monstrosities had taken place? Climbing blindly, Hanna wiped the sweat from her brow. She rattled the doorknob to the tower, the highest point of the colossal home. It was locked. "Margaret!" Hanna cried out. "Can you open this door?"

She turned around, searching for a weapon. She had been so foolish not to find a hunting rifle or to take a knife from the kitchen. Heaving her body against the door with all her might, Hanna listened as the wood groaned. But it did not break. Again she slammed into the door, sending a shock of pain through her shoulder.

"Open it!" Hanna screamed.

She dropped to the ground, her fingers clawing at the dusty floorboards. But in the crevices between the boards, Hanna found no key. Beneath her, heavy footsteps creaked on the spiral staircase. Someone was coming. Blood rushed to her ears. Grabbing the back of her head, Hanna pulled a metal hairpin from her topknot and shoved it into the lock.

She jiggled it back and forth. "Please, please!" she whispered, begging the lock to give. With a click, the doorknob turned in Hanna's palm. Twisting it open, she pushed her way into the room, falling to her knees in the darkness.

The stench hit her immediately, rotten and pungent. Her eyes darted from the windows, hung with black lace, to the dusty porcelain dolls and children's toys scattered about the floor. Black crepe had been draped over the mirror on the wooden vanity in the corner. Mourning cloth.

Rising to her feet, Hanna walked slowly toward the bed, covering her mouth as the thick air of death filled her pores and lungs. Propped against the pillows, surrounded by dried roses, Margaret lay naked, her red hair spilling over the satin and her white skin glowing pale as the moon. Mottled bruises covered Margaret's neck, and her beautiful blue eyes stared vacantly at the ceiling, lifeless.

"No!" Hanna screamed, taking Margaret's limp hand. Sobs racked Hanna's body. Margaret had been dead for some time. She had come too late.

"I see you've found her."

Hanna gasped. Robert stood in the doorway, lamplight from the hall illuminating his narrow shoulders. He stepped into the room, shutting the door behind him.

"You monster," Hanna cried, dropping Margaret's hand. "You've murdered her!"

"Don't disturb my Clara," Robert said, taking a step forward. "She's sleeping."

Hanna took in his high cheekbones, smooth forehead, and long regal nose—the face of a killer. His green eyes glinted with menace.

"She is not Clara," Hanna growled. "She is Margaret O'Brien, my dearest friend. Why did you do such a thing?"

Robert's body twitched, like he could not control his own movement. "Stop speaking," he spat. "You can see it is Clara. Look at her lovely red hair."

Hanna looked down at Margaret and the bruises covering her body. How had she suffered at Robert's hands? Heat rose within her, blurring her vision.

"You deserve to die!" Hanna screamed, running toward Robert. Slamming her fists against his chest, she sobbed. "You will hang for this crime, you sick monster. You know this is not Clara. It is Margaret!"

Robert pulled back, slapping Hanna hard across the cheek. She stumbled, clutching her face where it stung. Lunging, Robert grabbed Hanna's wrists, his eyes lucid now. His breath hot on her neck, Robert looked at her with hatred.

"Yes, I killed her," he said, his voice harsh as gravel. "Just as I killed the other red-haired whore. Such teases, women are. Even little Clara, she had eyes like a harlot. I smothered her in her sleep so she would never tempt a man."

Hanna's insides writhed like they were full of worms. "You vile beast! Your sister was only a child! Was she never sick?"

Robert laughed, gripping Hanna tighter. "Katja will be

next. She's quite a pretty girl. I'll let you watch as I snap her neck."

"No!" Hanna screamed, looking wildly about the room. Twisting back and forth, she fought against the vise hold of Robert's fists. "Lucas, help!"

A reptilian smile formed on Robert's lips. "He cannot hear you. He's with his father and mother in the drawing room, downstairs. You see, Frances informed me of your state, and so I asked her to shut the doors and draw the curtains. Our home is quite soundproof. Even you couldn't hear Margaret's screams whilst she was still alive."

"Help me!" Hanna yelled, louder this time, her voice hoarse. The smell of rotting flesh and fermented roses overpowered her, bringing on a wave of nausea.

Robert clucked his tongue. "This was Clara's room. No one comes here anymore, as if they would rather forget. I haven't forgotten. She will forever be my little girl."

Gagging, Hanna struggled to breathe. She could not faint, not now.

Robert's green eyes flashed with hatred. "I've already placed our best family silver in your chamber. It shan't be difficult to convince Lucas you've stolen it. I know of the ring he's bought you, the fool."

Hanna tugged as hard as she could, but Robert would not let go.

He threw his head back and laughed. "To marry a low-born slattern is unheard of, especially one as dirty as you." He smiled like a madman, his teeth sharp as points. "I will have you thrown in jail for thievery, and your siblings shall become street urchins. Except for Katja, whom I'll keep close."

Rage filled Hanna like fire, to the point where she couldn't see anything other than red. With all her might, she rammed the top of her head against Robert's nose. Pain flooded her skull, and a crack sounded. Robert yelped, releasing her wrists. Staggering backward, Hanna seized the moment to escape.

Picking up her skirts, she ducked as Robert lunged for her, feeling a whoosh of air where his hands nearly grabbed ahold of her neck.

"You little bitch," Robert growled, blood dripping onto his suit.

Hanna's heart pounded against her rib cage as she darted to the door. The stench of death clung to her hair and clothing. Shoving the door open, she ran down the hall. In a flurry of curse words, she heard Robert fall to the ground behind her, but she didn't dare pause to turn around. She had to find the children! Fear surged within her body like waves in a storm as her feet thundered down the staircase.

Reaching the third level of the mansion, Hanna ran through every room. "Hans!" she cried, entering the chamber where her brother and sister had been playing earlier with blocks and marbles. "Katja, where are you?"

Her breath came in ragged gasps, and her head spun. She wiped the tears from her cheeks, turning in circles. A tall figure emerged from the shadows. Hanna brought a hand to her mouth, muffling a scream.

"It's me," Martin said, stepping into the light. He held Hans by the hand and carried Katja on his shoulders. His worried eyes met Hanna's. "Clive told me to find you and to take the children. He said we must leave right now."

"Yes," Hanna said breathlessly. "As fast as we can."

Clutching Hans in her arms, she followed Martin down the stairs. She fought back tears as she felt her heart splinter into a million pieces. Though she longed to tell Lucas the horrible truth, she knew there would be no justice for Margaret. Hanna's blood ran cold, recalling the eve of Margaret's disappearance. During her carriage ride with Lucas, he had spoken of wealthy men who enjoyed bawdy shows, whilst pretending to attend meetings at the Young Men's Christian Association.

"What the rich don't want to believe, they ignore, even if it's taking place right under their noses."

The Havensworth family could never endure a scandal such as this. And no matter what Robert's crime, they would not bring it to light. An innocent man would likely hang for Margaret's murder. Perhaps it would be Clive or Kieran McClaren.

Hugging Hans close, Hanna pressed her tear-stained cheek against his. She couldn't bear holding such a terrible secret inside. And Lucas couldn't bear learning the monstrous nature of his beloved cousin. Hanna would spare him that truth, even if it cost her the future she had envisioned.

Martin pushed open the door to the kitchen, and the four of them ran together across the lawn, toward the road. Hanna breathed in a deep gulp of fresh air, like a fish that had been beached finally returned to the ocean. Clive waited with the carriage ready. Martin hoisted Katja inside, and then Hans.

"Where are we going?" Hans asked, scrambling into the seat.

Katja stopped sucking her thumb and looked at Hanna with wide, frightened eyes. "Lucas come with us?"

"No, my loves," Hanna said, a lump forming in her throat. "We will go on our own."

Martin climbed aboard the driver's seat, sliding in next to Clive. "Hanna," he said, his eyes darting nervously to the house. "It's time."

He reached out his hand. With a creak, the front door to the mansion opened, and Georgina stepped outside. Hanna's breath caught in her throat. Georgina hurried down the steps, the silken skirts of her gown rustling. Her beautiful face creased with worry as she ran forward, like a princess in a fairy story.

"Hanna," Georgina called. "Wait! You will leave us so abruptly? Whatever is the reason? I thought we were to sit down to supper."

"Get in, girl," Clive yelled, tugging on the leather bridle of the horse.

Hanna took a step toward Georgina, reaching into the bodice of her dress. "Please tell him I am sorry," Hanna said, a tear trickling down her cheek as she placed the ring in Georgina's palm. "But I cannot marry him."

Georgina's mouth fell open. She stared at the jewel, the emerald sparkling beneath the streetlamps, surrounded by its halo of diamonds.

Lifting up her skirt, Hanna took Martin's hand. Her brother

pulled her into the carriage, where she slid in beside the children.

"Go now!" Hanna cried.

With a whistle, Clive tugged the reins and the carriage lurched forward. As the horses began to trot, Hanna wiped the tears from her cheeks. Her lips trembled. But nothing prepared her for the moment when she saw Lucas standing in the doorway.

Her chest clamped.

"Hanna!" Lucas cried, running down the steps. "Stop, at once!"

His eyes shone with desperation as he ran down the street, his legs pumping as he tried to catch up with the carriage.

"I love you," Hanna whispered, placing both hands over her heart, which seared like an open wound. "Forgive me."

Turning away so she would not see Lucas, Hanna sobbed into her palms. The carriage rocked as it bumped along the cobblestones. How she had deceived herself! The daughter of a blacksmith could never strive to become a rich man's wife. No matter how deeply she loved Lucas, she'd been foolish to imagine herself a Havensworth. And just as she'd always believed, Hanna could not be foolish if she wished to survive.

Chapter 21

Sarah, *Present Day*

When I opened the door to my apartment, my stomach filled with dread. I could tell from the look on Hunter's face that he'd already read the article. He sat at our kitchen island, running his hands back and forth across his face—his telltale gesture for whenever he was nervous. I tried to swallow, but my throat was too dry.

"Hey," I said in a weak voice.

"Hey," Hunter answered, his hazel eyes following me as I walked toward the teapot. "Are you going to tell me what's going on?"

I bit my lip hard, tugging a packet of Earl Grey from the cupboard and putting it inside a mug. "What do you mean?" I said, my voice too high, too scared to turn around and look my husband in the eye.

"Sarah." Hunter's voice was soft. "My father talked to me about an email he received today. It's pretty serious."

Setting down my mug, I turned to face my husband, my arms wrapped across my chest as if I could protect myself. "Your *father*? Who sent it to him?"

Hunter blew out his breath, puffing his cheeks. "Dad said it was a tip-off from his HR team at the firm. Someone reported you on LinkedIn. Look, I know you don't work for him, but because you share our last name, HR was worried."

My stomach plummeted. Every suspicion I'd had that James was blackmailing me had been confirmed. He had gone too far. I had threatened his job by asking Jen to report him, and instead he'd reported me first.

"What did they say?" I asked.

Hunter grimaced. "Um, well, there was an article attached about a teenage driver who killed a three-year-old. They said the driver was *you*. Is it true?"

I braced myself against the countertop, worried my legs would give out underneath me. It would be so easy to lie. The article didn't name me. James couldn't prove anything. But I had been lying for so long. I couldn't do it anymore.

A rock-hard lump rose in my throat. I closed my eyes. "Yes."

My voice had come out barely louder than a whisper, but it felt like I'd spoken to a crowded room while holding a microphone.

When I opened my eyes, Hunter's face was covered in judgment, just like the man at the scene of the accident. In that moment, I knew I was no longer the person Hunter thought he'd married. I covered my trembling mouth.

"Sarah," Hunter said, the color draining from his face. "Are you serious?"

I couldn't stop myself from seeing Connor's limp leg, his tiny foot missing a shoe. I saw him in my sleep, at the grocery store, and sometimes even sitting at my desk while I tried to write. I pressed my hands to my heart, feeling the rising panic. "Stop asking me that! I already told you it was true, didn't I?"

Hunter sat there, his mouth hanging open. "You killed him?"

I nodded, tears streaming down my cheeks. "I was late to work. I was speeding in the rain when I shouldn't have been. I rear-ended the car in front of me. At first I thought it wasn't so bad—maybe I'd given the driver whiplash. But then . . ."

Hunter lifted his head to the ceiling and bit his lip. Then he looked at me like the policemen had at the station, like I had killed a child on purpose.

My lip trembled. "Please say something?"

Hunter rubbed his face with his hands. "I don't understand. Why didn't you tell me about this before? Why the hell would my dad have to tell me the news before I knew about it? Sarah, you're my wife!"

I sank to the floor, the lights of our kitchen ceiling shining too brightly, exposing me. "Because I didn't tell anyone."

"But I'm not just anyone," Hunter said. "I'm your husband!"

My body began to shake, and I hugged my knees to my chest. "I thought if I told you, you would leave me. I wanted to tell you early on, but then you mentioned your friend Andy who got fired, and said something about how you couldn't have him associated with your father's company or your family name. I got scared, because I didn't want to lose you and *I* have a criminal record too."

Hunter groaned, his face shifting from sadness to anger. "You didn't tell me because of something I *said*? Sarah. This shows me you don't trust me. We're supposed to be a team! Do you know how much this scares me?"

"I'm sorry," I whispered.

Hunter glared at me. "How many times have I helped you through your panic attacks?" He scoffed. "You don't have social anxiety, do you? Every single time I've rubbed your back and asked you to tell me what was wrong, you refused."

"I'm so sorry," I said, my stomach twisting. This was the end for us. I could feel it. And worst of all, I deserved it. My voice broke into a sob. "I was lucky I didn't get sentenced to more jail time. And I feel guilty every day!"

Hunter stopped pacing. "I could have helped you! But considering you don't even trust me enough to share your life with me, I feel duped and angry."

"I never meant to make you feel that way," I said, tears wet against my cheeks. "But think of how I feel. I didn't mean to hurt anyone! It was an accident. I swear, Hunter. I know it was selfish, but I didn't tell you because I was afraid you'd look at me the way you're looking at me now, like I'm a murderer."

Hunter's eyes shone with tears. The anger left his face and his hands hung by his sides. "I need some time to process this. My dad thinks we should get a divorce."

I shook with sobs, burying my face in my hands. Walter had hated me since the beginning, just like most of my high school class. I'd become a pariah, lost every single one of my friends. I'd begged my mom to let me drop out, but she'd forced me to keep going, staying up late with me to help me finish my homework. My parents already had so little, and then I'd drained their savings with my legal bills. I worked so hard to expunge the crime from my record and to get a good job so I could make it up to them. Then they died one after the other. Now I was losing Hunter too.

"I guess I'm being punished for what I've done," I said, choking on my sobs. "Of course you want a divorce."

"No," Hunter said, shaking his head. "You're punishing yourself. *And* you're twisting my words. So why don't you be honest with me about something else. Is this why you're not ready to have kids?"

I nodded, tears trickling down my face. I longed to throw my arms around my husband's neck and to breathe in the piney scent of his skin. I needed Hunter to tell me everything would be okay, like he always did. But it wouldn't. Not this time.

I tugged my emerald ring from my finger and held the family heirloom out to him. "You should take this back."

"Sarah," Hunter said, his eyes widening. "What are you doing? You're not thinking straight. Seriously, you need to calm down."

"Just take it," I said.

Hunter's fingers closed around the ring. "So this is what you want?"

His words sucked the air out of my lungs. What if I was making the biggest mistake of my life? I loved him, so much. But the damage was done.

"Yes," I said.

I watched my husband's face collapse, the lie piercing me like shards of glass. Now that Hunter knew the truth, it wouldn't take him long to realize he deserved someone better. Because who could love a murderer? Like ripping off a scab, I'd inflicted the pain on myself.

"I'll be at my parents' house," Hunter said, his eyes shining with tears. "You've made it pretty clear you don't want me here anymore."

I watched stupefied while Hunter threw his clothing into a bag, and then slammed the door to our apartment behind him. But as soon as I heard his car pull away from the curb, a wail escaped my throat. I hugged Redford and buried my face in his fur. The cat rubbed his head against my chin, purring.

Setting Redford down, I looked around for my purse, and then found it sitting on the kitchen table. Unscrewing the cap on my Klonopin bottle, I popped two pills in my mouth and downed them with a glass of water. Then I waited for the hazy fog to envelop me so I could dissolve into it, disappearing forever, like Hanna and Margaret.

Chapter 22

Sarah, *Present Day*

My palms began to sweat as I held Gwyneth's house key in my hand. Even though everything important in my life had come crashing down around me, I had committed to turning in my master's thesis on time. My throat tightened. I needed one more piece of evidence to confidently write my article.

When I pushed open the heavy door, the parquet floors gleamed in the sunlight, polished to a high gloss by Rosa. If I saw her, I'd tell her I was looking for family photos, which wasn't exactly a lie. With a picture of the Havensworth carriage driver, I could find his name and see if he had a criminal record.

I shut the door behind me, and my footsteps echoed in the large hall. The grand staircase leading to the bedrooms on the second floor looked like the one from the movie *Titanic*. Once upon a time, women in beautiful gowns probably used this wooden handrail. My chest ached, thinking Hunter was the last person to touch it.

Had he slept well last night, or had he stayed up late, thinking about me? I tried to shake my sadness as I climbed the stairs. What the hell had I done? Walking down the hall, I stopped and then peeked into Hunter's childhood bedroom. It didn't have any of the normal memorabilia of most guys his age—sports trophies or posters of nineties bands.

Gwyneth had gotten rid of everything, reupholstered the furniture in peach, and redecorated with expensive floral wallpaper imported from France. If the redesign had hurt Hunter's feelings, he hadn't said anything. That was his mom's way, to hide what she found unsightly, burying the past under layers of paint.

My lip quivered, looking at Hunter's gym bag splayed open on the ground. A few T-shirts and pairs of boxer briefs spilled out. I stepped inside and picked up the pillow on his bed. It smelled like his hair pomade. Setting it down, I burst into tears.

But I hadn't come here to smell my husband's things and cry. Gwyneth would probably keep the photo albums downstairs in one of the living room cabinets. After shutting the door, I walked down the hall.

I was taking the spiral staircase this time. It couldn't be that bad, could it? Servants had probably been forced to stay out of sight while invited guests had the pleasure of making a grand entrance in their beaded gowns. A thrill ran through me as I pushed open the wooden door leading inside. A dark, dizzying passageway wound downward like something out of a dream.

From what I could see, nothing was rotting or broken.

Aside from being slightly cramped and spooky, the narrow staircase seemed structurally sound. My footsteps creaked as I descended the steps. Walter and Gwyneth would be at the country club for another hour or so, and I still had time to avoid them. Telling my in-laws about my separation from Hunter was too painful to think about. It would make everything real—and I wasn't sure I wanted that.

When my heel hit the next step, the sound echoed. *Huh?* Climbing up to the previous stair, I tapped the plank with my toe. The wood thumped flatly. Crouching low, I inspected the step that had made the noise, rapping my knuckles on the wood. The sound was distinctly hollow.

Taking a deep breath, I turned my palms upward, pressing against the lip of the stair with my fingertips. With a creak, it swung open. I gasped, then coughed, sucking in a puff of dust. I looked into the dark hollow. It was shallow, only about six inches deep—a hidden compartment under the stair. Well, I'd be damned. Had this been what Gwyneth didn't want me to find?

At first the hole appeared empty. But when I reached my hand inside, I discovered that the edges of the compartment went farther back than I'd thought. Tucked against the far corner was the square edge of a book. I picked it up, pulling it out and blowing the debris off its cover. The leather-bound book looked nearly as old as the house itself. Gently I cracked the spine, reading the first page.

Diary of Georgina Havensworth Chapman, 1876.

Sitting down on a step, I carefully flipped through the pages, afraid to damage an amazing piece of history. My breathing grew shallow as I read Georgina's descriptions of lavish society dinners and balls, of carriage rides with her husband, and Georgina's fears that her son Marcus was not a good boy.

I shook my head. This diary would make a wonderful addition to any San Francisco history museum—and Gwyneth loved contributing to the arts. She was a member of San Francisco's preservation society! So why had she taken such pains to keep it hidden?

Turning the page, I read the next entry, curious to see if Georgina's young son had cursed at his governess during their math lesson. "Oh my *God*," I whispered, bringing a hand to my mouth.

January 12, 1876

Today the oddest occurrence took place. Just before supper, Lucas arrived at the door with a family of immigrants from Prussia. One was a lovely dark-haired girl about my age named Miss Hannelore Schaeffer, and the other three were her younger siblings, Martin, Hans, and Katja. At first I didn't know what to make of them. Father surely had quite the fright when Lucas introduced Miss Schaeffer as his "friend."

The impropriety of it! He believed her to be unmarried with three children, and thought Lucas had brought her to the house to be employed as a servant. But the dear girl had lost her own parents and found herself in need of a place to sleep. To act as any good Christian would, I suggested to Father that he allow the family to stay. Lucas appeared quite keen on the girl, whom he had come to know at a shop in town.

Despite her lowborn station in life, she is bright and well spoken. I do enjoy her company and I have lent her several of my old dresses. Life here has been rather dull lately and I am quite excited to have a friend to converse with, though I cannot call her a friend yet, for I hardly know the girl. But I should like to know her better, and the young children are lovely and shall make good playmates for Marcus and Annabelle.

The look on Mother's face at supper when Hanna mentioned her father's trade as a blacksmith! Truly, it was priceless. For weeks I have listened to nothing other than dull talk between Charles and Father of financial things, such as fighting over in-shares. How refreshing to hear tales of a woman's life outside the home!

Gertrude remarked that Hanna had never seen a copper bath with indoor plumbing. Imagine! I suspect dreadful circumstances have befallen poor Hanna, for she appears as though she has not eaten in weeks, and she is forever looking about as if someone is watching. What could she be running from? Dear diary, it is late now, and I must be off to bed.

Georgina

"Are you kidding me?" I cried out in the empty stairwell. My surroundings became hazy, like the outside world had faded away. Had Hanna stayed in one of the very guest bedrooms I'd slept in with Hunter? She'd been in this house! Setting down the diary, I rubbed my arms, which prickled goose bumps.

Picking up the diary, I turned the page, reading Georgina's words as if she had written a bestseller I couldn't put down.

January 13, 1876,

Today I extended an invitation to Miss Schaeffer to join Mother and me in the drawing room. I had hoped for lively conversation, as Hanna is employed as a seamstress. An unmarried girl's life is surely far from dull. How gay it must be to work in a shop! But the poor dear had a fainting spell and took to her chamber.

In the afternoon, Lucas accompanied Hanna on a carriage ride into town, so that the fresh air could restore her health. She returned quite rosy cheeked. From the way those two looked upon one another, I suspect the beginnings of a courtship. Papa would have the vapors, and Mother a fit, but I like to think myself a modern woman. Love does not discriminate, and Lucas may court whomever he pleases!

Hanna is so taken by the fabric of my dresses and the workings of a bustle and hoopskirt, I'm afraid she's never worn fine things. I often tire of the mindless chatter of Miss Delia Heathcoate and Miss Juliet

Livingston. They only wish to gossip, complain of their mundane lives, and speak ill of other people.

> *Oh! I am called to assist the children with their lessons. I shall write more when time allows.*

As I turned the page, Hanna's world unfolded before my eyes. How out of place she must have felt at formal dinner with the Havensworths, just like I did. The uncanny parallel between our lives brought a shiver from the crown of my head down to my toes. Had I always been meant to find her?

On the next entry, big round water droplets smeared the ink. The words feathered out, like Georgina had been crying.

January 13, 1876—continued

Tonight has been awful. I know not where to begin. My dear brother, Lucas, was to announce his betrothal to Hanna at supper. He had purchased the most gorgeous ring—a three-carat emerald flanked by twelve diamonds and set in rose gold.

My mouth went dry. I didn't need to look at my bare finger to know that the ring was mine. And it had belonged to Hanna.

Of course it came as a shock that their courtship progressed so quickly, yet such whirlwind romances are not unheard of. Father is firmly opposed to the notion of marrying below one's class, and Lucas quite rightly possessed the strong conviction to defy him. It is for these reasons I believe my dear brother truly loved the girl. And that is why my tears fall freely upon the page.

Just before supper, I heard a commotion upstairs, like a herd of cattle thundering down the servant's staircase. Mother, Father, Charles, and I sat with Lucas in the drawing room, awaiting his announcement. Robert could not be found—he is such a strange, brooding man, and I know not what plagues my cousin's conscience.

When the door slammed shut with such force, Lucas and I stood to attention. I ventured outside into the garden, finding Hanna, her hair askew and her face streaked with tears. After all the kindness I had shown, she had hopped into our very own carriage, with Clive at the reins, for an unannounced and early departure!

With the most pained expression, Hanna reached into her bodice and produced the emerald ring. Giving it to me, she said, "Forgive me. But I cannot marry him." I stood there aghast. My parents may not have approved of the union, but to leave my poor Lucas in such a state is unconscionable. Lucas ran to the porch just as the carriage pulled away. My brother's heart is shattered, and his spirit crushed.

What's more, Robert has a broken nose from a fall down the stairs, and has produced the family silver, which Hanna intended to steal. Apparently, she hoarded it in her chamber beneath the bedclothes. And to think I *had believed her to be a nice girl. Perhaps she is naught more than a common thief making a fool of Lucas.*

Calling a second carriage to the house, Robert sent a rather fearful scar-faced man to search for Miss Schaeffer. I have never seen this driver before in my life, nor do I wish to again. He gives me the willies, yet Robert assures me the man is trustworthy. What's more, his carriage bore a terrible stench, like death!

Thankfully, the scar-faced man did not return. Sadly, Lucas did not attend supper, so deep was his sorrow. At dinner, Robert announced the morbid news that an Irish shopgirl had been found dead in the water at California Street Wharf. How horrid indeed!

All in all it has been a very dark day. In spite of the revelation that Hanna was not who she appeared to be, I fear Lucas will never love again. He pines for her now, crying softly in his bedchamber.

Regrettably,
Georgina

I set the diary in my lap, not knowing whether minutes or hours had passed. Then I sucked in my breath. *Clive!* He was the Havensworths' carriage driver, possibly Margaret's killer. But something did not sit right. Georgina had described an Irish shopgirl found dead in the water, a girl sounding suspiciously like Margaret.

Fumbling for my phone, I brought up the snapshot I'd taken of the newspaper article reporting Margaret's death. Zooming in to look at the date, I read "January 14, 1876"—a day after Georgina's diary entry.

Rubbing my temples, I tried to concentrate. In the late 1800s, the wharves were notorious for crime and gangs—the Sydney Ducks, shady characters of San Francisco's underworld. These were not the type of people Robert Havensworth would associate with. Plus, Georgina had said he'd never left the house.

So how would he have heard the news?

I tapped my lips. If Hanna had loved Lucas and wanted a better life for herself and her siblings, why wouldn't she have waited for Lucas to announce their engagement? Even if his parents had rejected her because of class differences, why would she have run away without saying good-bye—not giving Lucas the ring in person, but giving it to Georgina instead? Hanna hadn't even taken the silver when she fled.

It all felt very rushed, very frantic. The sound of people running down the stairs, the silver in her bedroom, Robert's broken nose . . . nothing added up.

Sighing, I set the diary down on the step. Hanna wouldn't have gotten into a carriage with a murderer. She was smarter than that. Besides, if Clive was concealing Margaret's body, getting ready to dispose of it, the stench would have alerted Hanna right away. I gasped, my eyes zipping to Georgina's handwriting.

Calling a second carriage to the house, Robert sent a rather fearful scar-faced man to search for Miss Schaef-

*fer. I have never seen this driver before, nor do I wish
to again. He gives me the willies, yet Robert assures me
the man is trustworthy. What's more, his carriage bore
a terrible stench, like death!*

Wait a minute. How would Robert have known that the
murder victim was Irish and a shopgirl a day *before* Margaret's
death was announced in the paper? And he'd called a suspi-
cious guy, whose carriage smelled like *death*. Given the time
Lucas had spent courting Hanna and the fact men and women
in Victorian times were rarely alone together until they married, Robert had probably met Margaret.

I covered my mouth. It wasn't Clive who had killed Margaret. It was Robert Havensworth. Hanna hadn't left Lucas
because she hadn't loved him. She'd left him because she'd
wanted to protect him from the truth. What if Robert Havensworth had taken an interest in Margaret, gotten this scar-faced
man to kidnap her, and then later asked him to dispose of her
body?

The Havensworths were murderers.

My phone pinged, startling me so badly that I jumped.
Swiping the screen, I found a text message from Nick.

Hey chica. I searched that IP address for you. The emails from
Anonymous are coming from an address in Pacific Heights. 2713
Pacific Avenue.

I dropped my cell phone, watching it clatter down the stairs
all the way to the landing. The emails had come from inside
this house. My eyes pricked with tears. James hadn't ruined my

marriage, Walter Havensworth had. Of course Walter wanted to hide the fact that his wealthy ancestor had murdered a poor young Irish immigrant. As a board member of the Irish National Gallery, Walter couldn't risk losing face with his cronies by appearing to be a giant hypocrite.

I stood up, ready to grab my fallen cell phone, when the front door slammed. A single set of footsteps crossed the foyer. Sucking in my breath, I knocked over the diary. It fell with a thud into the dusty compartment beneath the stairs, its pages splayed open. I quietly shut the lid, hoping to retrieve the diary later. The footsteps came closer.

Tiptoeing up the servants' staircase, I made my way back to the second floor. Without thinking, I darted down the hallway toward Hunter's bedroom, my breath hot and shallow. Opening the door to his room, I stepped inside and shut it behind me. Why hadn't I run downstairs instead? Walter wasn't going to hurt me, was he?

Before I could make a move, the doorknob twisted. Taking a step backward, I looked at the window. The bedroom was two stories up, with no way to get out, and I didn't have my phone to call the police.

The door swung open, and I tried to scream. But the sound never escaped my mouth. Hunter stood before me wearing a pair of shorts, golf shoes, and a sweaty polo shirt. "Sarah," he said, his eyes widening. "What are you doing here?"

"I'm—I'm—" I stammered, staring at my husband. "What are you doing here? I thought you would be at work?"

Hunter stepped toward me, holding both my shoulders.

The kindness in his eyes enveloped me, along with the familiar piney scent of his cologne. My muscles went rigid as I prepared myself for the worst. No matter how much I wanted Hunter to forgive me, I didn't know if he could.

"I took a long lunch to go golfing," Hunter said, his hazel eyes locked on mine. "I needed to clear my head. And I want to talk to you about last night." He sighed. "I said my *dad* wants us to get a divorce, not that I want one. I don't give a damn what my dad thinks." Hunter touched his nose to mine. "I realized how I might have made you feel attacked, and how you lashed out at me because of it. I'm so sorry about how I spoke to you. I should have been more understanding."

My muscles began to relax one by one. My husband's words washed over me like warm water. We stayed there for a moment, hugging each other close.

"I'm an idiot," I said, a tear trickling down my cheek. "I didn't mean what I said when I gave you back the ring. I don't ever want you to leave me. I'm so sorry that you had to find out about my past from your father. I was ashamed. I've never been able to forgive myself, and I didn't think you'd look at me the same way again."

Hunter stroked my cheek, his eyes sad. "You're too hard on yourself, you know that? Listen to me. I forgive you. Do you hear me, Sarah? I forgive you. You need to forgive yourself too."

My lip trembled, and tears slipped over my cheeks. Hunter wiped them away with his thumb. "Tell me the truth," he said quietly. "Is the reason you don't want kids because you don't think you deserve them?"

I nodded. Hunter slid his hands down, holding me tightly by the waist. "I want you to know that I love you no matter what. Your past is in your past. I only care about our future. Personally, I think you'd make a great mom."

"You don't hate me?"

He smiled, indenting his dimple. "Of course I don't hate you."

I leaned against Hunter's strong chest. "Does that mean you're willing to work through this?" I dropped my voice to a whisper. "Because I want to. I'm so sorry for not being open with you earlier about my accident. I didn't feel like I could be."

"Hey," Hunter said, murmuring into my hair. "I don't ever want to lose you, Kiddo. I want you to feel like you can talk to me about anything, even if it scares you, even if my dad gives us a hard time. That's what I'm here for. No more secrets, okay?"

"Thank you," I said, tracing the familiar curve of my husband's jaw. "When I married you, I felt like I had a family again. *You* are my family."

"And you're my family too. You're my whole universe."

Hunter tilted his head, his lips so close I could feel his breath on my face.

"Aren't you going to kiss me?" I whispered.

Hunter's nose brushed against mine. "Not until I give you this."

Reaching into his pocket, he pulled out a closed fist, and then opened his palm.

My eyes welled with tears. "You brought that with you to the golf course?"

Hunter nodded. "I've been carrying it in my pocket all day, hoping I'd have the chance to give it back to you."

The large emerald surrounded by a halo of diamonds sparkled in the sunlight. Never had the Havensworth family heirloom looked so beautiful.

"Will you take this ring," Hunter asked, "and me to be your husband? I know I'm not always the easiest guy to be around, but I love you with all my heart."

"I love you too," I said, my voice breaking. "More than I've ever loved anyone."

Sliding the ring onto my finger, Hunter looked at me with the same expression I'd seen on our wedding day, letting me know he'd always be there for me, accepting me flaws and all. Closing my eyes, I kissed him.

Could I forgive myself, like he had asked me to?

Hunter didn't think I was a monster. He thought I was a good person who'd had very bad luck. And for the first time in my life, I began to believe it too. As we kissed each other, the air filled with the scent of lavender. I had the strangest sensation that Hanna was smiling at me, knowing her ring had found its rightful place.

Epilogue

Trees blurred past as Hunter turned his BMW off Highway 49 and onto a long dirt road. I rolled down my window, breathing in the crisp mountain air. It smelled like pine needles and campfire smoke, so different from the city fog. Quaint clapboard buildings stood next to barns with faded paint. Passing through the mining town in the Sierra Nevada foothills felt like traveling back in time to the nineteenth century.

"Are you nervous?" I asked, squeezing Hunter's hand.

His eyes crinkled at the corners as he smiled. "A little bit. Are you?"

"Yeah. But it's a good kind of nervous."

Shifting gears, Hunter pulled the steering wheel to the right, driving us into a residential neighborhood. My stomach had been doing flips for the past hundred miles, but I hadn't taken my Klonopin. Now when I felt my anxiety coming on, I reached for Hunter's hand or my therapist's phone number. Today, I'd pinned my bangs back into my ponytail, showing my forehead for the first time in years. My scar exposed me for what I was—not a cold-blooded killer, but a human being who'd made a mistake.

"I think we turn right here," I said, pointing to a farm building, its sheet metal corroded with rust. "He said right at the fork."

Horses flicked their tails and watched us with curious eyes as Hunter's tires crunched along the gravel. Swaying in the breeze, tall golden oats lined both sides of the road. A flock of birds formed a V in the sky. Smiling, I watched them soar higher and higher. Today I felt just as free, making my own way in the world.

Jen had reported James, and he'd resigned from his post as editor in chief. It turns out he'd been harassing a few of the interns as well, and Jen had given them the courage to come forward with their stories.

As for my master's thesis, I'd passed my final exam with flying colors. Mariko had encouraged me to submit it to local magazines, and "The Lost Dressmakers of the Barbary Coast" had been the *San Francisco Chronicle*'s most-read article to date. With Bill McClaren's follow-up call, I'd gotten the employment paperwork necessary to clear Kieran McClaren of Margaret's murder. Kieran had been in Alameda on the night of her disappearance, working at the shipyard.

I didn't name Robert as the killer. To the public, the story of Margaret O'Brien and Hannelore Schaeffer remained an unsolved mystery. But at the very least, I'd shed light on their lives and the conditions of working-class women during the Victorian era. No matter how many tech companies set up shop in the city, San Francisco would never lose its soul. I'd devoted myself to the forgotten history of its unrecognized heroes. My next article focused on the first labor organization led by African Americans.

I felt confident working as a freelance journalist with my master's degree under my belt. I had a flexible schedule, which allowed me to help Hunter with his start-up, and I was very lucky to write the stories I felt passionate about.

"I'm proud of you, Kiddo," Hunter said, turning to me.

"Thank you, Sweetie."

"Forget those Kardashians," Hunter said, chuckling. "I'm pretty sure you're the one who broke the Internet. How many hits does your article have now?"

"Don't know," I said, grinning. "A lot."

"Mom and Dad are meeting with a lawyer today," Hunter said, "about filing the paperwork. I'm glad you finally got them on board."

Sticking my arm out the window to feel the breeze, I smiled. "Well, considering how your dad tried to *blackmail* me into keeping the truth about Robert Havensworth a secret, I'd say it's a pretty fair trade."

Hunter's brows drew together. "I'm still so angry with him. No matter what his intentions were, it was wrong. Especially him following you around."

I shrugged. "It is what it is."

Hunter hadn't spoken to his father for over two months. I'd shown him the emails from "Anonymous" and Nick's text confirming the IP address. Later, Walter had apologized to me in private, explaining how he cared only about his son's well-being and had Hunter's best interests in mind. Honestly, his apology felt insincere, but I decided to forgive him on one condition.

Walter was now the proud president of a nonprofit where art education was free to any student with the drive to pursue it. Lucas had founded Havensworth Art Academy for Hanna, as an act of his undying devotion. What began as an NPO had been restored to what Lucas intended it to be: a school for all people, no matter their background.

While Hunter's car bumped along the road, I thought back on the pages of Georgina's diary, which had taught me so much. Though Lucas eventually married Juliet Livingston, he never forgot Hannelore Schaeffer, the woman he truly loved. Every day, he gazed upon Hanna's painting in his study. According to Georgina, it was his most prized possession, worth more to him than every Monet in the house.

"Hey, do I turn right here?" Hunter asked, peering at the faded sign.

"Yep, this is the street," I said, my thoughts shifting back to the present. I bit my lip. "I'm so excited."

"Easy there, Tiger," Hunter said, steering the car slowly. "You don't want to scare the poor guy. He was pretty cool to invite us up here."

"That's the house," I said, pointing out the window at a Victorian cottage, fish-scale shingles painted a sunny yellow. "Pull over."

Hunter turned off the car, and I smiled. All of my research

had brought me to this tiny mountain town, where Hanna's story continued. Opening the door, I took a deep breath. Birds chirped in the trees and the sun warmed my shoulders. Purple shadows dappled the ground, pine needles crunching beneath my feet. I could see why Hanna had chosen this place to start over. The rocking chair on the front porch looked like a comfortable spot to sit with a glass of iced tea.

I followed Hunter up the creaky porch steps. Lavender bloomed in the yard, the sweet scent filling the air. Everywhere I looked seemed to burst with color. In the exhibit of gold rush artifacts, where I'd found Hanna's plate fragment, initially I'd overlooked something important. At the site of Tomkinson's livery and stable, there'd also been a ledger from the boarding-house above.

Hannelore Schaeffer was not listed among the names of guests who'd stayed there. But Hanna Mueller was. And on a hunch, I had Googled her. An Internet search revealed census results for Hanna Mueller, a widow in Sutter Creek, California. In addition to her "children" Martin, Hans, and Katja, she had another child, a son named Luke, born October 17, 1876.

Hunter rapped his knuckles on the screen door. The knob turned and it swung open. With his height and tanned skin, the man standing in the doorway could have passed for Hunter's brother. They even had the same wavy dark hair.

"Mike Bauer?" Hunter asked, sticking out his hand.

"That's me," Mike said, giving Hunter a hearty handshake and then gripping my palm in his. "And you must be Sarah. Come on in."

"Thanks," I said. "Really, I appreciate this so much."

Mike waved us inside. "We're family, after all. Right?"

Hunter laughed. "Yeah, man, we are."

I'd begged Mike not to hang up on me when I'd called to tell him that he and my husband shared the same great-great-great-grandfather, Lucas Havensworth. Mike had listened, and then he'd invited me to the home where Hannelore Schaeffer had spent the remainder of her life. I'd been so excited when I'd gotten off the phone with Mike that I'd danced around the kitchen.

Stepping inside the sun-drenched living room, I gazed at pictures in silver frames, which sat on the mantel of an old brick fireplace. Oil paintings of landscapes and portraits of men, women, and children hung from the walls. Ticking in the corner, a large grandfather clock stood watch, at least a century old.

I stepped closer, admiring a painting of the riverbank at dawn, the water sparkling in the sunlight. In another, an old barn stood next to hay bales round as bread rolls. My eyes settled on the next, where a woman with chestnut hair and blue-gray eyes stared off into the distance. A slight smile rested on her lips.

Mike nodded. "My grandma's grandma painted those. That one is a self-portrait."

"It's Hanna," I murmured.

Seeing Hanna as a grown woman, long after she'd left San Francisco and the Barbary Coast behind, I felt emotional. "She's beautiful."

Walking over to the mantel, I picked up a framed sepia photograph. A dimpled towheaded boy stood in front of a woman with dark hair and a long dress. *Hanna.* She looked straight at the camera, a fierce determination in her eyes. With her hands on the boy's shoulders, she looked prepared to protect him with her life.

Setting the picture down, I looked at the next photo. Two young women stood arm in arm against the railing of a wooden bridge. Behind them, boys cast fishing poles into the water, and schooners bobbed in the distance. The girl with long curly hair threw her head back in laughter, while the other girl, with two braids pinned up, smiled shyly. I touched the glass, my throat tightening. I didn't have to ask to know this was a picture of Hanna and Margaret.

Turning my gaze to the rocking chair, which sat empty by the window, I wondered how many times Hanna had waited there, thinking of Margaret and Lucas, the loved ones she'd lost.

"Cool furniture," Hunter said. "Are these antiques?" He trailed his fingers along a wooden end table. "Man, people had such an appreciation for craftsmanship back then."

"Yeah," Mike said. "My brother wants to sell this place, but I don't mind taking care of the old house. I like keeping it the way it is."

I turned to Mike. "That's what I would do too."

"So," Mike asked, looking at us. "Can I get you anything? Lemonade, beer?"

"I'll take a beer," Hunter said.

"I'll have a lemonade," I answered. "Thanks."

I'd gone off the pill. My therapist helped me see that even though Connor died, his death didn't mean I didn't deserve kids of my own. Hunter and I made love differently now, giddy with the possibility of what might happen. I knew he'd make a wonderful father—I'd always known it. Hunter smiled at me, squeezing my hand.

Mike disappeared into the kitchen. He returned with two bottles of Sierra Nevada and a glass of lemonade. We sat down together at a long table in the living room.

"I'd love to hear your stories about Hanna," I said, scooting my chair closer. "After all this research, I feel like I know her. But I only know a small part of her life."

Mike swigged his beer, and then set it down to rest on a coaster. "My grandma always told me that her Oma, Hanna, was a resourceful pioneer woman. Hanna Mueller came here as a widow and opened her own shop in Sutter Creek."

I pictured Hanna forging her independence far away from the gritty streets of San Francisco, and how much bravery that must have taken. It must have been hard for her to let go of her old life, her friendships, and her love for Lucas.

I chewed my lip. "She wasn't actually a widow, though. I think she told the townspeople that because it was easier. Did she ever marry?"

Mike nodded. "She married a Swiss immigrant named Peter Bauer. They built this house together and lived here until old age."

"That's wonderful," I said, clasping my hands.

Domestic life offered love in small moments. It wasn't passionate or fiery, but it was real. Raising a family together, running a store, building a home—those things forged a strong bond between two people. Yet I couldn't help but wonder if the fireworks Hanna shared with Lucas smoldered like embers in her heart.

"The business they opened kept growing. Our family still owns it. Bauer's Hardware, right over on Main Street in town."

Hunter raised his beer glass. "We passed it when we drove in. That's so cool. We'll have to check it out on the way back. And I bet there were lots of customers back then, because of the miners."

Mike smiled. "Yeah, there were. Hanna and Peter did well for themselves. They had a happy life, kids, and grandkids." His eyes brightened, looking at me. "Speaking of which, I found some stuff you might be interested in. Hang on a sec."

"Okay," I said, watching Mike get up from the table.

After Mike disappeared into the other room, I let my eyes roam the interior of Hanna's home, drinking in every detail: the blue-painted plates, the lace curtains, the beautiful hand-carved chairs made from sturdy oak. Maybe Hanna's husband, Peter, had built them. I wanted to touch everything, to feel closer to her.

Mike reemerged with a shoebox in his hands. Blowing dust off the lid, he set it down on the table. "When I was cleaning out the back bedroom, I found this box of stuff that's so old I think it must've belonged to Hanna. I thought you might be interested."

"May I?" I asked, reaching for the box.

"Of course," he said. "Open it up."

Hunter leaned forward on his elbows as I lifted the lid. Setting it down, I peered inside. My breath hitched when I saw the small treasures—a smooth stone, a pinecone, a green marble. Lifting a blue jay feather, I twisted it between my fingers. Maybe Hanna's son had brought it to her after playing outside beneath the pine trees.

My throat tightened, thinking of the picture above the fireplace. Little Luke had big eyes and a contagious smile. How Hanna must have loved him, and how heartbreaking for her that he'd never known his real father. Had Peter discovered the truth of the romance between Hanna and Lucas?

I set the blue jay feather down. Maybe Peter had, and maybe he hadn't. The truth could've been an unspoken secret between husband and wife. Reaching into the box, I picked up a sepia-toned photograph of a bearded man holding a boy tightly around his middle. Both smiled widely. The caption read, "Peter and Luke." I smiled. Peter had loved his stepchild as his own. There was no doubt about it.

"I think that's everything," Mike said. "Just the picture and a few trinkets. I'm not sure what meaning they held for her, but I figured they belonged to Hanna because this photo is of Hanna's husband, Peter, and their son."

"Um," I said, pressing my lips together.

"Oh jeez," Mike said, rubbing his face. "I mean Lucas Havensworth's son. Sorry, it's still tough for me to wrap my head around."

"It's okay, man," Hunter said, patting Mike's shoulder.

"When Sarah was writing her article, I could barely keep the facts straight. She'd try to tell me about it and I'd just get this blank look."

Mike laughed. As he and Hunter started talking about the Giants and whether or not they could win the World Series a fourth time, I tilted the box forward. Something rattled in the bottom. Scraping my fingers along the edge, I pulled out a tightly rolled tube of paper. When I undid the rubber band, out tumbled a silver ring.

I gasped. The worn metal had become thin with age. Placing it in my palm, I looked at the intricate design: two hands held a heart topped with a crown. I recognized it as an Irish claddagh ring—a very old one. Hunter and Mike's conversation receded as I held the beautiful antique.

For reasons I couldn't explain, I wanted to cry. Gently setting the ring down on the table, I unfurled the thin piece of paper, smoothing it out with my fingers. In shaky cursive, someone had written a letter.

Dearest Margaret,

I miss you more with every passing day. I keep your grandmother's ring with me always, so that you will stay close to my heart. I am an old woman now, with a husband, Peter, a son, two daughters, and grandchildren of my own. I love them dearly, but they do not know of the life we shared in San Francisco.

in a time that is now forgotten. Those days were grim, Margaret, but you were my light in the darkness. My little girl, Maggie, reminds me so much of you.

Remember how you helped me into the green dress we borrowed from Miss Delia? I can still feel the velvet. My mind might be as old and cloudy as an unpolished looking glass, but I will never forget what fun we had together. For heaven's sake, you convinced me to steal the dress! (And Miss Delia, such a cow, she deserved it.) You taught me to dare to see myself as a fine woman, worthy of a fine man.

I loved Lucas Havensworth with all my heart, even though I could not keep him. But I see him in my dreams, and I see his soul in our child's eyes. That is not to say I do not love my dear Peter, but it is different. You understand. How much love have I experienced in this life? To think I used to fear love would make me weak.

I was a fool, Margaret.

Instead, love has made me strong enough to leave that place of sadness and to start my life anew. Both Lucas and I are better for it, I am sure. Many days while rolling dough for brötchen, I have longed to feel him standing at my back, and to see you out the kitchen window, walking up the drive. You are wearing your green dress, rosy-cheeked and smiling, just as beautiful and young as I remember you. It was but a mirage. Yet in my heart, I've always known you were by my side.

Now death knocks at my door. I fear it not, for I know I will see you both again. And there, in whatever lies yonder, I will embrace you. Do you know how many years I have waited to see your smile, dear Margaret? I have not forgotten you, silly hen. Please tell me you will be there waiting.

Your friend forever,
Hannelore Schaeffer

I wiped a tear from my cheek. Hanna felt Margaret and Lucas in the same way I sensed my mother and father always watching over me. Whether separated by distance or death— love, loyalty, and friendship bound us together. Like Margaret's claddagh ring, we had formed an unbreakable circle of hearts and hands.

About the author

About the book

Insights,
Interviews
& More . . .

Meet Meredith Jaeger

Erika Pino Photography

MEREDITH JAEGER has lived and traveled around the world, spending periods in the Netherlands, the Czech Republic, and Australia. She is a native of the San Francisco Bay Area, born and raised in Berkeley, California. A graduate of the University of California, Santa Cruz, Meredith holds a BA in modern literature. While working at a San Francisco start-up, Meredith fulfilled a lifelong dream to write a novel, the result of which was *The Dressmaker's Dowry*. Like the character Hannelore Schaeffer, Meredith is also the daughter of a European immigrant who moved to California in search of a better life. Meredith lives in the San Francisco Bay Area with her husband, their infant daughter, English bulldog, and elderly cat. She's currently at work on her next novel. ❧

Behind the Scenes
with Meredith Jaeger

ON MY HONEYMOON IN GREECE, overlooking the Aegean Sea, I opened a leather notebook, plotted out my novel, and developed its characters. I have always been drawn to the gritty, dark underbelly of cities, and to the urban immigrant experience—particularly the lives of working-class Victorians and the photojournalism of Jacob Riis.

With the sparkling blue expanse of ocean before me, I envisioned narrow cobblestone streets, horse-drawn carriages, smoke-filled saloons, and the infamous Barbary Coast of 140 years ago, where citizens were murdered in the street.

It was my first vacation in years. I had been working long hours for a San Francisco startup while simultaneously planning my wedding. To have the freedom and space to let my words flow felt like sweet relief.

As a native of the Bay Area, I grew up across the water from "the City," a place filled with artists and musicians, dive bars, quirky cafés, and family-owned businesses. But while I walked to work in 2013, it became apparent to me that San Francisco had changed. I heard constant talk of apps, series C funding, and large tech companies setting up shop.

Did the influx of new residents have any idea that San Francisco has a rich and colorful history dating from before the time of Twitter? I wanted to paint ▶

a picture for them. Immigrants—
Chinese, German, Irish, Dutch, and
Mexican—built the bones of our
bustling metropolis. These laborers lived
a life far removed from the millionaires
of Nob Hill. In fact, the San Francisco of
1876 mirrors the San Francisco of today:
a place of magnificent wealth displayed
against dire poverty.

I knew immediately that my character
Hannelore Schaeffer would be a German
immigrant. My father immigrated to
California from Switzerland in the
1960s, the son of German parents. He
didn't come from much, but his
adventurous spirit shone like the gold
flakes he panned from the Feather River.
(He went on to earn his PhD in business
from UC Berkeley, but always had a little
bit of cowboy dust in his soul.) Hanna
would be poor, and she would have the
drive to make a better life for herself in
this precarious land of opportunity.
Allowing Hanna to fall for a
businessman with a silver fortune from
the Comstock Lode, I let class and
societal differences to come into play.

My inspiration for Sarah
Havensworth, Hanna's present-day
counterpart, came from my own
heirloom engagement ring. When my
husband proposed to me with a delicate
cluster of diamonds from 1903, I fell in
love—with him, with the beautiful piece
of family jewelry, and with a story idea.
What if I didn't know whom this ring
had once belonged to? (He assured me

his great-aunt Peg was a very nice woman.) What if there was an incredible tale behind how the ring came to be passed down to me?

And so my novel unfolded. It wasn't a stretch to make Sarah a writer like myself. And I had the advantage of being able to explore every street and alleyway that Hanna traversed in her frantic search for her missing friend, Margaret. I even stopped for beers at the Saloon, San Francisco's oldest bar, which I've renamed the Tavern in *The Dressmaker's Dowry*. On my lunch break from work, I often wander around Jackson Square, a chic neighborhood in the shadow of the Transamerica Pyramid, admiring the brick buildings that used to be dance halls, secret opium dens, and brothels. No matter how many startups move to San Francisco, its storied past will never be erased. ❧

Behind the Book: Historical Facts and Fiction

I chose to explore San Francisco's Barbary Coast because it represents a bawdy, brawling time in the city's early history, so different from today's sleek skyscrapers, ubiquitous Starbucks cafés, and trendy restaurants in what is now the Financial District and Jackson Square. I love writing historical fiction because I get to bring forgotten time periods to life, and to make unknown voices heard.

During the gold rush of 1849 and continuing into the twentieth century, San Francisco was filled with crime, gambling, opium dens, bordellos, gangs, and men getting "shanghaied"—drugged and put aboard merchant ships, where they were forced to work on the crew. A far cry from today's businessmen ordering lattes!

In my research, I read *The Barbary Coast* by Herbert Asbury. San Francisco's wild past felt palpable, its characters jumping off the page. Asbury describes the Barbary Coast as roughly bounded "on the east by waterfront and East Street, now the Embarcadero; on the south by Clay and Commercial streets; on the west by Grant Avenue and Chinatown; and on the north by Broadway, with occasional overflows into the region around North Beach and Telegraph Hill."

One of the helpful films I watched was *Sin, Fire & Gold! The Days of San Francisco's Barbary Coast.* In this KQED documentary, host Greg Sherwood joins tour guide and historian Daniel Bacon in uncovering San Francisco's fascinating past. Lucky for me, I had easy access to the former Barbary Coast (I've worked in San Francisco's Financial District on and off for years), and I spotted a series of bronze medallions marking the Barbary Coast Trail. Daniel Bacon, the founder of the trail, has devoted himself to creating the path of 180 plaques.

Barbary Coast Trail medallion, Gold Street, San Francisco. (Courtesy of the author)

Behind the Book: Historical Facts and Fiction (*continued*)

I imagined my character Hanna walking along these gritty streets in her frantic search for Margaret, and how frightening and dangerous it must have been. The 3.8-mile trail winds from the beginning of Market Street through the Financial District, Chinatown, Jackson Square, and North Beach up to Fisherman's Wharf.

Rather than have Hanna follow this exact path, I focused on Broadway, Pacific, Jackson, Kearny, and Dupont Street, which is now Grant Street in Chinatown. Broadway was known for bars so dangerous they were called "deadfalls" because patrons didn't always emerge alive. Some saloons reportedly had trapdoors in the floor for shanghaiing sailors. Hanna visits pubs and dance halls mentioned in Asbury's *The Barbary Coast,* such as the Billy Goat Saloon and the Opera Comique. The owner of the latter, Happy Jack Harrington, was a real person, infamous for his drunken antics. The location of the Opera Comique on Jackson and Kearney was known as "Murderer's Corner." In the 1870s, the Jackson Square neighborhood was called Devil's Acre.

Modern-day bar named after the old neighborhood. The Devil's
Acre, 256 Columbus Avenue, at the corner of Broadway. (Courtesy
of the author)

Behind the Book: Historical Facts and Fiction *(continued)*

Broadway today, dotted with strip clubs reminiscent of its bawdy past. (Courtesy of the author)

San Francisco's oldest bar, the Saloon, renamed the Tavern in my novel. 1232 Grant Avenue, San Francisco. (Courtesy of the author)

Both Hanna and Sarah visit the Tavern, which I based off the Saloon, San Francisco's oldest bar. Just like the Tavern in *The Dressmaker's Dowry,* the Saloon hosts live blues, and it is one of the few businesses in San Francisco that hasn't been touched by gentrification. I love the rumor that the upstairs once operated as a brothel, the reason the building was saved from the raging fire following the 1906 earthquake!

Before Hanna begins her search for Margaret, we see a bit of her life in the city. She works at 42 Montgomery Street at Walton's Tailor Shop. Here is how the street appeared in 1870:

Montgomery Street from Market, San Francisco. (Photo from the New York Public Library)

Behind the Book: Historical Facts and Fiction *(continued)*

Montgomery Street from Market, San Francisco. (Courtesy of the author)

Hanna lives on Telegraph Hill, now a coveted residential address for the wealthy, but once an area home to stevedores, fishermen, and immigrant warehouse workers. They built modest homes on the hill's slopes, and a few still exist today. While breathtaking views of the Bay can still be enjoyed from Coit Tower, Hanna also looked out at the ocean and wharf below when she painted her ship.

View from Telegraph Hill, 1870. (Photo from the New York Public Library)

Napier Lane, the street Hanna lived on. (Photo by Melisa Smith)

Hanna meets her love interest, Lucas Havensworth, at Lotta's Fountain, a cast iron monument commissioned by the actress Lotta Crabtree as a gift to the city of San Francisco. It still stands at the intersection of Market, Kearney, and Geary Streets.

Lotta's Fountain. (Courtesy of the author)

Behind the Book: Historical Facts and Fiction *(continued)*

Lotta's Fountain. (Courtesy of the author)

A mural in the Embarcadero Center depicting how Lotta's Fountain once appeared. (Courtesy of the author)

Behind the Book: Historical Facts and Fiction *(continued)*

Before enlisting Lucas's help to find Margaret, Hanna visits him at the Merchants Exchange, his place of employment.

Merchants Exchange, south side of California Street, between Leidesdorff and Montgomery Streets. (Photo from the New York Public Library)

The Merchants Exchange Building. 465 California Street. (Courtesy of the author)

Lucas and Hanna traverse the streets of the Barbary Coast together. One they might have walked down is Osgood Place, which serves as a lovely juxtaposition of the past and present— the Transamerica Pyramid looming over the brick buildings that used to be saloons, brothels, and opium dens.

Osgood Place, a street in Jackson Square, the former Barbary Coast. (Courtesy of the author)

Behind the Book: Historical Facts and Fiction *(continued)*

Pieces of Sarah's research are grounded in real life. I visited the California Historical Society at 678 Mission Street, just like Sarah did, to look through the directories from 1876. And guess what I found? A dressmaker named O'Brien!

1876 San Francisco directory. (Courtesy of the author)

The exhibit of Victorian artifacts found at the construction site of the Transbay Transit Center is real as well. Sadly, I did not get to see it. But I could vividly imagine a fragment of Hanna's mother's blue plate, and the boardinghouse ledger in which Hanna would have written her name.

Construction site of new Transbay Transit Center, where Victorian artifacts were found, and luxury condos in the distance. (Courtesy of the author)

Behind the Book: Historical Facts and Fiction (*continued*)

And if you're ever in San Francisco, be sure to window shop at Lang Antiques. They have an incredible 3-carat emerald ring surrounded by diamonds from the 1800s (not to mention lots of other exquisite Edwardian, Victorian, and Art Deco jewelry!) that I used as the inspiration for Sarah's beautiful ring: Lang Antiques, 309 Sutter Street, San Francisco.

I hope you'll take the time to walk the Barbary Coast Trail, and to think about San Francisco's wild and forgotten history. ᐧᐧᐧ

Reading Group Discussion Questions

1. The novel is set in 1876, years before the 1906 San Francisco earthquake and fire. Margaret says, "There's enough sin in this city for it to burn someday." Is there anything about this time period in San Francisco's history that surprised you? Do you think it was more dangerous to be a working-class woman at that time than a woman of society?

2. Hanna's position as a seamstress allows her to provide an income for her family. What other jobs do you think were available to women in the 1870s? Did Hanna's education help her?

3. At the wharves, a street child expresses anti-Chinese sentiment to Hanna. She fears the gangs that are opposed to foreigners living in the city. Did immigrants have a more difficult time finding jobs and assimilating into American culture than natives? Can you trace the arrival of your own ancestors to the United States? ▶

3. Sarah is hiding a dark and painful secret from her husband. What was your reaction to finding out Sarah's secret? Did she have a right to conceal the truth from Hunter? Did it change your opinion of her character?

4. Lucas and Hanna's relationship crosses a social divide, and is unconventional due to both class and cultural differences. What were your thoughts as their relationship developed?

5. When Hanna discovers that Robert murdered Margaret, she makes the difficult decision to leave Lucas without ever telling him the truth. She believes someone else will hang for the crime—Kieran McClaren or Clive—and Robert will get away with it. Did you agree with Hanna's heartbreaking choice? How was her decision influenced by her position in society and Lucas's position?

6. Sarah talks a lot about the wave of change taking over San Francisco: large tech companies moving in, rents rising, and the original residents, such as working-class families, being pushed out. Meanwhile, her husband is passionate about helping the city's many homeless. How does the San

Francisco of today compare to the San Francisco of 1876? Is there still a large gap between the wealthy and the poor?

7. Hanna is steadfast in her devotion to finding Margaret. What did you like about their friendship? Were you surprised that Margaret kept her pregnancy a secret from Hanna? Why do you think she did?

8. Sarah receives threatening e-mails and is blackmailed into keeping the truth about Margaret's murder a secret. Why does Walter Havensworth want to hide Robert's crime? Why do appearances matter to him?

9. In the beginning of the novel, Sarah hides the scar on her forehead and takes medication for her anxiety. In the end, she pins her bangs back into her ponytail and is no longer on medication. What caused her character transformation? What does this symbolize?

10. In the epilogue, we learn that Hanna escaped San Francisco and made a new life for herself in Sutter's Creek under a new name. She remarries, and continues to paint. Do you believe she is happy? How is this life different from the one she would have had with Lucas?

Behind the Scenes with Meredith Jaeger
(continued)

11. In the Victorian era, postmortem
photography was common. Do you
find this practice creepy? Did it
surprise you? Why do you think
these photos were taken? ∾

Discover great authors,
exclusive offers, and more
at hc.com.